the unbecoming of mara dyer

the unbecoming of mara dyer

MICHELLE HODKIN

SIMON & SCHUSTER BFYR

New York London Toronto Sydney New Delhi

SIMON & SCHUSTER BFYR
An imprint of Simon & Schuster Children's Publishing Division
1230 Avenue of the Americas, New York, New York 10020

For information about special discounts for bulk purchases, please contact Simon & Schuster Special Sales at 1-866-506-1949 or business@simonandschuster.com.
The Simon & Schuster Speakers Bureau can bring authors to your live event. For more information or to book an event, contact the Simon & Schuster Speakers Bureau at 1-866-248-3049 or visit our website at www.simonspeakers.com.
Also available in a SIMON & SCHUSTER BFYR hardcover edition
Book design by Lucy Ruth Cummins
The text for this book is set in Caslon.
Manufactured in the United States of America
First SIMON & SCHUSTER BFYR paperback edition October 2012
18 20 19
The Library of Congress has cataloged the hardcover edition as follows:
Hodkin, Michelle.
The unbecoming of Mara Dyer / Michelle Hodkin.
p. cm.
Summary: Seventeen-year-old Mara cannot remember the accident that took the lives of three of her friends but, after moving from Rhode Island to Florida, finding love with Noah, and more deaths, she realizes uncovering something buried in her memory might save her family and her future.
ISBN 978-1-4424-2176-9 (hc)
[1. Supernatural—Fiction. 2. Murder—Fiction. 3. High schools—Fiction. 4. Schools—Fiction. 5. Post-traumatic stress disorder—Fiction. 6. Family life—Florida—Fiction. 7. Florida—Fiction.] I. Title.
PZ7.H66493Unb 2011
[Fic]—dc22
2010050862
ISBN 978-1-4424-2177-6 (pbk)
ISBN 978-1-4424-2178-3 (eBook)

For Grandpa Bob, who filled my imagination with stories,
for Janie, who made all the other kids jealous;
and for my mother, who loves me too much.

My name is not Mara Dyer, but my lawyer told me I had to choose something. A pseudonym. A nom de plume, for all of us studying for the SATs. I know that having a fake name is strange, but trust me—it's the most normal thing about my life right now. Even telling you this much probably isn't smart. But without my big mouth, no one would know that a seventeen-year-old who likes Death Cab for Cutie was responsible for the murders. No one would know that somewhere out there is a B student with a body count. And it's important that you know, so you're not next.

Rachel's birthday was the beginning. This is what I remember.

"Mara Dyer"

, New York City

1

BEFORE

Laurelton, Rhode Island

THE ORNATE SCRIPT ON THE BOARD TWISTED in the candlelight, making the letters and numbers dance in my head. They were jumbled and indistinct, like alphabet soup. When Claire pushed the heart-shaped piece into my hand, I startled. I wasn't normally so twitchy, and hoped Rachel wouldn't notice. The Ouija board was her favorite present that night, and Claire gave it to her. I got her a bracelet. She wasn't wearing it.

Kneeling on the carpet, I passed the piece to Rachel. Claire shook her head, oozing disdain. Rachel put down the piece.

"It's just a game, Mara." She smiled, her teeth looking even whiter in the dim light. Rachel and I had been best friends since preschool, and where she was dark and wild, I was pale and cautious. But less so when we were together. She made me feel bold. Usually.

"I don't have anything to ask dead people," I said to her. And at sixteen, we're too old for this, I didn't say.

"Ask whether Jude will ever like you back."

Claire's voice was innocent, but I knew better. My cheeks flamed, but I stifled the urge to snap at her and laughed it off. "Can I ask it for a car? Is this like a dead Santa scenario?"

"Actually, since it's my birthday, I'm going first." Rachel put her fingers on the piece. Claire and I followed her.

"Oh! Rachel, ask it how you're going to die."

Rachel squealed her assent, and I shot a dark look at Claire. Since moving here six months ago, she'd latched onto my best friend like a starving leech. Her twin missions in life were now to make me feel like the third wheel, and to torture me for my crush on her brother, Jude. I was equally sick of both.

"Remember not to push," Claire ordered me.

"Got it, thanks. Anything else?"

But Rachel interrupted us before we could descend into bickering. "How am I going to die?"

The three of us watched the board. My calves prickled from kneeling on Rachel's carpet for so long, and the backs of my knees felt clammy. Nothing happened.

Then something did. We looked at each other as the piece

moved under our hands. It semi-circled the board, sailing past *A* through *K*, and crept past *L*.

It settled on *M*.

"Murder?" Claire's voice was soaked with excitement. She was so sketchy. What did Rachel see in her?

The piece glided in the wrong direction. Away from *U* and *R*.

Landing on *A*.

Rachel looked confused. "Matches?"

"Mauling?" Claire asked. "Maybe you start a forest fire and get eaten by Smokey the Bear?" Rachel laughed, briefly dissolving the panic that had slithered into my stomach. When we first sat down to play, I had to resist the urge to roll my eyes at Claire's melodramatics. Now, not so much.

The piece zigzagged across the board, cutting her laughter short.

R.

We were silent. Our eyes didn't leave the board as the piece jerked back to the beginning.

To *A*.

Then stopped.

We waited for the piece to point out the next letter, but it remained still. After three minutes, Rachel and Claire withdrew their hands. I felt them watching me.

"It wants you to ask something," Rachel said softly.

"If by 'it' you mean Claire, I'm sure that's true." I stood up, shaking and nauseous. I was done.

"I didn't push it," Claire said, wide-eyed as she looked at Rachel, then at me.

"Pinky swear?" I asked, with sarcasm.

"Why not," Claire answered, with malice. She stood and walked closer to me. Too close. Her green eyes were dangerous. "I didn't push it," she said again. "It wants *you* to play."

Rachel grabbed my hand and pulled herself up off the floor. She looked straight at Claire. "I believe you," she said, "but let's do something else?"

"Like what?" Claire's voice was flat, and I stared right back at her, unflinching. Here we go.

"We can watch *The Blair Witch Project*." Claire's favorite, naturally. "How about it?" Rachel's voice was tentative, but firm.

I tore my eyes away from Claire's and nodded, managing a smile. Claire did the same. Rachel relaxed, but I didn't. For her sake, though, I tried to swallow my anger and unease as we settled in to watch the movie. Rachel popped in the DVD and blew out the candles.

Six months later, they were both dead.

2

AFTER

Rhode Island Hospital
Providence, Rhode Island

I OPENED MY EYES. A PERSISTENT MACHINE BEEPED rhythmically to my left. I looked to my right. Another machine hissed beside the bedside table. My head ached and I was disoriented. My eyes struggled to interpret the positions of the hands on the clock hanging next to the bathroom door. I heard voices outside my room. I sat up in the hospital bed, the thin pillows crinkling underneath me as I shifted to try and hear. Something tickled the skin under my nose. A tube. I tried to move my hands to pull it away but when I looked at them, there were other tubes. Attached to needles. Protruding from my skin. I felt a tugging tightness as I moved my hands and my stomach slithered into my toes.

"Get them out," I whispered to the air. I could see where the sharp steel entered my veins. My breath shortened and a scream rose in my throat.

"Get them out," I said, louder this time.

"What?" asked a small voice, whose source I couldn't see.

"Get them out!" I screamed.

Bodies crowded the room; I could make out my father's face, frantic and paler than usual. "Calm down, Mara."

And then I saw my little brother, Joseph, wide-eyed and scared. Dark spots blotted out the faces of everyone else, and then all I could see were the forest of needles and tubes, and felt that tight sensation against my dry skin. I couldn't think. I couldn't speak. But I could still move. I clawed at my arm with one hand and ripped out the first tube. The pain was violent. It gave me something to hold on to.

"Just breathe. It's okay. It's okay."

But it wasn't okay. They weren't listening to me, and they needed to get them out. I tried to tell them, but the darkness grew, swallowing the room.

"Mara?"

I blinked, but saw nothing. The beeping and hissing had stopped.

"Don't fight it, sweetie."

My eyelids fluttered at the sound of my mother's voice. She leaned over me, adjusting one of the pillows, and a sheet of black hair fell over her almond skin. I tried to move, to get out of her way, but I could barely hold my head up. I glimpsed two dour-faced nurses behind her. One of them had a red welt on her cheek.

"What's wrong with me?" I whispered hoarsely. My lips felt like paper.

My mother brushed a sweaty strand of hair from my face. "They gave you something to help you relax."

I breathed in. The tube under my nose was gone. And the ones from my hands, too. They were replaced by gauzy white bandages wrapped around my skin. Spots of red bled through. Something released itself from my chest and a deep sigh shuddered from my lips. The room shifted into focus, now that the needles were out.

I looked at my father, sitting at the far wall, looking helpless. "What happened?" I asked hazily.

"You were in an accident, honey," my mother answered. My father met my eyes, but he didn't say anything. Mom was running this show.

My thoughts swam. An accident. When?

"Is the other driver—" I started, but couldn't finish.

"Not a car accident, Mara." My mother's voice was calm. Steady. It was her psychologist voice, I realized. "What's the last thing you remember?"

More than waking up in a hospital room, or seeing tubes attached to my skin—more than anything else—that question unnerved me. I stared at her closely for the first time. Her eyes were shadowed, and her nails, usually perfectly manicured, were ragged.

"What day is it?" I asked quietly.

"What day do you think it is?" My mother loved answering questions with questions.

I rubbed my hands over my face. My skin seemed to whisper on contact. "Wednesday?"

My mother looked at me carefully. "Sunday."

Sunday. I looked away from her, my eyes roaming the hospital room instead. I hadn't noticed the flowers before, but they were everywhere. A vase of yellow roses were right beside my bed. Rachel's favorite. A box of my things from the house sat in a chair next to the bed; an old cloth doll my grandmother had left to me when I was a baby lounged inside, resting its limp arm around the rim.

"What do you remember, Mara?"

"I had a history test Wednesday. I drove home from school and . . ."

I rifled through my thoughts, my memories. Me, walking into our house. Grabbing a cereal bar from the kitchen. Walking to my bedroom on the first floor, dropping my bag and taking out Sophocles' *Three Theban Plays*. Writing. Then drawing in my sketchbook. Then . . . nothing.

A slow, creeping fear wound its way around my belly. "That's it," I told her, looking up at her face.

A muscle above my mother's eyelid twitched. "You were at The Tamerlane—" she started.

Oh, God.

"The building collapsed. Someone reported it at about three a.m. Thursday. When the police arrived, they heard you."

My father cleared his throat. "You were screaming."

My mother shot him a look before turning back to me. "The way the building fell, you were buried in a pocket of air, in the basement, but you were unconscious when they reached you. You might have fainted from dehydration, but it's possible that something fell and knocked you out. You do have a few bruises," she said, pushing aside my hair.

I looked past her, and saw her torso reflected in a mirror above the sink. I wondered what "a few bruises" looked like when a building fell on your head.

I pushed myself up. The silent nurses stiffened. They were acting more like guards.

My joints protested as I craned my head over the bed rails to see. My mother looked in the mirror with me. She was right; a bluish shadow blossomed over my right cheekbone. I pushed my dark hair back to see the extent of it, but that was it. Otherwise I looked—normal. Normal for me, and normal, period. My gaze shifted to my mother. We were so different. I had none of her exquisite Indian features; not her perfect oval face or her lacquer-black hair. Instead, my father's patrician nose and jaw were reflected in my own. And except for the one bruise, I did not look like a building had collapsed on me at all. I narrowed my eyes at my reflection, then leaned back against the pillows and stared at the ceiling.

"The doctors said you're going to be fine." My mother smiled faintly. "You can come home tonight, even, if you feel well enough."

I lowered my gaze to the nurses. "Why are they here?" I asked my mother, staring straight at them. They were creeping me out.

"They've been taking care of you since Wednesday," she said. She nodded at the nurse with the welt on her cheek. "This is Carmella," she said, then indicated the other nurse. "And this is Linda."

Carmella, the nurse with the welt on her cheek, smiled, but it wasn't warm. "You have some right hook."

My forehead crumpled. I looked at my mother.

"You panicked when you woke up before, and they had to be here when you woke up just in case you were . . . still disoriented."

"Happens all the time," Carmella said. "And if you're feeling like yourself now, we can go."

I nodded, my throat dry. "Thank you. I'm sorry."

"No problem, sweetie," she said. Her words sounded fake. Linda hadn't said a word the whole time.

"Let us know if you need anything." They turned and

walked synchronously out of the room, leaving me and my family alone.

I was glad they were gone. And then I realized that my reaction to them was probably not normal. I needed to focus on something else. My eyes swept the room, and finally landed on the bedside table, on the roses. They were fresh, unwilted. I wondered when Rachel brought them.

"Did she visit?"

My mother's face darkened. "Who?"

"Rachel."

My father made a strange noise and even my mother, my practiced, perfect mother, looked uncomfortable.

"No," my mother said. "Those are from her parents."

Something about the way she said it made me shiver. "So she didn't visit," I said softly.

"No."

I was cold, so cold, but I had started to sweat. "Did she call?"

"No, Mara."

Her answer made me want to scream. I held out my arm instead. "Give me your phone. I want to call her."

My mother tried to smile and failed miserably. "Let's talk about this later, okay? You need to rest."

"I want to call her now." My voice was close to cracking. I was close to cracking.

My father could tell. "She was with you, Mara. Claire and Jude, too," he said.

No.

Something tightened around my chest and I could barely find the breath to speak. "Are they in the hospital?" I asked, because I had to, even though I knew the answer just looking at my parents' faces.

"They didn't make it," my mother said slowly.

This wasn't happening. It couldn't be happening. Something slimy and horrible began to rise in my throat.

"How? How did they die?" I managed to ask.

"The building collapsed," my mother said calmly.

"*How?*"

"It was an old building, Mara. You know that."

I couldn't speak. Of course I knew. When my father moved home to Rhode Island after law school, he'd represented the family of a boy who had been trapped inside the building. A boy who died. Daniel was forbidden from going there, not that my perfect older brother ever would. Not that *I* ever would.

But for some reason, I had. With Rachel, Claire, and Jude.

With Rachel. *Rachel.*

I had a sudden image of Rachel walking boldly into kindergarten, holding my hand. Of Rachel turning out the lights in her bedroom and telling me her secrets, after she had listened to mine. There was no time to even process the words "Claire and Jude, too," because the word "Rachel" filled my mind. I felt a hot tear slide down my cheek.

"What if—what if she was just trapped, too?" I asked.

"Honey, no. They searched. They found—" My mother stopped.

"What?" I demanded, my voice shrill. "What did they find?"

She considered me. Studied me. She said nothing.

"Tell me," I said, a knife's edge in my voice. "I want to know."

"They found . . . remains," she said vaguely. "They're gone, Mara. They didn't make it."

Remains. Pieces, she meant. A wave of nausea rocked my stomach. I wanted to gag. I stared hard at the yellow roses from Rachel's mother instead, then squeezed my eyes shut and searched for a memory, any memory, of that night. Why we went. What we were doing there. What killed them.

"I want to know everything that happened."

"Mara—"

I recognized her placating tone and my fingers curled into fists around my sheets. She was trying to protect me but she was torturing me instead.

"You have to tell me," I begged, my throat filled with ash.

My mother looked at me with glassy eyes and a heart-broken face. "I would if I could, Mara. But you're the only one who knows."

3

Laurelton Memorial Cemetery, Rhode Island

THE SUN REFLECTED OFF THE POLISHED mahogany of Rachel's coffin, blinding me. I stared, letting the light sear my corneas, hoping the tears would come. I should cry. But I couldn't.

Everyone else could, though, and did. People she never even spoke to, people she didn't even like. Everyone from school was there, claiming a piece of her. Everyone except Claire and Jude. Their memorial service was that afternoon.

It was a gray and white day, a biting New England winter day. One of my last.

The wind blew, lashing my curls against my cheeks. A handful of mourners separated me from my parents, silhouettes of black against the colorless, unbroken sky. I hunched into my coat and wrapped it tighter around my body, shielding myself from my mother's unblinking stare. She'd been watching my reactions since they released me from the hospital; she was the first to reach me that night when my screaming woke the neighbors, and she was the one who caught me crying in my closet the next day. But it was only after she found me two days later, dazed and blinking and clutching a shard of a broken mirror in my bloody hand, that she insisted on getting me help.

What I got was a diagnosis. Post-traumatic stress disorder, the psychologist said. Nightmares and visual hallucinations were my new normal, apparently, and something about my behavior in the psychologist's office made him recommend a long-term care facility.

I couldn't let that happen. I recommended moving instead.

I remembered the way my mother's eyes narrowed when I brought it up a few days after the disastrous appointment. So wary. So *cautious*, like I was a bomb under her bed.

"I really think it will help," I said, not believing that at all. But I had been nightmare-free for two nights, and the mirror episode I didn't remember was apparently the only one. The psychologist was overreacting, just like my mother.

"Why do you think so?" My mother's voice was casual and even, but her nails were still bitten down to the beds.

I tried to recall the mostly one-sided conversation I'd had with the psychologist.

"She was always in this house—I can't look at anything

without thinking about her. And if I go back to school, I'll see her there, too. But I want to go back to school. I need to. I need to think about something else."

"I'll talk to your father about it," she said, her eyes searching my face. I could see in every crease of her forehead, every tilt of her chin, that she didn't understand how her daughter could have gotten here—how I could have snuck out of the house and ended up in the last place I should. She had asked me as much, but of course I had no answer.

I heard my brother's voice out of nowhere. "I think it's almost over," Daniel said.

My heartbeat slowed as I looked up at my older brother. And as he predicted, the priest then asked us all to bow our heads and pray.

I shifted uncomfortably, the brittle grass crunching under my boots, and glanced at my mother. We weren't religious and frankly, I wasn't sure what to do. If there was some protocol for how to behave at your best friend's funeral, I didn't get the memo. But my mother tilted her head, her short black hair falling against her perfect skin as she appraised me, examined me, to see what I'd choose. I looked away.

After an eternity of seconds, heads lifted as if eager for it to be over, and the crowd dissolved. Daniel stood beside me while my classmates took turns telling me how sorry they were, promising to stay in touch after the move. I hadn't been in school since the day of the accident, but some of them had come to visit me in the hospital. Probably just out of curiosity. No one asked me how it happened, and I was glad because I couldn't tell them. I still didn't know.

Squawking pierced the funeral's hushed atmosphere as hundreds of black birds flew overhead in a rush of beating wings. They settled on a cluster of leafless trees that overlooked the parking lot. Even the trees were wearing black.

I faced my brother. "Didn't you park under those crows?"

He nodded, and started walking to his car.

"Fabulous," I said as I followed him. "Now we're going to have to dodge crap from the whole flock."

"Murder."

I stopped. "What?"

Daniel turned around. "It's called a murder of crows. Not a flock. And yes, we're going to dodge avian fecal matter, unless you want to go with Mom and Dad?"

I smiled, relieved without knowing why. "Pass."

"Thought so."

Daniel waited for me and I was grateful for the escape. I glanced back to make sure my mother wasn't watching. But she was busy talking to Rachel's family, whom we'd known for years. It was too easy to forget that my parents were leaving everything behind too; my father's law practice, my mother's patients. And Joseph, though only twelve, accepted without much explanation that we were moving and agreed to leave his friends without complaint. When

I thought about it, I knew I had won the family lottery. I made a mental note to behave more charitably toward my mother. After all, it wasn't her fault we were leaving.

It was mine.

4

EIGHT WEEKS LATER

Miami, Florida

"You're killing me, Mara."

"Give me a minute." I squinted at the spider that stood between me and my breakfast banana. She and I were working out an arrangement.

"Let me do it, then. We're going to be late." Daniel was getting his panties in a bunch at the thought. Mr. Perfect was always punctual.

"No. You'll kill it."

"And?"

"And then it will be dead."

"And?"

"Just imagine it," I spoke, my eyes never leaving my arachnid opponent. "The spider family bereft of their matriarch.

Her spider children waiting in their web, watching for Mother for days on end before they realize she's been murdered."

"She?"

"Yes." I tilted my head at the spider. "Her name is Roxanne."

"Of course it is. Take Roxanne outside before she meets the Op-Ed section of Joseph's *Wall Street Journal*."

I paused. "Why is our brother getting the *Wall Street Journal*?"

"He thinks it's funny."

I smiled. It was. I turned to stare at Roxanne, who had sidestepped an inch or two in response to Daniel's threat. I held out the paper towel and reached for her, but recoiled involuntarily. For the past ten minutes, I'd been repeating this motion: reaching and withdrawing. I wanted to shepherd Roxanne to freedom, to deliver her from our kitchen and lead her to a land flowing with the blood of myriad flying insects. A land otherwise known as our backyard.

But it seemed I was not up to the task. I was still hungry, though, and wanted my banana. I reached for her again, my hand stuck in midair.

Daniel heaved a melodramatic sigh and stuck a cup in the microwave. He pressed a few buttons and the tray began revolving.

"You shouldn't stand in front of the microwave."

Daniel ignored me.

"You could get a brain tumor."

"Is that a fact?" he asked.

"Do you want to find out?"

Daniel examined my hand, still suspended between my body and Roxanne's, paralyzed. "Your level of neuroses will only find love in a made-for-TV movie."

"Perhaps, but I'll be tumorless. Don't you want to be tumorless, Daniel?"

He reached into the pantry and withdrew a cereal bar. "Here," he said, and tossed it at me, but lately I was useless before noon. It fell with a thud on the countertop beside me. Roxanne scurried away, and I lost track of her.

Daniel grabbed his keys and sauntered toward the front door. I followed him into the blinding sunlight, breakfastless.

"C'mon," he said with false cheer. "Don't tell me you aren't psyched beyond belief for our first day of school." He dodged the tiny lizards that scurried across the slate walkway of our new house. "Again."

"I wonder if it's snowing in Laurelton right now?"

"Probably. That, I won't miss."

Just when I thought it wasn't possible to get any hotter, the interior of Daniel's Civic proved me wrong. I choked on the heat and motioned for Daniel to open the window while I sputtered.

He looked at me strangely.

"What?"

"It's not *that* hot."

"I'm dying. You're not dying?"

"No . . . it's like *seventy-two* degrees."

"Guess I'm not used to it yet," I said. We'd moved to Florida only a few weeks ago, but I wouldn't recognize my old life in a lineup. I hated this place.

Daniel's eyebrows were still lifted, but he changed the subject. "You know, Mom was planning to drive you to school separately today."

I groaned. I didn't want to play the patient this morning. Or any morning, actually. I contemplated buying her knitting needles, or a watercolor set. She needed a hobby that didn't involve hovering over me.

"Thanks for taking me instead." I met Daniel's eyes. "I mean it."

"No problemo," he said, and flashed a goofy smile before turning onto I-95 and into traffic.

My brother spent a large portion of the agonizingly slow drive to school banging his forehead on the steering wheel. We were late, and as we pulled into the full parking lot, there wasn't a single student among the glossy luxury cars.

I reached behind me for Daniel's neat and tidy backpack, which was positioned in the backseat like a passenger. I grabbed it for him and launched myself out of the car. We approached the elaborately scrolled iron gate of the Croyden Academy of the Arts and Sciences, our new institution of higher learning. A giant crest was wrought into the gate—a shield in the center with a thick band extending from the top right to the bottom left, separating it into halves. There was a knight's helmet crowning the shield, and two lions on either side. The school looked oddly out of place, considering the run-down neighborhood.

"So, what I didn't tell you is that Mom's picking you up this afternoon," Daniel said.

"Traitor," I mumbled.

"I know. But I need to meet with one of the guidance counselors about my college applications and she's only free after school today."

"What's the point? You know you're going to get in everywhere."

"That is far from certain," he said.

I squinted one of my eyes at Daniel.

"What are you doing?" he asked.

"This is me, giving you the side eye." I continued to squint.

"Well, you look like you're having a stroke. Anyway, Mom's going to pick you up over there," my brother said, pointing to a cul-de-sac on the other side of the campus. "Try to behave."

I stifled a yawn. "It's too early to be such an asshat, Daniel."

"And watch your language. It's unbecoming."

"Who cares?" I lolled my head back as we walked, reading the names of illustrious Croyden alumni inscribed in the brick archway above our heads. Most were along the lines of Heathcliff Rotterdam III, Parker Preston XXVI, Annalise Bennet Von—

"I heard Joseph call someone that the other day. He's picking it up from you."

I laughed.

"It's not funny," Daniel said.

"Please. It's just a word."

He opened his mouth to respond when I heard Chopin emerge from his pocket. The sound of Chopin, not the actual Chopin, thank God.

Daniel picked up his phone and mouthed *Mom* to me, then pointed at the glass wall that housed the administration office of Croyden Academy.

"Go," he said, and I did.

Without my brother distracting me, I was able to fully absorb the campus in its immaculate, overlandscaped splendor. Fat blades of emerald grass anchored the grounds, clipped within a millimeter of uniformity. A sprawling courtyard divided the campus into blooming, flower-framed quadrants. One section housed the gaudily becolumned library, another the cafeteria and windowless gymnasium. The classrooms and administration office dominated the last two quadrants. Open-air archways and brick paths connected the structures and led to a gurgling fountain in the center of the lawn.

I half-expected to see woodland creatures burst forth from the buildings and break into song. Everything about the place shrieked *WE ARE PERFECT HERE AND YOU WILL BE TOO!* No wonder my mother chose it.

I felt grossly underdressed in my T-shirt and jeans; uniforms were required at Croyden, but thanks to our late transfer ours hadn't arrived yet. Switching from public school to private as a junior—and in the middle of the trimester, no less—would have been torment enough without the added insult of plaid skirts and kneesocks. But my mother was a snob, and didn't trust the public schools in such a big city. And after everything that had happened in December, I was in no shape to argue coherently about it.

I picked up our schedules and maps from the school secretary and headed back outside as Daniel hung up the phone.

"How's Mom?" I asked.

My brother half-shrugged. "Just checking in." He looked over the paperwork for me. "We've missed first period so your first class is . . ." Daniel fumbled with the papers and declared, "Algebra II."

Perfect. Just perfect.

His eyes scanned the open-air campus; the classroom doors led directly outside, like the structure of a motel. After a few seconds, Daniel pointed to the farther building.

"It should be there, on the other side of that corner. Listen," he said, "I might not see you until lunch. Do you want to eat with me or something? I have to speak to the principal and the head of the music department but I can find you after—"

"No, it's fine. I'll be fine."

"Really? Because there's no one I'd rather eat mystery meat with."

My brother smiled, but I could tell he was anxious. Daniel had kept a big-brotherly eye on me ever since I was released from the hospital, though he was less obvious about it, and therefore less irritating, than our mother. But as such, I had to work extra hard to reassure him that I would not crack today. I put on my best mask of adolescent ennui and wore it like armor as we approached the building.

"Really. I'm fine," I said, rolling my eyes for effect. "Now go, before you fail out of high school and die poor and lonely." I shoved him lightly, for emphasis, and we separated.

But as I walked away, my little facade started to crumble. How ridiculous. This wasn't my first day of kindergarten, though it was my first day of school without Rachel . . . ever. But it was the first of many. I needed to get a grip. I swallowed back the ache that rose in my throat and tried to decipher my schedule:

AP English, Ms. Leib, Room B35

Algebra II, Mr. Walsh, Room 264

American History, Mrs. McCreery, Room 4

Art, Mrs. Gallo, Room L

Spanish I, Ms. Morales, Room 213

Biology II, Mrs. Prieta, Annex

Hopeless. I wandered the path to the building and scanned the room numbers, but found the vending machines before I found my Algebra classroom. Four of them in a row, pushed up against the back of the building, facing a series of tiki huts that dotted the grounds. They reminded me that I'd skipped breakfast. I looked around. I was already late. A few more minutes couldn't hurt.

I set the papers down on the ground and dug in my bag for change. But as I inserted one quarter in the machine, the other one I held in my hand fell. I bent to search for it, as I had only enough money to buy one thing. I finally found it, placed it in the machine, and clicked on the letter-number combination that would provide my salvation.

It stuck. Unbelievable.

I clicked the numbers again. Nothing. My M&M's were trapped by the machine.

I grabbed the sides of the machine and tried to shake it. No dice. Then I kicked it. Still nothing.

I glared at the machine. "Let them *out*." I punctuated my statement with a few more useless kicks.

"You have an anger-management problem."

I whipped around at the sound of the warm, lilting British accent behind me.

The person it belonged to sat on the picnic table under the tiki hut. His general state of disarray was almost enough to distract me from his face. The boy—if he could be called that, looking like he belonged in college, not high school—wore Chucks with holes worn through, no laces. Slim charcoal pants and a white button-down shirt covered his lean, spare frame. His tie was loose, his cuffs were undone, and his blazer lay in a heap beside him as he lazily leaned back on the palms of his hands.

His strong jaw and chin were slightly scruffy, as though he hadn't shaved in days, and his eyes looked gray in the shade. Strands of his dark chestnut hair stuck out every which way. Bedroom hair. He could be considered pale in comparison to everyone else I'd observed in Florida thus far, which is to say he wasn't orange.

He was beautiful. And he was smiling at me.

5

SMILING AT ME LIKE HE KNEW ME. I TURNED my head, wondering if there was anyone behind me. Nope. No one there. When I glanced back in the boy's direction, he was gone.

I blinked, disoriented, and bent to pick up my things. I heard footsteps approach, but they stopped just before they reached me.

The perfectly tanned blond girl wore heeled oxfords and white kneesocks with her just-above-the-knee charcoal and navy plaid skirt. The fact that I'd be wearing the same thing in a week hurt my soul.

She was linked arm-in-arm with a flawlessly groomed, startlingly enormous blond boy, and the two of them in their Croyden-crested blazers looked down their perfect noses with their perfect smattering of freckles at me.

"Watch it," the girl said. With venom.

Watch what? I hadn't done anything. But I decided not to say so, considering I knew exactly one person at the school, and we shared a last name.

"Sorry," I said, even though I didn't know what for. "I'm Mara Dyer. I'm new here." Obviously.

A hollow smile crept over Vending Machine Girl's puritanically pretty face. "Welcome," she said, and the two of them walked away.

Funny. I did not feel welcome at all.

I shook off both strange encounters, and, map in hand, circled the building with no results. I climbed the stairs, and circled it again before finally finding my classroom.

The door was closed. I did not relish the idea of walking in late, or at all, really. But I'd already missed one class, and I was there, and the hell with it. I opened the door and stepped inside.

Cracks appeared in the classroom walls as twenty-something heads turned in my direction. The fissures spidered up, higher and higher, until the ceiling began to crumble. My throat went dry. No one said a word, even though dust filled the room, even though I thought I would choke.

Because it wasn't happening to anyone else. Just to me.

A light crashed to the floor right in front of the teacher, sending a shower of sparks in my direction. Not real. But I tried to avoid them anyway, and fell.

I heard the sound of my face as it smacked against the polished linoleum floor. Then pain punched me between my eyes. Warm blood gushed out of my nostrils and swirled over my mouth and under my chin. My eyes were open, but I still couldn't see through the gray dust. I could hear, though. There was a collective intake of breath from the class, and the sputtering teacher tried to determine just how hurt I was. Oddly, I did nothing but lie on the cool floor and ignore the muffled voices around me. I preferred my bubble of pain to the humiliation I would surely face upon standing.

"Umm, are you okay? Can you hear me?" The teacher's voice grew increasingly panicky.

I tried to say my name, but I think it sounded more like "I'm dying" instead.

"Someone go get Nurse Lucas before she bleeds to death in my classroom."

At that, I scrambled up, shifting woozily on alien feet. Nothing like the threat of nurses and their needles to get my ass into gear.

"I'm fine," I announced, and looked around the room. Just a normal classroom. No dust. No cracks. "Really," I said. "No need for the nurse. I just get nosebleeds sometimes." Chuckle, chuckle. Laugh it off. "I don't even feel anything. The bleeding's stopped." And it had, though I probably looked like a freak show.

The teacher eyed me warily before he answered. "Hmm. You

really aren't hurt, then? Would you like to go to the restroom to clean up? We can formally introduce ourselves upon your return."

"Yeah, thanks," I answered. "I'll be right back." I willed myself out of my dizziness, and snuck a glance at the teacher and my new classmates. Every face in the room registered a mixture of surprise and horror. Including, I noticed, Vending Machine Girl. Lovely.

I vacated the classroom. My body felt wiggly as I walked, like a loose tooth that could be dislodged by the slightest force. When I no longer heard the whispers or the teacher's shaky voice, I almost broke into a run. I even missed the girls' bathroom at first, barely registering the swinging door. I doubled back and, once inside, focused on the pattern of the hideous yolk-colored tile, counted the number of the stalls, did anything I could to avoid looking at myself in the mirror. I tried to calm myself, hoping to stave off the panic attack that would follow the sight of blood.

I breathed slowly. I did not want to clean myself up. I did not want to return to class. But the longer I was gone, the higher the likelihood that the teacher would send the nurse after me. I *really* didn't want that, so I positioned myself in front of the wet counter, which was covered in wads of crumpled paper towels, and looked up.

The girl in the mirror smiled. But she wasn't me.

6

It was Claire. Her red hair spilled over my shoulders where my brown hair should have been. Then her reflection bent, sinister in the glass. The room tilted, pitching me to the side. I bit my tongue, then braced my hands on the counter. When I looked up at the mirror, it was once again my face that stared back.

My heart pounded against my rib cage. It was nothing. Just like the classroom was nothing. I was okay. Nervous about my first day of school, maybe. My disastrous first day of school. But at least I was unsettled enough that my stomach forgot to churn at the sight of the drying blood on my skin.

I grabbed a handful of paper towels from the dispenser and wetted them. I brought them to my face to clean it up, but the pungent wet paper towel smell finally set my stomach roiling. I willed myself not to vomit.

I failed.

I had the presence of mind to pull back my long hair from my face as I emptied the meager contents of my stomach into the sink. At that moment, I was glad that the universe had thwarted my attempts at breakfast.

When I finished dry heaving, I wiped my mouth, gargled some water, and spit it into the sink. A thin film of sweat covered my skin, which had that unmistakable just-puked pallor. A charming first impression, to be sure. At least my T-shirt had escaped my bodily fluids.

I leaned on the sink. If I skipped the rest of Algebra, the teacher would just rustle up a mathlete posse to find me and make sure I hadn't died. So I bravely headed out into the relentless heat and made my way back. The classroom door was still open; I'd forgotten to close it after my unceremonious departure, and I heard the teacher droning on about an equation. I took a deep breath and carefully walked in.

In seconds, the teacher was at my side. His thick glasses gave his eyes an insectlike quality. Creepy.

"Oh, you look much better! Please, have a seat right here. I'm Mr. Walsh, by the way. I didn't catch your name before?"

"It's Mara. Mara Dyer," I said thickly.

"Well, Ms. Dyer, you certainly know how to make an entrance."

The class's low chuckle hovered in the air.

"Yeah, um, just clumsy, I guess." I sat down in the first row, where Mr. Walsh had indicated, in an empty desk parallel to the teacher's and closest to the door. Every seat in the row was unoccupied, except mine.

For eight painful minutes and twenty-seven infinite seconds, I sat sweltering in the seventh circle of my own personal inferno, motionless at my desk. I listened to the sound of the teacher's voice but heard nothing. Shame drowned him out, and every pore of my skin felt painfully naked, open for exploitation by the pillaging eyes of my classmates.

I tried not to focus on the assault of whispers that I could hear but not decipher. I patted the back of my tingling head, as if the heat of the anonymous stares managed to burn through my hair, exposing my scalp. I looked desperately at the door, wishing to escape this nightmare, but I knew that the whispers would only spread as soon as I was outside.

The bell rang, marking the end of my first class at Croyden. A resounding success indeed.

I hung back from the mass exodus toward the door, knowing I'd need a book and a briefing on where the class was in the syllabus. Mr. Walsh told me ever so politely that I was expected to take the trimester exam in three weeks like everyone else, then returned to his desk to shuffle papers, and left me to face the rest of my morning.

It was blissfully uneventful. When lunch rolled around, I

gathered my book-laden messenger bag and heaved it over my shoulder. I decided to look around for a quiet, secluded place to sit and read the book I'd brought with me. My vomiting shenanigans had ruined my appetite.

I hopped down the stairs two at a time, walked to the edge of the grounds, and stopped at the fence that bordered a large plot of undeveloped land. Trees towered above the school, casting one building entirely in shadow. The eerie screech of a bird punctured the breezeless air. I was in some preppy *Jurassic Park* nightmare, definitely. I violently opened my book to where I'd left off, but found myself reading and rereading the same paragraph before I gave up. That lump rose in my throat again. I slumped against the chain-link fence, the metal scoring marks in my flesh through the thin fabric of my shirt, and closed my eyes in defeat.

Someone laughed behind me.

My head snapped up as my blood froze. It was Jude's laugh. Jude's voice. I stood slowly and faced the fence, the jungle, as I hooked my fingers in the metal and searched for the source.

Nothing but trees. Of course. Because Jude was dead. Like Claire. And Rachel. Which meant that I'd had three hallucinations in less than three hours. Which wasn't good.

I turned back to the campus. It was empty. I glanced at my watch and panic set in; only a minute to spare before my next class. I swallowed hard, grabbed my bag and rushed to the nearest building, but as I rounded the corner, I stopped cold.

Jude stood about forty feet away. I knew he couldn't be there, that he wasn't there, but he *was* there, unfriendly and unsmiling beneath the brim of the Patriots baseball cap he never took off. Looking like he wanted to talk.

I turned away and picked up my pace. I walked away from him, slowly at first, then ran. I glanced over my shoulder once, just to see if he was still there.

He was.

And he was close.

7

By some stroke of luck, I flung open the door to the closest classroom, 213, and it turned out to be Spanish. And judging by all of the taken desks, I was already late.

"Meez Dee-er?" the teacher boomed.

Distracted and disturbed, I pulled the door closed behind me. "It's Dyer, actually."

For my correction or for my lateness, I'll never know, the teacher punished me, forced me to stand at the front of the room while she fired question after question at me, in Spanish, to which I could only respond, "I don't know." She didn't even introduce herself; she just sat there, the muscles twitching in her veiny forearms as she scribbled self-importantly in her teacher book. The Spanish Inquisition took on a whole new meaning.

And it continued for a solid twenty minutes. When she finally stopped, she made me sit in the desk next to hers, in the front of the class, facing all of the other students. Brutal. My eyes were glued to the clock as I counted the seconds until it was over. When the bell rang, I bolted for the door.

"You look like you could use a hug," said a voice from behind me. I turned around to face a smiling short boy wearing an open, white button-down shirt. A yellow T-shirt that said I AM A CLICHÉ was beneath it.

"That's very generous of you," I said, plastering a smile on my face. "But I think I'll manage." It was important to act not crazy.

"Oh, I wasn't offering. Just making an observation." The boy pushed his wild dreadlocks out of his eyes and held out his hand. "I'm Jamie Roth."

"Mara Dyer," I said, though he already knew.

"Wait, are you new here?" A mischievous grin reached his dark eyes.

I matched it. "Funny. You're funny."

He gave an exaggerated bow. "Don't worry about Morales, by the way. She's the world's worst teacher."

"So she's that heinous to everyone?" I asked, after we were a safe distance away from the classroom. I scanned the campus for imagined dead people as I shifted my bag to my other shoulder. There were none. So far so good.

"Maybe not *that* heinous. But close. You're lucky she didn't throw any chalk at you, actually. How's your nose, by the way?"

Had he been in Algebra II this morning?

"Better, thanks. You're the first person to ask. Or say anything nice at all, actually."

"So people have said not-nice things, then?"

I thought I glimpsed a flash of silver in his mouth when he spoke. A tongue stud? Interesting. He didn't seem the type.

I nodded as my eyes drank in my new classmates. I knew there were variants of the school uniform—different shirt, blazer, and skirt/pants options, and sweater vests for the really adventurous. But when I looked for any telltale signs of cliques—wild shoes, or students with dyed black hair and makeup to match, I saw none. It was more than the uniforms; everyone somehow managed to look exactly alike. Perfectly groomed, perfectly well-behaved, not a hair out of place. Jamie, with his dreadlocks and tongue stud and exposed T-shirt, was one of the only standouts.

And, of course, the disheveled-looking person from this morning. I felt an elbow in my ribs.

"So, new chick? Who said what? Don't leave a fella hangin'."

I smiled. "There was this girl earlier who told me to 'watch it.'" I described Vending Machine Girl to Jamie and watched his eyebrows rise. "The guy she was with was equally unfriendly," I finished.

Jamie shook his head. "You went near Shaw, didn't you?"

Then he smiled to himself. "God, he really is something."

"Uh . . . does this Shaw happen to have an overabundance of muscles and wear his shirt with a popped collar? He was on the arm of said girl."

Jamie laughed. "That description could fit any number of Croyden douches, but definitely not Noah Shaw. Probably Davis, if I had to guess."

I raised my eyebrows.

"Aiden Davis, lacrosse all-star and *Project Runway* aficionado. Pre-Shaw, he and Anna used to date. Until he came out of the metaphorical closet, and now they're BFFs forevah." Jamie batted his eyelashes. I kind of loved him.

"So what did you do to Anna?" he asked.

I gave him a look of mock horror. "What did *I* do to *her*?"

"Well, you did *something* to get her attention. You'd normally be beneath her notice, but the claws will come out if Shaw starts sniffing around you," he said. He took a long look at me before he spoke again. "Which he will, having exhausted Croyden's limited female resources already. Literally."

"Well, she needn't trouble herself." I shuffled my schedule and my map, then looked around, trying to locate the annex for Biology. "I have no interest in stealing someone's boyfriend," I said. Or dating at all, I didn't say, considering my last boyfriend was now dead.

"Oh, he's not her boyfriend. Shaw dropped her ass last year after a couple of weeks. A record for him. Then she went even crazier—like the rest of them. Hell hath no fury like a woman scorned, and all that jazz. Anna used to be the abstinence poster girl, but post-Shaw, you could write a comic book about the many adventures of her vagina. It could wear a cape."

I snorted. My eyes scanned the buildings in front of me. None of them looked like an annex. "And the guy she was all cozy with has no problem with this?" I asked, distracted.

Jamie quirked an eyebrow at me. "The Mean Queen? That would be no."

Ah. "How'd he earn the nickname?"

Jamie looked at me like I was an idiot.

"I mean, specifically," I said, trying not to be one.

"Let's just say I tried to make friends with Davis once. In the platonic sense," Jamie clarified. "I'm not his type. Anyway, my jaw still clicks when I yawn." He demonstrated it for me.

"He hit you?"

The fountain burbled behind us as we crossed the quad, and stopped in front of the building farthest from the administration offices. I inspected the labels on the classroom doors. Completely random. I would never figure this place out.

"Indeed. Davis has a *vicious* right hook."

We had that in common, apparently.

"I got him back later, though."

"Oh?" Jamie wouldn't stand a chance in a knife fight with Aiden Davis if all Aiden had was a roll of toilet paper.

Jamie smiled knowingly. "I threatened him with Ebola."

I blinked.

"I don't actually *have* Ebola. It's a biosafety Level Four hot agent."

I blinked again.

"In other words, impossible for teenagers to obtain, even if your father is a doctor." He looked disappointed.

"Riiight," I said, not moving.

"But Davis believed it and almost soiled himself. It was a defining moment for me. Until that rat bastard tattled to the guidance counselors. Who believed him. And called my dad, to verify I didn't actually have Ebola at home. Idiots. One little joke involving hemorrhagic fever and they brand you 'unstable.'" He shook his head, then his mouth tilted into a smile. "You're, like, totally freaked out right now."

"No." I was, just a tad. But who was I to be picky in the friend department?

He winked and nodded. "Sure. So what class do you have next?"

"Biology with Prieta? In the annex, wherever the hell that is."

Jamie pointed to an enormous flowered bush about a thousand feet away. In the opposite direction. "Behind the bougainvillea."

"Thanks," I said, peering at it. "I never would have found it. So what's your next class?"

He shrugged out of his blazer and button down. "AP Physics, normally, but I'm skipping it."

AP Physics. Impressive. "So . . . are you in my grade?"

"I'm a junior," Jamie said. He must have registered my skepticism because he quickly added, "I skipped a grade. Probably absorbed my parents' short genes by osmosis."

"Osmosis? Don't you mean genetics?" I asked. "Not that you're short." A lie, but harmless.

"I'm adopted," Jamie said. "And please. I'm short. No biggie." Jamie shrugged, then tapped his watchless wrist. "You'd better get to Prieta's class before you're late." He waved. "See ya."

"Bye."

And just like that, I made a friend. I mentally patted myself on the back; Daniel would be proud. Mom would be prouder. I planned to offer this news to her like a cat presenting a dead mouse to its owner. It might even be enough to help stave off therapy.

If, of course, I kept today's hallucinations to myself.

8

I MANAGED TO SURVIVE THE REST OF THE DAY without being hospitalized or committed, and, after school ended, Mom was waiting for me at the cul-de-sac exactly as Daniel said she would be. She excelled at those small "mom" moments, and didn't disappoint today.

"Mara, honey! How was your first day?" Her voice bubbled with overenthusiasm. She pushed up her sunglasses over her hair and leaned in to give me a kiss. Then she stiffened. "What happened?"

"What?"

"You have blood on your neck."

Damn. I thought I'd washed it all off.

"I had a nosebleed." The truth, but not the whole truth, so help me.

My mother was quiet. Her eyes were narrowed, and full of concern. Par for the course, and so irritating.

"*What?*"

"You've never had a nosebleed in your life."

I wanted to ask "How would you know?" but, unfortunately, she *would* know. Once upon a time I used to tell her everything. Those days were over.

I dug my heels in. "I had one today."

"Out of nowhere? Randomly?" She gave me that piercing therapist stare, the one that says *You're full of it*.

I wasn't going to admit that I thought I saw my classroom fall apart the second I walked in it. Or that my dead friends reappeared today, courtesy of my PTSD. I'd been symptom-free since we'd moved. I went to my friends' funerals. I packed up my room. I hung out with my brothers. I did everything I was supposed to do to avoid being Mom's project. And what happened today wasn't remotely worth what telling her would cost.

I looked her in the eye. "Randomly." She still wasn't buying it. "I'm telling you the truth," I lied. "Can you leave me alone now?" But as soon as I spoke the words, I knew I'd regret them.

I was right. We drove the rest of the way home in silence, and the longer we went without speaking, the more obviously she stewed.

I tried to ignore her and focus on the route home, since I'd be driving myself to school in a few days thanks to Daniel's long-overdue dentist appointment. It was only mildly comforting that Mr. Perfect had a penchant for cavities.

The houses we passed were all low-slung and blocky, with plastic dolphins and hideous Greek-style statues dotting their lawns. It was as if the city council convened and voted to manufacture Miami to be utterly devoid of charm. We passed generic strip mall after generic strip mall, all proclaiming *Michaels! Kmart! Home Depot!* with their collective might. I couldn't for the life of me fathom why anyone would need more than one set of them within a fifty-mile radius.

We arrived at our new home after a gut-wrenching hour of traffic, which made my stomach roll with nausea for the second time that day. After pulling all the way into the driveway, my mother exited the car in a huff. I just sat there, motionless. My brothers weren't home yet, my dad definitely wouldn't be home yet, and I didn't want to enter the lion's den alone.

I stared at the dashboard, melodramatically stewing in the juices of my own bitterness, until a knock on the car door made me fly out of my skin.

I looked up and out at Daniel. The daylight had dwindled into evening, leaving the sky behind him a deep royal blue. Something inside me flipped. How long had I been sitting there?

Daniel peered at me through the open window. "Rough day?"

I tried to push my unease aside. "How'd you guess?"

Joseph slammed the door of Daniel's Civic, then walked

over with a huge smile on his face, his overstuffed backpack hooked between both arms. I got out of the car and clapped my little brother on the shoulder. "How was your first day?"

"Awesome! I made the soccer team and my teacher asked me to try out for the school play next week and there are some cool girls in my class but there's also a really weird one who started talking to me but I was nice to her anyway."

I grinned. Of course Joseph would sign up for every extracurricular activity. He was outgoing and talented. Both of my brothers were.

I compared the two of them, walking side-by-side toward the house with their matching gangly strides. Joseph looked more like our mother, and shared her stick-straight hair, unlike me and Daniel. But the two of them inherited her complexion, while I had my father's Whitey McWhiterson skin. And there was no family stamp of similarity in our faces. It made me kind of sad.

Daniel opened the door to the house. When we moved here a month ago, I was surprised to discover that I actually liked it. Boxwood topiaries and flowers framed the gleaming front door, and the lot was huge. I remember my father saying that it was almost an acre.

But it wasn't home.

The three of us entered together, a united front. I could hear my mother stalking in the kitchen but when she heard us come in, she appeared in the foyer.

“Boys!” she practically shouted. “How was your day?” She hugged them both, pointedly ignoring me while I hung back.

Joseph rehashed every detail with juvenile enthusiasm, and Daniel waited patiently for Mom to lob questions in his direction while he followed them to the kitchen. Seeing an opportunity for escape, I detoured down the long hallway that led to my bedroom, passing three sets of French doors on one side and several family photographs on the other. There were pictures of my brothers and me as infants and toddlers, and a few obligatory, awkward elementary school photos too. After that were pictures of other relatives and my grandparents. Today, one of them caught my eye.

An old black-and-white photograph of my grandmother on her wedding day stared back at me from its gilt frame. She was sitting placidly with her hennaed hands folded in her lap, her shining, jet-black hair parted severely in the middle. The flash in the photo made the bindi sparkle between her perfectly arched eyebrows, and she was swathed in extravagant fabric, the intricate patterns dancing on the edges of her sari. A strange sensation was there and gone before I could identify it.

Then Joseph came running down the hallway, two inches from knocking me over.

“Sorry!” he shouted, and raced around the corner. I tore my eyes from the picture and escaped into my new bedroom, closing the door behind me.

I plopped down onto my fluffy white comforter and

pushed off my sneakers using my footboard. They fell to the carpet with a dull thud. I stared back at the dark, bare walls of my bedroom. My mother had wanted my room pink, like my old room; some psychological nonsense about anchoring me in the familiar. So stupid. A paint color wasn't going to bring Rachel back. So I played the pity card and Mom let me choose an emo midnight blue instead. It made the room feel cool and my white furniture looked sophisticated in it. Small ceramic roses dripped from the arms of the chandelier my mother had installed, but against the dark walls, it didn't overly feminize the room. It worked. And I had my own bathroom for the first time, which was a definite perk.

I hadn't hung any sketches or pictures on the walls and didn't plan to. The day before we left Rhode Island, I dismantled the quilt of photos and drawings I'd tacked up, saving a pencil sketch of Rachel's profile for last. I stared at the solitary picture of her then, and marveled at how serious she looked. Especially compared to her giddy expression in school, the last time I remembered seeing her alive. I didn't see what she looked like at the funeral.

It was closed-casket.

9

"Honey? Are you sleeping?"

I startled at the sound of my mother's voice. How much time had passed? I was instantly anxious. A rivulet of sweat rolled down the back of my neck, even though I wasn't hot.

I pushed myself up on my bed. "No."

Her eyes searched my face. "Are you hungry?" she asked. All traces of her earlier irritation with me were gone. She looked worried now. Again. "Dinner's almost ready," she said.

"Is Dad home?"

"Not yet. He's working on a new case. He probably won't be home for dinner for a while."

"I'll be in the kitchen in a few."

My mother took a tentative step into my room. "Was the first day awful?"

I closed my eyes and sighed. "Nothing unexpected, but I'd rather not talk about it."

She looked away and I felt guilty. I loved my mother, truly. She was devoted. She was nurturing. But in the last year, she'd become painfully present. And in the past month, her hovering was all but unbearable. The day of our move, I spent the sixteen-hour drive to Florida silent, even though it was for my benefit—I was afraid to fly, and of heights in general. And when we arrived, Daniel told me that after my release, he overheard Mom and Dad arguing about the possibility of hospitalization. Mom was for it, naturally. Someone would be watching me all the time! But I had no desire to study for the SATs in a padded cell, and since the effect of my grand gesture—attending the funerals—had obviously worn off, I needed to keep my crazy in check. It seemed to be working. For now.

Mom let the conversation drop and kissed my forehead before returning to the kitchen. I got out of bed and padded down the hallway in my socks, careful not to slip on the lacquered wood floor.

My brothers had set the table already and my mother was still working on dinner, so I made my way to the family room and sank into the deep leather sofa before turning on the television. The news was on the picture-in-picture view, but I tuned it out as I clicked over the programs in the guide.

"Mara, turn that up for a second?" Mom asked. I complied.

Three photographs floated in the corner of the screen. "With the help of the Laurelton Police Department's Search and Rescue Unit, the bodies of Rachel Watson and Claire Lowe were recovered this morning, but investigators are having trouble recovering the remains of seventeen-year-old Jude Lowe due to the wings of the landmark that are still standing, but could collapse at any moment."

I squinted at the television. "What the—" I whispered.

"Hmm?" My mother walked into the family room and took the remote from my hand. When she did, the pictures of my friends vanished. In their place was a photograph of a dark-haired girl smiling happily in the corner of the screen next to the female news anchor.

"Investigators are pursuing new leads in the case of murdered tenth grader Jordana Palmer," the female anchor trilled. "The Metro Dade Police Department is conducting a new search for evidence with a team of K-9 units in the area bordering the Palmers' property, and Channel Seven has the footage."

The image on the screen flashed to a shaky video of a team of police in beige uniforms, accompanied by large German shepherds patrolling a sea of tall grass that stretched behind a row of small, new houses. "Sources say that the fifteen-year-old's autopsy reveals disturbing insights into the manner of her death, but officials wouldn't release any details."

"The leads, like I said, are the result of talking to witnesses that have come forward, and we will be following up on those leads today," said Captain Ron Roseman of the Metro Dade Police Department. "Other than that, I can't divulge anything that might compromise our investigation."

The anchors then cheerily transitioned to discussing some new literacy initiative in the Broward school district. Mom handed the remote back to me.

"Can I change it?" I asked, careful to keep my voice even. Seeing my dead friends on television had left me shaken, but I couldn't let it show.

"Might want to turn it off. Dinner's ready," she said. She looked anxious, more so than usual. I was starting to think she was the one who should be taking medication, and not for the first time.

My brothers pulled up to the table and I pasted on a lopsided grin as I joined them. I tried to laugh at their jokes as we ate, but I couldn't blot out the images of Rachel, Jude, and Claire I'd just seen. No, not seen. Hallucinated.

"Something wrong, Mara?" my mother asked, snapping me out of my trance. The expression on my face must have matched my feelings.

"No," I said breezily. I stood up, tilting my head forward so that my hair veiled my face. I picked up my plate and made my way to the sink to rinse it off before putting it in the dishwasher.

The dish slipped in my soapy hands and broke against the stainless steel. In my peripheral vision, I saw Daniel and my mother exchange a glance. I was a goldfish without a castle to hide in.

"You okay?" Daniel asked me.

"Yeah. It just slipped." I picked the shards out of the sink and threw them in the trash before excusing myself to do homework.

As I walked back down the hallway to my bedroom, I shot a look at my grandmother's portrait. Her eyes stared back, following me. I was being watched. Everywhere.

10

THAT SAME CREEPING, WATCHFUL FEELING escorted me to school the next day. I just couldn't shake it. As Daniel pulled into the school parking lot, he said, "You know, you should think about getting some sun."

I shot him a look. "Seriously?"

"I only mention it because you're looking a little peaked."

"Duly noted," I said dryly. "We're going to be late if you don't find a spot, you know."

Rachmaninoff floated softly from the speakers, doing nothing to settle my jangled mood.

Or Daniel's, apparently. "I am seriously itching to start playing bumper cars, here," he said, his jaw clenched. Even though we left early, it still took us forty minutes to drive to school, and there was already an egregiously long line of luxury cars waiting to pull into the entrance.

We watched as two of them vied on opposite ends of the lot for the same space; one of the waiting vehicles, a black Mercedes sedan, squealed its tires as the driver propelled it forward into the spot, cutting off the other car, a blue Focus. The Focus driver pounded one long, sharp note on the horn.

"Crazy," Daniel said.

I nodded as I watched the driver of the Mercedes exit the car along with another passenger. I recognized the immaculate sheet of blond hair on the driver even before I saw her face. Anna, naturally. Then I recognized the sour expression of her omnipresent companion, Aiden, as he emerged from the front passenger seat.

When we finally found a space, Daniel smiled at me before we parted.

"Just text me if you need me, okay? The lunch offer still stands."

"I'll be fine."

The door was still open when I arrived at AP English, but most of the seats were already filled. I sat down at one of the only available desks in the second row and ignored the snickers of a couple of students I recognized from Algebra II. The teacher, Ms. Leib, was busy writing something on the board. When she finished, she smiled at the class.

"Good morning, guys. Who can tell me what this word means?"

She pointed to the board, where the word "hamartia" was written. My confidence grew, having already had this lesson. Point one for the Laurelton public school system. I briefly looked around the class. No one raised a hand. Oh, what the hell. I raised mine.

"Ah, the new student."

I really, really needed that uniform.

Ms. Leib's smile was genuine as she leaned against her desk. "Your name?"

"Mara Dyer."

"Nice to meet you, Mara. Have at it."

"Fatal flaw," someone else called out. In a British accent.

I half-turned in my seat and would have recognized the boy from yesterday immediately even if he hadn't looked as distinctly rumpled as before, with his collar open, his tie knotted loosely around it and his shirtsleeves rolled up. He was still beautiful, and still smiling. I narrowed my eyes at him.

The teacher did the same. "Thank you, Noah, but I called on Mara. And 'fatal flaw' isn't the most precise definition, anyway. Care to take a shot at it, Mara?"

I did, particularly now that I knew that British Boy was the notorious Noah Shaw. "It means mistake or error," I said. "Sometimes called a tragic flaw."

Ms. Leib gave a congratulatory nod of her head. "Very

good. I'm going to go out on a limb here and assume you've read the *Three Theban Plays* at your previous school?"

"Yep," I said, fighting self-consciousness.

"Then you're ahead of the game. We've just finished *Oedipus Rex*. Can someone—not Mara—tell me what Oedipus' tragic flaw was?"

Noah was the only one to raise his hand.

"Twice in one day, Mr. Shaw? That's out of character. Please, demonstrate your dazzling intellect for the class."

Noah stared straight at me as he spoke. I was wrong yesterday—his eyes weren't gray, they were blue. "His *fatal* flaw was his lack of self-knowledge."

"Or his pride," I volleyed back.

"A debate!" Ms. Leib clapped her hands. "Love it. I would love it more if the rest of you would look alive, but hey." The teacher turned back to the board and wrote my answer and Noah's on the board, under "hamartia." "I think there are arguments to support both claims; that Oedipus' failure to acknowledge who he was—to know himself, as it were—caused his downfall, or that his pride, or more correctly, his hubris, led to his tragic fall. And for next Monday, I want a five-page paper from each of you with your brilliant analysis of the subject."

There was a collective groan from the class.

"Save it. Next week we start antiheroes."

Then she continued on with her lecture, most of which I'd

heard before. A bit bored, I took out my thoroughly dog-eared and well-loved copy of *Lolita* and hid it behind my notebook. The air conditioner in the class must not have been working, and the atmosphere grew increasingly stuffy as the minutes ticked by. When the bell finally rang, I was fiending for some fresh air. I sprung out of my seat, knocking it over. I crouched to lift it and set it right, but my chair was already in someone's hands.

Noah's hands.

"Thanks," I said as our eyes met.

He gave me the same familiar, knowing look as yesterday. Slightly ruffled, I broke the stare and gathered my things before hurrying out of the classroom. A throng of oncoming students jostled me and my book fell to the ground. A shadow darkened the cover before I could reach for it.

"You have to be an artist and a madman, a creature of infinite melancholy, in order to discern, at once, the little deadly demon among the wholesome children," he said, his British accent melting around the words, his voice smooth and low. "She stands unrecognized by them and unconscious herself of her fantastic power."

I stood there staring, openmouthed and speechless. I would have laughed—the whole thing was sort of ridiculous. But the *way* he said it, the way he was looking at me, was shockingly intimate. Like he knew my secrets. Like I *had* no secrets. But before I could think of a reply, Noah crouched and picked up my book.

"*Lolita*," he said, turning my book over in his hands. His eyes wandered over the pink-lipped mouth on the cover, then handed it to me. Our fingers brushed, and a warm current coursed through them. My heart thundered so loud he could probably hear it.

"So," he said, his eyes meeting mine again. "You're a smuthound with daddy issues?" The corner of his mouth turned up in a slow, condescending smile.

I wanted to smack it off of his face. "Well, *you're* quoting it. And incorrectly, by the way. So what does that make you?"

His half-smile morphed into a whole grin. "Oh, I'm *definitely* a smuthound with daddy issues."

"I guess you nailed me, then."

"Not yet."

"Asscrown," I muttered under my breath as I headed to my next class. I wasn't proud of swearing at a complete stranger, no. But he started it.

Noah matched my pace. "Don't you mean 'assclown'?" He looked amused.

"No," I said, louder this time. "I mean asscrown. The crown on top of the asshat that covers the asshole of the assclown. The very zenith in the hierarchy of asses," I said, as though reading from a dictionary of modern profanity.

"I guess you nailed me, then."

Not yet.

The words popped into my mind without permission, and I

ducked into my Algebra classroom and away from him the second I saw the door.

I sat in the back, hoping to hide from yesterday's stares and lose myself in the incomprehensibility of the lecture. I cracked *Lolita*'s spine and hid it under my bag. I took out my graph paper, then took out my pencil. Then exchanged that pencil for another pencil. Noah was getting under my skin. Not healthy.

But then Anna primly entered the classroom, accompanied by her not-so-little friend, and cut off my thoughts. The pair walked in like a matched set of evil. She caught me staring and I quickly looked away, but not without blushing. Out of the corner of my eye, I watched her watching me as she sat in the third row of desks.

I was flooded with relief when Jamie slipped into the seat next to me. My only friend at Croyden thus far.

"How goes it?" he asked, grinning.

I smiled back. "No nosebleeds."

"Yet," Jamie said, and winked. "So who else have you met? Anyone interesting? Besides me, obviously."

I lowered my voice and scratched at my graph paper. "Interesting? No. Assholish, yes."

The dimple in Jamie's cheek deepened. "Let me guess. A certain unkempt bastard with a panty-dropping smile?"

Maybe.

Jamie nodded. "That blush of yours tells me it is decidedly so."

"Maybe," I said casually.

"So you've met Shaw. What did he say?"

I wondered why Jamie was so interested. "He's an asshole."

"Yeah, you mentioned that. Now that I think about it," Jamie started, "that's what they all say. And yet that boy is drowning in pu—"

"All right class, take out your problems and pass them to the front, please." Mr. Walsh rose, and wrote out an equation on the blackboard.

"Nice visual," I whispered to Jamie. He winked, just as Anna turned to glare at me.

My second day passed in a sea of dreary mundanity. Lectures, homework, bad teacher jokes, homework, in-class assignments, homework. When it ended, Daniel was waiting for me at the campus perimeter and I was glad to see him.

"Hey, you," he said. "Walk faster so we can have a prayer of getting out of here before the cars clog up the only exit." When I complied, he asked, "Second day any better than the first?"

I thought about yesterday. "Mildly," I said. "But can we not talk about me? How was *your* day?"

He shrugged. "The usual. People are the same everywhere. Not many stand out."

"Not *many*? So some people actually stood out?"

He rolled his eyes at me. "A few."

"Come on, Daniel. Where's that Croyden enthusiasm? Let's hear it."

Daniel dutifully gave me the rundown of his senior class, and was in the middle of telling me about a brilliant female violinist in his music study when we arrived back home. The news blared from the living room, but my parents weren't home yet. Must be the little brother.

"Joseph?" Daniel shouted over the din.

"Daniel?" he shouted back.

"Where's Mom?"

"She went out to get dinner; Dad's coming home early tonight."

"Did you do your homework?" Daniel rifled through the mail on the kitchen table.

"Did you?" Joseph asked, without looking up.

"I'm about to, but nevertheless, I'm not the one engrossed in—what are you *watching*?"

"CNBC."

Daniel paused. "Why?"

"They recap the day's market trends," Joseph replied, without missing a beat.

Daniel and I exchanged a glance. Then he held up an incredibly thick envelope with no return address. "Where did this come from?"

"Dad's new client dropped it off like two seconds before you got here."

A look passed over Daniel's face.

"What?" I asked him.

And then it was gone. "Nothing."

He made his way to his room, and after a minute, I made my way to mine, leaving Joseph to face the consequences of being caught watching television before doing his homework. He'd charm his way out of them in about five seconds.

Some time later, a loud knock startled me from the depths of my Spanish textbook, which I'd decided was my most hated subject. Even worse than math.

My dad peeked in through a crack in my door. "Mara?"

"Dad! Hey."

My father walked into my bedroom, obviously tired but not at all rumpled despite spending the day in a suit. He sat down on the bed next to me, his silk tie catching the light.

"So how's the new school?"

"Why does everyone always ask me about school?" I said. "There are other things to talk about."

He feigned bafflement. "Like what?"

"Like the weather. Or sports."

"You hate sports."

"Ah, but I hate school more."

"Point taken," my dad said, smiling.

He then launched into a story about work, and midway through telling me about the lambasting of a clerk for wearing "hooker heels" by a judge today, my mother called us in for dinner. It was so much easier to laugh with my dad around, and that night I drifted off to sleep easily.

But I didn't stay asleep for long.

Before

I opened one eye when the pounding on my window grew too loud to ignore. The figure in my window brought his face up to the glass, peering. I knew who it was, and I wasn't surprised to see him. I buried myself under the warm covers, hoping he'd go away.

He knocked on it again. No such luck.

"I'm sleeping," I mumbled under my blanket.

He pounded on the glass even louder, and the old window rattled in its wooden frame. He was either going to break it, or wake my parents. Both scenarios were undesirable.

I inched over to my bedroom window and opened it a crack.

"I'm not home," I whispered loudly.

"Very funny." Jude opened the window, shocking me with a jet of cold air. "I'm freezing my ass off out here."

"That problem has a simple solution." I crossed my arms over my tank top.

Jude looked confused. His eyes were shaded under the brim of his baseball cap, but it was obvious that he was scanning my nighttime attire.

"Oh my God. You're not even dressed."

"I am dressed. I am dressed for bed. I am dressed for bed because it's two in the morning."

He looked at me, his eyes wide and mocking. "You forgot?"

"Yeah," I lied. I leaned out the window slightly and checked the driveway. "Are they waiting in the car?"

Jude shook his head. "They're at the asylum already. It's just us. Come on."

11

I WOKE IN THE MIDDLE OF THE NIGHT WITH A scream in my throat and an anchor on my chest, soaked in sweat and terror. I remembered. I *remembered*. The flood of recognition was almost painful. Jude at my window, there to pick me up and bring me to a waiting Rachel and Claire.

That was how I got there that night. The memory wasn't frightening, but the fact that it existed almost was. Or maybe not frightening—maybe *thrilling*. I knew with everything in me that my sleeping mind hadn't invented it—that the memory was real. I probed the edges of my consciousness for something more but there was nothing, no hint of why we'd gone.

My veins were flooded with adrenaline and I could not fall

back asleep. The dream—the memory—kept replaying itself on a loop, disturbing me more than it should have. Why now, all of a sudden? What could I do about it? What *should* I do about it? I needed to remember the night I lost Rachel—for her sake. For mine. Even though my mother wouldn't agree; my mind was protecting itself from the trauma, she'd say. Trying to force it was "unhealthy."

After the second night of the same dream, the same terror, I silently began to agree with her. I was a basket case in school that day, and the day after that. The Miami breeze blew hot but I felt the frigid December air of New England on my arms instead. I saw Jude at my window when I closed my eyes. I thought of Rachel and Claire waiting for me. At the asylum. The *asylum*.

But with everything on my plate at Croyden, I needed, more than anything, to relax. And so it was that I focused on little details that Friday morning; the swirling column of gnats that I almost choked on when exiting Daniel's car in the parking lot. The air swollen with humidity. Anything to avoid thinking about the new dream, memory, whatever, that had become a part of my nightly repertoire. I was glad Daniel had a dentist appointment this morning. I did not want to talk.

When I arrived at school, the parking lot was still empty. I'd overestimated the amount of time it would take to get there in traffic. Lightning flashed in distant purple clouds that spread over the sky like a dark quilt. It was going to rain, but

I couldn't sit still. I had to do something, to move, to shake off the memory that gnawed at my mind.

I threw open the car door and walked, passing more than a few empty, scraggly lots and some run-down houses. I don't know how far I'd gone before I heard the whimper.

I stopped and listened for the sound again. A chain-link fence stood in front of me, punctuated by barbed wire. There was no grass, only light brown, tightly packed dirt and mud in places where the ground was wet with last night's rain. Junk littered the space: machinery parts, pieces of cardboard, and some garbage. And a very large pile of lumber. Nails were scattered across the dirt.

I crept up to the barbed wire and tried to stand on my toes to see the entire expanse of the space. Nothing. I crouched, hoping to gain a different vantage point. My eyes panned over a cluster of car parts and moved across the scattered garbage to the lumber pile. The dog's short, fawn-colored fur almost blended into the dust under the precariously stacked wood. She was emaciated, every bone in her spine protruding from her patchy coat. Curled up into a tiny ball, the dog trembled despite the oppressive heat. Her black muzzle had numerous scars, and her ears were torn, and almost invisible behind her head.

She was in really, really bad shape.

I looked for a way inside the yard but saw none. I crouched and called her to me in the kindest, highest voice I could muster. She crawled out of the pile and walked to the fence with halting, tentative steps, looking through the metal with liquid brown eyes.

I had never seen anything so pathetic in my life. I couldn't leave her there, not like that. I would have to skip school and get her out.

That's when I noticed the collar.

The leather collar was secured with a padlock, attached to a chain so heavy it was incredible the dog could even stand. It didn't even need to be staked into the ground; she was going nowhere.

I petted her muzzle through the fence and tried to assess whether I could slip the collar over her large, bony head. I cooed to her, getting her to come closer so I could feel how tight it was, but just as I gained purchase under it, a nasal drawl interrupted the silence from just a few feet away.

"What the hell d'ya think you're doin' with my dog?"

I looked up. The man stood on my side of the fence, and he was close. Too close. It was not good that I didn't hear him approach. He wore a stained wife-beater and torn jeans, and his long greasy hair receded into a skullet.

What do you say to someone whose dog you plan to steal?

"Hi."

"I asked what you're doin' with my dog." He squinted at me with bloodshot, watery blue eyes.

I tried to swallow my desire to bludgeon him to death with

a tree limb and stalled, leaving his question hanging in the air. My options, being a teenage girl and not knowing whether this asshole had a knife or gun in his pocket, were limited.

I used my best innocent-dumb-girl voice. "I was just on my way to school and saw your dog! She's so sweet, what kind is she?" I hoped this would be enough to deter him from pillaging me for breakfast. I held my breath.

"She's a pit bull, ain't you never seen one before?" He ejected a wad of some foul substance from his mouth onto the dirt.

Not one that skinny. I'd never seen any dog, or any animal, that thin. "Nope. What a great dog! Does she eat much?" An obscenely stupid question. My lack of filter was going to get me killed one of these days. Maybe today.

"Whadda you care?"

Oh, well. Go big, or go home.

"She's starving, and that chain around her neck is too heavy. She has bites on her ears and scars on her face. Is this really the best you can do for her?" I said, my voice growing shrill. "She doesn't deserve this." I was losing it.

His jaw clenched along with the muscles in his body. He walked right up to my face. I held my breath but didn't move.

"Who the hell d'ya think you are?" he said, his voice a raspy hiss. "Get outta here. And if I see you 'round here again, I ain't gonna be this nice next time we meet."

I inhaled without meaning to, and a noxious odor wafted in my direction. I looked down at the dog, cringing away from her owner. I didn't want to leave her, but I couldn't see how to get around the obstacles: the barbed wire, the padlocked collar and heavy chain. Her owner. So I tore my eyes away and began to leave.

Then I heard a scream.

When I whipped around, the dog cowered so low she hugged the ground. Her owner held the heavy chain. He must have jerked it.

The sick bastard smiled at me.

I swelled with loathing, brimmed with it. I'd never hated anyone as much as I hated him in that moment; my fingers itched with the violence they wanted to do but couldn't. So I turned and ran, to give my trembling limbs some relief from the fury that boiled up from a dark place I didn't know existed. My feet pounded the pavement, wishing they could trample the smile on that piece of filth's face. And as the thought spiked through my brain, I saw it. The redneck's skull caved in, leaving a gaping, pulpy hole in the side of his head. A thick cloud of flies clogging his mouth. Blood staining the sandy dirt by the lumber pile in a wide, darkening pool around his body.

He deserved to die.

12

Sweaty and breathless, I rounded the parking lot by the school entrance and checked my watch. Seven minutes to spare before English. I grabbed my bag from the car, sprinted to class and made it a minute before the bell rang. Slick.

Ms. Leib closed the door behind me and I settled into the nearest available desk. Noah was there, looking as bored and careless and disheveled as ever. He sat at his desk without his book or notes, but that didn't stop him from answering each of Ms. Leib's questions correctly when she called on him. Show-off.

My mind wandered against the backdrop of the lecture. I had to do something about the dog. Help her, somehow. I'd just started to envision a dubious plan involving wire cutters, a ski mask, and mace when the bell rang. I made my way toward the door, anxious to get to my next class, but a throbbing mass of students had already assembled in front of it, crowding the exit.

When I finally escaped the confines of the classroom, I found myself staring directly into Anna's face. Her nose wrinkled in disgust.

"Don't you shower?"

I probably did smell ripe after this morning's sprint, but I was in no mood for her garbage. Not today. I opened my mouth, ready to let the abuse fly.

"I vastly prefer the unshowered to the overperfumed, don't you, Anna?"

That voice could only be Noah's. I turned around. He stood behind me wearing an almost imperceptible smile.

Anna's blue eyes went wide. Her face transformed from evil to innocent. Like magic, only more nefarious.

"I guess if those are your only two choices, Noah, then yes. But I'm partial to neither."

"Could have fooled me," Noah said.

That did not seem to be the response she'd been expecting from him. "Wh-whatever," she stammered, refocusing her gaze in my direction and staring daggers before she walked away.

Fabulous. Now she and I were definitely going to have a Thing.

I turned to face Noah. He shot an insolent smile at me, and

I bristled. "You didn't have to do that," I said. "I was handling it."

"A simple thank-you would suffice."

Rain began to spatter the roof of the walkway. "I really need to get to class," I said, and picked up my pace. Noah matched it.

"What do you have next?" he asked lightly.

"Algebra II." Go away. I'm smelly. And you bother me enormously.

"I'll walk with you."

Fail. I shifted my bag to my other shoulder, bracing myself for an uncomfortably silent walk. Out of nowhere, Noah tugged on my messenger bag, jerking me into a halt.

"Did you draw that?" he asked, indicating the graffiti on my messenger bag.

"Yep."

"You're talented," he said. I looked at his face. No sarcasm. No amusement. Was it possible?

"Thanks," I said, disarmed.

"Now it's your turn."

"For what?"

"To compliment me."

I ignored him.

"We can continue to walk in silence, Mara, or you can ask me a bit about myself until we reach the classroom."

He was infuriating. "What makes you think I'm at all curious about you?" I asked.

"Nothing," he replied. "In fact, I'm quite sure you're not at all curious. It's intriguing."

"Why's that?" My classroom was at the end of the hall. Not much longer, now.

"Because most girls I meet here ask me where I'm from when they hear my accent. And they're usually thrilled to have the pleasure of my conversation."

Oh, the arrogance.

"It's English, by the way."

"Yeah, I caught that." Only ten feet left.

"I was born in London."

Seven feet left. Not going to respond.

"My parents moved here from England two years ago."

Four feet.

"I don't have a favorite color, though I strongly dislike yellow. Horrid color."

Two feet.

"I play the guitar, love dogs, and hate Florida."

Noah Shaw played dirty. I smiled despite myself. And then we reached the classroom.

I darted to the back of the room and planted myself at a desk in the corner.

Noah followed me in. He wasn't even *in* this class.

Noah took the seat next to me, and I pointedly ignored the fit of his clothes on his narrow frame as he slid by. Jamie walked in and sat on my other side, giving me a long look before shaking his head. I took out my graph paper and prepared to calculate. Which meant that I doodled until Mr. Walsh came around to collect last night's homework. He stopped at the desk Noah was now occupying.

"Can I help you, Mr. Shaw?"

"I'm auditing your class today, Mr. Walsh. I'm in desperate need of an Algebraic brush-up."

"Uh-huh," Mr. Walsh said dryly. "Do you have a note?"

Noah stood and left the room. He returned as Mr. Walsh reviewed last night's homework, and, sure enough, handed the teacher a piece of paper. The teacher said nothing, and Noah sat back down next to me. What kind of school was this?

When Mr. Walsh began to speak again, I doodled furiously in my notebook again and ignored Mr. Walsh. The dog. Noah had distracted me, and I needed to figure out how to save her.

Thoughts of the dog consumed my morning. I didn't think about Noah, even though he stared at me in Algebra with the single-minded focus of a kitten playing with a ball of yarn. I didn't look at him once as I took notes, and didn't notice his permanently amused expression while I fidgeted in my seat.

Or the way he ran his long fingers through his hair every five seconds.

Or how he rubbed his eyebrow whenever Mr. Walsh asked me a question.

Or the way he leaned his coarse cheek into his hand and just . . .

Stared at me.

When class finally ended, Anna looked primed for murder, Jamie booked it before I could say a word, and Noah waited as I gathered my things. He had no things. No notebooks. No books. No bag. It was bizarre. My confusion must have shown on my face because that delinquent grin was back.

I resolved to wear something yellow the next time I saw him. Yellow from head to toe, if I could manage it.

We walked in silence until a swinging door ahead caught my eye.

The bathroom. An ingenious idea.

When we reached it, I turned to Noah.

"I'm going to be in here for a while. You probably don't want to wait."

I only briefly caught the horrified expression on his face before I pushed open the door with overwhelming force. Win.

There were a few girls in the bathroom of indeterminate age, but they paid no attention to me as they left. I was glad to get away from Noah, so I stifled the part of me that wanted to know his favorite song to play on guitar. Jamie had warned me about this nonsense; Noah was toying with me, and I'd be foolish to forget it.

And none of this was important. The dog was important. During Algebra, while ignoring Noah, I'd decided to call Animal Control and file a complaint against Abuser Douche. I took out my cell phone. Surely someone would be sent to follow up on my complaint, and see that the dog was on the brink of death. Then they'd get her out of there.

I dialed information, asking for the number of the city's Animal Control office and scribbled it down on my hand. The phone rang three times before a female voice answered.

"This is Animal Control Officer Diaz, can I help you?"

"Yes, I am calling to complain about a neglected dog."

It was impossible to sit still during the rest of the day, knowing that after school I had to check on the dog to make sure she was safe. I fidgeted in my chair in every class, earning me extra homework in Spanish.

When school ended, I flew down the slick stairs and almost broke my neck. The rain had stopped, for now, but it had infiltrated the covered walkways, making my progress treacherous. I was halfway to the parking lot when my cell phone rang; it wasn't a number I recognized, and I needed to concentrate on my footing anyway. I ignored it and jogged in the direction of the dog's house. But lights flashed ahead as I rounded the corner. My stomach flip-flopped. It could be a good sign. Maybe they arrested the guy. Still, I slowed to a walk as I approached, my fingers trailing the crumbling wall on the opposite side of the chain-link fence. I listened to the voices and the tinny sound of the police radio in front of me. As I neared the house, I saw a cruiser with the lights on and an unmarked car.

And an ambulance. The hair stood up on the back of my neck.

When I reached the yard, the front door of the house was open. People stood next to the cars by the quiet ambulance. My eyes scanned the property, looking for the dog, but as they reached the lumber pile, my blood froze.

You couldn't see his mouth at all, with the teeming mass of flies bubbling over it and the side of the pulpy mess that had been the man's scalp. The ground under his caved-in head was completely black, and the stain blossomed red at the edges of his dingy wife-beater.

The dog's owner was dead. Exactly as I had imagined it.

13

THE TREES, SIDEWALK, AND THE FLASHING lights spun around me as I felt it: the first unmistakable snarl in the delicate fabric of my sanity.

I laughed. I was that crazy.

Then I threw up.

Large hands grabbed my shoulders. Out of the corner of my eye, I saw a woman in a suit and a man in a dark uniform approach, but they were out of focus. Whose hands were on me?

"Great, just great. Get her out of here, Gadsen!" the female voice said. She sounded so far away.

"Shut it, Foley. You could have set up a perimeter just as easily," said the man's voice from behind me. He spun me around as I wiped my mouth. He was also in a suit. "What's your name?" he asked, with authority.

"M-Mara," I stammered. I could barely hear myself.

"Can you bring the EMTs over here?" he shouted. "She might be in shock."

I snapped to attention. No paramedics. No hospitals.

"I'm fine," I said, and willed the trees to stop dancing. I took a few deep breaths to steady myself. Was this even happening? "I've just never seen a dead body before." I said it before I even realized it was true. I hadn't seen Rachel, Claire, and Jude at their funerals. There wasn't enough of them left to see.

"Just to take a look," the man said. "While I ask you some questions, if that's all right." He signaled to the EMT.

I knew it wasn't a fight I could win. "Okay," I said. I closed my eyes but still saw the blood. And the flies.

But where was the dog?

I opened my eyes and looked for her, but didn't see her anywhere.

The EMT approached me and I tried to focus on not appearing insane. I breathed slowly and evenly as he flashed his penlight in both of my eyes. He looked me over, but just as he seemed to be wrapping it up, I overheard the female detective speak.

"Where the hell is Diaz?"

"She said she'll be here soon." The voice belonged to the man who'd been talking to me a minute ago.

"You want to go and tie up that dog better?"

"Uh, no?"

"I didn't want to touch it," the woman said. "I could see the fleas crawling in its fur."

"Ladies and gentlemen, Miami's finest."

"Go to hell, Gadsen."

"Calm down. The dog's not going anywhere. It can barely walk, let alone run away. Not that it matters. It's a pit bull, they're just going to euthanize it."

What?

"There's no *way* that dog did it. The guy tripped and cracked his skull open on the stake by the lumber pile—see? Don't even need to wait for the techs to tell us that."

"I didn't say the dog did it. I just said they're going to euthanize it anyway."

"Shame."

"Least it'll be put out of its misery."

After everything she'd been through, the dog was going to be put to sleep. Killed.

Because of me.

I felt sick again. My hand trembled as the EMT took my pulse.

"How are you feeling now?" he asked in a quiet voice. His eyes were kind.

"Fine," I lied. "Really. I'm all right now." I hoped that saying it would be enough to convince him that it was actually true.

"Then we're all done. Detective Gadsen?" The male detective

and the suited woman made their way over to us, and the man, Detective Gadsen, thanked the EMT as he headed back to the ambulance. Other people milled about around it, some in uniform and some not, and a truck had pulled up, with the words MEDICAL EXAMINER stenciled on the back. A slimy fear coated my tongue.

"Mara, is it?" Detective Gadsen asked me as his partner took out her notepad. I nodded. "What's your last name?"

"Dyer," I answered. His partner wrote it down. The armpits of her tan suit were darkened with sweat. So were his. But for the first time in Miami, I wasn't hot. I shivered.

"What brought you here this afternoon, Mara?" he asked.

"Um." I swallowed. "I was the one who called in the complaint about the dog." No point lying about that. I left my name and phone number with the Animal Control office.

His eyes didn't waver from my face, but I noticed a change in his expression. He waited for me to continue.

I cleared my throat. "I just wanted to stop by after school and see if Animal Control had picked her up."

At that, he nodded. "Did you see anyone else when you were here this morning?"

I shook my head.

"Where do you go to school?" he asked.

"Croyden."

The female detective wrote that down too. I hated when she did that.

He asked me a few more questions, but I couldn't keep my eyes from searching for the dog. The body must have been moved while I was being examined, because it was now gone. A metallic door slammed shut, and I jumped. I hadn't noticed that Detective Gadsen had stopped speaking. He was waiting for me to say something.

"Sorry," I said, as a few fat raindrops pelted the metal and tin scraps like bullets. It was going to pour again, and soon. "I didn't hear you."

Detective Gadsen studied my face. "I said my partner will walk you back to campus." The female detective looked like she wanted to go inside the house.

"I'm really fine." I smiled, demonstrating just how fine I was. "It's not far at all. But thank you anyway," I said.

"I'd be much more comfortable if—"

"She said she's fine, Vince. Come and take a look at this, will you?"

Detective Gadsen eyed me carefully. "Thanks for calling it in."

I shrugged. "I had to do something."

"Of course. If you remember anything else," the detective said handing me his business card, "call me anytime."

"I will. Thank you." I walked away, but when I turned the corner, I leaned against the cool stucco wall and listened.

One pair of footsteps crunched on gravel, soon accompanied by a second. The detectives talked to each other, and a third voice joined them, one I didn't remember hearing.

Someone must have been in the house before I got there.

"Best guess, he died about seven hours ago."

"So around nine a.m., then?"

Nine. Just a few minutes after I'd left him. I couldn't swallow, my throat was so dry.

"That's my guesstimate. The heat and the rain don't help. You know how it is."

"I know how it is."

I heard something then about temp and lividity and tripping and trajectories over the loud rush of blood pounding in my ears. When the footsteps and voices faded away, I chanced a peek around the wall.

They were gone. Inside the house, possibly? And from this angle, I could see the dog. She was tied loosely to a tire at the far end of the yard, her fur blending in with the dirt. The rain now fell steadily, but she didn't even flinch.

I ran to her without thinking. My cotton T-shirt was quickly soaked through. I dodged garbage and car parts, stepping as gingerly as I could, grateful for the rain that masked the sound of my steps. But if anyone in the house was paying attention, I'd probably be heard. And I'd definitely be seen. When I reached the dog, the sky opened vengefully as I knelt and untied her lead from the tire. I tugged on it lightly. "Come," I whispered by her ear.

The dog didn't move. Maybe she couldn't. Her neck was raw and seeping where they cut away the heavy collar and I didn't want to pull on it. But then the voices grew louder as they approached us. We had no time.

I snaked one arm under the dog's ribs and lifted her into a standing position. She was weak, but stayed up. I whispered to her again and pushed gently on her rump to urge her forward. She took a step, but went no farther. My cells buzzed with panic.

So I lifted her into my arms. She wasn't as heavy as she should have been, but she was still heavy. I lurched forward, taking huge strides until we were out of the yard. Sweat and rain slicked my hair to my forehead and my neck. I was panting by the time we rounded the block. My knees shook as I set her down.

I wasn't sure I could carry her all the way back to Daniel's car. And what would I do then? I hadn't thought that far ahead, but now the enormity of the situation I'd stepped in hit me. The dog needed a vet. I had no money. My parents weren't animal people. I'd stolen something from a crime scene.

A crime scene. An image of the bright watermelon insides of the man's skull spilling over into the dirt appeared again in my mind. He was definitely dead. Only hours after I wished it. Exactly the way I wished it.

A coincidence. Had to be.

Had to be.

The dog whined, snapping me back to reality. I reached down to pet her and took a tentative step forward, careful not to let the leash rub against her neck. It looked so painful.

I urged her forward and reached into my pocket for my cell phone. I had one new voice message. From my mother, at her new office. I couldn't call her back yet; I needed to get the dog to an animal hospital. I'd call 411 to find a vet close by. Then I'd figure out how to break the news to my parents that—surprise!—we have a dog. They had to take pity on their screwed-up daughter and her pathetic companion. I was not above milking my tragedy for a higher purpose.

The rain stopped again as suddenly as it had started, leaving only a fine mist in its wake. And as we turned the corner before the parking lot, I noticed the particular lope of a particular boy as he headed in my direction. He raked those fingers through his rain-drenched hair and fiddled with something in his shirt pocket. I tried to duck behind the nearest parked car to avoid him, but the dog barked at that exact second. Busted.

"Mara," he said as he approached us. He inclined his head and the shadow of a smile made his eyes crinkle at the corners.

"Noah," I replied, in the flattest voice I could muster. I kept walking.

"You going to introduce me to your friend?" His clear gaze settled on the dog. His jaw tightened as he took in the details—her knobby spine, her patchy fur, her scars—and for a second he looked coldly, quietly furious. But then it was replaced by a careful blankness.

I tried to appear casual, like I always went on my afternoon constitutional in the rain, accompanied by an emaciated animal. "I'm otherwise occupied, Noah." Nothing to see here.

"Where are you going?"

There was an edge to his voice that I didn't like. "My God, you're like the plague."

"A masterfully crafted, powerfully understated, and epic parable of timeless moral resonance? Why, thank you. That's one of the nicest things anyone's ever said to me," he said.

"The disease, Noah. Not the book."

"I'm ignoring that qualification."

"Can you ignore it while getting out of my way? I have to find a vet."

I lowered my eyes to the dog. She was staring at Noah, and weakly wagged her tail as he leaned down to pet her.

"For the dog I found." My heart pounded as my tongue formed my lie.

Noah raised an eyebrow at me, then checked his watch. "It's your lucky day. I know a vet six minutes from here."

I hesitated. "Really?" How random.

"Really. Come along. I'll drive you."

I debated the situation. The dog needed help, and badly. And she'd get looked at much, much sooner if Noah drove. With my sense of direction, I could end up driving aimlessly around South Miami until four in the morning.

I would go with Noah. "Thanks," I said and nodded at him. He smiled, and the three of us walked over to his car. A Prius.

He opened the back door, took the leash from my hands

and, despite the dog's patchy coat and the fact that she was infested with fleas, scooped her up and placed her on the upholstery.

If she peed all over his car, I would die. I had to warn him.

"Noah," I said, "I just found her two minutes ago. She's . . . a stray, and I don't know anything about her or if she's housebroken or anything and I don't want her to rui—"

Noah placed his forefinger above my upper lip and his thumb below my bottom lip, and applied the slightest pressure, cutting me off. I felt lightheaded, and my eyelids might have fluttered closed. So embarrassing. I wanted to kill myself a little.

"Shut up," he said quietly. "It doesn't matter. Let's just get her checked out, all right?"

I nodded feebly, my pulse galloping in my veins. Noah walked over to the passenger side and opened the car door for me. I climbed in.

14

I SETTLED INTO THE SEAT, ACUTELY AWARE OF MY proximity to him. Noah fumbled in his pocket and pulled out a pack of cigarettes, then a lighter. I spoke before I could help myself.

"You *smoke*?"

He flashed a small, mischievous smile at me. "Would you like one?" he asked.

Whenever he arched his eyebrows like that, his forehead creased in the most appealing way.

There was something wrong with me, absolutely. I chalked it up to my deteriorating sanity and avoided his eyes.

"No, I would not like one. Cigarettes are disgusting,"

Noah placed the pack back in the top pocket of his shirt. "I don't have to smoke if it bothers you," he said, but the way he said it set me on edge.

"It doesn't bother *me*," I said. "If *you* don't mind looking forty years old at twenty, smelling like an ashtray, and getting lung cancer, why should I?" The words tumbled out of my mouth. So obnoxious, but I couldn't help it; Noah brought out the worst in me. Feeling a tad guilty, I snuck a glance at him to see if he was annoyed.

Of course not. He just looked amused.

"I find it hilarious that whenever I light up, Americans look at me like I'm going to urinate on their children. And thanks for your concern, but I've never been ill a day in my life."

"How nice for you."

"It is nice, yes. Now, do you mind if I drive this starving dog in the back of my car to the veterinarian?"

And the guilt was gone. A rush of heat spread from my cheeks to my collarbone. "I'm sorry, is driving and talking too complicated? No problem, I'll shut up."

Noah opened his mouth as if to speak, then closed it again and shook his head. He pulled out of the parking lot and we sat in awkward silence for nine minutes, thanks to a train.

When we reached the vet's office, Noah left the car and started walking to the passenger side. I flung my door open, just in case he had a mind to open it. His coltish gait didn't change; instead, he opened the back door and reached for the dog. The upholstery was mercifully free of canine bodily fluids as he lifted the dog out. But instead of placing her on the ground, Noah carried her all the way to the door of the building. She nuzzled into his chest. Traitor.

As we neared the door, he asked me what her name was.

I shrugged. "I have no idea. I told you, I found her ten minutes ago."

"Yes," Noah said, cocking his head to one side. "You did tell me that. But they're going to need a name to register her under."

"Well, pick one, then." I shifted my weight from foot to foot, growing nervous. I didn't have a clue how I was going to pay for the vet visit, or what I would say once we went inside.

"Hmm," Noah murmured. He looked at the dog with a serious expression. "What's your name?"

I threw my head back in exasperation. I just wanted to get this over with.

Noah ignored me, taking his sweet time. After an eternity, he smiled. "Mabel. Your name is Mabel," he told the dog.

She didn't even look up at him; she was still curled up comfortably in his arms.

"Can we go in now?" I asked.

"You're a piece of work," he declared. "Now be a gentleman and open the door for me. My hands are full."

I complied, sulking the whole time.

When we walked in, the receptionist's eyes widened as she took in the dog's appearance. She rushed off to get the vet and my mind raced, trying to think of what I could possibly say to finagle treatment for the dog without having to pay for it. A cheerful voice from the other side of the large waiting area startled me from my scheming.

"Noah!" A petite woman emerged from one of the examining rooms. Her face was pleasant, alight with surprise. "What are you doing here?" she asked, beaming at him as he bent over and kissed both her cheeks. Curious.

"Hello, Mum," Noah said. "This is Mabel." He nodded down at the dog tucked into his arms. "My schoolmate Mara found her near campus."

It took a conscious exertion of will to nod my head. Noah's smile suggested that he noticed my bewilderment, and enjoyed it.

"I'm going to take her in the back to weigh her."

She motioned to the veterinary assistant, who gently extracted the dog from Noah's arms. Then it was just me and Noah in the waiting area. Alone.

"So," I started. "You didn't think to mention that your mother was the vet?"

"You never asked," he said. He was right, of course. But still.

When his mother came back into the room, she outlined the various treatments she was going to administer, which included keeping the dog over the weekend for observation. I silently thanked the heavens. That would buy me some time to figure out what I was going to do with her.

After she finished ticking off a list of Mabel's ailments, Noah's mother looked at me expectantly. Guess I couldn't delay the payment discussion any further.

"Umm, Dr. Shaw?" I hated the sound of my voice. "I'm sorry, I don't—I don't have any money with me, but if the receptionist can give me an estimate, I can get to the bank and—"

Dr. Shaw cut me off with a smile. "That won't be necessary, Mara. Thank you for . . . catching her, did you say?"

I swallowed and my eyes flicked to my shoes before I met her gaze. "Yes. I found her."

Dr. Shaw looked skeptical, but she smiled. "Thank you for bringing her in. She wouldn't have lasted much longer."

If she only knew. An image of her owner's body lying on blood-darkened mud flickered in my mind again, and I tried not to let it show in my face. I thanked Noah's mother profusely and then he and I headed back to the car. Noah's stride was twice as long as mine and he got there first, opening the passenger door for me.

"Thanks," I said, before glancing at his smug, self-satisfied expression. "For everything."

"You're welcome," he said, his voice laced with obnoxious triumph. As expected. "Now, are you going to tell me how you really found the dog?"

I turned away from his stare. "What are you talking about?" I hoped he wouldn't notice that I couldn't look him in the eye.

"You were walking Mabel on a slip lead when I saw you. There's no way she was wearing that, from the wounds on her neck. Where'd you get it?"

Being trapped, I did what any self-respecting liar would do. I changed the subject. My eyes fell on his clothes.

"Why do you always look like you just rolled out of bed?"

"Because usually I have." And the way he raised his eyebrow at me made me blush.

"Classy," I said.

Noah leaned back and laughed. The sound was raucous. I loved it immediately, then mentally flogged myself for the thought. But his eyes crinkled at the corners and his smile illuminated his entire face. The light changed, and Noah, still smiling, took his hands off the steering wheel and reached into his pocket, withdrawing the cigarettes. He drove with his knee as he tapped one out in his hand, flicked open a small silver lighter and lit up in one fluid movement.

I tried to ignore the way his lips curved around the cigarette, how he held it pinched between thumb and third finger, and drew it almost reverently to his mouth.

That *mouth*. Smoking was a bad habit, yes. But he looked *so* good doing it.

"I hate uncomfortable silences," Noah said, interrupting my less-than-clean thoughts. He tilted his head back slightly and a few strands of his spiking, curling hair caught a shaft of sunlight that filtered through his car window. "They make me nervous," he said.

That comment warranted an eye-roll. "I have a hard time believing anything makes you nervous." The words rang true. It was impossible to imagine that Noah was anything but comfortable, all the time. And not just comfortable—bored. Bored.

And gorgeous. And I was sitting next to him. Close.

My pulse raced to catch up with my thoughts. There was some villainy afoot, absolutely.

"It's true," he continued. "I totally freak out when people look at me, as well."

"I call shenanigans," I said, as the sounds of Miami floated in through the window.

"What?" Noah looked at me, all innocence.

"You're not shy."

"No?"

"No," I said, narrowing my eyes. "And pretending to be makes you look like a jackass."

Noah feigned offense. "You've wounded me to the core with your profane characterization."

"Pass the tissues."

Noah broke into an easy smile as the cars in front of us lurched forward. "All right. Maybe 'shy' isn't the right word," he said. "But I do get—anxious—when there are too many people around. I don't really like attention." He then studied me carefully. "A vestige of my dark and mysterious past."

It was a struggle not to laugh in his face. "Really."

He took another long drag on his cigarette. "No. I was just an awkward kid. I remember being, like, twelve or thirteen and all my friends had little girlfriends. And I'd go to sleep and feel like a loser, wishing that one day I could grow up and just be fit."

"Fit?"

"Yeah. Fit. Hot. Anyway, I did."

"Did what?"

"I woke up one morning, went to school, and the girls noticed me back. Rather unnerving, actually."

His candor caught me a little off guard. I tried not to let it show. "Poor Noah," I said, and sighed.

He smirked and stared straight ahead. "I figured out what to do with it eventually, but not until we moved here. Unfortunately."

"I'm sure you worked it out just fine."

He turned to me and arched an eyebrow. "The girls here are boring."

And the arrogance was back. "We Americans are so uncouth," I said.

"Not Americans. Just the girls here, at Croyden."

I noticed then that we were back in the parking lot. And parked. How did that happen?

"Most of them, anyway," Noah finished.

"You seem to be managing."

"I was, but things are looking up this week in particular."

So awful. I shook my head slowly, not even bothering to hide my grin.

"You're not like other girls."

I snorted. "Seriously?" And Jamie said he was smooth.

"Seriously," he replied, missing my sarcasm. Or ignoring it.

Noah took a final drag on his stub of a cigarette, breathed the smoke out of his flared nostrils and flicked the remains of the cancer stick out the window.

My mouth fell open. "Did I just see you litter?"

"I'm driving a hybrid. It cancels out."

"You're horrible," I said, without conviction.

"I know," Noah said, with it. He smiled, then reached over my lap to open my door, brushing my arm with his as he leaned across my body. He cracked my door open but didn't move away. His face was inches from mine, and I could see hints of gold in his perpetual five o' clock shadow. He smelled like sandalwood and ocean, but only faintly of smoke. My breath caught in my throat.

When my cell phone rang, I jumped so forcefully that my head hit the roof of Noah's car. "Whatthef—!"

The phone continued to ring, ignorant of my pain. The lyrics of Tupac's "Dear Mama" that Joseph had programmed for my ringtone indicated the culprit.

"I'm sorry, I have to—"

"Wait—" Noah started.

My heart galloped in my chest and only partly from surprise. Noah's lips were inches away from my face, my phone was protesting in my hand, and I was in trouble.

15

I MUSTERED UP EVERY OUNCE OF FREE WILL I HAD and extracted myself from his car. I gave him a half-hearted wave as I shut the door behind me. I answered the phone.

"Hello?"

"Mara! Where are you?" My mother sounded frantic.

I turned the key in the ignition of Daniel's car and glanced at the clock. I was seriously late. Not good.

"I'm driving home now." My tires squealed as I reversed out of the spot, and almost hit a parked black Mercedes in the spot behind me.

"Where have you been?" she asked.

She was counting every nanosecond I hesitated, so I went

with the truth. "I found a starving dog near the school and she was in really bad shape so I had to take her to the vet." There.

There was silence on her end before she finally asked, "Where is it now?"

Some jerk honked behind me as I turned onto the expressway. "Where is what?"

"The dog, Mara."

"Still at the vet."

"How did you pay for it?"

"I didn't—a classmate saw me and he took me to his mom, a vet, and she treated her for free."

"That's convenient," she said.

There it was; that edge to her voice. I was in it, and deep. I didn't respond.

"I'll see you when you get home," my mother said. Abruptly.

I was not looking forward to it, but I slammed on the gas at the first opportunity anyway. I dared the cops to pull me over, pushing ninety when I could. I wove in and out of lanes at every opportunity. I ignored the irritated honking. Miami was infecting me.

It wasn't long before I pulled into the driveway at home. I crept into the house like a criminal, hoping to be able to sneak into my room without being seen, but my mother was perched on the arm of the sofa in the sunken living room. She'd been waiting for me. Neither of my brothers was within sight or hearing. Curse them.

"Let's talk." Her expression was unnaturally calm. I braced myself for the onslaught.

"You have to answer the phone when I call. Every time."

"I didn't realize it was you calling before. I didn't recognize the number."

"It's my office number, Mara. I told you to program it in as soon as we moved, and left you a voice mail."

"I didn't have time to listen to it. Sorry."

My mother leaned forward, and her eyes searched my face. "Is there really a dog?"

I stared straight back into them, defiant. "Yes."

"So if I call the vet's office tomorrow morning and ask about it, they'll confirm?"

"You don't trust me?"

My mother didn't respond. She just sat there, eyebrows raised, waiting for me to say something.

I gritted my teeth, then spoke. "The vet's name is Dr. Shaw, and her office near school," I said. "I don't remember the street address."

Her expression didn't change.

I was sick of this. "I'm going to my room," I said. When I turned around, she let me go.

I closed the door a bit too forcefully. Trapped in my room, I couldn't delay thinking about what happened today any longer. Noah. Mabel. Her owner. His death.

Things were changing. Sweat pebbled my skin, even though

I knew it wasn't possible. It wasn't *possible*. I was in class at nine this morning, when that bastard died. He had to have died earlier. The coroner, or whoever he was, was wrong. Even *he'd* said he was just guessing.

That was it. I imagined my conversation with him. I'd thought he snuck up on me too quietly, but he didn't sneak up on me at all. He was already dead. The whole thing was just another hallucination—par for the course, really, considering my PTSD.

But still. Today felt . . . different. Confirmation that I was now crazier than I'd known it was possible for me to be. My mother worked with only the mildly disturbed. I was full on delusional. Abnormal. Psychotic.

When I joined my family for dinner that night, I felt strangely, disturbingly calm as I ate, as if watching the whole thing from a distance. I even managed to be polite to my mother. In a way, it was oddly comforting, the conviction of my insanity. The man died before I met him this morning. Wait, no—I *never* met him. I invented the conversation between us to give me a feeling of power over the situation in which I felt powerless; my mother's words, but they sounded about right. I was powerless to bring Rachel back, she'd said, after I was released from the hospital. Right before she mentioned—pushed—the idea of counseling and/or drugs to help me cope. And of course now, I was powerless to leave Florida and go back home. But a skinny, neglected, abandoned dog was something I could fix.

So that was it, then. I was *truly* crazy. But then why did I feel like there was something else? Something I was missing?

My mother's laughter at the dinner table brought me back to the present. Her whole face lit up when she smiled, and I felt guilty for freaking her out. I decided not to tell her about my little adventure today; if she watched me any closer, she'd turn into the Eye of Sauron. And then she'd follow through on her threat of therapy and medication. Neither option sounded particularly appealing, and really, now that I knew what was happening, I could deal with it.

Until I fell asleep.

16

BEFORE

We pulled into a long driveway guarded by a rusting iron gate. Thick branches of leafless trees twisted over the car, rasping in the wind. Our headlights provided the only light on the silent road. Despite the artificial heat, I shivered.

Jude put his arm around me and turned down Death Cab on the speakers. I looked out the window. The headlights flashed over an idling car about twenty feet away, and I instantly recognized it as Claire's. The glass was fogged and she cut the engine as we pulled up. I reached for the door and Jude reached for my waist. I gritted my teeth. I was already on edge, and wasn't up to fending him off again tonight.

I twisted away. "They're waiting for us."

He didn't let me go. "You sure you're ready?" He looked skeptical.

"Hell, yes," I lied. I smiled for emphasis.

"Because we can turn around if you want."

I can't say his suggestion wasn't appealing. Warm covers usually win over midnight excursions in the freezing cold.

But tonight was different. Rachel had been begging me to do this since last year. And now that she had Claire in her corner, my neuroses could cost me my best friend.

So instead of saying yes, emphatically yes, I rolled my eyes. "I said I was in. I'm in."

"Or, we could stay here." Jude pulled me toward him but I turned my head so that he caught my cheek.

"Do *you* want to turn around?" I asked, even though I knew the answer.

Jude pulled away, irritated. "I've already done this. It's just an old building. Big deal."

He launched himself out of the car and I followed. He'd be pissy later, but it was worth it. We'd been dating for only two months, and during the first one, I actually liked him. Who wouldn't? He was the picture of all-American wholesomeness. Dark blond hair and green eyes, same as Claire's. Big linebacker shoulders. And he was sweet. Syrup sweet. For the first month.

But lately? Not as much.

The passenger door of Claire's car slammed and Rachel bounded out to meet me, her dark hair flouncing behind her.

"Mara! I'm so glad you came. Claire thought you'd chicken out at the last minute." She hugged me.

I glanced at Claire, still huddled by the car. Her eyes narrowed slightly in return. She looked unfriendly and disappointed, likely hoping that I wouldn't show up.

I lifted my chin. "And miss my chance to spend the night in this illustrious insane asylum? Never." I placed an arm over Rachel and grinned at her. Then looked pointedly at Claire.

"What took you so long?" Claire asked us.

Jude shrugged. "Mara overslept."

Claire smiled coldly. "Why am I not surprised?"

I opened my mouth to say something obnoxious, but Rachel took my hand which had frozen solid in the few moments I'd been outside and spoke first.

"It doesn't matter, she's here now. This is going to be *so* much fun, I promise."

I looked up at the imposing Gothic building in front of us. Fun. Oh, yes.

Jude blew into his hands and pulled his gloves on. I steeled myself in anticipation of the long-ass night to come. I could do this. I would do this. Claire had made fun of me for freaking out after Rachel's birthday party for the last time. I was sick of hearing about the Ouija board incident. And after tonight, I wouldn't have to.

As I stared at the building, fear seeped into my bloodstream.

Rachel withdrew her camera from her pocket and opened the shutter, then took my right hand again as Jude moved to hold my left. Still, their company and the contact didn't make what we were about to do less terrifying. But I'd be damned before I freaked out in front of Claire.

Claire took out her video camera from her backpack before slinging it over her shoulder. She started walking toward the building and Rachel followed, pulling me along behind her. We reached a dilapidated fence with several NO TRESPASSING signs plastered along the length of the weathered wood, and I reflexively looked back up at the ominous institution above me, towering over us like something out of a Poe poem. The architecture of the Tamerlane State Lunatic Asylum was formidable, made more sinister by the creeping ivy that snaked its way along the front steps and expansive brick walls. The stone window facades crumbled in decay.

The plan was to spend the night in the abandoned building and head home at dawn. Rachel and Claire wanted to thoroughly explore it, and try to find the children's wing and the rooms where shock therapy was administered. According to Rachel's canonical horror literature, those would be the rooms most likely to contain any paranormal activity, and she and Claire planned to document our adventure for posterity. Hooray.

Jude inched closer to me, and I was actually grateful for his presence as Rachel and Claire scaled the rotting wood fence.

Then it was my turn. Jude gave me a lift but I hesitated as I grabbed the fragile wood. After a few words of encouragement, I finally hoisted myself over with his help. I landed hard, into a rustling pile of decaying leaves.

The easiest way into the building was through the basement.

17

I KNEW RACHEL WANTED TO GO TO THE ASYLUM. But until the night after Mabel's piece of shit owner died, I didn't remember why I agreed.

On Saturday I tried to prepare myself to dream more, to remember more—to watch her die. I crawled into my sheets shaking, wanting and not wanting to see her again. I did, but it was the same dream. Nothing new on Sunday night, either.

It was a good sign, the remembering. It was happening slowly, but it was happening nonetheless. And without a psychologist or mind-altering chemicals. My mind was obviously altered enough.

I was almost glad to have Mabel to wonder and worry about all weekend, even if I couldn't bring myself to try and find out Noah's phone number. I figured I'd ask him how the dog was in English on Monday, but when I got to class, he wasn't there.

Instead of listening, my mind and my pencil wandered over my sketchbook, drifting lazily as Ms. Leib collected our papers and discussed the difference between tragic heroes and antiheroes. Each time a student left or entered the classroom, my gaze shifted to the door, waiting for Noah to stroll in before the next bell rang. But he never did.

When class ended, I glanced at the drawing before closing the book and stuffing it in my bag.

Noah's charcoal eyes squinted at me from the page, cast downward, the skin around them crinkled in laughter. His thumb grazed his bottom lip as his hand curled in a lazy fist at his brilliantly smiling mouth. He looked almost shy as he laughed. The pale plain of his forehead was smooth, relaxed mid-chortle.

My stomach churned. I flipped to the previous page, and noted with horror that I'd traced Noah's elegant profile perfectly, from his high cheekbones down to the slight bump in his solemn nose. And on the page before that, his eyes stared back at me, aloof and unattainable.

I was afraid to keep looking. I needed serious help.

I shoved the sketchbook in my bag and glanced furtively over my shoulder, hoping no one saw. I was halfway to Algebra before I felt a light tap on my back. But when I turned around, no one was there. I shook my head. I felt strange all of a sudden, like I was floating through someone else's dream.

By the time I arrived at Mr. Walsh's classroom, I was surrounded by laughter. Some guys whistled when I walked in the room. Because I was finally wearing an iteration of the school uniform? I didn't know. Something was happening, but I didn't understand it. My hands trembled at my sides so I balled them into fists as I sat at the desk next to Jamie's. That was when I noticed the sound of crunching paper behind me. The crunching of the paper that was taped to my back.

So someone *did* bump into me earlier. That, at least, I hadn't hallucinated. I reached around and pulled the sign off my back, where the word "slut" was scrawled on a sheet of looseleaf. The quiet snickers then erupted into laughter. Jamie looked up, confused, and I flushed as I crumpled the paper in my fist. Anna threw her head back and roared with laughter.

Without thinking about it, I unfurled one of my fists and placed the wad of paper in my flat palm.

And then I flicked it in her face.

"Creative," I said to her as it hit its target.

Anna's tan cheeks turned red first, and then a vein protruded from her forehead. She opened her mouth to fling an insult my way but Mr. Walsh cut her off before she began. Score.

Jamie grinned and clapped me on the shoulder as soon as class ended. "Well played, Mara."

"Thanks."

Aiden pushed past Jamie on his way out the door, slamming Jamie's shoulder into the door frame. Aiden turned before leaving the room.

"Don't you have a lawn you should be decorating?"

Jamie glared after him and rubbed his shoulder. "He needs a knife in the eye," he muttered, once Aiden was gone. "So. A-holes aside, how's your first week?"

Oh, you know. Saw a dead guy. Losing my mind. Same old. "Not too bad."

Jamie nodded. "Big change from your old school, is it?"

When he asked me that, a still frame of Rachel materialized in my brain. "Is it that obvious?"

"You've got public school written all over you."

"Uh, thanks?"

"Oh, that's a compliment. I've sat in class with these douches for most of my waking life. It's nothing to be proud of. Trust."

"Going to private school or going to Croyden?" I asked as we made our way to his locker.

"From what I've heard from friends at other schools, I believe this level of asshattery is unique to Croyden. Take Anna, for example. She's only a few IQ points above a corpse, and yet she sullies our Algebra II class with her stupidity."

I decided not to mention that I was probably just as confounded by the homework as she was.

"The amount your parents donate is directly proportional

to how much murder you're allowed to get away with," Jamie said as he exchanged his books. When a shadow blocked the light filtering in from the midday sun, I looked up.

It was Noah. As always, the top button of his collar was undone, his shirtsleeves were carelessly rolled up, and today he wore a skinny, knitted tie loosely knotted around his neck. I could just make out the black cord that hung around his neck, peeking out from beneath the open collar of his shirt. It was a good look for him. A great look, actually, despite the shadows that stained the skin under his eyes. His hair was in its permanent state of disarray as he ran a hand over his rough jaw. When he caught me staring, I blushed. He smirked. Then walked away, without saying a word.

"So it begins." Jamie sighed.

"Shut up." I turned around so he couldn't see me flush a deeper shade of red.

"If he wasn't such a dick, I'd applaud," Jamie said. "You could start a fire with the heat between you two."

"You're mistaking bitter animosity for heartfelt affection," I said. But when I thought about last week, and how Noah had been with Mabel, I wasn't so sure if I was right.

Jamie answered with a sad shake of his head. "It's only a matter of time."

I shot him a poisonous look. "Before . . . ?"

"Before you're doing the walk of shame out of his den of iniquity."

"Thanks for thinking so highly of me."

"It's not your fault, Mara. Girls can't help falling for Shaw, especially in your case."

"My case?"

"Noah is clearly smitten with you," Jamie said, his voice dripping with sarcasm. He shut his locker and I spun around to walk away. Jamie followed behind me. "And that ass don't hurt, neither."

I smirked over my shoulder at him. "What's your deal with him, anyway?"

"You mean, aside from the fact that his attention already has Anna Greenly gunning for you?"

"Aside from that."

He considered his words, the mulch crunching under our feet as we cut across one of the flower beds to the picnic tables. "Noah doesn't date. He'll screw you—literally and figuratively. Everyone knows it—his conquests know it—but they pretend not to care until he moves on to the next one. And then they're alone and their reputations are shot to hell. Anna's a prime example, but she's only one of many. I heard that a senior from Walden tried to commit suicide after he—well. After he got what he came for, pun intended, and didn't call again."

"Sounds like a *major* overreaction on her part."

"Maybe, but I wouldn't want to see that happen to you," Jamie said. I raised my eyebrows. "You have enough problems," Jamie said, and a wide grin spread across his face.

I returned it. "How magnanimous of you."

"You're welcome. Consider yourself warned. Much good may it do you."

I shifted my bag to my other shoulder. "Thanks for telling me," I said to Jamie. "I'm *not* interested, but it's good to know."

Jamie shook his head. "Uh-huh. When you're all broken-hearted and listening to sad kill-yourself music after it ends, just remember I told you so." He walked off and left me at the door to History. Wise were his words, but forgotten in the face of my next class.

Lunchtime found me once again scrounging for scraps from the snack machine. I rooted around in my bag for change when I heard footsteps approach. Somehow, I didn't need to turn to know who it was.

Noah reached around me, brushing my shoulder as he placed a dollar in the machine. I sidestepped out of his way.

"What shall I get?" he asked.

"What do you want?"

He looked at me and tilted his head, and one corner of his mouth lifted into a smile. "That's a complicated question."

"Animal crackers, then."

Noah looked confused, but he pressed E4 anyway and the machine obeyed. He handed me the box. I handed it back to him, but he laced his hands behind his back.

"Keep it," he said.

"I can buy my own, thanks."

"I don't care," he said.

"What a surprise," I said. "How's Mabel, by the way? I meant to ask you about her this morning but you weren't in class."

Noah gave me a blank look. "I had a previous engagement. And she's hanging in. She's not going anywhere for a while, though. Whoever let her get that way ought to die a slow, painful death."

Suddenly queasy, I swallowed hard before speaking. "Thank your mom again for taking care of her," I said, trying to shake it off as I made my way to a picnic table. I sat on its pitted surface and opened the box of crackers. Maybe I just needed to eat. "She was amazing." I bit the head off an elephant. "Just let me know when I should pick her up?"

"I will."

Noah loped onto the picnic table and sat beside me, leaning back on his arms but staring straight ahead. I munched next to him in silence.

"Have dinner with me this weekend," he said out of nowhere.

I almost choked. "Are you asking me out?"

Noah opened his mouth to respond just as a group of older girls burst forth from the stairwell. When they saw him, they arrested their breakneck pace and sashayed suggestively as they walked past us, tossing a chorus of "Hey, Noah"s behind them. Noah seemed to ignore them, but then, the tiniest twitch of a traitorous smile began at the corners of his lips.

That was all the reminder I needed. "Thanks for the invitation, but I'm afraid I must decline."

"Already have plans?" His voice suggested he was merely waiting to hear my excuse.

I delivered. "Yeah, a date with all of the crap I've missed in school," I said, then tried to recover. "You know, from transferring in late." I didn't want to talk about that now. Especially not with him. "The trimester exams are twenty percent of our grade, and I can't afford to screw them up."

"I can help you study," Noah said.

I looked at him. The dark lashes that framed his gray-blue eyes weren't helping my situation. Neither was the slightly mischievous smile on his lips. I turned away. "I do better studying on my own."

"I don't think that's true," he said.

"You don't know me well enough to make that assessment."

"So let's change that, then," he said matter-of-factly. He continued to stare straight ahead as a few strands of hair fell forward into his eyes.

He was killing me. "Look, Shaw—"

"We're starting with the surname nonsense, are we?"

"Hysterical. Ask someone else."

"I don't want to ask someone else. And you don't really want me to either."

"Wrong." I hopped off the table and walked away. If I didn't look at him, I'd be fine.

Noah caught up to me in two long strides. "I didn't ask you to marry me. I asked you for dinner. What, are you afraid I'll ruin the image you're cultivating here?"

"What image," I said flatly.

"Angsty, solitary, introspective emoteen, staring off into the distance as she sketches withered leaves falling from bare branches and . . ." Noah's voice trailed off, but the look of cool amusement on his face didn't.

"No, that was lovely. Please, continue."

I rushed ahead until another girls' bathroom appeared. I pushed the door open, planning to leave Noah outside while I collected myself.

But he followed me in.

Two younger girls were standing at the mirror applying lip gloss.

"Get out," Noah said to them, his voice laced with boredom. As if they were the ones who didn't belong in the girl's bathroom. But they didn't wait to be told twice. They scooted out so fast that I would have laughed if I hadn't been so shocked myself.

Noah directed his gaze at me, and something flickered behind his eyes. "What's your problem?" he asked in a low voice.

I looked at him. Gone was the casual indifference. But he wasn't angry. Or even annoyed. More like . . . curious. His quiet expression was ruinous.

"I don't have a problem," I said confidently. I took a step

forward, eyes narrowed at Noah. "I'm problem-free."

His long frame, accentuated by the spare line of his untucked shirt and slim cut pants looked so out of place against the ugly yellow tile. My breathing accelerated.

"I'm not your type," I managed to say.

Noah then took a step toward me, and a deviant smile teased the corner of his mouth. Damn. "I don't have a type."

"That's even worse," I said, and I swear I tried to sound mean when I said it. "You're as indiscriminate as they say."

But I wanted him closer.

"I've been slandered." His voice was barely above a whisper. He took another step, so close that I felt the warm aura of his chest. He looked down at me, all sincere and open and with that chaos hair in his eyes and I wanted and didn't want and I had to say something.

"I doubt it" was the best I could do. His face was inches from mine. I was going to kiss him, and I was going to regret it.

But at that moment, I couldn't bring myself to care.

18

I HEARD HE E-MAILED HER A PICTURE OF HIS—OH. Hi, Noah." The voice stopped mid-sentence, and I could hear the coy smile in it.

Noah closed his eyes. He stepped away from me and turned to face the intruders. I blinked, trying to bring everything back into focus.

"Ladies," he said to the openmouthed girls and nodded. Then he walked out.

The girls giggled, stealing sidelong glances at me while they fixed their melting makeup in front of the mirror. I was still slack-jawed and shell-shocked, staring at the door. Only when the bell rang did I finally remember how to walk.

I didn't see Noah again until Wednesday night.

I spent the day mildly freaked out from lack of sleep, general malaise, and angst over what had happened between us. On Monday, he'd walked out on me like it was nothing. Like Jamie warned me he would. And I'd be lying if I said it didn't sting.

I had no idea what, if anything, I was going to say to Noah when I saw him. But English came and went, and he didn't show. I dutifully took notes from Ms. Leib and loitered outside of the class when it ended, scanning the campus for Noah without understanding why.

In Algebra, I tried to focus on the polynomials and parabolas but it was becoming painfully clear that while I could coast in Bio, History, and English, I was struggling in math. Mr. Walsh called on me twice in class and I gave a grievously wrong answer each time. Each homework assignment I'd submitted was returned with angry red pencil marks all over it, punctuated by a disgraceful score at the bottom of the page. Exams were in a few weeks, and I had no hope of catching up.

When class ended, an odd bit of conversation caught my attention, scattering my thoughts.

"I heard she was eaten after he killed her. Some kind of cannibal thing," a girl said behind me. She punctuated her remark with a crack of her gum. I turned around.

"You're an idiot, Jennifer," a guy named Kent, I think, shot back at her. "Eaten by alligators, not the pedophile."

Before I could hear more, Jamie dropped his binder on my desk. "Hey, Mara."

"Did you hear that?" I asked him, as Jennifer and Kent left the classroom.

Jamie looked confused at first, but then understanding transformed his face. "Oh. Jordana."

"What?" The name rang a bell, and I tried to remember why.

"That's who they were talking about. Jordana Palmer. She was a sophomore at Dade High. I know someone who knows someone who knew her. Kind of. It's really sad."

The pieces clicked into place. "I think I heard something about it on the news," I said quietly. "What happened to her?"

"I don't know the whole story. Just that she was supposed to show up at a friend's house and then . . . didn't. They found her body a few days later, and she was definitely murdered, but I haven't heard how, yet. Her dad's a cop, and I think they're keeping it quiet or something. Hey, you okay?"

That was when I tasted the blood. Apparently I'd chewed on the skin of my bottom lip until it split. I flicked out my tongue to catch the drop.

"No," I said truthfully, as I made my way outside.

Jamie followed me. "Care to share?"

I didn't. But when I met Jamie's eyes, it was like I didn't have a choice. The weight of all the weirdness—the asylum, Rachel, Noah—all of it just bubbled up, trying to claw its way out of my throat.

"I was in an accident before we moved here. My best friend

died." I practically vomited the words. I closed my eyes and exhaled, appalled by my overshare. What was wrong with me?

"I'm sorry," Jamie said, lowering his eyes.

I'd made him feel awkward. Fabulous. "It's okay. I'm okay. I don't know why I just said that."

Jamie shifted uncomfortably. "It's cool," he said. Then he smiled. "So when do you want to study Algebra?"

A random segue, and a ridiculous one. There was no way Jamie would benefit from having me as a study partner; not when he nailed each and every question Mr. Walsh lobbed at him.

"You are aware that my math skills are even more lacking than my social skills?"

"Impossible." Jamie's mouth spread into a mocking grin.

"Thanks. Seriously, you must have better things to do with your life than waste it on the hopeless?"

"I've already learned Parseltongue. What else is there?"

"Elvish."

"You're like, a gen-u-wine nerd. Love it. Meet me at the picnic tables during lunch. Bring your brain, and something for it to do," he said as he walked away. "Oh, your flap's open, by the way," he called over his shoulder.

"Excuse me?"

Jamie pointed at my messenger bag with a grin, then strolled to his next class. I closed my bag.

When I met him at the appointed time, math textbook in

hand, he was all smiles, ready and waiting to bear witness to my idiocy. He took out his graph paper and textbook but my mind glazed over as soon as I glanced at the numbers on the glossy page. I had to will myself to focus on what Jamie was saying as he wrote out the equation and explained it patiently. But after only minutes, as if a switch had been flipped in my brain, the numbers began to make sense. We worked through problem after problem until all of the week's homework was finished. Half an hour for what would normally have taken me two and netted me an F for my efforts, and my work was perfect.

I gave a low whistle. "Damn. You're good."

"It's all you, Mara."

I shook my head. He nodded his.

"All right," I acquiesced. "Either way, thanks."

He bent into an exaggerated bow before we headed to Spanish. We made meaningless small talk on the way, steering clear of dead people as a topic of conversation. When we reached the classroom, Morales lumbered up from her desk to the blackboard and wrote down a series of verbs for us to conjugate. Characteristically, she called on me first. I answered wrong. She threw a piece of chalk at me, scattering my good mood from my lunchtime study session into a million pieces.

When class ended, Jamie offered to help me with Spanish, too. I accepted.

At the end of the day, I stuffed my now unnecessary textbook in my locker. I needed to spend some quality time with my sketchbook *not* drawing Noah, not drawing anyone. I shifted my books to one side of the locker and searched through a week's worth of refuse, but didn't see it. I leafed through my messenger bag, but it wasn't there, either. Irritated, I dropped my bag so I could focus, and it slid against the bottom row of lockers, dislodging some pink fliers taped to the metal before it hit the concrete. Still nothing. I started pulling out my books one at a time as raw, arctic fear coiled in my stomach. Faster and faster, I tore through my things and let them fall to the ground until I was staring at my empty locker.

My sketchbook was gone.

Tears threatened my eyes, but a bunch of students walked into the locker niche and I refused to cry in public. Sluggishly, I put my books back into my locker and removed the flier that was now stuck to the front of my Algebra textbook. A costume party on South Beach hosted by one of Croyden's elite, in honor of the teacher workday tomorrow. I didn't bother reading the rest of the details before letting it fall to the ground again. Not my scene.

None of this was my scene. Not Florida and its hordes of tan blonds and mosquitoes. Not Croyden and its painfully generic student body. I'd made a friend in Jamie, but I missed Rachel. And she was gone.

Screw it. I ripped a flier off of another locker and shoved it in my messenger bag. I needed a party. I jogged to the back gate to meet Daniel. He looked uncharacteristically cool in the Croyden uniform, and happy until he saw me—then his face transformed into a mask of brotherly concern.

"You're looking unusually glum this afternoon," he said.

I got in the car. "I lost my sketchbook."

"Oh," he said. And after a beat, "Was there anything important in it?"

Other than the several detailed sketches of the most infuriatingly beautiful person in our school? No, not really.

I changed the subject. "What were you looking so happy about before I curdled your good mood?"

"Did I look happy? I don't remember looking happy," he said. He was stalling. And speeding. I glanced at the odometer; he was doing over fifty miles per hour before we got to the highway. Living dangerously for Daniel. Very suspicious.

"You looked happy," I said to him. "Spill."

"I'm going to the party tonight."

I did a double take. It definitely wasn't *Daniel's* scene. "Who are you going with?"

He blushed and shrugged. No way. Did my brother have a . . . crush?

"Who?!" I demanded.

"The violinist. Sophie."

I stared at him, mouth agape.

"It's not a date," he added immediately. "I'm just meeting her there."

The beginnings of an idea sprouted as we turned off the

highway. "Mind if I tag along?" I asked. Now it was Daniel's turn to double take. "I promise not to interfere with your amorous advances."

"You know, I was going to say yes, but now..."

"Oh, come on. I just need a ride."

"All right. But who are *you* going to see, pray tell?"

Huh. I hadn't planned to see anyone. I just wanted to dance and sweat and forget and—

"What the hell?" Daniel whispered, as we rounded the corner of our street.

A massive gathering of news vans and people lined the pavement in front of our driveway. Daniel and I looked at each other, and I knew we shared the same thought.

Something was wrong.

19

THE SEA OF REPORTERS PARTED FOR DANIEL'S car as he pulled into the driveway. They peered at us as we rolled by; the cameramen seemed to be packing up their equipment, and the satellites on the vans had been retracted into the vehicles. Whatever had happened, they were getting ready to leave.

As soon as Daniel came to a stop, I rocketed out of the car toward the front door, passing both my mother and father's car. My father's car. Which didn't belong here this early.

I was ready to be sick when I finally burst into the house with Daniel behind me. Electronic machine gunfire and video game music met my ears, and the familiar shape of our little brother's head stared up at the screen from his cross-legged position on the floor. I closed my eyes and breathed through flared nostrils, trying to slow my heart before it exploded in my chest.

Daniel was the first to speak. "What the hell is going on?"

Joseph half-turned to look at Daniel, annoyed at the interruption. "Dad took on some kind of big case."

"Can you turn that off?"

"One sec, I don't want to die." Joseph's avatar bludgeoned a mustachioed villain into a thick, oozing puddle of goo.

My parents appeared soundlessly in the door frame of the kitchen.

"Turn it off, Joseph." My mom sounded exhausted.

My brother sighed and paused the game.

"What's happening?" Daniel asked.

"A case of mine is going to trial soon," my father said, "and I was announced as the defendant's new counsel today."

A shadow of comprehension passed over my older brother's face, but I didn't get it.

"We just moved here," I said. "Isn't that, like, unusually fast?"

My mother and father exchanged a look. There was definitely something I was missing.

"What? What's going on?"

"I took over the case for a friend of mine," my father said.

"Why?"

"He withdrew."

"Okay."

"Before we moved here."

I paused to absorb what I was hearing. "So you had the case before we moved to Florida."

"Yes."

That shouldn't matter, unless . . .

I swallowed, and asked the question I already knew the answer to. "What is it? What case?"

"The Palmer murder."

I massaged my forehead. No big deal. My father had defended murder cases before, and I tried to calm the nausea that unsettled my stomach. My mother started assembling ingredients from the pantry for dinner, and for no reason, no good reason at all, I pictured human body parts on a plate.

I shook my head to clear it. "Why didn't you tell us?" I asked my father. Then glanced at Daniel, wondering why he was so quiet.

He avoided my gaze. Ah. They didn't tell *me*.

"We didn't want you to have to worry about it. Not after—," he started, then stopped. "But now that things are heating up, I guess it's better this way. You remember my friend Nathan Gold?" my father asked me.

I nodded.

"When he found out we were moving, he asked me to take the case for him. I'm going to be doing some press conferences over the next couple of weeks. I don't know how they got the address here—I should have had Gloria send out a release about the substitution before it leaked," he said, mostly to himself.

And that was all fine, but I hated that they were treating me like some delicate, fragile thing. And let's be honest; it probably wasn't "they." I had no doubt my mother, as my unofficial treating psychologist, was responsible for the information that did and did not flow my way.

I turned to her. "You could have told me, you know." She silently hid behind the open refrigerator. I talked to her anyway. "I miss my friends and yeah, it's messed-up that this girl died, but it has nothing to do with what happened to Rachel. You don't have to keep me in the dark about stuff like this. I don't understand why you're treating me like I'm two."

"Joseph, go do your homework," my mother said.

My brother had been inching his way back into the living room, having almost reached the controller by the time she said his name.

"But there's no school tomorrow."

"Then go to your room."

"What did I do?" he whined.

"Nothing, I just want to talk to your sister for a minute."

"Mom," Daniel interrupted.

"Not now, Daniel."

"You know what, Mom? Talk to Daniel," I said. "I have nothing else to say."

My mother didn't speak. She looked tired; beautiful, as usual, but tired. The recessed lighting haloed her dark hair.

After a pause, Daniel spoke again. "So there's a party tonight and—"

"You can go," my mother said.

"Thanks. I thought I'd take Mara with me."

My mother turned her back to me and gave Daniel her full attention. Daniel made eye contact with me over her shoulder and shrugged, as if to say, *It's the least I can do.*

My mother hesitated before saying, "It's a school night." Of course that only bothered her when *I* was the subject of the conversation.

"There's no school tomorrow," Daniel said.

"Where is it?"

"South Beach," Daniel said.

"And you're going to be there the whole time?"

"Yes. I won't leave her alone."

She turned to my father. "Marcus?"

"It's fine with me," my dad said.

My mother then looked at me carefully. She didn't trust me for a hot minute, but she trusted her perfect eldest child. A conundrum.

"All right," she said finally. "Be home by eleven, though. No excuses."

It was an impressive display of Daniel's influence, I'll admit. Not quite enough to make me forget how irritated I was with our mother, but the prospect of getting out of the house and going somewhere that wasn't school did lift my mood. Maybe tonight I could actually have fun.

I left the kitchen to shower. The hot water scalded my thin shoulder blades, and I slumped against the tile and let the water glide over my skin. I needed to think of a costume; I did not want to be the only person wearing the wrong thing again.

I stepped out of the shower and threw on a T-shirt and yoga pants before untangling my rat's nest of wet hair. Rifling through my dresser would be hopeless. Same with my closet.

But my mother's closet . . .

Most of the time, she wore suit pants or a skirt and a button-down shirt. Always professional, thoroughly American. But I knew she had a sari or two buried somewhere in that enormous, monochromatic wardrobe of hers. It could work.

I tiptoed to my parents' room and cracked open the door. They were still in the kitchen. I began searching through my mother's clothes, looking for something suitable.

"Mara?"

Oops. I turned around. The stress was evident in my mother's face, her skin taut over her high cheekbones.

"I was just looking for something to wear," I said. "Sorry."

"It's okay, Mara. I just wish we could—"

I inhaled slowly. "Can we do this later? Daniel said there's going to be traffic and I have to figure out a costume."

My mother's forehead creased. I knew she wanted to say something but I hoped she'd let it go, just this once. I was surprised when a conspiratorial smile slowly transformed her face.

"It's a costume party?" she asked.

I nodded.

"I think I might have something," she said. She brushed past me and disappeared into the depths of her walk-in closet. After a few minutes, my mother emerged holding a garment bag that she cradled like a small child, and a pair of perilously high, strappy heels that dangled from her fingers. "This should fit you."

I eyed the bag warily. "It's not a wedding gown, is it?"

"No." She smiled and handed it to me. "It's a dress. One of my mother's. Take my red lipstick and pin up your hair, and you can go as a vintage model."

A smile spread across my face, matching my mother's. "Thanks," I said, and meant it.

"Just do me this one favor?"

I raised my eyebrows, waiting for the caveat.

"Stay with Daniel."

Her voice was strained, and I felt guilty. Again. I nodded and thanked her again for the dress before I made my way back to my room to try it on. The firm plastic of the garment bag rustled as I unzipped it, and dark, emerald green silk shimmered from inside. I withdrew the dress from the bag and my breath caught in my throat. It was stunning. I hoped it fit.

I went to my bathroom to attempt to put on mascara without impaling my eyeball, but when I looked in the mirror, Claire stood behind my reflection.

She winked. "You two kids have fun."

20

I SHOT OUT OF MY BATHROOM AND SAT ON MY BED, my mouth dry and my hands trembling. I wanted to scream, but I closed my eyes and forced myself to breathe. Claire was dead. She was not in my bathroom, and there was nothing to be scared of. My mind was playing tricks on me. I was going to go to a party tonight, and I needed to get dressed. One thing at a time.

Makeup first. I made my way back to the mirror behind my bedroom door, but stopped. There was no one there. Just the PTSD.

But why risk it?

I padded down the hallway back to my parents' bedroom. "Mom?" I asked, poking my head in the door. She sat in her bed, legs crossed, as she typed on her laptop. She looked up. "Will you do my makeup?" I asked her.

Her smile couldn't have been more enthusiastic. She ushered me into her bathroom and sat me down on a chair in front of the vanity. I tilted away from the mirror, just in case.

I felt my mother line my eyes, but when she pulled out her lipstick, I stopped her. "Pass. It makes me feel like a clown."

She nodded with mock seriousness and went back to work, twisting and pinning my hair behind my head so tightly that my face ached. When she was done, she told me to look in the mirror.

I smiled at her, the exact opposite of my internal reaction. "You know what? I trust you," I said, and kissed her on the cheek before leaving the room.

"Wait a second," my mother called after me. I stopped, and she opened her jewelry box. She withdrew a pair of earrings; a single emerald at the center of each stud, surrounded by diamonds.

"Oh my God," I said, staring at them. They were incredible. "Mom, I can't—"

"Just to borrow, not to keep," she said with a smile. "Here, stand still."

She fastened the studs to my ears. "There," she said, her hands on my shoulders. "You look beautiful."

I smiled. "Thank you."

"You're welcome. But don't lose them, okay? They were my mother's."

I nodded, and went back to my room. It was time to deal with the dress. I withdrew it from its garment bag. Stepping into it would be safest—that way, I could stop if it threatened to tear. To my great surprise, it slid on easily. But it dipped dangerously low in front and dangerously low in back, exposing more skin than I was used to. Much more.

Too late now. A glance at the clock told me I had only five minutes before Daniel had to leave to meet his little nerdlet. I slipped on the shoes my mother had given me. They were slightly too tight but I ignored that and, balancing mostly on my toes, walked into the foyer. I met Joseph as he headed to his room.

"Ohmigod, DANIEL! You have to see Mara!"

Blushing furiously, I pushed past him and stood by the front door, itching to fling it open and wait in the car for my older brother. But he had the keys. Of course he did.

Daniel materialized from the hallway in a business suit with his hair slicked back and wet-looking, and my mother appeared shortly after. They stood there and stared for much longer than was necessary while I fidgeted, feigning boredom to hide my embarrassment.

Finally, Daniel spoke. "Wow, Mara. You look like . . . you look like . . ." His face scrunched as he searched for words.

A look passed over my mother's face, but vanished before I could interpret it. "Like a model," Mom said brightly.

"Uh, I was going to say a lady of ill repute." I shot Daniel a look of pure poison. "But, sure."

"She does not, Daniel. Stop it." The golden boy was scolded. I smirked.

"You look beautiful, Mara. Older, too. Daniel," my mother said, and turned to look him in the eye. "Watch her. Don't let her out of your sight."

He raised his hand in a salute. "Yes, ma'am."

Once we were in the car, Daniel put on some Indian music. He knew I was not a fan.

"Can I change it?"

"No."

I glared at him, but he ignored me as he pulled out of the driveway. We didn't talk until we reached the highway.

"So what are you supposed to be, anyway?" I asked him as we lined up behind the mass of cars, stalled and blinking in the traffic.

"Bruce Wayne."

"Ha."

"I'm sorry, by the way." He paused, still watching the road. "For not telling you about the case."

I didn't say anything.

"Mom asked me not to."

I stared straight ahead. "So naturally, you listened."

"She thought she was doing the right thing."

"I wish she'd stop."

Daniel shrugged, and we were silent for the rest of the drive. We crept along in traffic until we finally turned onto Lincoln

Road. It really was captivating. Neon lights illuminated the buildings, some sleek and some gaudy. Drag queens glittered down the sidewalks next to scantily clad revelers. Parking was impossible, but we eventually found a space near the club and paid an obscene amount of money for the privilege. As I got out of the car, my feet crunched on the broken glass that dusted the pavement.

I walked behind Daniel slowly and carefully, knowing that one misstep would send me hurtling toward the glass-and-cigarette littered concrete, thereby ruining my normal teenager excursion. And the dress.

We stood in line and waited our turn. When we reached the stereotypically muscled bouncer, we handed over our cash for the cover charge and he stamped our hands without ceremony. Daniel and I walked past the rope into the pulsing club and I could tell his confidence had worn a bit thin. In our lack of partying experiences, at least, we were equals.

The room was a wall-to-wall, throbbing mass of bodies. They writhed synchronously around us as we pushed our way in shoulder-to-shoulder. The level of undress was truly impressive; a handful of whorish angels, devils, and fairies teetered toward the bar in stilettos, sucking in their torsos and puffing out their twinkling cleavage. Much to my dismay, I spotted Anna among them. She had shed her usually wholesome ensemble for a staggeringly sparse angel getup with the requisite halo and wings. She overdid it on the makeup, the push-up bra, and the heels, and looked well on her way to ending up as some accountant's midlife crisis. I grabbed my brother by the arm and he steered us to the other side of the bar where we were supposed to meet his crush.

As we waited, I recognized the song being sampled in the remix that thrummed from the speakers and smiled to myself. Daniel tapped me on the shoulder a few minutes later, and I followed his eyes until he smiled at a petite blond girl dressed in overalls with fake greasepaint smudged on her face. She mouthed or screamed my brother's name—it was impossible to tell. The music swallowed up every other sound in the space.

Her short hair bounced and swayed under her chin as she made her way over. When she reached us, Daniel leaned into her ear to introduce us.

"This is Sophie!" he shouted.

I nodded and smiled at her. She was cute. Daniel did nicely.

"Nice to meet you!" I screamed.

"What?" she screamed back.

"Nice to meet you!"

The look on her face revealed that she still couldn't hear me. All righty then.

The music changed to a slower rhythmic beat and Sophie started to pull Daniel away from me and into the throng of people. He turned to me—for approval, I assumed—and I waved him on. When he was gone, though, I began to feel awkward. I pressed into the bar that wouldn't serve me, with no discernible purpose or reason for being there. What did I expect? I came to dance, and I came with my brother who was meeting someone else. I should have asked Jamie. I was stupid. Now I had no choice but to just plunge into the crowd and start gyrating. Because that wouldn't be weird.

I lolled my head back in hopelessness and leaned back into the dull edge of the metal bar. When I righted myself, two guys—one in a Miami Heat jersey and the other in what I hoped was an ironic portrayal of a perpetually shirtless, moronic reality TV person—made eye contact. Completely not interested. I looked away, but in my peripheral vision saw that they were edging themselves closer. I gracelessly darted into the crowd and only narrowly avoided being elbowed in the face by a girl attired in what could only be described as "slutty Gryffindor" apparel. So wrong.

When I finally reached the far wall, my eyes swept the crowd, absorbing the near-naked bodies and the costumes and trying to see if I recognized anyone not heinous from school.

I did.

Noah was fully clothed and, as far as I could tell, uncostumed. He wore dark jeans and a hoodie, apparently, despite the heat. And he was talking to a girl.

A stunningly beautiful slip of a girl, all legs crowned by a tiny, twinkling dress and fairy wings. She looked oddly familiar but I couldn't place her; she probably went to our school. Noah listened raptly to whatever she was saying, and a semicircle of costumed girls surrounded her; a devil, a cat, an angel, and . . . a carrot? Huh. I liked vegetable girl, but the rest of them I hated.

At precisely that moment, Noah's head lifted and he saw me staring. I couldn't read his expression, even as he leaned over to the fairy and said something in her ear. She turned to look at me; Noah reached out to stop her but not before my eyes met hers. She giggled and covered her mouth before turning back around.

Noah was making fun of me. Humiliation spread from the pit of my stomach and lodged in my throat. I twisted around and pushed my way through the bodies that had encroached into my bubble of personal space. As badly as I had wanted to come tonight, I now wanted to leave.

I found Daniel and screamed in his ear that I wasn't feeling well and asked Sophie if she could give him a ride back. Daniel was worried; he insisted on driving me home but I wasn't having it. I told him I just needed to get some air, and eventually he handed me the keys and let me go.

I bit back my embarrassment and hurried toward the exit. As I pushed through the throng, I thought I heard my name shouted behind me. I stopped, swallowed, and against my better judgment, turned around.

No one was there.

21

BY THE TIME I ARRIVED BACK AT THE HOUSE, I'd composed myself. Coming home with a tear-streaked face, and without Daniel, would not help my situation with my mother, and we were just starting to make some progress. But when I pulled into the driveway, her car wasn't there. Neither was my father's. The lights inside the house were off too. Where were they? I went to the front door and reached out to unlock it.

The door swung in. Before I touched it.

I stood there, my fingers mere inches from the handle. I stared, my heart in my throat, and raised my eyes slowly up the length of the door. Nothing unusual. Maybe they just forgot to lock it.

With one hand, I pushed the door open the rest of the way and stood in the door frame, peering into the dark house. The lights in the foyer, living room, and dining room were off, but a sliver of light peeked out from around the corner toward the family room. They must have left that one on.

My eyes roamed. The art was still on the wall. The antique ebony and mother-of-pearl Chinese screen was in the same place as when I left. Everything was where it should be. I inhaled, closed the door behind me and flipped on all of the front lights in quick succession.

Better.

When I went into the kitchen to get something to eat, I noticed the note on the refrigerator door.

Took Joseph to see a movie. Be back around 10:30.

A glance at the clock told me it was only nine. They must have just left. Joseph was probably the last one out and forgot to lock the front door. No big deal.

I stared into the refrigerator. Yogurt. Chocolate milk. Cucumbers. Leftover lasagna. My head ached, reminding me of the one thousand bobby pins my mother had stuck into my scalp. I grabbed a container of yogurt and a spoon, then made my way to my bedroom to change. But the second I entered the hallway, I froze.

When I had left the house with Daniel, all of the family

pictures had been hung on the left side of the wall, opposite three sets of French doors on the right.

But now all of the pictures were on the right. And the French doors were on the left.

The yogurt fell from my hands, spattering the wall. The spoon clattered to the floor and the sound snapped me back into reality. I had a bad night. I was imagining things. I backed out of the hall, then ran to the kitchen and snatched a dish towel from the oven handle. When I went back to the hallway, everything would be where it should be.

I went back to the hallway. Everything was where it should be.

I hurried to my bedroom, closed the door behind me, and sank onto my bed. I was upset. I shouldn't have gone out; the party was not, in fact, what I needed. The whole thing was nervous-making and stressful and was probably causing a PTSD episode. I needed to relax. I needed to get out of these clothes.

The heels went first. My feet were not used to that kind of torment, and once I slipped them off, my whole body sighed with relief. Everything was sore; my heels, calves, thighs. Still dressed, I padded to my bathroom and turned on the tub faucet. The hot water would unwind my muscles. Unwind me. I flicked the heat lamp on, casting a womblike, reddish glow over the white tile and sink. The roar of water drowned out my thoughts, and I inhaled the steam curling up from the tub. I began to remove the bobby pins, and they collected there in the corner of my sink like skinny black caterpillars. I went to the closet to slip off my dress, but then I froze.

An opened box sat on the closet floor. I had no memory of taking it down from the shelves. No memory of ripping the tape off the flaps and opening it since we'd moved. Did I leave it out? I must have. I kneeled in front of the box. It was the one my mother had brought to the hospital, and underneath bits of my old life—notes, drawings, books, the old cloth doll I've had since I was a baby—I found a stack of glossy pictures carelessly bound by a rubber band. A few of them escaped, fluttering to the floor, and I picked one up.

The photograph was from last summer. I saw the composition of that moment as if it was happening in real time. Rachel and I leaned our cheeks together as we faced the camera she held away from our faces. We were laughing, our mouths open, teeth glinting in the sun, the wind teasing the glowing strands of our hair. I heard the snap of her shutter creating an imprint on film, which she insisted on using that summer because she wanted to learn to develop it. Then the print went dark, leaving the two of us in white, skeletal in the negative image.

I placed the picture carefully on my empty desk, put the box back into my closet and shut the door. When I noticed the silence, it stole the air from my lungs. I backed away from the closet and peered into the bathroom. The faucet was off. A single drop of water fell, sounding like a bomb in the stillness.

The bathtub had overflowed, making the ceramic tile reflect the light like glass.

I didn't remember turning the water off.

But I must have.

But there was still no *way* I was getting in.

I could barely breathe as I grabbed two towels and threw them on the floor. They darkened as they absorbed the water, and saturated in seconds. The water seeped through to my feet. The bathtub drain needed to be unplugged. I made my way over to it carefully, but everything inside me screamed *bad idea*. I leaned over the edge.

The emerald and diamond earrings glinted at the bottom. I raised my hands to my ears.

Yup, gone.

I heard my mother's voice in my mind. *"Don't lose them, okay? They were my mother's."*

I squeezed my eyes shut and tried to breathe. When I opened them, I would be brave.

I tested the water with my finger. Nothing happened.

Of course nothing happened. It was only a bathtub. The pictures had distracted me and I let it overflow, then turned it off without remembering it. Everything was fine. I plunged my arm in.

For a second, I could not think. It was as if all feeling beneath my elbow had been cut off. Like the rest of my arm never even existed.

Then the scalding pain clawed at my skin, my bones, inside out, outside in. A soundless scream misshaped my mouth and I struggled to pull my arm out but it wouldn't move. I couldn't move. I crumpled against the side of the bathtub. My mother found me there an hour later.

"How did you say it happened?" The ER doctor looked my age. He looped the gauze over the red, swollen skin of my forearm as I clenched my teeth, fighting off a scream.

"Bathtub," I managed to croak. He and my mother exchanged a glance.

"Your arm must have been in there for some time," he said, meeting my eyes. "These are some serious burns."

What could I say? That I tested the water before reaching in and it didn't seem that hot? That it felt like something grabbed me and held me under? I could see in the doctor's eyes that he thought I was crazy—that I did it on purpose. Anything I could say to explain what happened wouldn't help.

So I looked away.

I didn't remember much about the ride to the hospital, except that Joseph and both of my parents were with me. And thankfully I didn't remember my mother picking me up off the bathroom floor, or getting me in the car as she must have. I could barely look at her. When the doctor finished with my bandage, he pulled her into the hallway.

I focused on the searing pain in my arm to avoid thinking about where I was. The antiseptic smell invaded my nostrils, the hospital air leached into my skin. I clenched my jaw against the nausea and leaned against the window to feel the cool glass on my cheek.

My father must have been filling out paperwork, because Joseph sat and waited out there, all alone. He looked so small. And still. His eyes were downcast and his face—God. His face was so scared. A hard ache rose in my throat. I had a glimpse of how terrified he must have been when I was in the hospital the last time, seeing his big sister swallowed up in a hospital bed. And now here we were again, not even three months later. It was a relief when my mother finally returned to lead me out of the room. We were all silent on the ride home.

When we arrived back at the house, Daniel was there. He rounded on me when I walked in the door. "Mara, are you okay?"

I nodded. "Just a burn."

"I want to talk to Mara for a bit, Daniel," my mother said. "I'll come to your room in a while."

Her voice was a threat, but Daniel looked unperturbed, more worried about me than anything else.

My mother led the way down the hall to my bedroom and sat on my bed. I sat on my chair.

"I'm making an appointment for you to talk to someone tomorrow," she said.

I nodded, as Joseph's terrified face appeared in my mind's eye. He was just a kid. I'd put him through enough. And between the burn, the mirrors, the laughter, the nightmares—maybe it was time to do things my mother's way. Maybe talking to someone would help.

"The doctor said you must have held your arm under water for a long time to get second-degree burns. And you stayed there until I found you?" she asked, her voice raw. "What were you thinking, Mara?"

My voice was laced with defeat. "I was going to take a bath, but the earrings—" I took a shaky breath. "The earrings you lent me fell into the tub. I had to get them before I could unplug the drain."

"Did you?" my mother asked.

I shook my head. "No." My voice cracked.

My mother's eyebrows knit together. She walked over to me and put her hand on my earlobe. I felt her finger unhook the back of an earring. She held the emerald and diamond stud in her flat palm. I lifted my hand to my other ear; that one was in too. I removed the earring and placed it in her hand as tears welled in my eyes.

I'd imagined the whole thing.

22

"MARA DYER?" THE RECEPTIONIST CALLED OUT.

I shot up. The magazine I'd been not-reading fell to the floor, open to an NC-17 photograph of two naked models straddling a handsomely suited actor. Rather racy for a psychiatrist's office. I picked up the magazine and set it on the coffee table, then walked over to the door the smiling receptionist was pointing at. I went in.

The psychiatrist took off her glasses and set them on her desk as she rose. "Mara, it's nice to meet you. I'm Rebecca Maillard."

We shook hands. I stared at the seating options. An armchair. The obligatory couch. A desk chair. Probably some kind of test. I chose the armchair.

Dr. Maillard smiled and crossed her legs. She was thin. My mother's age. Maybe they even knew each other. "So, what brings you here today, Mara?" she asked.

I held out my bandaged arm. Dr. Maillard raised her eyebrows, waiting for me to speak. So I did.

"I burned myself."

"Do you mean, you were burned, or you burned yourself?"

She was quick, this one. "I was burned, but my mother thinks I burned myself."

"How did it happen?"

I took a deep breath and told her about the earrings and the bathtub. But not the unlocked front door. Or the box in my closet that I didn't remember taking down. One thing at a time.

"Has anything like that happened before?"

"Like what?" I scanned the books on her shelves; the diagnostic manual, pharmacological volumes, journals. Nothing interesting or unusual. It could have been anyone's office. There was no personality.

Dr. Maillard paused before answering. "Was last night the first time you've been in the hospital?"

I narrowed my eyes at her. She sounded more like a lawyer than a psychiatrist. "Why ask if you already know the answer?"

"I don't already know the answer," Dr. Maillard said, unruffled.

"My mother didn't tell you?"

"She told me that you moved here recently because you experienced a trauma back in Rhode Island, but I didn't get a chance to speak with her for very long. I had to switch one of my other patients to see you on such short notice."

"I'm sorry," I said.

Dr. Maillard furrowed her eyebrows. "There's nothing to be sorry for, Mara. I just hope I can help."

I hoped so too, but I was starting to doubt it. "What do you have in mind?"

"Well, you can start by telling me if you've ever been in the hospital before," she said, clasping her hands in her lap. I nodded.

"What for?" She looked at me with only casual interest. She wrote nothing down.

"My friends died in an accident. My best friend. I was there, but I wasn't hurt."

She looked confused. "Why were you in the hospital, then?"

"I was unconscious for three days." My mouth didn't seem to want to form the word "coma."

"Your friends," she said slowly. "How did they die?"

I tried to answer her, to repeat what my mother had told me, but had trouble with the words. They were buried in my throat, just beyond my reach. The silence grew more and more awkward as I struggled to pull them out.

Dr. Maillard leaned in. "It's okay, Mara," she said. "You don't have to tell me."

I took a deep breath. "I don't remember how they died, honestly."

She nodded her head. A strand of dark blond hair fell over her forehead. "Okay."

"Okay?" I shot her a skeptical look. "Just like that?"

Dr. Maillard smiled softly, her brown eyes kind. "Just like that. We don't have to talk about anything you don't want to talk about in this room."

I bristled a bit. "I don't mind talking about it. I just don't remember."

"And that's okay. Sometimes, the mind has a way of protecting us from things until we're ready to deal with them."

Her assumption bothered me, more than it should have. "I feel ready to deal with it."

She tucked her hair behind her ear. "That's fine too. When did all of this happen?"

I thought for a minute—it was so hard to keep track of time. "A few months ago? December?"

For the first time, Dr. Maillard's demeanor changed. She seemed surprised. "That's pretty recent."

I shrugged and looked away. My eyes fell on a plastic-looking plant in the corner of the room that had caught the sunlight. I wondered if it was real.

"So how have you been doing since the move?"

A slight smile twitched at the corner of my mouth. "Aside from the burn, you mean?"

Dr. Maillard grinned back. "Aside from that."

The conversation could play out a hundred different ways. Dr.

Maillard was being paid to listen to me—it was her job. Just a job. When she went home to her family, she wouldn't be Dr. Maillard. She'd be Mom. Becca, maybe. Someone else, just like my mother. And she wouldn't think about me until I saw her next.

But I was there for a reason. The flashbacks—the dreams—I could handle. The hallucinations, I could deal with. But the burn upped the ante. I thought of Joseph, looking so scared and small and lost in the hospital. I never wanted to see him look that way again.

I swallowed hard and went for it. "I think something's happening to me." My grand declaration.

Her expression didn't change. "What do you think is happening to you?"

"I don't know." I felt the urge to sigh and rake my hands through my hair, but resisted. I didn't know what kind of signal it would send, and didn't want to send the wrong one.

"All right, let's back up for a minute. *Why* do you think something is happening to you? What makes you think that?"

I struggled to maintain eye contact with her. "Sometimes I see things that aren't there."

"What kinds of things?"

Where to begin? I decided to go in reverse chronological order. "Well, like I told you, I thought the earrings my mother lent me fell in the bathtub, but they were in my ears."

Dr. Maillard nodded. "Go on."

"And before I went to the party last night, I saw one of my dead friends in the mirror." *Zing.*

"What kind of party was it?"

If Dr. Maillard was shocked by my revelation, she didn't show it.

"A—a costume party?" I didn't mean for it to sound like a question.

"Did you go with anyone?"

I nodded. "My brother, but he was meeting someone else." The room started to feel warm.

"So you were alone?"

An image of Noah whispering to the fairy girl flashed before my eyes. Alone, indeed. "Yes."

"Have you gone out much since you've moved?"

I shook my head. "Last night was the first time."

Dr. Maillard smiled slightly. "Sounds like it could be stressful."

At that, I snorted. Couldn't help it. "Compared to what?"

Her eyebrows lifted. "You tell me."

"Compared to having your best friend die? Or moving away from everyone you've ever known? Or starting at a new school so late in the year?"

Or finding out your father is representing an alleged murderer of a teenage girl? The thought appeared in my mind without warning. Without precedent. I pushed it away. Dad's work was *not* going to be a problem for me. I couldn't let myself be *that* damaged—if my mother noticed me stressing about it, she might make him drop the case, his first one since we moved. And with three kids in private school now, they probably needed the money. I'd screwed up their lives enough already. I decided not to mention it to Dr. Maillard. What we said was confidential, but still.

Her face was serious when she spoke. "You're right," she said, shifting back in her chair. "Let me ask you this: Was last night the first time you saw something, or someone, that wasn't there?"

I shook my head, somewhat relieved that the focus of the conversation had shifted.

"Do you feel comfortable telling me about other things you've seen?"

Not particularly. I picked idly at the thread in my worn jeans, knowing how crazy I would sound. How crazy I already sounded. I said it anyway.

"I saw my old boyfriend, Jude, at school, once."

"When?"

"My first day." After I saw my Algebra classroom collapse. After Claire first appeared in the mirror. I bit my lip.

"So, you were already pretty stressed out."

I nodded.

"Do you miss him?"

Her question caught me off guard. How did I answer that? When I was awake, I barely thought about Jude. And when I dreamed—it wasn't exactly pleasant. I lowered my eyes, hoping Dr. Maillard wouldn't notice my burning face, the only evidence of my shame. I was a bad person.

"Sometimes these things are complicated, Mara," she said. Guess she noticed after all. "When we lose people who were important to us, there's a whole range of emotions we might experience."

I shifted in my seat. "Can we talk about something else?"

"We can, but I'd really like to stay with this for a little while. Can you tell me a little bit about your relationship?"

I closed my eyes. "It wasn't much of one. We were only together for a couple of months."

"Was it a good couple of months?"

I thought about it.

"Okay," Dr. Maillard said, moving on. The answer must have been written all over my face. "How about your relationship with your best friend? You saw her since she died too, right?"

I shook my head. "That was Claire. She only moved to Laurelton last year. She was Jude—my boyfriend's—sister. She was close with Rachel."

Dr. Maillard's eyes narrowed. "Rachel. Your best friend?"

I nodded.

"But she wasn't close with you?"

"Not so much."

"And you haven't seen Rachel."

I shook my head.

"Is there anything else? Anything you've seen that you shouldn't have? Anything you've heard that you shouldn't have?"

My eyes narrowed. "Like voices?" She definitely thought I was crazy.

She shrugged. "Like anything."

I looked at my lap and tried to stifle a yawn. I failed. "Sometimes. Sometimes I hear my name being called."

Dr. Maillard nodded. "How do you sleep?"

"Not so great," I admitted.

"Nightmares?"

You could call them that. "Yes."

"Do you remember any of them?"

I rubbed the back of my neck. "Sometimes. Sometimes I dream about that night."

"I think you're pretty brave to be telling me all of this." She didn't sound patronizing when she said it.

"I don't want to be crazy," I told her. Truthfully.

"I don't think you're crazy."

"So it's normal to see things that aren't there?"

"When someone's been through a traumatic event, yes."

"Even though I don't remember it?"

Dr. Maillard raised an eyebrow. "Any of it?"

I rubbed my forehead, then pulled the hair off the back of my neck into a knot. I said nothing.

"I think you are starting to remember it," she said. "Slowly, and in a way that it doesn't hurt your mind too much to process. And even though I want to explore this more if you decide to see me again, I think it's possible that you seeing Jude and

Claire could be your mind's way of expressing the unresolved feelings you have about them."

"So what do I do? To make it stop?" I asked her.

"Well, if you think you'd like to see me again, we can talk about making a plan for therapy."

"No drugs?" I figured my mother had taken me to a psychiatrist for a reason. Probably figured she needed to bring out the big guns. And after last night, I couldn't exactly argue with her.

"Well, I do usually prescribe medication to be used in conjunction with therapy. But it's your choice. I can recommend you to a psychologist if you don't want to pursue medication just yet, or we can give it a try. See how you do."

The things that had been happening since we moved—the dreams, the hallucinations—I wondered if a pill could really make it go away. "Do you think it will help?"

"On its own? Maybe. But with cognitive behavioral therapy, chances are higher that you'd feel better sooner, although it's definitely a long-term process."

"Cognitive behavioral therapy?"

Dr. Maillard nodded. "It changes your way of thinking about things. How to deal with what you've been seeing. What you're feeling. It will also help with the nightmares you've been having."

"The memories," I corrected her. And then a thought materialized. "What if—what if I just need to remember?"

She leaned forward in her chair slightly. "That could be

part of it, Mara. But it's not something you can force. Your mind is already working on it, in its own way."

A smile tugged at the corner of my mouth. "So, we won't be doing any hypnotherapy or anything here?"

Dr. Maillard grinned. "I'm afraid not," she said.

I nodded. "My mother doesn't believe in it either."

Dr. Maillard took a pad off of her desk and wrote something on it. She tore a piece of paper off and handed it to me. "Have your mother fill this. If you want to take it, great. If not, that's okay too. It might not kick in for a few weeks, though. Or it might kick in a few days after you start. Everyone's different."

I couldn't read Dr. Maillard's handwriting. "Zoloft?"

She shook her head. "I don't like to prescribe SSRIs for teenagers."

"How come?"

Dr. Maillard's eyes scanned the calendar on her desk. "There have been some studies that show a link between SSRIs and suicide in adolescents. Can you meet next Thursday?"

The dates flew by in my mind. "Actually, I have exams coming up. Huge chunk of my grade."

"That's a lot of pressure."

I barked out a laugh. "Yeah. I guess so."

She picked up her glasses and put them back on. "Mara, have you ever thought about taking some time off from school?"

I stood up. "So I can sit around and think about how much I miss Rachel all day? Screw up my chance to graduate on time? Ruin my transcripts?"

"Point taken." Dr. Maillard smiled and stood. She extended her hand, and I shook it but couldn't meet her eyes. I was too embarrassed by my impromptu pity party.

"Try to watch the stress, though," she said, then shrugged. "As much as you can. PTSD episodes tend to be triggered by moments of it. And call me when exams are over, especially if you decide to start taking the medication. Or before, if you need me." She handed me her card. "It was nice to meet you, Mara. I'm glad you came in."

"Thanks," I said, and meant it.

My mother was waiting for me outside when the appointment ended. Surprisingly, she didn't pry. I handed her the prescription and her face tensed.

"What's wrong?" I asked her.

"Nothing," she said, and faced the road. We stopped at a pharmacy on the way home. She placed the bag in the center console.

I opened it and looked at the pill bottle. "Zyprexa," I read out loud. "What is it?"

"It should help make things a little easier to deal with," my mother said, still staring ahead. A non-answer. She said nothing else on the way home.

My mother took the bag in the house with her, and I went to my room. I turned on my computer and typed "Zyprexa" into Google. I clicked on the first website I found, and my mouth went dry.

It was an antipsychotic.

23

I DIDN'T KNOW HOW TO REACT TO NOAH IN CLASS the next day. The costume party seemed like a lifetime ago, but my humiliation was fresh. I was grateful for the long-sleeved dress shirt I had to wear—it minimized the impact of the bandage on my left arm, at least. My mother had become the Keeper of the Pills, and she doled out the Tylenol with codeine before I left that morning. I ached all over but I didn't take it, and didn't plan on starting the Zyprexa just yet, either. I needed a clear head.

When I walked into English, Noah was already there. Our eyes met for a second before I dropped my gaze and walked past him. I had to find out about Mabel—was it only a week since I'd taken her?—and figure out how to spring her on my parents now, considering what had happened. But I didn't know how to bring it up to Noah, how to talk to him after the party. I sat down at a desk on the other side of the room, but he stood and followed me, sitting behind my chair. As Ms. Leib began her lecture, I found myself tapping my pencil on my desk. Noah cracked his knuckles behind me, setting my teeth on edge.

When the bell rang, I threaded through the students, eager for Algebra for the first time in my life. Noah drove girls crazy, and I was already crazy. I needed to let it go. Let him go. As Jamie had so astutely said, I had enough problems.

I was so relieved to see Jamie in Algebra that I might have actually smiled. With teeth. But the glimmer of my good mood didn't last; Noah caught up with me as soon as the bell rang.

"Hey," he said, as he fell into a graceful lope beside me.

"Hey." I gave him the stare-ahead. Ask about the dog. Ask about the dog. I tried to find the words but clenched my teeth instead.

"Mabel isn't doing so well," Noah said, his voice even.

My stomach dropped and I slowed my pace by a fraction. "Is she going to be okay?"

"Think so, but it's probably better if she stays with us for a while. So my mother can care for her," he said, as he ran his hand over the back of his neck. "Do you mind?"

"No," I said, shifting the weight of my bag on my shoulder

as I approached my next class. "That's probably the best thing."

"I wanted to ask—" Noah started, then lifted a hand to his hair, twisting the strands. "My mother wanted to know if maybe we could keep her? She's gotten attached."

I tilted my head sideways to see him. He either didn't notice my bandaged hand or was ignoring it. He seemed indifferent to everything. Remote. His words didn't match his tone.

"I mean, she's your dog," he said, "whatever you want we'll do—"

"It's okay," I cut him off. I remembered the way Mabel had curled into his chest as he carried her. She'd be better off with him. Definitely. "Tell your mom I said it's fine."

"I was going to ask you when I saw you at the party, but you left."

"I had somewhere else to be," I said, avoiding his eyes.

"Right. What's wrong?" he asked, still sounding utterly disinterested.

"Nothing," I said.

"I don't believe you."

"I don't care." Not true.

"All right. Have lunch with me, then," he said casually.

I paused, torn between yes and no. "No," I said finally.

"Why not?"

"I have a study date," I said. Hopefully Jamie would oblige.

"With who?"

"Why do you care?" I asked with an edge. We could have

been discussing molecular physics for all the interest he seemed to be paying to the conversation.

"I'm starting to wonder that myself," Noah said, and walked away. He didn't look back.

Fine.

I drew my bandaged hand in Art, even though we were supposed to be working on faces. And when lunch arrived, I didn't look for Jamie, choosing solitude instead. I withdrew the banana I brought, peeled it, and took a slow bite as I wandered to my locker, letting my teeth graze against the flesh. I was glad to be free of Noah. Relieved, even, as I went to exchange my books.

Until I saw the note.

Folded so that it fit through the slats of my locker, innocently perched on a tower of my books. A thick piece of paper with my name on it.

Acid free, bright white paper.

Sketchbook paper.

I unfolded the note and recognized one of my drawings of Noah immediately. The other side simply said:

I HAVE SOMETHING THAT BELONGS TO YOU.
MEET AT THE VENDING MACHINES AT LUNCH IF YOU WANT IT BACK.

A rush of heat ignited my skin. Did Noah steal my sketchbook? My sudden fury surprised me. I'd never punched anyone before, but there was a first time for everything. I punctuated the thought with a ringing, metallic slam of my locker door.

I don't remember how I got to the bottom of the stairs. One minute I was by my locker, and the next minute I was rounding the corner by the vending machines. And then a horrible thought occurred to me; what if it wasn't Noah? What if it was someone else? Like—oh, no. Like Anna. I imagined her dissolving into a fit of giggles as she showed my sketches of Noah to her friends.

Sure enough, when I arrived, Anna stood waiting with a smug, satisfied sneer on her generically pretty face. Flanked by Aiden, they blocked my way, dripping with gloat.

When I saw them there, I was still confident I could handle it. I'd almost come to expect her bullshit.

What I didn't expect were the dozens of students assembled to watch this train wreck unfold.

And what sent a piercing scream through my spine was the sight of Noah, centered in a halo of admirers, male and female.

At that moment, the magnitude of Anna's machinations insulted my mind. My stomach turned as it all snapped into place; why everyone was there, why Noah was there. Anna had been constructing this three-ring circus since Noah first spoke to me on day one. It was *her* black Mercedes I almost hit last week—she saw me get out of Noah's car. And now, all she needed to complete her ringmaster role was a top hat and a monocle.

Oh, Anna. I underestimated you.

All eyes were on me. My move. If I played.

My eyes scanned the assembled students as I stood there,

debating. Finally, I simply looked at Anna and dared her to speak. She who speaks first loses. She didn't disappoint.

"Looking for this?" she chirped innocently, as she held up my sketchbook.

I reached for it but she snatched it away. "You crotch-pheasant," I said through gritted teeth.

Anna feigned shock. "My, my, Mara. What language! I'm simply returning a lost item to its rightful owner. You are the rightful owner, aren't you?" she asked, as she flipped the sketchbook open to the inside cover. "'Mara Dyer,'" she read loudly. "That's you," she added with emphasis, punctuating the declaration with a sneer. I said nothing. "Aiden here was nice enough to pick it up when you left it in Algebra by mistake."

Aiden smiled on cue. He must have snatched it from my bag.

"Actually, he stole it."

"I'm afraid not, Mara. You must have carelessly misplaced it," she said, and tsked.

Now that she had set the stage, Anna began to flip through my sketchbook. If I hit her, Aiden would snatch the sketchbook and Noah would still see what I'd drawn. And let's be honest, I've never hit anyone in my life. There would be nothing I could say to minimize the damage, either. The sketches were so accurate, snapshots of him so adoringly rendered that they'd betray my obsessive infatuation the second they were revealed. The humiliation would be perfect, and she knew it.

Defeat bloomed in my cheeks, staining my throat and my

collarbone. I could do nothing but suffer through the emotional skinning and stand there, flayed before the entire school until Anna was drunk on her overdose of cruelty.

And collect my sketchbook when she was finished. Because it was mine, and I would get it back.

I didn't want to see Noah's face when Anna finally turned to the page where he made his first appearance. Seeing him smirk or smile or laugh or roll his eyes would undo me and I could not cry here today. So I fixed my stare on Anna's face, and watched her tremble with gleeful malice as she held the sketchbook and made her way over to him. The crowd shifted from a rough semicircle into a wedge, with Noah at the point.

"Noah?" she cooed.

"Anna," he replied flatly.

She flipped from page to page and I could hear the whispers rise into a murmur and could hear a ringing laugh somewhere from the far side of the tiki hut, but it died down. Anna turned the pages slowly for effect, and like some demonic schoolmarm, held the book at an angle to provide maximum exposure to the assembled crowd. Everyone needed to have the opportunity to catch a long, languorous glimpse of my disgrace.

"This looks *so* much like you," she said to Noah, pressing her body against his.

"My girl is talented," Noah said.

My heart stopped beating.

Anna's heart stopped beating.

Everyone's heart stopped beating. The buzzing of a solitary gnat would have sounded obscene in the stillness.

"Bullshit," Anna whispered finally, but it was loud enough for everyone to hear. She hadn't moved an inch.

Noah shrugged. "I'm a vain bastard, and Mara indulges me." After a pause, he added, "I'm just glad you didn't get your greedy little claws on the *other* sketchbook. *That* would have been embarrassing." His lips curved into a sly smile as he slid from the picnic table he'd been sitting on. "Now, get the fuck off me," he said calmly to a dumbfounded, speechless Anna as he pushed past her, plucking the sketchbook roughly from her hands.

And walked over to me.

"Let's go," Noah ordered gently, once he was at my side. His body brushed the line of my shoulder and arm protectively. And then he held out his hand.

I wanted to take it and I wanted to spit in Anna's face and I wanted to kiss him and I wanted to knee Aiden Davis in the groin. Civilization won out, and I willed each individual nerve to respond to the signal I sent with my brain and placed my fingers in his. A current traveled from my fingertips through to the hollow where my stomach used to be.

And just like that, I was completely, utterly, and entirely, His.

Neither of us spoke until we were out of earshot and out of sight of the shocked and awed student body. We were standing next to a bench by the basketball court when Noah stopped, finally letting go of my hand. It felt empty, but I barely had time to process the loss.

"Are you all right?" he asked softly.

I nodded, staring past him. My tongue felt numb.

"Are you sure?"

I nodded again.

"Are you positive?"

I glared at him. "I'm fine," I said.

"That's my girl."

"I am not your girl," I said, with more venom than I intended.

"Right, then," Noah said, and looked at me with a curious stare. He raised an eyebrow. "About that."

I didn't know what to say, so I said nothing.

"You like me," he finally said. "You *like* me, like me." He was trying not to smile.

"No. I hate you," I said, hoping that saying it would make it so.

"And yet, you draw me." Noah was still smug, completely undeterred by my declaration.

This was torture; worse somehow than what just happened, even though it was only the two of us. Or *because* it was only the two of us.

"Why?" he asked.

"Why what?" What could I say? Noah, despite you being an asshole, or maybe because of it, I'd like to rip off your clothes and have your babies. Don't tell.

"Why everything," he continued. "Start with why you hate me. And then continue until you get to the part about the drawings."

"I don't really hate you," I said in defeat.

"I know."

"Then why are you asking?"

"Because I wanted you to admit it," he said, grinning crookedly.

"Done," I said, feeling hopeless. "Are we finished?"

"You're the most ungrateful person alive," he mused.

"You're right," I said, my voice flat. "Thanks for the save. I should go." I started to walk away.

"Not so fast." Noah reached for my good wrist. He took it gently and I turned around. My heart was sickeningly aflutter. "We still have a problem."

I looked at him, uncomprehending. He was still holding my wrist and the contact interfered with my cerebral functioning.

"Everyone thinks we're together," Noah said.

Oh. Noah needed a way out. Of course he did; we weren't, in fact, together. I was just—I don't know what I was to him. I looked at the ground, digging the toe of my sneaker into the paved walkway like a sullen child while I thought about what to say.

"Tell your friends you dumped me on Monday," I said finally.

Noah let go of my wrist, and looked genuinely confused. "What?"

"If you tell them that you broke up with me over the weekend, everyone will forget about this eventually. Tell them I was too needy or something," I said.

Noah arched his eyebrows slightly. "That wasn't exactly what I had in mind."

"Fine," I said, confused myself. "I'll go along with whatever you want, okay?"

"Sunday."

"Excuse me?"

"I want Sunday. My parents are having a thing on Saturday, but Sunday I'm free."

I didn't understand. "And?"

"And you're going to spend the day with me."

That was not what I expected. "I am?"

"Yes. You owe me," he said. And he was right; I did. Noah wouldn't have had to do anything to make Anna's dream and my nightmare come true. He could have sat there and shrugged and stared, and it would have been enough to perfect my school-wide humiliation.

But he didn't. He saved me, and I could not fathom why.

"Is there any point asking what you're going to make me do on Sunday?"

"Not really."

Okay. "Is there any point asking what you're going to do to me?"

He grinned wickedly. "Not really."

Fabulous. "Does it involve the use of a safe word?"

"That will depend entirely on you." Noah moved impossibly closer, just inches away. A few freckles disappeared into the scruff on his jaw. "I'll be gentle," Noah added. My breath caught in my throat as he looked at me from beneath those lashes, ruining me.

I narrowed my eyes at him. "You're evil."

In response, Noah smiled, and raised his finger to gently tap the tip of my nose.

"And you're mine," he said, then walked away.

24

After school, I found Daniel waiting for me at the back gate. He shifted his overloaded backpack to his other shoulder.

"Well, well. If it isn't the talk of the town."

"News travels fast 'round these parts?" I asked, but as I did, I noticed quite a bit of staring from other Croyden students as we made our way to his car.

"On the contrary, dear sister. I didn't hear about the showdown at Tiki Corral until a half an hour after it ended," he said as we reached the car. "Are we going to talk about it?"

I barked out a laugh as I pulled my car door open and ducked inside. "No."

Daniel followed in less than a second. "Noah Shaw, huh?"

"I said no."

"When did that happen?"

"No means no."

"You don't actually think you're going to be allowed out of the house with this guy without my help, do you?"

"Still no."

Daniel pulled out of the parking lot. "Something tells me you'll come around," he said, and smiled at the road in front of us the whole way home. So annoying. When he pulled into the driveway, I shot out of the passenger seat, almost missing the fact that our younger brother was crouched over the bushes that separated our house from the neighboring property. Daniel was already inside.

I made my way over to Joseph. As of yesterday, he'd seemed fine. Like the hospital never happened. I wanted to make sure it stayed that way.

"Hey," I said as I walked up to him. "What's—"

A black cat he'd been petting slit its yellow eyes and hissed at me. I took a step back.

Joseph withdrew his hand and turned, still crouched. "You're scaring her."

I raised my hands defensively. "Sorry. You coming inside?"

The cat issued a low meow and then darted away. My brother stood and wiped his hands on his shirt.

"I am now."

Once in the house, I dropped my bag by the front table,

ignoring the crunch of some unidentifiable object inside the canvas, and strolled into the kitchen. The phone rang. Joseph darted to pick it up.

"Dyer residence," he answered formally.

"Hold please," he said as he covered the mouthpiece. He really was hilarious. "It's for you, Mara," he said. "And it's a booooy," he sing-songed.

I rolled my eyes but wondered who it could be. "I'm taking it in my room," I said as Joseph erupted in giggles. Horrible.

Out of his field of vision, I jogged the rest of the way and lifted my phone. "Hello?"

"Hello," Noah answered, mimicking my American accent. But I'd know that voice anywhere.

"How did you get my phone number?" I blurted, before I could stop myself.

"It's called research." I could hear him smirking over the phone.

"Or stalking."

Noah chuckled. "You're adorable when you're bitchy."

"You're not," I said, but smiled despite myself.

"What time shall I pick you up on Sunday? And where exactly do you live?"

Noah meeting my family could not happen. I would never hear the end of it. "You don't have to pick me up," I said in a rush.

"Considering you have no idea where we're going and I

have no intention of telling you, I'm quite sure that I do."

"I can meet you somewhere centrally located."

Noah sounded amused. "I promise to press my trousers before meeting your family. I'll even bring flowers for the occasion."

"Oh, God. Please don't," I said. Maybe honesty would be the best policy. "My family is going to screw with my life if you come over." I knew them far too well.

"Congratulations—you just made the prospect all the more enticing. What's your address?"

"I hate you more than you can know."

"Give it up, Mara. You know I'll find it anyway."

I sighed, defeated, and gave it to him.

"I'll be there at ten."

"Oh," I said, surprised. "For some reason I thought this was a day thing."

"Hilarious. Ten in the morning, darling."

"Can't a girl sleep in on the weekend?"

"You don't sleep. See you Sunday, and don't wear stupid shoes." Noah said, and hung up before I could reply.

I stood, staring at the phone. He was so *aggravating*. But a nervous thrill traveled through my stomach. Me and Noah. Sunday. Just us.

My mother poked her head into my room and spoke, startling me. "Dad's going to be home for dinner tonight. Can you help set the table? Or does your arm hurt too much?"

My arm. My mother. Would she still let me go?

"Be right there," I said, putting down the phone. Seems I'd need Daniel's help after all.

I walked down the hallway and slipped into his room. He was on his bed, reading a book.

"Hi," I said.

"Hi." He didn't look up.

"So, I need your help."

"With what, pray tell?"

He was going to make this as difficult as possible. Awesome. "I'm supposed to go out with Noah on Sunday."

He laughed.

"Glad I amuse you."

"I'm sorry, I'm just—I'm impressed."

"God, Daniel, am I really that hideous?"

"Oh, come on. That's not what I meant. I'm impressed that you actually agreed to go out. That's all."

I sulked, and raised my arm. "I don't think Mom is ever going to let me out of her sight again."

At this, Daniel finally looked at me and raised an eyebrow. "She was supremely pissed Wednesday night, but now that you're, you know, talking to someone, I could work some magic, I think." His grin spread. "If you spilled the proverbial beans, that is."

If anyone could work our mother, it was Daniel. "Fine. What?"

"Did you know it was coming?"

"My sketchbook went missing on Wednesday."

"Nice try. How about the part where Shaw declared to practically the entire school that you'd been using him to practice your nudes?"

I sighed. "Complete surprise."

"That's what I thought when I heard it. I mean, really. You've barely left the house. . . ." He trailed off, but I heard the things he didn't say—you've barely left the house except to run away from a party, to visit the emergency room, to visit a psychiatrist.

I interrupted the awkward silence. "So are you going to help me or not?"

Daniel tilted his head sideways and smiled. "You like him?"

This was unbearable. "You know what, forget it." I turned to leave.

Daniel sat up. "All right, all right. I'll help you. But only out of guilt." He made his way over to me. "I should have told you about Dad's case."

"Well, consider us even, then," I said, then smiled. "If you help me set the table."

"So what's the special occasion?" I asked my father at dinner that night. He gave me a questioning look. "It's, like, the third time you've been home this early since we moved."

"Ah," he said, and smiled. "Well, it was a good day at the office." He took a bite of curried chicken, then swallowed.

"Turns out my client's the real deal. The so-called eyewitness is a hundred years old. She is not going to hold up on cross."

My mother stood to retrieve more food from the kitchen. "That's lovely, Marcus," she said, watching me. I kept my face carefully composed.

"Well, what do you want me to say? Lassiter has an alibi. He has roots in the community. He's one of the most well-respected land developers in south Florida, he's given hundreds of thousands of dollars to conservancy groups—"

"Isn't that, like, oxymoronic?" Joseph chimed in.

Daniel grinned at our little brother, and then piped up. "I think Joseph's right. Maybe that's all just a pretense. I mean, he's a developer and he's donating to the groups who hate him? It's obviously just for show—probably bought him good will at his bail hearing."

I decided to join in, to keep up appearances. "I agree. Sounds like he has something to hide." I sounded suitably jovial. My mother even gave me a thumbs-up from the kitchen. Mission accomplished.

"All right," my father said, "I know when I'm being ganged up on. But it's not very funny, guys. The man's on trial for murder, and the evidence doesn't add up."

"But Dad, isn't it your job to say that?"

"Knock it off, Joseph. You tell him, Dad," Daniel said to our father. When my dad's back was turned, Daniel winked at our little brother.

"What I'd like to know," my mother said as my father opened his mouth to retort, "is where my eldest son will be attending college next year."

And then Daniel was in the spotlight. He reported on the college acceptances he expected, and I tuned him out while shoveling some basmati rice onto my plate. I'd already taken a bite when I noticed something fall through the prongs of my fork. Something small. Something pale.

Something moving.

I froze mid-chew as my gaze slid over my plate. White maggots writhed on the porcelain, half-drowned in curry. I covered my mouth.

"You okay?" Daniel asked, then ate a forkful of rice.

I looked at him wide-eyed with my mouth still full, and then back down at my food. No maggots. Just rice. But I couldn't bring myself to swallow.

I got up from the table and walked slowly to the hallway. Once I turned the corner, I raced to the guest bathroom, and spit out the food. My knees trembled and my body felt clammy. I splashed cold water over my pale, sweaty face and looked in the mirror out of habit.

Jude stood behind me, wearing the same clothes he had on the night I last saw him and a smile that was completely devoid of warmth. I couldn't breathe.

"You need to take your mind off this place," he said, before I turned to the toilet and threw up.

25

MY ALARM SHOCKED ME AWAKE SUNDAY morning. I hadn't remembered falling asleep at all. I was still in the clothes I was wearing the day before.

I was just tired. And maybe a little nervous about meeting Noah today. Maybe. A little. I focused on my closet and surveyed my options.

Skirt, no. Dress, definitely not. Jeans it would be, then. I pulled on a destroyed pair and snatched a favorite T-shirt from my dresser drawer, yanking it over my head.

My heart beat wildly in sharp contrast to the sluggish movement of every other body part as I made my way to the kitchen that morning, as if everything was normal. Because it was.

My mother was putting slices of bread in the toaster when I walked in.

"Morning, Mom." My voice was so even. I gave myself an internal round of applause.

"Good morning, honey." She smiled, and pulled out a filter for the coffeepot. "You're up early." She tucked a strand of her short hair behind her ear.

"Yes." I was. And she didn't know why. Since Wednesday, I'd been trying to think of some way to mention today's non-plans to her, but my mind kept blanking. And now he was almost here.

"Got any plans today?"

Go time. "Yeah, actually." Keep it casual. No big deal.

"What are you up to?" She rummaged through the cabinets and I couldn't see her face.

"I don't really know." It was true; I didn't, though that is generally not what parents like to hear. Particularly not my parents. Particularly not my mother.

"Well, who are you going with?" she asked. If she wasn't suspicious yet, she would be soon.

"A boy from school . . ." I said, my voice trailing off as I braced myself for the third degree.

"Do you want to take my car?"

What?

"Mara?"

I blinked. "Sorry . . . I thought I said 'what?' What?"

"I asked if you wanted to take the Acura. I don't need it today, and you're off the codeine."

Daniel must have held up his side of the bargain. I'd have to ask how he finagled it later.

I declined to correct my mother and tell her I'd been off the codeine for days. The burn still hurt, but since Friday, it had subsided quite a bit. And under the dressings, it didn't look nearly as bad as I'd expected. The ER doctor told me I would probably scar, but my blisters already seemed to be healing. So far, so good.

"Thanks Mom, but he's actually picking me up. He'll be here in—" I checked the clock. Damn. "Five minutes."

My mother turned to look at me, surprised. "I wish you'd given me a bit more notice," she said, as she checked her reflection in the microwave's glass surface.

"You look great, Mom. He'll probably just honk or something anyway." I was tempted to sneak a quick glance at myself in the microwave too, but wasn't willing to chance who might be staring back. I poured myself a glass of orange juice and sat down at the kitchen table instead. "Is Dad here?"

"Nope, he left for the office. Why?"

Because that would leave one less person around to witness my coming humiliation. But before I could translate my thought into acceptable speech, Daniel sauntered in. He stretched, glancing his fingertips against the ceiling.

"Mother," he said, kissing Mom on the cheek, as he made

his way to the refrigerator. "Any plans today, Mara?" he asked, his head buried in the contents of the fridge.

"Shut up," I said, but my heart wasn't in it.

"Don't tease her, Daniel," my mother said.

Three knocks at the front door announced Noah's arrival.

Daniel and I looked at each other for a half a second. Then I shot up from the kitchen table and he slammed the refrigerator door. We both bolted for the foyer. Daniel got there first. Bastard. My mother was right behind me, rubbernecking.

Daniel opened the front door wide. Noah was a standing ovation in dark jeans and a white T-shirt, exuding his scruffy charm.

And he was carrying flowers. My face didn't know whether to blanch or blush.

"Morning," Noah said, flashing a brilliant smile at the three of us. "I'm Noah Shaw," he said, looking over my shoulder. He extended the bouquet of lilies to my mother, who reached past me to take it. It was stunning. Noah had good taste. "It's a pleasure to meet you, Mrs. Dyer."

"Come on in, Noah," she gushed. "And you can call me Indi."

I was dying. Daniel's shoulders shook with silent laughter.

Noah stepped inside and grinned at my brother. "You must be Daniel?"

"Indeed. Pleased to make your acquaintance," my brother said.

It was a slow, painful death.

"Please sit, Noah." My mother gestured at the sofas in the living room. "I'm going to put these in some water."

I saw a window of opportunity and latched on to it. "Actually, I think we have to—"

"I'd love to, thanks," Noah said quickly. He was trying to hide a smile and failing, while Daniel looked like a canary-eating feline. They both walked into the living room. Daniel sat in an overstuffed armchair as Noah settled himself into one of the sofas. I stood.

"So, what are you doing with my little sister today?" Daniel asked. I closed my eyes in defeat.

"I'm afraid I can't ruin the surprise," Noah said. "But I promise I'll return her intact."

He did not just say that. Daniel cackled, and the two of them somehow segued into a conversation. About music, I think, but I wasn't sure. I was too busy drowning in my embarrassment to pay much attention until my mother returned from the kitchen and breezed past me to sit directly across from Noah.

"So Noah, where in London are you from?" she asked.

This morning was full of surprises. How did she know where in England he was from? I looked at my mother and stared.

"Soho," Noah replied. "Have you been there?"

My mother nodded, as Joseph wandered into the living room in his pajamas. "My mother lived in London before she moved to the U.S.," she said. "We used to go every year when I was little." She pulled Joseph onto the sofa next to her. "This is my baby, by the way," she said, grinning.

Noah smiled at my younger brother. "Noah," he said, introducing himself.

"Joseph," my brother replied, and held out his hand.

My mother and Noah proceeded to chat like old mates about Mother England while I shifted from foot to foot, waiting for them to wrap it up.

My mother stood first. "It was so nice to meet you, Noah. Really. You'll have to come over for dinner sometime," she said, before I could stop her.

"I'd love to, if Mara will have me."

Four pairs of eyebrows arched in expectation, waiting for my answer.

"Sure. Sometime," I said, and pushed open the door.

Noah grinned unevenly. "Can't wait," he said. "It was an absolute pleasure, Indi. Daniel, we *must* talk. And Joseph, it was wonderful to meet you."

"Wait!" My little brother shot up from the coach and ran to his room. He returned with his cell phone. "What's your number?" he asked Noah.

Noah looked surprised, but he gave it to him anyway.

"What are you doing, Joseph?" I asked.

"Networking," my brother said, still concentrating on his phone. Then he looked up, and a smile brightened his face. "Okay, got it."

My mother smiled at Noah as he followed me out of the house. "Have a good time!" she called after us.

"Bye, Mom, we'll be back . . . later."

"Wait, Mara," my mother said as she took a few steps out the door. Noah's eyes lifted to us, but when my mother pulled me aside, he kept walking to his car, leaving us alone.

Mom held out her hand. A little round white pill was inside it.

"*Mom*," I whispered through gritted teeth.

"I'd feel better if you took it."

"Dr. Maillard said I didn't have to," I said, glancing over at Noah. He stood next to his car and looked away.

"I know honey, but—"

"Fine, fine," I whispered, and took it from her. Noah was waiting, and I did *not* want him to see. This was blackmail of the worst kind.

"Take it now, please?"

I tossed the pill in my mouth and held it under my tongue as I pretended to swallow. I opened my mouth.

"Thank you," she said, a sad smile on her face. I didn't respond, and walked away. When I heard the front door close, I extracted the pill from my mouth and threw it on the ground. I hadn't decided *not* to take the drugs, but I didn't want to be forced.

"Pre-date pep talk?" Noah asked as he sauntered over to open the passenger door for me. I wondered if he'd seen the pill exchange. If he did, he didn't act like it.

"This isn't a date," I said. "But that was quite a performance in there. She didn't even ask what time I'd be coming home."

Noah grinned. "Glad you enjoyed it." He glanced down at my clothes and nodded once. "You'll do."

"You're so fucking patronizing."

"You have such a filthy mouth."

"Does it bother you?" I smiled, pleased by the thought.

Noah grinned and shut the door behind me. "Not in the least."

26

I WAITED FOR NOAH TO LIGHT A CIGARETTE ONCE he started to drive. Instead, he handed me a plastic cup filled with iced coffee.

"Thanks," I said a little surprised. It looked like it had just the right amount of milk. I took a sip. And sugar. "So how long of a drive is it? To get wherever?"

Noah lifted his own cup and extracted the straw from it with his mouth. The muscles in his jaw worked as he chewed. I couldn't tear my eyes away. "We're stopping to see a friend, first," he said.

A friend. It didn't sound ominous, and truly, I tried not to be paranoid. But a part of me wondered if I was being set up for something. Something bigger than what Anna had planned. I swallowed hard.

Noah clicked on his iPod with one hand while he kept the other on the wheel.

"Hallelujah," I said, smiling.

"What?"

"The song. I love this cover."

"Really?" Noah looked obnoxiously surprised. "Doesn't seem like your thing."

"Oh? What's my thing?"

"I had you pegged for a closeted pop fan."

"Bite me."

"If I must."

The song ended and something classical came on. I reached for the iPod. "May I?" Noah shook his head in exaggerated disappointment, but waved me on anyway. "Calm yourself. I wasn't going to change it, I just wanted to see." I scrolled through his music; Noah had excellent but consistent taste. I was much more diverse. I smiled with satisfaction.

Noah arched an eyebrow. "What are you smirking about, over there?"

"I'm more well-rounded than you."

"Not possible. You're American," he said. "And if it is true, it's only because you like crap."

"How is it that you have friends, Noah?"

"I ask myself that daily." He chomped down on the plastic straw.

"Seriously. Inquiring minds want to know."

Noah's brow creased, but he stared straight ahead. "I guess I don't."

"Could have fooled me."

"That wouldn't be difficult."

That stung. "Go to hell," I said quietly.

"Already there," Noah said calmly, pulling out the straw from his mouth and chucking it on the floor.

"So why are you doing this?" I asked, careful to keep my voice even, but an unpleasant image of myself at a prom night soiree covered in pig's blood crept into my mind.

"I want to show you something."

I turned away and looked out the window. I never knew which Noah to expect from day to day. Or hell, minute to minute.

Tangled overpasses wove around and above us, the hulking concrete monstrosities the only scenery on this part of I-95. We were heading south, and Noah and I didn't speak most of the way.

At some point, the urban landscape gave way to ocean on both sides of the highway. It narrowed from four lanes to two and a steep, high bridge loomed in front of us.

Very steep. Very high.

We climbed behind the swarm of brake lights that crawled up the overpass in front of us. My throat closed. I gripped the center console with my bandaged hand, the pain screaming under my skin as I tried not to look straight ahead or to either side, where the turquoise water and the Miami skyline receded into smallness.

Noah placed his hand on mine. Just slightly. Barely touching.

But I felt it.

I tilted my head to look at his face, and he half-smiled while staring straight ahead. It was contagious. I smiled back. In response, Noah laced his fingers in between my bandaged ones, still resting on the plastic. I was too preoccupied by his hand on mine to feel any pain.

"Are you afraid of anything?" I asked.

His smile evaporated. He nodded his head once.

"Well?" I prodded. "I showed you mine . . ."

"I'm afraid of forgeries."

I turned away. He couldn't even reciprocate. Neither of us spoke for about a minute. But then.

"I'm afraid of being fake. Empty," Noah said tonelessly. He released my fingers and the palm of his hand rested on the back of mine for a moment. My entire hand would fit almost completely into his. I flipped mine over and laced our fingers together before I realized what I was doing.

Then I realized what I was doing. My heart skipped a beat. I watched Noah's face for something. A sign, maybe. I honestly didn't quite know what.

But there was nothing there. His expresion was smooth, his forehead uncreased. Blank. And our fingers were still entwined. I didn't know if mine were holding his in place by force and if his were just resting or—

"There's nothing I want. There's nothing I can't do. I don't care about anything. No matter what, I'm an impostor. An actor in my own life."

His sudden candor floored me. I had no idea what to say, so I said nothing.

He extracted his hand from mine and pointed to an enormous gold dome across the water. "That's the Miami Seaquarium."

Still nothing.

Noah's free hand searched in his pocket. He tapped out a cigarette and lit it, exhaling the smoke through his nose. "We ought to go."

He wanted to take me back home. And to my surprise, I didn't want that. "Noah, I—"

"To the Seaquarium. They have a killer whale there."

"Okay . . ."

"Her name's Lolita."

"That's . . ."

"Twisted?"

"Yeah."

"I know."

And let the awkward silence ensue. We turned off the highway, in an opposite direction from the Seaquarium, and the street curved into a busy neighborhood filled with peach, yellow, orange, and pink stucco boxes—houses—with bars on the windows. Everything was in Spanish; every sign, every storefront. But even as I looked, I felt Noah sitting next to me, inches away, waiting for me to say something. So I did.

"So, uh, have you seen—Lolita?" I asked. I wanted to punch myself in the face.

"God, no."

"Then how'd you hear about her?"

He ran his fingers through his hair and a few strands fell into his eyes, catching the mid-morning sunlight. "My mother's somewhat of an animal rights activist."

"Right, the vet thing."

"No, from before that. She became a vet because of the animal business. And it's more than that, anyway."

I knit my eyebrows together. "I don't think it's possible to be any more vague."

"Well, I don't know how to describe it, honestly."

"Like animal rescue and stuff?" I wondered if Noah's mother had pulled any dog theft capers like mine with Mabel.

"Kind of, but not what you're thinking."

Ha. "So, what then?"

"Ever hear of the Animal Liberation Front?"

"Aren't they the ones that let all of those lab monkeys out of their cages and they spread this virus that turns people into zombies . . . ?"

"I think that's a movie."

"Right."

"But that's the general idea."

I conjured an image of Dr. Shaw in a ski mask freeing lab animals. "I like your mom."

Noah smiled slightly. "Her primate freedom fighting days ended after she married my father. The in-laws didn't approve," he said with mock solemnity. "But she still gives money to those groups. When we moved here, she was all riled up about Lolita and she had a few fundraisers to try and raise enough money to get a bigger tank."

"What happened?" I asked, as Noah took a long drag on his cigarette.

"The bastards kept raising their price with no guarantee that they'd actually build the thing," Noah said, exhaling the smoke through his nose. "Anyway, because of my dad, she just gives money now, I think. I've seen the return envelopes in the outgoing mail."

Noah took a sharp right, and I reflexively glanced out the window. I hadn't been paying attention to the scenery—I was sitting inches away from Noah, after all—but now noticed that somewhere along the way, North Cuba had transformed into East Hampton. Sunlight filtered through the leaves of the enormous trees that lined both sides of the street, dappling our faces and hands through the glass of the windshield and sunroof. The houses here were experiments in excess; each one was more ostentatious and absurd than the next, and there was no uniform look to them whatsoever. The only thing the modern, glass house on one side of the street had in common with its opposite, a stately Victorian, was the scale. They were palaces.

"Noah?" I asked slowly.

"Yes?"

"Where are we going?"

"I'm not telling you."

"And who is this friend?"

"I'm not telling you."

Then, after a beat, "Don't worry, you'll like her."

I looked down at the shredded knees of my jeans and my worn sneakers. "I feel ridiculously underdressed for a Sunday brunch scenario. Just saying."

"She won't care," he said as he ran his fingers through his hair. "And you're perfect."

27

ROWS OF PALM TREES SPRUNG UP FROM THE sides of the narrow street, and the ocean peeked out from the spaces in between homes. When we drove to the end of the cul-de-sac, an enormous automated iron gate opened for us. A camera was perched at the entrance. The day was getting weirder.

"So . . . what does this friend do, exactly?"

"You could call her a lady of leisure."

"Makes sense. You probably don't have to work if you can afford to live here."

"No, probably not."

We passed an enormous, garish fountain in the center of the property; a muscled, barely clothed Greek man clasping the waist of a girl who reached into the sky. Her arms transformed into branches and spouted pale, golden water in the sunlight. Noah pulled all the way up to the front entrance, where a man in a suit was waiting.

"Good morning, Mr. Shaw," the man said, as he nodded to Noah, and then moved toward the passenger side door to open it for me.

"Morning, Albert. I got it."

Noah exited the car and opened the door for me. I narrowed my eyes at him, but he avoided my stare.

"You must be here often," I said cautiously.

"Yes."

Albert opened the front door for us and Noah breezed right in.

As extravagant as the landscaping, fountain, driveway, and gate were, nothing, *nothing* could have prepared me for the mansion's interior. On either side of us, arches and columns towered into a double balcony. My Chucks squeaked on the flawless patterned marble floor, and there was another Greek-inspired fountain in the center of the inner courtyard, with three women carrying watering jugs. The sheer enormousness of the place was staggering.

"No one can possibly live here," I said to myself.

Noah heard me. "Why's that?"

"Because this is not a house. This is like . . . a set. For some mafia movie. Or a tacky wedding venue. Or . . . *Annie*."

Noah tilted his head. "A scathing, yet accurate analysis.

Alas, I am afraid people do actually live here."

He sauntered carelessly to the end of the courtyard and turned left. I followed him, wide-eyed and wondrous, into an equally expansive hallway. I didn't notice the small, black streak of fur hurtling in my direction until she was only a few feet away. Noah whisked the dog into the air just as it charged me.

"You little bitch," Noah said to the snarling dog. "Behave."

I raised an eyebrow at him.

"Mara, meet Ruby." The squirming mass of fat rolls and fur strained for my jugular, but Noah held her back. The pug's smushed face only magnified the sounds of her fury. It was disturbing and hilarious at the same time.

"She's . . . charming," I said.

"Noah?" I turned around to see Noah's mother standing about twenty feet behind us, barefooted and impeccably dressed in white linen. "I thought you were out for the day," she said.

Out for the day?

"Like an idiot, I left the keys here."

Left the keys . . . here.

That was when I first noticed the fawn-colored dog trying to hide behind Dr. Shaw's knees.

"Is that . . . ?" I looked from the dog to Noah. His face broke into a smile.

"Mabel!" he called loudly.

She whined in and stepped backward, farther behind the fabric of Dr. Shaw's dress.

"Come here, gorgeous."

She whined again.

Still looking at the dog, Noah said, "Mum, you remember Mara?" He tilted his head in my direction while he crouched, trying to call the dog over.

"I do," she said, smiling. "How are you?"

"Good," I said, but I was too absorbed in the scene unfolding before me to really focus. The vicious pug. Mabel's terror. And the fact that Noah lived here. *Here.*

He walked over to where his mother stood and reached down to pet Mabel, with Ruby still struggling in his other arm. Mabel thumped her tail against Dr. Shaw's legs. It was incredible how much better she looked after just over a week. Her spine and hip bones still protruded, but she was already starting to fill out. And her coat looked impossibly healthier. Amazing.

"Would you take her?" He offered the little dog to his mother, who held her arms out. "Since I had to double back, I thought I'd let Mara and Mabel get reacquainted while we're here."

Mabel wanted no part of that plan, and Dr. Shaw seemed to know it. "Why don't I take them both upstairs while you two—"

"It's Ruby fussing that's making her nervous. Just take her, we'll be fine." Noah crouched down to pet Mabel.

Dr. Shaw shrugged. "It was nice to see you again, Mara."

"You too," I said quietly, as she walked out.

Noah lifted Mabel in a football carry before she could bolt after Dr. Shaw. The poor dog's legs paddled as if she were running on a phantom treadmill. A memory of a hissing black cat flared in my mind.

"You're scaring her," Joseph had said.

Mabel was scared too. Of me.

My breath caught in my throat. That was a crazy thing to think. Why would she be scared of me? I was being paranoid. Something else was freaking her out. I tried not to let the hurt leak into my voice when I spoke. "Maybe your mom's right, Noah."

"She's fine, Ruby just made her nervous."

The whites of Mabel's eyes were visible by the time Noah carried her over to where I stood. He looked at me, confused. "What did you do, bathe in leopard urine before you left the house this morning?"

"Yes. Leopard urine. Never leave home without it."

Mabel whined and yelped and strained against Noah's arms. "All right," he said finally. "Mission aborted." He placed Mabel on the floor and watched her scramble out of the hall, her claws clicking on the marble. "She probably doesn't remember you," Noah said, still looking in Mabel's direction.

I dropped my gaze. "I'm sure that's it," I said. I didn't want Noah to see that I was upset.

"Well," he said finally. He rocked back on his heels and studied me.

I willed myself not to blush under his stare. "Well." Time to change the subject. "You are a lying liar who lies."

"Oh?"

I looked around us, at the towering ceiling and sweeping balconies. "You kept all of this a secret."

"No, I didn't. You just never asked."

"How was I supposed to guess? You dress like a hobo."

At this, a mocking grin crept over Noah's mouth. "Haven't you heard not to judge a book by its cover?"

"If I'd have known it was Trite Proverb Day, I would have stayed home." I rubbed my forehead and shook my head. "I can't believe you didn't say anything."

Noah's eyes challenged me. "Like what?"

"Oh, I don't know. Like, 'Mara, you might want to wear some makeup and put on heels because I'm going to take you to my family's palace in Miami Beach on Sunday.' Something like that."

Noah stretched his lithe frame, locking his fingers and raising his arms above his head. His white T-shirt rose, exposing a sliver of stomach and the elastic of his boxers above the low waistband of his jeans. Button fly, I noticed.

Well played.

"First, you don't need makeup," he said as I rolled my eyes. "Second, you wouldn't last an hour in heels, where we're going. Speaking of which, I have to get the keys."

"Oh, yes, the mysterious keys."

"Are you going to go on about this the entire day now? I thought we were making progress."

"Sorry. I'm just a tad rattled by the pug attack and Mabel's freak-out. And the fact that you live in the Taj Mahal."

"Rubbish. The Taj Mahal is only a hundred eighty-six square feet. This house has twenty-five thousand."

I stared at him blankly.

"I was kidding," he said.

I stared at him blankly.

"All right, I wasn't kidding. Let's go, shall we?"

"After you, my liege," I said.

Noah gave an exaggerated sigh as he started walking to an enormous staircase with an intricately carved banister. I followed him up, and shamefully enjoyed the view. Noah's jeans were loose, barely hanging on to his hips.

When we finally reached the top of the staircase, Noah took a left down a long corridor. The plush Oriental rugs muffled our footsteps, and my eyes drank in the detailed oil paintings that hung from the walls. Eventually, Noah stopped in front of a gleaming wooden door. He reached to open it, but we heard the careless slam of a door behind us and turned.

"Noah?" asked a sleep-ridden voice. Female.

"Hey, Katie."

Even with pillow creases on her face, the familiar girl was absolutely stunning. She looked as otherworldly standing there in a camisole and shorts set as she had in her fairy getup. Without the costume and the pulsing lights in the club, it was obvious that she shared Noah's extraterrestrial beauty. Her hair was the same dark honey brown color as his, only longer; the ends skimmed the lace bottom of her camisole. Her blue eyes widened in surprise as they met mine.

"I didn't know you had company," she said to Noah, suppressing a smile.

He shot her a look, then turned to me. "Mara, my sister Katie."

"Kate," she corrected him, then gave me a knowing glance. "Morning."

I couldn't manage much more than a nod. At that moment, a perky, blond cheerleader was doing cartwheels in my vena cava. His sister. His *sister*!

"It's almost noon, now, actually," Noah said.

Kate shrugged and yawned. "Well, nice meeting you, Mara," she said, and winked at me before heading down the stairs.

"You too," I managed to breathe. My heart rioted in my chest.

Noah opened the door all the way and I tried to compose myself. This changed nothing. Nothing at all. Noah Shaw was still a whore, still an asshole, and still painfully out of my league. This was my inner mantra, the one I repeated on a loop until Noah tilted his head and spoke.

"Are you coming in?"

Yes. Yes I was.

28

Noah's room was startling. A low, modern platform bed dominated the center of it but otherwise, there was no furniture except for a long desk that blended inconspicuously into an alcove. There were no posters. No laundry. Just a guitar leaning against the side of the bed. And the books.

Rows upon rows of books, lining built-in shelves that stretched from the floor to the ceiling. Sunlight spilled through the enormous windows that overlooked Biscayne Bay.

I never imagined what Noah's room would look like, but if I had, I wouldn't have imagined this. It was gorgeous, definitely. But so . . . bare. Unlived in. I circled the room, trailing my fingers along some of the spines as I went.

"Welcome to the private collection of Noah Shaw," he said.

I stared at all of the titles. "You have not read all of these."

"Not yet."

I cracked a smile. "So it's a tail-chasing tactic."

"Pardon?" I could hear the amusement in his voice.

"Vanity books," I said without looking at him. "You don't actually read them, they're just here to impress your . . . guests."

"You're a mean girl, Mara Dyer," he said, standing in the middle of his room. I felt his eyes on me, and I liked it.

"I'm wrong?" I asked.

"You are wrong."

"All right," I said, and pulled a random book from the shelf. "*Maurice*, by E.M. Forster. What's it about? Go."

Noah told me about the gay protagonist who attended Cambridge in turn-of-the-century Britain. I didn't believe him, but I hadn't read it so I moved on.

"*A Portrait of the Artist as a Young Man*?"

Noah belly-flopped on to his bed, affecting a bored tone as he rattled off another synopsis. My eyes followed the thousand-mile stretch of his back and my feet itched with the confusing impulse to walk over and join him. Instead, I pulled out another book without reading the spine first.

"*Ulysses*," I called out.

Noah shook his head, his face buried in the pillow.

Satisfied, I smiled to myself, put the book back on the shelf and reached for another. The dust jacket was missing, so I read the title from the cover. "*The Joy of* . . . crap." I read the rest of the full title of the thick, nondescript volume to myself and felt myself redden.

Noah turned over on to his side and said with mock seriousness, "I have never read *The Joy of Crap*. Sounds disgusting." I blushed deeper. "I have, however, read *The Joy of Sex*," he continued, a mischievous smile transforming his face. "Not in a while, but I think it's one of those classics you can come back to again . . . and again."

"I don't like this game anymore," I said as I placed the book back on its shelf.

Noah reached over to the floor next to his bed, near the acoustic guitar that was propped up against a sticker-covered case. He jangled the keys. "Well, we can go now. You can come back and grill me on the library's contents later," he said, his grin still in place. "You hungry?"

I was, actually, and nodded. Noah walked to a well-disguised intercom and pressed his finger on the call button.

"If you order some servant to bring food, I'm leaving."

"I was going to make sure Albert hadn't moved the car."

"Oh, right. Albert the butler."

"He's a valet, actually."

"You are not helping yourself."

Noah ignored me and glanced at the clock by his bed. "We really ought to have been there by now; I want you to have time to get the full experience. But we can stop at Mireya's on the way."

"Another friend?"

"A restaurant. Cuban. The best."

When we reached the car, Albert smiled as Noah opened my door for me. After the mansion was out of sight, I screwed up the courage to attack Noah with the questions that plagued me since learning of his assets. The financial sort.

"So who are you people?" I asked.

"You people?" He slipped on his sunglasses.

"Cute. Your family. Supposedly, the only people who live here are basketball players and has-been pop singers."

"My father owns a company."

"Okaaay," I said. "What kind of company?"

"Biotechnology."

"So where was Daddy Warbucks this morning?"

Noah's face was curiously blank. "Don't know, don't care," he said easily. He stared straight ahead. "We're not . . . close," Noah added.

"Clearly." I waited for him to elaborate, but he lifted his sunglasses and hid his eyes instead. Time to change the subject. "So why doesn't your mother have a British accent?"

"She doesn't have an *English* accent because she's American."

"Oh my God, really?" I mocked. I saw Noah's smile in profile. He paused before continuing.

"She's from Massachusetts. And she is not actually my biological mother." He looked at me sideways, gauging my reaction. I kept my face even. I didn't know much about Noah, aside from his rumored extracurricular activities. But I realized then that I wanted to. I had no idea what to expect this morning when he picked me up, and to an extent, I still didn't. But I no longer thought it would be some nefarious plot, and that made me curious.

"My mother died when I was five and Katie was almost four."

The revelation knocked me out of my thoughts. And made me feel like a jackass, after picking not one but two unpleasant topics of conversation. "I'm sorry," I said lamely.

"Thanks," he said, staring at the bright road ahead of us. "It was a long time ago, I don't really remember her," he said, but his posture had stiffened. He didn't speak for a minute, and I wondered if I was supposed to say something. But then I remembered everyone telling me how sorry they were when Rachel died, and how little I wanted to hear it. There was just nothing to say.

Noah surprised me by continuing. "Before my mother died, she and my dad and Ruth," he tipped his head back toward the house, "were all really close. Ruth spent high school in England, so that's how they met, and they stayed friends while at Cambridge, wreaking havoc and organizing protests."

I raised my eyebrows.

"Ruth told me my mother was the most . . . enthusiastic. Chaining herself to trees and breaking into university science departments and freeing lab animals and such," Noah said, as he placed a cigarette between his lips. "The three of them ran around doing it together—incomprehensible, if you know my father—and somehow, he convinced my mother to marry him." The cigarette dangled from his lips as he spoke, drawing my eyes like a magnet. "While they were still in college. Some ultimate act of rebellion or something." He lit the cigarette, opened his window, and inhaled. His face was carefully impassive beneath the dark lenses as he spoke.

"My grandparents were unenthused. They're old money, were not fans of my mother's to start, and thought my father was ruining his prospects. Et cetera, et cetera. But they married anyway. My stepmother moved back to the U.S. for vet school, and my parents lived *la vie bohème* for a while. When they had kids, my grandparents were happy. Katie and I were so close together that I think they were hoping my mother would go on maternity leave from civil disobedience." Noah fed the ash of his cigarette to the expanse of highway behind us. "But my mother didn't slow down at all. She just took us with her wherever she went. Until she died. She was stabbed."

Oh my God.

"At a protest."

Jesus.

"She made my father stay home to watch Katie that day, but I was with her. I'd just turned five a few days before, but I don't remember it. Or much of her at all, really. My father won't even mention her name, and he loses it if anyone else does," Noah said, without inflection.

I was speechless. Noah's mother died—was murdered—and he was there when it happened.

Noah breathed smoke through his nose, and it billowed around him before escaping through the open window. It was a gorgeous day, blue and cloudless. But there could have been a hurricane outside for all I cared. In an instant, Noah became different to me. I was riveted.

"Ruth went back to England when she heard about my mother. A long time ago, she told me that after my mother died, my father was useless. Couldn't take care of us, couldn't take care of himself. Literally a disaster—this was, of course, before he sold his soul to the shareholders. And she stayed, and they got married, even though he doesn't deserve her, even though he'd become someone else. And here we are now, one big happy family."

His expression was inscrutable behind his sunglasses, and I wished I could see it. Did anyone at school know about his mother—about him? And then it occurred to me that Noah didn't know about what happened to *me*. I looked at my lap, fidgeting with the shredded knee of my jeans. If I told him now, it might sound like I was comparing tragedies—like I thought losing a best friend was comparable to losing a parent, which I didn't. But if I said nothing, what would he think?

"I just—" I started. "I don't even—"

"Thanks," he said, cutting me off coolly. "It's all right."

"No, it isn't."

"No, it isn't," he said plainly. Noah pushed his sunglasses up, but his face was still guarded. "However, there are benefits to having a corporate sellout of a father."

He was flippant, so I was too. "Like getting a car on your sixteenth birthday?"

Noah's grin was full of mischief. "Katie has a Maserati."

I blinked. "She does not."

"She does. She's not even old enough to drive it legally."

I raised my eyebrow. "And your car? Is it your brand of teenage rebellion or something?"

The corner of Noah's mouth curved up into a slight smile. "Sad, isn't it?" He said it lightly, but there was something haunted about his expression. His eyebrows drew together, and I wanted so badly to reach over and smooth them apart.

"I don't think so," I said instead. "I think it's brave. There's so much *stuff* you could buy with that much money. Not taking it is—it's pretty moral."

Noah feigned horror. "Did you just call me moral?"

"I believe I did."

"Little does she know," he said, and turned up the volume on his iPod.

"Death Cab?" I asked. "Really?" I asked.

"You sound surprised."

"I wouldn't have thought you liked them."

"They're one of the only modern bands I do like."

"I'm going to have to broaden your musical tastes," I said.

"It's too early for threats," Noah said as he turned on to a bustling, narrow road. It was alive with people out enjoying the weather. Noah parked on the street just as the song ended, and I let him open the door for me. I was starting to get used to it. We passed a small park where a handful of old men sat, playing dominoes. A large, colorful mural was painted on one wall, and striped tents covered the game tables. I'd never seen anything like it before.

"It doesn't mean anything, you know," Noah said out of nowhere.

"What doesn't?"

"The money."

I looked around, at the mostly shabby storefronts and cars parked on the street. Noah's might have been the newest one. "I think your perspective is somewhat skewed because, you know, you actually have it."

Noah stopped walking, and stared straight ahead. "It's shut-up money," he said, and there was an edge to his voice. "So my father doesn't have to spend any time with us." But then his tone lightened. "Even if he gave me nothing, there's still the trust I come into when I turn eighteen."

"Nice. When's that?" I asked.

Noah started walking again. "December twenty-first."

"I missed your birthday." And that made me sad, for some reason.

"You did."

"What do you think you'll do with the money?"

Noah flashed a grin. "Convert it to gold coins and swim in it. But first," he said, taking my hand, "lunch."

29

MY BODY WARMED AT THE CONTACT AS Noah led the way into the bustling restaurant. I watched him in profile, talking to the host. Somehow, he didn't look like the same person I'd met two weeks ago. He didn't look like the same person who picked me up this morning. Noah—sarcastic, distant, untouchable Noah—cared. And that made him real.

I wondered if anyone else knew, but enjoyed a fleeting moment thinking that I might be the only one as we were led to a table by the window. But then Noah's grip tightened on my hand. I looked up at him. The color had drained from his face.

"Noah?" His eyes were tightly shut, and I began to feel scared without knowing why. "Are you okay?"

"Give me a minute," he said, not opening his eyes. He dropped my hand. "I'll be right back."

Noah threaded back the way we'd come in and disappeared out of the restaurant. A bit dazed, I sat down at the table and perused the menu. I was thirsty, though, and lifted my head to scan the restaurant for a waiter when I saw him.

Jude.

Staring at me from under the brim of his hat. In the middle of a throng of people waiting for a seat.

He started walking toward me.

I squeezed my eyes shut. He wasn't real.

"How does it feel to be the most beautiful girl in the room?"

I jumped at the accented voice. Not Noah's. And definitely not Jude's. When I opened my eyes, a fair-skinned guy with blond hair and hazel eyes was standing next to the table with an earnest expression. He was cute.

"Mind if I join you?" he asked as he slipped into the seat across from me. Apparently he had no intention of waiting for my answer.

I narrowed my eyes at him. "Actually, I'm here with some-one," I said. Where was Noah?

"Oh? A boyfriend?"

I paused before answering, "A friend."

His grin widened. "He's a fool."

"What?"

"If he's just a friend, he's a fool. I don't think I could stand being just your friend. I'm Alain, by the way."

I snorted. Who was this guy? "Luckily, Alain," I said, mispronouncing his name on purpose, "I don't foresee that being a problem."

"You don't? Why's that?"

"Because you were just leaving," Noah said from behind me. I half-turned and looked up. Noah stood inches away, leaning over me just slightly. The tension was evident in the set of his shoulders.

Alain stood, and fished for something in the pocket of his jeans, withdrawing a pen. "In case you get tired of friends," he said, scrawling something on a napkin, "here's my number." He slid it over the surface of the table in my direction. Noah's hand reached over my shoulder and took it.

Alain's eyes narrowed at Noah. "She can make her own decisions."

Noah stood still for a second, staring at him. Then he relaxed, and a spark of amusement lit his eyes. "Of course she can," he said, and raised an eyebrow at me. "Well?"

I stared at Alain. "That seat's taken."

Alain grinned. "It certainly is."

Noah turned to him too casually and said something in French—I watched Alain's expression grow increasingly anxious. "Still care to join us?" Noah asked him, but Alain was already leaving.

Noah slipped into the now-empty seat and smiled. "Tourists," he said, shrugging lazily.

I glared at him, even though I wasn't mad. I was calm, actually. Unusually so, for my post-hallucinatory state. I was glad Noah was back. But I couldn't let him off so easily. "What did you say to him?"

Noah picked up the menu and spoke while studying it. "Enough."

But I wasn't having it. "If you're not going to tell me, then give me his number."

"I told him you were in high school," he said, without looking up.

"That's it?" I was skeptical.

A hint of a smile appeared on Noah's lips. "Mostly. You look too old for your own good."

My eyebrows shot up. "You're one to talk."

He grinned and placed the menu on the table. Then stared out the window. Distracted.

"What's wrong?"

He glanced up at me and gave me a tight smile. "Nothing."

I didn't believe him.

The waiter appeared then, and Noah plucked the menu from my hands and handed it over, rushing off our order in Spanish. The waiter departed for the kitchen.

I shot him a dark look. "I hadn't decided yet."

"Trust me."

"Guess I don't have much of a choice." A devious smile formed on his lips. I took a deep breath and, for the sake of peace, let it go. "So, Spanish *and* French?"

Noah answered with a slow, arrogant grin. I had to concentrate to prevent myself from melting in the plastic-covered seat.

"Do you speak anything else?" I asked.

"Well, what level of fluency are we talking about here?"

"Anything."

The waiter returned, and brought two empty, frosted glasses along with dark bottles of something. He poured the caramel-colored drinks for us, then left.

Noah took a sip before answering. Then said, "German, Spanish, Dutch, Mandarin, and, of course, French."

Impressive. "Say something in German," I said, and took a sip of the drink. It was sweet with a spicy, sharp finish. I wasn't sure I liked it.

"*Scheide*," Noah said.

I decided to give the drink another shot. "What does that mean?" I asked, then sipped.

"Vagina."

I almost choked, and covered my mouth with my hand. After I composed myself, I spoke. "Lovely. Is that all you know?"

"In German, Dutch, and Mandarin, yes."

I shook my head. "Why, Noah, do you know the word for vagina in every language?"

"Because I'm European, and therefore more cultured than you," he said, taking another swig and trying not to smile.

Before I could smack him, the waiter then brought a basket of what looked like banana chips accompanied by a viscous, pale yellow sauce.

"*Mariquitas*," Noah said. "Try one, you'll thank me."

I tried one. And I did thank him. They were savory with just a hint of sweet, and the garlic-burn of the sauce made my tongue sing.

"God, these are good," Noah said. "I could snort them."

The waiter returned and loaded our table with food. I couldn't identify anything except for the rice and beans; the oddest looking were plates of glistening fried dough balls of some sort, and a dish of some white fleshy vegetable smothered in sauce and onions. I pointed to it.

"Yuca," Noah said.

I pointed to the dough balls.

"Fried plantains."

I pointed to a low bowl filled with what purported to be stew, but then Noah said, "Are you going to point, or are you going to eat?"

"I just like to know what I'm putting in my mouth before I swallow."

Noah arched an eyebrow, and I wanted to crawl into a hole and die.

Shockingly, he let it slide. Instead, he explained what everything was as he held the dishes out for me to take from. When I was full to bursting, the waiter arrived with the check, setting it down in front of Noah. In an echo of his earlier gesture with Alain's number, I slid the check my way as I dug in my pocket for cash.

A look of horror dawned on Noah's face. "What are you doing?"

"I am paying for my lunch."

"I don't understand," Noah said.

"Food costs money."

"Brilliant. But that still doesn't explain why you think you're paying for it."

"Because I can pay for my own food."

"It was ten dollars."

"And, wouldn't you know, I have ten dollars."

"And I have an American Express Black Card."

"Noah—"

"You have a little something right here, by the way," he said, pointing to the side of his scruffy jaw.

Oh, how horrible. "Where? Here?" I grabbed a napkin from the dispenser on the table and rubbed at the location where the offending food bit seemed to be lurking. Noah shook his head, and I rubbed again.

"Still there," he said. "May I?" Noah indicated the napkin dispenser and leaned over the table at eye level, ready to wipe my face like a food-spattered toddler. Misery. I squinted my eyes shut out of shame and waited for the feel of the paper napkin on my skin.

I felt his fingertips on my cheek instead. I stopped breathing, and opened my eyes, then shook my head. How embarrassing.

"Thanks," I said quietly. "I'm completely uncivilized."

"Then I suppose I'm going to have to civilize you," Noah said, and I noticed then that the check had disappeared.

One look at Noah told me he'd taken it. Very slick.

I narrowed my eyes at him. "I was warned about you, you know."

And with that half-smile that wrecked me, Noah said, "But you're here anyway."

30

A HALF-HOUR LATER, NOAH DROVE UP TO the front entrance of the Miami Beach Convention Center and parked next to the curb. On top of the words NO PARKING emblazoned on the asphalt. I gave him a skeptical look.

"A perk of being Baby Warbucks," he said.

Noah withdrew the keys from his pocket and walked over to the door like he owned the building. Hell, he probably did. It was pitch-black inside, and Noah felt for the lights and flipped them on.

The art took my breath away.

It was everywhere. Every surface was covered; the floors themselves were pieces, geographic patterns painted beneath our feet. There were installations everywhere. Sculpture, photography, prints; anything and everything.

"Oh my God."

"Yes?"

I smacked his arm. "Noah, what *is* this?"

"An exhibition funded by some group my mother's on the board of," he said. "Two thousand artists are being shown, I think."

"Where is everyone?"

"The show doesn't open for five days. It's just us."

I was speechless. I turned to Noah and stared at him, mouth agape. He looked deliriously pleased with himself.

"Another perk," he said, and grinned.

We walked the labyrinth of exhibits, weaving our way through the industrial space. It was like nothing I'd ever seen. Some of the *rooms* were art; walls twisted with metalwork, or entirely crocheted in a walk-in tapestry.

I wandered over to a sculpture installation, a forest of tall, abstract pieces that surrounded me. They looked like trees or people, depending on the angle, copper and nickel mingling together, towering over my head. I was amazed at the scale of it, the amount of effort it must have taken the artist to create something like this. And Noah brought me here, knowing I would love it, arranging the whole day for me. I wanted to run over and give him the hug of his life.

"Noah?" My voice bounced off the walls in a hollow echo. He didn't answer.

I turned around. He wasn't there. The giddiness I'd felt slipped away, replaced by a low buzzing of fear. I walked to the far wall looking for a way out and registered the soreness of my calves and thighs for the first time. I must have been walking for a while. The vastness of the space swallowed my footsteps. The wall was a dead end.

I needed to go back the way I came, and tried to remember which way that was. As I passed the trees—or were they people?—I felt their faceless, misshapen trunks twist in my direction, following me. I stared straight ahead, even while their limbs reached out to grab me. Because they weren't reaching. They weren't moving. It wasn't real. I was just scared and it wasn't real and maybe I would start taking the pills when I got home later.

If I got home later.

I escaped the metal forest unscathed, of course, but then found myself surrounded by enormous photographs of houses and buildings in various stages of decay. The images stretched from floor to ceiling, making it seem like I was walking on a real sidewalk beside them. Ivy crept over brick walls, and trees bent and leaned into the structures, sometimes swallowing them whole. The grass might have edged on to the concrete floor of the Convention Center, too. And there were people in the pictures. Three people with backpacks, scaling a fence at the border of one of the properties. Rachel. Claire. Jude.

I blinked. No, not them. No one. There were no people in the picture at all.

The air pressed in on me and I quickened my pace, my head pounding, my feet sore, and rushed through the photographs, detouring at a sharp corner to try and find the exit. But when I turned, I faced another photograph.

Thousands of pounds of brick and concrete rubble were strewn along the wooded grounds. It was a picture of destruction, as if a tornado had hit a building and all that was left was a pile of rubble and the vague sense that there were people beneath it. It was reverent—each ray of sunlight that filtered through the trees cast a perfect, distorted shadow on the snow-covered ground.

And then the dust and bricks and beams began to move. Darkness pressed in on the edges of my vision as the snow and sunlight receded, leaving dead leaves in their wake. The dust curled back in on itself and the bricks and beams flew and towered and reassembled themselves. I couldn't breathe, couldn't see. I lost my balance and fell, and when I hit the floor, my eyes flew open at the shock of the impact. But I was no longer in the Convention Center.

I was no longer in Miami at all. I was standing right beside the asylum, right next to Rachel and Claire and Jude.

31

BEFORE

RACHEL HELD OUT THE MAP SHE'D PULLED from the Internet, which showed a detailed blueprint of the facility. It was huge, but navigable if you had enough time. The plan was to enter through the cellar door, make our way through the basement storage area, and climb up to the main level, which would bring us to the industrial kitchen. Then, another staircase would lead us to the patient and treatment rooms in the children's wing.

Rachel and Claire were giddy with excitement as they pried open the basement door with a groaning creak. The Laurelton Police Department had mostly given up securing the place, beyond some cursory CONDEMNED notices, which suited Rachel perfectly; she was itching to write our names on the blackboard inside one of the patient rooms. It bore the names of other thrill-seekers—or idiots, flip a coin—who had dared to spend the night.

Claire was first to walk down the steps. The light on her video camera cast shadows in the basement. I must have looked as freaked out as I felt, because Rachel smiled and promised, again, that everything would be fine. Then she followed Claire.

I walked behind them down to the lowest level of the asylum and felt Jude loop his finger through the belt hole in the back of my jeans. I shivered. The basement was covered in debris, the crumbling brick walls peeled and cracked. Exposed, broken pipes jutted from the ceiling, and evidence of a rat infestation was pronounced. As we walked through the skeletal remains of some kind of shelving system, our lights pierced random columns of steam or fog or something that I tried vainly to avoid.

At the opposite wall of this section of the basement, a full stairway with a rotten wood banister twisted up to the main floor. On the first landing, only five steps up, was a random, high-backed wooden wing chair. It was placed like some kind of eerie sentinel, blocking access to the second floor of the stairs. *Snap.* The flash on Rachel's camera went off as she took a picture. I shivered in my coat, and my teeth must have chattered because I heard Claire snort.

"Oh my God, she's freaking out already and we're not even in the treatment rooms yet."

Jude rushed to my defense. "Leave her alone, Claire. It's freezing down here."

That shut her up. Rachel pushed the chair out of the way and the sound of it as it scraped against the hard floor set my teeth on edge. We wound our way up the staircase, which groaned under our weight. The climb was steep, the stairs felt loose, and I held my breath the whole way. When we reached the top I almost collapsed with relief. We stood in an enormous pantry now. Claire kicked decades-old insulation and garbage out of her way, careful to avoid the obvious sections of rotting wood floor as she walked through the institutional kitchen and open cafeteria. *Snap*. Another picture. I felt dizzy as I followed Rachel, and imagined stern-faced nurses and orderlies doling out bland mush to drooling, twitching patients from behind the long counter that stretched from one end of the vast room to the other.

An impossibly large and imposing pulley system announced our entry into the hall that led to the first floor of patient rooms. The levers that controlled it were on the right, the hulking weights that balanced them visible behind the desk of the nurses station. The system's cables ran up to the ceiling and stretched down the hall, deviating at the entrance of each individual room. Culminating in thousand-pound iron doors. *Don't mess with the pulley system*, the website had warned. A kid exploring alone got trapped on the wrong side. His body was found six months later.

Of course, I didn't need the warning. My father had told me and my brothers plenty of times how dangerous the old building was. Before he switched to criminal law, he'd sued the property owners and the township on behalf of the boy's family, and he should have won; his files overflowed with evidence. But inexplicably, the jury found against the boy's family. Maybe they thought the boy should have known better. Maybe they thought the town needed an example.

But all I thought about was what it must have felt like to hear the slam of those doors—to feel the reverberations in the rotting floor, in the walls, as thousands of pounds of iron separated you from the rest of your life. What it must have felt like to know no one was coming for you. What it must have felt like to starve.

Rachel and Claire's delight reached a higher pitch as we passed the roped cables and levers. *Snap*. The flash illuminated the cavernous hall. Jude and I walked together behind the two of them, sticking to the middle. Patient rooms flanked us, and I didn't want to go anywhere near them.

We followed slowly, the beam of Jude's flashlight bouncing over the walls as we advanced toward the impenetrable black hole that yawned in front of us. When Rachel and Claire disappeared behind a corner I sped up, terrified to lose them in the labyrinthine passageways. But Jude had stopped altogether, and lightly jerked the waistband of my jeans. I turned.

He grinned. "We don't have to follow them, you know."

"Thanks, but I've seen enough horror movies to know that

splitting up is not the best idea." I started forward again, but he didn't release me.

"Seriously, there's nothing to be scared of. It's just an old building."

Before I could reply, Jude grabbed my hand and tugged me behind him. His flashlight illuminated the number on the room in front of us. 213.

"Hey," he whispered, as he pulled me in.

"Hey," I grumbled.

Jude cocked an eyebrow at me. "You need to take your mind off of this place." I shrugged and took a step backward. My foot hitched on something, and I fell.

32

I tried to open my eyes. They were wet and swollen, and the dark blue-black world rocked around me. I could see only pieces of it. Somehow, I was very warm, but my body was curled up.

"Mara?" Noah asked. I was inches away from his face. My head rested on his shoulder in the crook between his neck and his ear. He was carrying me. Not inside the asylum. Or the Convention Center.

"Noah," I whispered.

"I'm here."

He folded me into the passenger seat and brushed a few strands of hair out of my face as he leaned over me. His hand lingered.

"What happened?" I asked, even though I knew. I passed out. I had a flashback. And now I was shaking.

"You fainted during my grand gesture." His voice was light, but he was obviously rattled.

"Low blood sugar," I lied.

"You screamed."

Busted. I leaned back against the passenger seat. "Sorry," I whispered. And I was. I couldn't even go on a date without crumbling into pieces. I felt like a tool.

"There's *nothing* to be sorry about. Nothing."

I smiled, but it was hollow. "Admit it. That was weird."

Noah said nothing.

"I can explain," I said, as the fog in my brain receded. I *could* explain. I owed him that.

"There's no need," he said quietly.

I barked out a laugh. "Thanks, but I'd rather you didn't think that's my typical reaction to art shows."

"I don't think that."

I sighed. "Then what do you think?" I asked, eyes closed.

"I don't think anything," he said. His voice was even.

It didn't make sense that Noah was so nonchalant about my little episode. I opened my eyes to look at him. "You're not at all curious?" It was slightly suspicious.

"No." Noah stared straight ahead, still standing outside the car.

Not slightly suspicious. *Very* suspicious. "Why not?" My

pulse raced as I awaited his answer. I had no idea what Noah was going to say.

"Because I think I know," he said, and looked down at me. "Daniel."

I rubbed my forehead, not sure I heard him correctly. "What? What does he have to do with—"

"Daniel told me."

"Told you what? You just met—"

Oh. *Oh.*

I'd been set up.

Which was why Noah never once asked about my old school. My old friends. Not a single question about the move, even though he was relatively new to Miami, too. He hadn't even asked about my arm. Now I understood why; Daniel told him everything. My brother would not hurt me on purpose, but this wouldn't be the first time he'd acted like Mom's little henchman. Maybe he thought I needed a new friend and he didn't think I'd make one on my own. Self-righteous ass.

Noah closed my passenger door and climbed into the driver's seat, but didn't start the car. Neither of us said anything for a long time.

When I found my voice again, I asked, "How much do you know?"

"Enough."

"What kind of answer is that?"

Noah closed his eyes, and for a split second, I felt guilty. I looked out the window at the inky sky instead of at his face. Noah lied to me. *He* should feel guilty.

"I know about—about your friends. I'm sorry."

"Why didn't you just tell me?" I asked quietly. "Why lie?"

"I suppose I thought you'd mention it when you were ready."

Against my better judgment, I looked at him. Noah's legs were stretched out languidly in front of him. He cracked his knuckles, completely unfazed. Unmoved. I wondered why he'd bothered with any of this.

"What did Daniel bribe you with to get you to take me out?"

Noah turned to me, incredulous. "Are you insane?"

I had no good answer to that question.

"Mara, I asked Daniel," Noah said.

I blinked. "What?"

"I asked *him*. About you. When you swore at me after English. I remembered you from—I found out you had a brother and talked to him and—"

I cut him off. "I appreciate what you're trying to do, but you don't have to cover for Daniel."

Noah's expression hardened. The streetlight above us cast the shadow of his eyelashes on his cheeks. "I'm not covering for him. You wouldn't talk to me and I didn't know—" Noah stopped, and fixed his gaze on me. "I didn't know what to do, all right? I had to know you."

Before my lips could even form the word "why," Noah rushed on. "When we were in the bathroom that day, do you remember?" He didn't wait for me to answer. "When we were there, I thought I had you." A sly smile appeared for a fraction of a second. "But then you said you'd heard—things—about me, and those girls walked in. I didn't want them talking shit about you. It was your first week, for Christ's sake. You shouldn't have had to deal with it, especially when no one knew you."

I was speechless.

"And then I saw you in South Beach. In that dress. And I just decided, fuck it, I'm a selfish bastard, who cares. Katie teased me for brooding that whole week, and I told her there that you were the reason. And then you just . . . ran out. So, no. I'm not covering for Daniel. I don't know what I *am* doing, but it's not that." He stared straight ahead into the dark.

The bathroom. The club. I was wrong about everything.

Or . . . was I? It, this, could just be another play. It was so hard to know what was real.

He leaned his head back against the headrest, his dark tousled hair twisted every which way. "So, I seem to be an idiot."

"Maybe."

He grinned crookedly, his eyes closed.

"But hey, it could be worse. You could be broken, like me." I hadn't meant to say that out loud.

"You're not broken," Noah said firmly.

Something inside of me began to tear. "You don't know that." I told myself to stop it—to shut up. It didn't work. "You don't know me. You only know what Daniel told you, and I don't let him see. There's something wrong with me." My voice cracked as my throat closed, drum tight with a sob that wanted to escape. Damn it.

"You've been through—"

And I lost it. "You don't know what I've been through," I said as two hot tears escaped. "Daniel doesn't know. If he did, he'd report to it our mother and I'd end up in a mental hospital. So please, *please* don't argue with me when I tell you that there is something seriously wrong with me." The words poured out, but once spoken, I felt the truth of them. I could take drugs, do therapy, whatever. But I knew enough to know that psychotics can't be cured, only managed. And the hopelessness of it was suddenly too much to take. "There's nothing anyone can do to fix it," I said quietly. Finally.

But then Noah turned to me. His face was uncharacteristically open and honest but his eyes were defiant as they held mine. My pulse raced without my permission.

"Let me try."

33

I EXPECTED SEVERAL DIFFERENT SCENARIOS AFTER my little freak-out. Noah rolling his eyes and laughing at me. Noah making a smart-ass comment, driving me home, and dumping me at my door.

His actual response was not one of them.

His question hung in the air. Let him try what? I didn't know how to answer because I didn't understand what he was asking. But Noah stared at me, expectant, with the barest suggestion of a smile on his lips and I needed to do *something*.

I nodded. That seemed to be enough.

When Noah pulled into my driveway, he got out of the car and strode quickly to the passenger door to open it for me. I gave him a look, but he interrupted me before I had the chance to speak.

"I like doing it for you. Try to remember so I don't have to sprint every time."

Every time. I felt strange as we walked up the brick path to my front door. Something had shifted between us.

"I'm picking you up tomorrow morning," Noah said, as he brushed a strand of hair from my face and tucked it behind my ear. His touch felt like home.

I blinked hard, and shook my head to clear it. "But it's out of your way."

"And?"

"And Daniel has to drive to school anyway."

"So?"

"So wh—"

Noah placed a finger on my lips. "Don't. Don't ask me why. It's annoying. I want to. That's it. That's all. So let me." Noah's face was so close. So close.

Focus, Mara. "Everyone's going to think that we're together."

"Let them," he said as his eyes searched my face.

"But—"

"But nothing. I want them to think that."

I thought of everything that would imply. Because it was Noah, people wouldn't just think that we were together, but that we were *together*, together.

"I'm a bad actress," I said by way of explanation.

Noah skimmed his fingers down the line of my arm and

lifted my hand to his mouth. His lips brushed over my knuckles, impossibly soft. He looked into my eyes and killed me.

"Then don't act. See you at eight." He let go of my hand and walked back to his car.

I stood on the doorstep, breathless as Noah drove away. I turned his words over in my mind. *Let me try. I want them to think that. Don't act.*

Something was starting between us. But it would finish me if it ended. When it ended, which would be soon, if Jamie was to be believed. Dazed, I went into the house, leaned against the back of the door, and closed my eyes.

"Welcome back." I heard the smile in Daniel's voice, even though I couldn't see it.

I tried to regain my equilibrium because my brother was in it deep, and I was not about to let it go just because my insides were mid-quiver. "You have some 'splainin' to do," was all I managed to say.

"Guilty," Daniel said, but he didn't look it. "Did you have fun?"

I shook my head. "I can't believe you did that to me."

"Did. You. Have. Fun?"

"That's. Not. The. Point," I said back.

Daniel's grin widened. "I like him."

"What does that have to do with anything? How could you tell him, Daniel?

"Okay, hold on a second here. First of all, the only thing I told him was why we moved from Laurelton. There was an accident, your friends died, and we moved to start over. You don't have the monopoly on that explanation, so relax." I opened my mouth to protest but Daniel continued. "Second, he's a good guy."

I agreed with him, but didn't want to. "Other people don't think so," I said instead.

"Other people are usually wrong."

I glared at him. "Moving on. Tell me what happened. Leave nothing out."

"After our first day of school, I went to discuss my independent music study with the teacher and Noah was there. He composes, by the way, and he's really freaking good. Sophie told me she did a few open mic nights with him last year."

I thought of little blond adorable Sophie, and felt a sudden urge to kick her in the shins and run away.

"Anyway, when he found out my name, he asked me about you."

I rewound my thoughts. "But I didn't meet him until our second day of school."

Daniel shrugged. "He knew you somehow."

I shook my head slowly. "Why lie, Daniel? Why pretend not to know each other this morning?"

"Because, I surmised—and correctly, I might add—that you would flip out. But really, Mara, you're overreacting. You were barely mentioned in our conversation. We spent most of the time discussing the Kafka-Nietzsche nexus and the parodic sonnets in *Don Quixote*."

"Don't try to distract me with your smart talk. You shouldn't have gone begging for friends for me. I'm not that pathetic."

"That's not what I did. But even if it was, have you exceeded your friend quota here in Miami already? Is there something I missed?"

I stiffened. "That's a dick thing to say," I said in a low voice.

"You're right. It is. But you're always insisting that everyone treat you normally, so answer the question. *Have* you made any other friends since we've been here?"

I gave him the death stare. "Yes, actually."

"Who? I want a name."

"Jamie Roth."

"The Ebola kid? I heard he's a little unstable."

"That was one incident."

"Not what I've heard."

I clenched my teeth. "I detest you, Daniel. I really do."

"Love you too, sister. Good night."

I went to my room and slammed the door.

When I awoke the next morning, I felt heavy, like I'd gotten too much sleep, but my head ached as though I hadn't. I glanced at my clock. 7:48 a.m.

I swore and stumbled out of bed, rushing to put on clothes. But when I passed my desk, I stopped. A small white pill floated on top of a napkin. I closed my eyes and inhaled. I hated the thought of taking it—*hated*. But the art show debacle was scary, not to mention the bathtub incident last week. And I didn't want to freak out in front of Noah again. I just wanted to be normal for him. For my family. For everyone.

Before I overthought it, I swallowed the pill and dashed out of my room. I collided with my father as he turned the corner, and sent the accordion file he'd been carrying flying. Papers scattered everywhere.

"Whoa, where's the fire?" he said.

"Sorry—gotta go, late for school."

He looked confused. "Daniel's car's not here. I didn't think anyone was home."

"A friend's taking me," I said as I bent to pick up the papers. I shuffled them and turned them over to my father.

"Thanks, honey. How've you been? I never see you anymore. Stupid trial."

I bounced a little on my feet, eager to meet Noah before he got out of his car. "When is it?"

"Opening arguments in two weeks, with one week scheduled on the docket," he said, and kissed my forehead. "We'll talk before I leave for base camp."

I raised my eyebrows.

"Moving to a hotel for trial prep."

"Ah."

"But don't worry, we'll talk before I leave. You go. Love you."

"Love you, too." I pecked him on the cheek and brushed

past him into the foyer, slinging my bag over my shoulder. But when I flung open the front door, Noah was already there.

These were the things that added up to Noah that morning, from bottom to top:

Shoes: gray Chucks.

Pants: charcoal tweed.

Shirt: slim cut, untucked, thin and pinstriped dress shirt. Super skinny tie, knotted loose around his open collar, exposing the shadow of a screen-printed t-shirt beneath it.

Days unshaven: somewhere between three and five.

Half-smile: treacherous.

Eyes: blue and infinite.

Hair: a beautiful, beautiful mess.

"Morning," he said, his voice warm and rich. God help me.

"Morning," I managed to reply, squinting. From the sun, or from staring at him for too long. Flip a coin.

"You need sunglasses," he said.

I rubbed my eyes. "I know."

Suddenly, he crouched down.

"What are you—"

In my rush, I hadn't tied my shoelaces.

Noah was now tying them for me. He looked up at me through his dark fringe of lashes and smiled.

The expression on his face melted me completely. I knew I had the goofiest grin plastered on my lips, and didn't care.

"There," he said as he finished tying the laces on my left shoe. "Now you won't fall."

Too late.

When we pulled into the school parking lot, I began to sweat despite the blast of the air conditioner. Dark clouds had filled the sky during our drive, and a few splatters of rain hit the windshield, prompting teeming multitudes of students to bolt to the front gates. I was nervous—terrified, really—to walk into school with Noah. It was so *public*.

"Ready?" he asked, with mock seriousness.

"Not really," I admitted.

Noah looked confused. "What's wrong?"

"Look at them," I said, indicating the hordes. "I just—everyone's going to be talking about it," I finished.

He half-smiled. "Mara. They're already talking about it."

That didn't make me feel any better. I chewed on my lower lip. "This is different," I said. "This is putting everything out there. On purpose. By choice."

And then Noah said just about the only thing that could make me feel better. "I won't leave you. I'll be there. All day."

He said it like he meant it. I believed him. No one seemed to care what Noah did at Croyden, so it was not a stretch to imagine him sitting in on my classes. But I'd die if it came to that.

Noah grabbed his blazer from the backseat, shrugged it

on, opened my door, and then there we were, standing side-by-side as every stray eye turned in our direction. Panic constricted my throat. I looked at Noah to gauge his reaction. He looked—happy. He *liked* it.

"You're getting off on this," I said, incredulous.

He arched an eyebrow at me. "I like being beside you. And I like everyone seeing us together." He placed an arm around my shoulders, drawing me closer to him, and my anxiety dissolved. Somewhat.

As we approached the gate, I noticed some guys loitering by their cars parked near the entrance. They all had the wide-eyed cud-chewing look in common as they turned to look at us.

"Dude!" A guy named Parker shouted to Noah as he jogged in our direction. Noah cocked an eyebrow at him.

Parker's eyes met mine for the first time since I'd arrived at Croyden. "'Sup?"

Did people really say that? "Hey," I returned.

"So you guys are like—?"

Noah glared at him. "Go away, Parker."

"Sure, sure. Hey, um, Kent just wanted to know if we're still on for tomorrow night?"

Noah half-turned his head to look at me and said, "Not anymore."

Parker looked at me pointedly. "That blows."

Noah rubbed the heel of his palm into his eye. "Are we finished?"

Parker smirked. "Yeah, yeah. See you guys later," he said, winking at me as he left.

"He seems . . . special," I said, while Parker went to rejoin his pack.

"He isn't," Noah said.

I laughed until a voice from behind cut it off.

"I'd hit that."

I kept walking.

"I'd hit it harder," said someone else. Blood whooshed in my ears but I didn't look back.

"I'd hit that so hard whoever pulled me out would become the King of England."

Noah was no longer by my side when I turned. He had Kent from Algebra pinned against the car.

"I should injure you considerably," he said in a low voice.

"Dude, chill." Kent was completely calm.

"Noah," I heard myself say. "It's not worth it."

Noah's eyes narrowed, but upon hearing my voice, he released Kent, who straightened his shirt and brushed the front of his khakis.

"Get fucked, Kent," Noah said as he turned away.

The idiot laughed. "Oh, I will."

Noah whirled around, and I heard the unmistakable impact of knuckles meeting face. Kent was on the concrete, his hands clutching his nose.

When he started to get up, Noah said, "I wouldn't. I'm

barely above kicking the shit out of you on the ground. Barely."

"You broke my nose!" Blood streamed down Kent's shirt and a crowd formed a small circle around the three of us.

A teacher parted the throng and called out, "Principal's office NOW, Shaw."

Noah ignored him and walked over to me, inordinately calm. He placed his good hand on the small of my back and my legs threatened to dissolve. The bell rang, and I looked at Noah as he leaned in and brushed his lips against my ear.

He whispered into my hair, "It was worth it."

34

THE TEACHER STOOD A FEW FEET AWAY. "I'M not kidding, Shaw. I don't care whose kid you are, you're going to Dr. Kahn's office."

Noah pulled back slightly and searched my face. "Will you be all right?"

I nodded. Noah's eyes lingered for a moment longer before he kissed the crown of my head and sauntered off.

After a dumbstruck moment, I collected myself and walked through the gauntlet of eyes alone. I made it to English just before Ms. Leib began the lecture. She was giving us a review of her term paper expectations, but I was the one that had the class's attention. Furtive glances were shot over shoulders, notes were passed among desks in a chain, and I sunk low in my seat, futilely trying to melt into the hard plastic. I thought of Noah in the principal's office, answering for his chivalry. His dick-measuring display. Whatever it was, I liked it. Much as I hated to admit.

Noah appeared halfway through English, and a ridiculous smile transformed my face the second I saw him. When class ended, he took my bag and slung it over his shoulder as we walked out the door.

"So what happened in Dr. Kahn's office?" I asked.

"I just sat there and stared at him for five minutes, and he sat there and stared back for five minutes. Then he told to me to try and learn to play well with others during my two-day suspension, and sent me on my merry way."

My face fell. "You're suspended?"

"After exams," he said, seemingly unconcerned. Then he grinned. "That's what I get for defending your honor."

I laughed. "That was *not* for me. That was you marking your territory," I said. Noah opened his mouth to say something but I cut him off before he could. "So to speak," I finished.

Noah grinned. "I neither confirm nor deny your assertion."

"You didn't have to do it, you know."

Noah shrugged lazily and stared straight ahead. "I wanted to."

"Is it going to screw with your transcripts or anything?"

"With my perfect GPA? Doubtful."

I turned to him slowly, just as we reached the door to my Algebra class. "Perfect?"

Noah smirked. "And you thought I was just a pretty face."

Unbelievable. "I don't understand. You never take notes. You never have your books with you."

Noah shrugged. "I have a good memory," he said, as Jamie appeared on his way into Algebra. "Hey," Noah said to him.

"Hi," Jamie said, and shot me a look as he slid past us.

If Noah noticed Jamie's reaction, he didn't mention it. "I'll see you after?" he asked me.

The thought warmed me up. "Yeah." I smiled, and walked into class.

Jamie was already at his desk and I sat next to him, dropping my bag on the floor with a thud.

"Much has changed since you last I saw," he said, without looking at me.

I decided to make him work for it. "I know," I said with a dramatic, exasperated sigh. "I cannot even tell you how much I am dreading exams."

"Not speaking of that, was I."

"Why are you Yoda-ing me this morning?"

"Why are you avoiding the subject du jour?" Jamie asked, filling out squares on his graph paper to form a really weird picture of a fire-breathing dragon with a human arm.

"I'm not avoiding it, there's just nothing to say."

"Nothing to say. The lonely new girl is suddenly kickin' it with Croyden's hottest piece of ass, and there's a sketchbook of Shawporn depicting this unlikely relationship? 'Nothing to say,' my tuchus." Jamie still refused to make eye contact.

I leaned in and whispered to Jamie, "There's no porn sketchbook. 'Twas a ruse."

Jamie finally looked at me and cocked an eyebrow. "It's all a sham?"

I sucked in my lips, then bit them, then said, "Not exactly." I wasn't sure how to explain what had happened between me and Noah yesterday, and wasn't even sure I wanted to.

Jamie turned back to his graph paper. "Well, at some point, you're gonna have to break this down for me real slow-like."

Anna interrupted my train of thought before I could respond to Jamie. "How long do you give it, Aiden?"

Aiden pretended to study me as he spoke to her. "The end of this week, if she gives it up. Otherwise, she might last a couple more."

"Jealous much?" I asked calmly, though inside I was furious.

"Of what you're going to go through once Noah's done with you?" Anna said, her prim little mouth curving into a malicious grin. "Please. But he *is* an awesome lay," Anna said to me in a stage whisper. "So enjoy it while you can."

Anna sat back down, Mr. Walsh walked in the room, and I seethed quietly in my seat as I pressed my pencil down on my notebook very, very hard. My stomach soured at the thought of Anna acquiring that particular piece of information about Noah. Jamie told me they'd dated. But that didn't *have* to mean—

I did and didn't want to know.

When the bell rang, I got up from my seat and another girl in the class, Jessica, elbowed me as she walked by. What was her problem? My arm hurt and I rubbed it before picking up my textbook and notebook from my desk. As I made my way to the door, someone knocked them out of my hands. I whirled around, but no one around me looked particularly guilty.

"What the hell?" I muttered under my breath as I bent down to pick up my things.

Jamie crouched with me. "You're unraveling the very fabric of Croyden society."

"What are you talking about?" I shoved my things into my messenger bag with unnecessary force.

"Noah drove you to school."

"So what?"

"Noah doesn't drive anyone to school."

"So what?" I asked, growing frustrated.

"He's acting like your boyfriend. Which makes the girls he treated like condoms a trifle jealous."

"Condoms?" I asked, confused.

"Used once and then discarded."

"Gross."

"He is."

I ignored that, knowing I'd make zero headway on this particular subject. "So what are you saying? I was invisible, but now I'm a target?"

Jamie tilted his head and laughed. "Oh, you were never invisible."

Noah was waiting for me when we made it out of the classroom. Jamie wordlessly stepped around us and headed to his next class. Noah didn't even notice.

The rain slanted in under the arch-covered path, but he walked on the outside anyway, not caring that he was getting wet. As soon as we were out of earshot, I couldn't hold in the question that had been nauseating me since Algebra. I looked up at him.

"So, you dated Anna last year, right?"

Noah's formerly content expression morphed into disgust. "I wouldn't exactly use the word 'dated.'"

So Jamie was right. "Gross," I muttered.

"It wasn't that awful," he said.

I wanted to bang my head against the brick arch. "I don't want to hear that, Noah."

"Well, what do you want to hear?"

"That she has scales underneath her uniform."

"I wouldn't know."

My heart leapt, but I tried to appear only mildly curious. "Really?"

"Really," Noah said, his tone amused.

"So, uh, what happened?" I asked so very casually.

Noah shrugged one shoulder. "She just sort of attached herself to me last year, and I suffered it until her general hideousness of character and my inability to translate her moron language got to be too much."

It was still too early to celebrate. "She said you were an awesome lay," I said, feigning interest in the gush of water that spilled out from the gutter by the lockers. My face would betray me if he saw it.

"Well, that's true," Noah said.

Lovely.

"But she wouldn't know from personal experience." Just then, Noah tilted my chin so that I faced him. "Why, Mara Dyer."

I bit my lip and looked down. "What?"

"I don't believe it," he said incredulously.

"*What?!*"

"You're jealous." I heard the smile in his voice.

"No," I lied.

"You *are*. I'd reassure you that there's nothing to worry about, but I think I kind of like this."

"I'm not jealous," I insisted, my face burning under the touch of Noah's fingers. I backed up against my locker.

Noah raised an eyebrow. "Then why do you care?"

"I don't. She's just so—so *malodorous*," I said, still looking at the ground. I finally screwed up the courage to look up at him. He wasn't smiling. "Why would you let her say she slept with you?"

"Because I never kiss and tell," he said, ducking slightly to meet my eyes.

I turned away from him and opened the locker door. "Then

anyone can say they've been doing anything with you," I said, into the dark space.

"Does that hurt your feelings?" He spoke in a low voice from behind my shoulders.

"I don't have feelings," I said, my face buried in my locker.

Noah's hand appeared on the locker next to me and I felt him lean toward my back. The air was thick with our electricity.

"Kiss me," he said simply.

"What?" I turned around and found myself just inches from him. My blood glowed under my skin.

"You heard me," Noah said.

I felt the stares of other students. In my peripheral vision, I saw them huddled under the covered path, waiting for the rain to let up. They gawked at Noah's long figure leaning over mine, his hand pressed on the steel by my ear. He didn't inch closer; he was asking, waiting for me to make the next move. But as my face burned with the feeling of his eyes and their eyes on me, the other students began to disappear one by one. And I don't mean they walked away. They *disappeared*.

"I'm not into kissing," I blurted, my eyes darting back to Noah's.

Noah's mouth tilted into the smallest of smiles. "Oh?"

I swallowed thickly, and nodded. "It's stupid," I said, checking for the once-assembled crowd. Nope. Gone. "Someone poking their tongue in someone else's mouth is stupid. And gross." Way to employ my AP English vocabulary. Mara doth protest too much.

Noah's eyes crinkled at the corners, but he wasn't laughing at me. He ran his free hand through his hair, twisting it as he went, but a few thick strands fell back over his forehead anyway. He didn't move. He was so close. I breathed him in, rain and salt and smoke.

"Have you kissed many boys before?" he asked quietly.

His question brought my mind back into focus. I raised an eyebrow. "Boys? That's an assumption."

Noah laughed, the sound low and husky. "Girls, then?"

"No."

"Not many girls? Or not many boys?"

"Neither," I said. Let him make of that what he would.

"How many?"

"Why—"

"I am taking away that word. You are no longer allowed to use it. How many?"

My cheeks flushed, but my voice was steady as I answered. "One."

At this, Noah leaned in impossibly closer, the slender muscles in his forearm flexing as he bent his elbow to bring himself nearer to me, almost touching. I was heady with the proximity of him and grew legitimately concerned that my heart might explode. Maybe Noah wasn't asking. Maybe I didn't mind. I closed my eyes and felt Noah's five o' clock graze my jaw, and the faintest whisper of his lips at my ear.

"He was doing it wrong."

35

Noah's lips pressed lightly on the skin of my cheek and lingered there. I was on fire. By the time I opened my eyes and my breathing returned to normal, Noah wasn't in front of me.

He hung casually from the archway in the locker nook, waiting for me to get my things for Art.

The bell rang.

I still stood there. I still felt the imprint of his lips on my cheek. I still stared like an idiot. Noah's smile spread into a smirk.

I closed my eyes, took a deep breath, and mustered up what dignity I had left before walking right past him, careful to avoid the rain slanting under the arches. I was glad Art was next. I needed to decompress, to watch my stress level as Dr. Maillard had said. And Noah was impossible to ignore. When we stood in front of my classroom, I told him I'd meet him later.

Noah's forehead creased as other students walked past us. "But I have a study period."

"So, go study."

"But I want to watch you draw."

I answered him by closing my eyes and rubbing my forehead. He was impossible.

"You don't want me there?" he asked. I opened my eyes. Noah looked crestfallen and adorable.

"You're distracting," I said truthfully.

"I won't be. I promise," Noah said. "I'll get some crayons and draw quietly. Alone. In a corner."

I couldn't help my smile and Noah saw his opening; he brushed right past me into the classroom. I calmly walked to a table at the far end of the room. Noah's eyes followed me as I sat at a stool and withdrew my graphite and charcoal.

I ignored him and went to my happy place. I opened my sketchbook, quickly flipping past the pages filled with Noah, as the substitute cleared her throat before speaking.

"Hi, guys! I'm Ms. Adams. Mrs. Gallo had a family emergency so I'm going to be your sub for the day." With her short bangs and glasses, she looked twelve years old. And sounded it.

When Ms. Adams took attendance and called out the name of an absent classmate, Noah's hand shot up. I watched him cautiously. After she finished roll call, Noah stood, completely unself-conscious as heads followed his progress to the front of the room.

"Um—" Ms. Adams checked her clipboard. "Ibrahim Hassin?"

Noah nodded. I died.

"What are you doing?" she asked.

Noah wore a bemused expression. "Didn't Mrs. Gallo tell you?" he asked her. "We're supposed to start working on live models today."

No, I was being tortured.

"Oh, umm. I didn't—"

"It's true," a girl in a cheerleading uniform piped up. Brittany, I think. "N—Ibrahim's supposed to go first. Mrs. Gallo said." A chorus of nodding and murmuring supported Brittany's assertion.

Ms. Adams looked baffled and a bit helpless. "Uh, okay, I guess. Do you guys know what to do?"

Noah flashed her a brilliant smile as he dragged a stool to the center of the room. "Definitely," he said. He sat down, and I looked at my blank page, feeling the pressure of his eyes on me the entire time.

"Um, wait—" the sub said, a note of desperation in her voice.

My eyes flitted up to the front of the classroom. Noah was in the process of unbuttoning his shirt. Sweet Jesus.

"I'm really not comfortable with—"

He pulled his tie loose. My female classmates tittered.

"Ohmigod!"

"Holy *hell*."

"Hot. So hot."

He lifted the hem of his T-shirt up. Good-bye, dignity. If Noah heard the girls, he made no indication. He caught my stare and shot me a sly smile.

"M-Mr. Hassin, please put your clothes back on," Ms. Adams stammered.

Noah paused, letting everyone enjoy the view a moment longer, then shrugged back into his T-shirt, then his dress shirt, redoing all of the buttons incorrectly and leaving the cuffs undone.

Ms. Adams exhaled audibly. "Okay, guys, get to work."

Noah's eyes held my face. I swallowed hard. The juxtaposition of him sitting in a room full of people while staring at no one but me was overwhelming. Something shifted inside of me at the intimacy of us, eyes locked amid the scraping of twenty graphite pencils on paper.

I shaded his face out of nothingness. I smudged the slope of his neck and darkened his delinquent mouth, while the lights accented the right angle of his jaw against the cloudy sky outside. I did not hear the bell. I did not hear the other students rise and leave the room. I did not even notice that Noah no longer sat at the stool.

I felt fingers whisper on my back. "Hey," Noah said. His voice was very soft.

"Hey," I answered. I remained hunched protectively over the page but half-turned to meet his stare.

"May I?"

I couldn't deny him and I didn't reply. I shifted out of the way so he could see.

I heard his intake of breath. Neither of us spoke for a long time. Then, "Is that what I look like?" Noah's expression was unreadable.

"It is to me."

Noah didn't speak.

"It's just how I saw you in that moment," I said.

Noah was still silent. I shifted uncomfortably. "If you looked at everyone else's drawings, they'd be completely different," I added.

Noah still stared.

"It's not *that* bad," I said, as I moved to close the sketchbook.

Noah stopped me. "No," he said in a low voice, barely perceptible.

"No?"

"It's perfect."

He was still staring at it, but he looked—distant. I closed the book and slipped it in my bag. When we left the classroom, his hand braceleted my wrist.

"May I have it?" he asked.

I arched an eyebrow.

"The picture?"

"Oh," I said. "Sure."

"Thank you," he said, a smile flirting with his mouth. "Would it be greedy to ask for one of you?"

"A self-portrait?" I asked. Noah smiled an answer. "I haven't done one in forever," I said.

"So it's about time, then."

I contemplated the idea. I'd have to draw myself without a mirror, now that I saw dead people in them these days. I shrugged noncommittally in Noah's general direction and focused on the drips of rain that fell from the thatched roof of the tiki hut above us.

I heard a low buzzing from Noah's pocket. He withdrew his phone and arched his eyebrow at it.

"Everything okay?"

"Mmm," he murmured, still staring at the phone. "It's your brother."

"Daniel? What does he want?"

"Joseph, actually," Noah said, texting something back. "And to offer a stock tip."

I have the strangest family.

Noah shoved his phone back in his pocket. "Let's eat in the dining hall," he said out of nowhere.

"Okay."

"I haven't exactly been—wait, what?" He looked bemused.

"If you want to go, we can go."

He raised an eyebrow. "That was easier than I expected. My body must have addled your good sense."

I sighed. "Why do you insist on making me hate you?"

"I'm not making you hate me. I'm making you love me."

Damn him for being right.

"So you're giving in?" he asked. "Just like that?"

I started walking. "How much worse could it be after everything else today?"

Noah stopped. "Worse?"

"Having everyone stare and wonder what sort of hijinks your vagina's been up to isn't as thrilling as one might imagine."

"I knew it," Noah said simply. He still had my hand. It felt tiny and warm in his. "I knew this would happen," he said again.

I pushed my hair back from my forehead. "I can take it."

"But you shouldn't have to," Noah said, his nostrils flaring. "I wanted to show them you were different. That's why—Christ," Noah said under his breath. "That's why everything. Because you *are* different," he said to himself. A shadow darkened his face and he was silent as he stared at me. Studied me. I was lost, but didn't have time to ask what he was talking about before his expression changed. He withdrew his hand from mine. "If you're getting hell for this—"

Without thinking, I took his hand back. "Then I'll put on my big-girl panties and deal." I indicated the cafeteria. "Shall we?"

Noah didn't speak the rest of the way, and I mulled over what I'd said and what it meant. People would think I was a slut. They likely already did. And even though Noah was different—seemed different—from the person Jamie had warned me about, that didn't mean our thing wouldn't be over tomorrow. Was it worth it? Noah's reputation didn't seem to ruffle Daniel, and I thought—hoped—that Jamie and I would stay friends anyway. And for now, there was Noah.

I decided that was enough.

We were still holding hands when we arrived at the cafeteria. As he opened the door for me, I finally understood why Noah called it the dining hall. The ceilings were chapel high and arches spanned the length of the space, housing floor-to-ceiling glass windows. The stark white of the walls contrasted with the burnished walnut floors. Nothing could have been further from the image the word "cafeteria" normally conjures.

"Any seating preferences?" Noah asked.

My eyes scanned the bustling room, filled with uniformed Croyden students. "You're kidding, right?"

Noah led me through the hall by the hand, and eyes turned up and followed us as we passed. He caught the eye of someone he knew in the far back and waved, and the person waved back.

It was Daniel. His eyes were wide with surprise and the table went silent as we wove through the chairs to meet him.

"Oh my God, if it isn't my baby sister. Here, in this very cafeteria!"

"Shut up." I sat down beside Noah and took out my lunch, too self-conscious to meet the eyes of the rest of the seniors assembled at the table.

"I see you've brought surly Mara out to play. Thanks for that, Noah."

Noah raised his hands defensively.

Daniel cleared his throat. "So, Mara." I looked up from my sandwich. "This is everyone," he continued. "Everyone, this is my sister Mara."

I mustered up some courage and looked around the table. I recognized Sophie but no one else. Noah slid into a chair across from my brother and I sat next to him, across from Sophie.

"Hey," I said to her.

"Hey," she answered, smiling mid-chew. She swallowed and introduced me to the rest of their group. Noah and my brother chatted away, Daniel's friends were incredibly nice, and after only a few minutes, Sophie had me laughing so hard I almost cried. When I caught my breath, Noah caught my eyes, took my hand under the table, and smiled. I smiled back.

I was happy. I wanted more than anything for it to last.

36

EXAMS WERE BRUTAL, AS EXPECTED. I KICKED ass in History and on my English paper, did not embarrass myself in Algebra, and dreaded Spanish, my second-to-last one.

Noah tried to study with me the first night of exam week, but he was an abject failure of a teacher; I ended up throwing a package of flash cards at him after ten minutes. Thank God for Jamie. We studied every day for hours, and by the end of the week, he was explaining Algebra to me in Spanish. He was amazing and I *felt* amazing, despite the stress. In the past week on Zyprexa, the nightmares had stopped, the hallucinations were gone, and I walked into Spanish feeling prepared, but still nervous.

The oral exam should have been straightforward; we were

assigned list of topics, and we were supposed to be able to speak about any of them, waxing poetic with proper grammar and pronunciation until Morales was satisfied. And naturally, the second Jamie and I walked into the classroom, Morales seized on me.

"Meez Dee-er," she sneered. She always said my name wrong and in English. Annoying. "You're next." She pointed at me, and then at the blackboard at the front of the classroom.

Jamie gave me a sympathetic look as I passed his desk. Vainly trying to calm my breathing, I trudged toward the front of the classroom. Morales was prolonging my misery, shuffling her papers, writing in her book, what have you. I braced myself for the coming onslaught, shifting my weight from foot to foot.

"Who was Pedro Arias Dávila?"

I stopped fidgeting. That wasn't one of the topics; we never even mentioned Dávila in class. She was trying to throw me. I lifted my gaze toward Morales, who was sitting alone in the front row, her body stuffed unceremoniously into the student chair. She was poised for the kill.

"We don't have all day, Meez Dee-er." She tapped her long fingernails on the metal surface of her desk.

A tingle of victory crept into my bloodstream. I took World History last year, and it just so happened my final project was on sixteenth-century Panama. What were the odds? I took it as a sign.

"Pedro Arias Dávila led the first major Spanish trip to the New World." I responded in flawless Spanish. I had no idea how, and I felt giddy. Everyone in the room was staring at me.

I paused to reflect on my genius, then continued. "He was a soldier in wars at Granada, Spain, and North Africa. King Ferdinand II made him leader of the trip in 1514." Mara Dyer for the win.

Morales spoke in a calm, cold voice. "You may sit down, Meez Dee-er."

"I'm not finished." I couldn't believe I actually said it. For a second, my legs threatened to bolt to the nearest desk. But as Morales quickly lost her composure, a juicy thrill coursed through my veins. I couldn't resist. "In 1519 he founded Panama City. He was part of the agreement with Francisco Pizarro and Diego de Almagro that allowed the discovery of Peru." Suck it, Morales.

"Sit down, Meez Dee-er." Morales began to huff and puff, strongly resembling a cartoon character. In thirty seconds, smoke would start radiating from her ears.

"I'm not finished," I said again, delighted by my own audacity. "In the same year, Pedro de los Ríos took over as governor of Panama. Dávila then died at the age of ninety-one in 1531."

"Sit down!" she screamed.

But I was invincible. "Dávila is remembered as a cruel man and as a liar." I emphasized each adjective and stared hard at Morales, watching the veins in her forehead threaten to explode. Her corded neck turned purple.

"Get out of my classroom." Her voice was quiet and furious. "Senor Coardes, you are next." Morales half-turned in the too-small chair and nodded at a freckled, openmouthed classmate.

"I'm not finished," I heard myself say. I was almost bouncing with energy. The room itself seemed sharp and alive. I heard the footfalls of individual ants scurrying to and from a prize piece of gum stuck to a bookshelf on my left. I smelled the sweat that trickled down the side of Morales's face. I saw the individual dreadlocks fall in slow motion over Jamie's face as he planted his forehead on his desk.

"GET OUT OF MY CLASSROOM!" Morales bellowed, stunning me with the force of it as she rose from her chair, knocking over the desk.

At that point, I could hold it in no longer. A smug smile lit up my face and I sauntered out of the room.

To the sound of applause.

37

I WAITED OUTSIDE FOR JAMIE UNTIL THE EXAM WAS over. As he walked out of the room, I snatched the strap of his backpack and pulled him over to me.

"How do you like them *cojones*?" My grin threatened to split my face in half as I held out my hand for a fist bump.

Jamie returned it. "That was—that was just . . ." He gazed at me, awestruck.

"I *know*," I said, high on victory.

"Stupid," he finished.

"*What*?" I'd been brilliant.

Jamie shook his head and stuffed his hands into the baggy pockets of his pants as we walked to the back gate. "She's going to try and fail you for sure now."

"What are you talking about? I *nailed* that answer."

He looked at me like I was an idiot. "It was an oral exam, Mara. Completely subjective." He paused, watching my face, waiting for it to sink in. "No one in that classroom is going to back up your story except little old me. And my word don't mean shit around here."

There it was. I *was* an idiot.

"Now you get it," he said.

Jamie was right. My shoulders sagged as if someone let all the air out of the smiley-face balloon that was my heart. Not so brilliant after all.

"It's a good thing I recorded you."

I whirled around. "No!" I said. *Yes!*

Jamie's grin matched my earlier one, tooth for tooth. "I thought you were going to freak out that you failed afterward, so I recorded an MP3 of your performance for posterity. Thought you'd want to dissect it later." He held up his iPhone as his smile grew impossibly wider. "Happy Purim."

I squealed for the first time in my life, like a piglet, and threw my arms around Jamie's neck. "You. Are. A. Genius."

"All in a day's work, sugar."

We stood there hugging and grinning and then things got awkward. Jamie cleared his throat and I dropped my arms, shoving them in my pockets. There may even have been some shuffling of feet before Jamie spoke. "Um, I think your brother might be waving at you. That, or trying to guide a plane to safety."

I turned. Daniel was indeed gesticulating wildly in my direction. "I guess I should—"

"Yeah. Um, do you want to hang out after school this week?"

"Sure," I said. "Call me?" I walked backward in Daniel's direction until Jamie nodded, then turned and waved over my shoulder. When I reached Daniel, he did not look pleased.

"You are in big trouble, young lady," Daniel said as we headed to his car.

"What now?"

"I heard about your performance in Spanish."

How was that even possible? Crap.

"Crap."

"Uh, yeah. You have *no* idea what you just stepped in," he said as we climbed in. "Morales is universally reviled for a reason," Daniel went on. "Sophie regaled me with horror stories after she broke the news."

I reminded myself to whine at Sophie for being a tattletale. My insides squirmed a little but my voice was collected when I spoke. "I'm not sure it could get much worse. The witch tortured me daily."

"What did she do?"

"She made me stand in front of the class while she hurled questions at me in Spanish on stuff we haven't even learned yet, and she would laugh when I answered incorrectly—" I stopped. Somehow, my arguments sounded less convincing out loud. Daniel looked at me sideways. "She laughed *meanly*," I added.

"Uh-huh."

"And she threw chalk at me."

"That's it?"

I grew irritated and shot him a look. "Says the student who has never been yelled at by a teacher."

Daniel said nothing and stared blankly ahead as he drove.

"It was pretty brutal. Guess you had to be there." I didn't want to think about Morales anymore.

"I guess," he said, and gave me a weird look. "What's with you?" he asked.

"Nothing," I mumbled.

"Liar liar, pants on fire."

"That hasn't been funny since you were five. Actually, it was never funny."

"Look, don't worry so much about the Morales thing. At least you don't have to apply to seven competitive internships for this summer."

"They're all going to accept you," I said quietly.

"Not true. I've been slacking on my independent study and Ms. Dopiko has *still* not written my recommendation—and I might have overestimated my AP load, and I don't know how I'll do on the exams. I might not get into my top schools."

"Well, if that's true, I don't have a prayer," I said.

"Well, maybe you should work on that now before it's too late," Daniel said, staring straight ahead.

"Maybe that wouldn't be so hard if I were a genius like my older brother."

"You're as smart as I am. You just don't work as hard."

I opened my mouth to protest but my brother cut me off.

"It's not just about the grades. What are you going to put on your college résumé? You don't do drama. Or music. Or the newspaper. Or sports. Or—"

"I draw."

"Well, do something with it. Enter some contests. Win some awards. And rack up other organizations, they need to see that you're well—"

"God, Daniel. I know, okay? I know."

We drove the rest of the way home in silence, but I felt guilty and broke it when we pulled into the driveway. "What's Sophie doing this weekend?" I asked.

"Dunno," Daniel said as he slammed his door. Fabulous. Now he was in a pissy mood too.

I walked into the house and went to the kitchen to rummage for food, while Daniel disappeared into his room, probably to limn the contours of some exquisite constellation of philosophical nonsense for his internship applications and gasp in the throes of his overachieving OCDness. I, meanwhile, mulled over a bleak future starring myself as a New York sidewalk sketch artist living off of ramen noodles and squatting in Alphabet City because I didn't have any extracurricular activities. Then the phone rang, interrupting my thoughts. I picked it up.

"Hello?"

"Tell your husband to drop the case," someone whispered on the other end of the line. So low I wasn't even sure I'd heard correctly.

But my heart thundered in my chest anyway. "Who is this?"

"You'll be sorry." The caller hung up.

I broke into a cold sweat and my mind went blank. When Daniel walked into the kitchen, I was still holding the phone, long after the dial tone went dead.

"What are you doing?" he asked as he passed me on his way to the fridge.

I didn't answer him. I checked the call history and scanned for the last one that came in. My mother's office, two hours ago. No record of any calls after that. What time was it now? I checked the clock on the microwave—twenty minutes had passed. I'd been standing there, holding the phone, for twenty minutes. Did I delete the call? *Was* there even a call?

"Mara?"

I turned to Daniel.

"Yeesh," he said, taking a step back. "You look like you've seen a ghost."

Or heard one.

I ignored him and took out my cell on the way to my room. I'd taken my pill this morning, just like I had every morning since the art show. But if the phone call was real, why wasn't it showing up in the call history?

Freaked out, I dialed my father just in case. He picked up on the second ring.

"I have a question," I blurted before even saying hello.

"What's up, kid?"

"If you wanted to drop the case now, would you be able to?"

My father paused on the other end of the line. "Mara, are you okay?"

"Yeah, yeah. Just an academic question," I said. And it was kind of true. For now.

"Okaaay. Well, it's highly unlikely the judge would allow a substitution of counsel at this point. In fact, I'm pretty sure she wouldn't allow it."

My heart sank. "How did the other lawyer get out of the case?"

"The client agreed to have me step in, otherwise Nathan would have been out of luck."

"And your client wouldn't let you back out now?"

"Doubtful. It would screw things up for him pretty badly. And the judge wouldn't let it happen—she'd have me sanctioned if I pulled something like that. Mara," he said, "are you sure you're all right? I meant to ask you about therapy last week but I got tied—"

He thought this was about him. About him not being here.

"Yeah. I'm fine," I said, as convincingly as I could.

"When's your next appointment?"

"Next Thursday."

"Okay. I gotta go, but we'll catch up on your birthday, all right?"

I paused. "You'll be home Saturday?"

"For as long as I can be. I love you, kid. Talk to you soon."

I hung up the phone. I paced in my room like a wild thing, running over the phone call in my mind. I was on antipsychotic medication for hallucinations and possibly, probably delusions. I'd been all right for the past week, but maybe the pressure of exams had gotten to me after all. If I told my parents about the phone call but there was no evidence for it, nothing to back me up, what would they think? What would they do? My father couldn't drop the case anyway, and my mother? My mother would want to pull me out of school to help me cope with the stress. And not being able to graduate on time or go to college right away—that would not help me cope with the stress.

I didn't mention it.

I should have.

38

Noah picked me up the next morning, but I was unsettled and silent on the way to school. He didn't push. Even though this had been our routine for virtually every day for over a week, all eyes were on us as we walked from the gate through the quad. Noah's arm never left my waist, but he did leave me at the door to Algebra, albeit reluctantly. Anna and Aiden breezed past us, making faces like they smelled something foul.

"You all right?" Noah asked me, tilting his head.

"What?" I was distracted, thinking about the call last night. And the metal forest at the art show. And Claire and Jude in mirrors. "Just thinking about my Bio exam later," I told Noah.

He nodded. "See you later, then?"

"Mmm-hmm," I said, and walked into class.

When I reached my desk, Jamie sauntered in and sat beside me. "You're still with that prideful ass?"

I dropped my head in my hands and tugged at my hair. "God, Jamie. Give it a rest."

He opened his mouth to say something, but Mr. Walsh had already started class. But I was sick of listening to Jamie whine about Noah, and today we were going to have it out. I narrowed my eyes at him and mouthed *lunch*. He nodded.

The rest of my morning classes flew by, and Jamie was waiting for me by the picnic tables at the appointed time. And for the first time I could remember, his eyes were level with mine.

"Did you get taller?" I asked him.

Jamie raised his eyebrows. "Did I? Crazy hormones. Better late than never, I guess," he said, shrugging. Then he narrowed his eyes at me. "But don't change the subject. We should be discussing your unfortunate taste in men."

"What is your problem?"

"I don't have a problem. You have a problem."

"Oh? What's my problem?"

"Shaw's playing you," Jamie said quietly.

I grew irritated. "I don't think so."

"How well do you really know him, Mara?"

I paused. Then said, "Well enough."

Jamie looked away. "Well, I've known him longer." He pushed

his dreadlocks out of his face and chewed on his lower lip.

I watched him closely as he sat there, and after a minute the evidence clicked into place. "Oh my God," I whispered. "You're jealous."

Jamie looked at me like I'd gone insane. "Are you insane?" he asked.

"Umm . . ." Maybe?

"No offense, sugar, but you're not my type."

I chuckled. "Not jealous of *him*, of me."

Jamie's face darkened. "I won't lie, the boy is hot, but no. I don't know how you stand him, honestly."

"What did he do, Jamie?"

He was silent.

"Did he sleep with your mom or something?"

Jamie's expression hardened. "My sister."

I opened my mouth, but no sound came out at first. Then, "I didn't know you had a sister."

"She graduated. She was a junior when Noah first started here."

"Maybe . . . maybe he liked her." I said. Something twinged in my chest.

Jamie barked out a laugh. "He didn't. He only used her to make a point."

"What point was that?"

Jamie leaned his head back and fixed his gaze on the thatched roof. "So you know I skipped a grade, right?" Jamie asked. I nodded. "Well, I used to be in his little sister Katie's class. When Noah and Katie first started here, she was kind of confused about the material. So I helped her."

"Like you helped me."

"Except there may or may not have been tonsil hockey involved. I don't remember," Jamie said, as I raised a skeptical eyebrow. "Anyway," he said pointedly, "Noah totally busted me with a hand up her skirt—she wears thongs, by the way. So hot. And the next day, I came home and all my extremely intelligent, pragmatic sister, Stephanie, could talk about was Noah."

I felt a pang of something in my chest. "Maybe she liked him," I said quietly.

"Oh, she did. A lot. Until she came home crying one Saturday night after they'd gone out." Jamie's eyes narrowed as he watched Noah approach us from the other building. "Noah humiliated her. She insisted on transferring out of Croyden, and my parents let her."

"Is she okay?"

Jamie laughed. "Yeah. I mean, she's in college, and it was a couple of years ago. But using her to make a point like that? Sick."

I didn't know what to say. I wanted to defend Noah, but could I, really? So I said something else. "What happened with you and Katie?"

"Nothing. I didn't want him screwing with Stephanie's life

more than he had, so I shut that shit down." Jamie sucked in his bottom lip. "I really liked her too." He tilted his head at me, his dreads falling to the side. "But none of this matters, because you're not going to listen to your token black Jewish bi friend, are you?"

My eyes connected with Noah's as he sauntered over. "I don't know," I said to Jamie, still watching Noah.

"It's your funeral." Jamie stopped talking a few seconds before Noah arrived.

"Roth," Noah said, inclining his head.

"Shaw." Jamie nodded back.

Noah stepped behind me and kissed my shoulder, just as Anna and Aiden appeared from behind the stairs.

"God, Mara, are you still holding out on him?" Anna said, tipping her head at Noah. She tsked. "Is that what I was missing, Noah?"

"The list of what you're missing, Anna, is longer than the South Beach Free Clinic's walk-in list," Jamie said, and I was surprised to hear his voice. "Though I'm sure your hookup résumé includes the same names."

Noah laughed silently against my back and I flashed Jamie a conspiratorial smile. He stood up for me. Even though he didn't agree with my choices. He was a good friend.

Anna stood there openmouthed before Aiden grabbed her shirt and pulled her in close for a whisper. An evil grin rearranged her face before they turned just as the bell rang.

It was only when I saw Noah's face as I walked out of my Bio exam that I realized something was wrong. Very wrong.

"What happened?" I asked, as he steered me away from the parking lot toward the lockers.

"Jamie wants to tell you himself. He asked me to get you," Noah said. "And he hasn't spoken more than one word to me in years, so let's go."

I was dumbstruck. What could have happened in the past two hours? When we rounded the corner by Jamie's locker, he was packing up his stuff. Not just his books, but his pictures, his notes . . . everything. Cleaning it out.

He shoved the script for the school play in his backpack and sighed when he saw me. "Aiden said I threatened him," he said in a rush.

"What?"

"With a knife. Anna backed him up." Jamie shoved a handful of papers into his bag. "One of them planted it in my backpack when I wasn't looking. I'm expelled."

"*What?*" My voice rang out, echoing against the metal. "That's bullshit! How can they just expel you?"

Jamie stopped and turned to me, his hands balled into fists. "Even if Croyden didn't have a zero-tolerance policy, I have a track record. The Ebola thing last year. My parents are already here to pick me up."

"Just like that?" I asked, my voice shrill.

"Just like that," he said, and slammed his locker shut. "Technically, I'm suspended pending review, but it's pretty much over—I was already on probation. So now I'm going to be doing all of my work by *correspondence*." He imitated Dr. Kahn's deep voice. "I saw Noah loitering near the administration building and asked him to get you. I've been informed that I'm grounded until I graduate. Or take my GED. Whichever comes first. It's going to completely fuck up my college applications next year."

My stomach plummeted. I couldn't believe this. It was beyond unfair.

"Well, well. If it isn't the school bully." I heard Aiden's voice and whipped around, furious. Anna stood beside him, looking triumphant.

So this was how it was going to be. In one stroke, they ruined Jamie's life, simply because he stood up for me. Because we were friends. And looking at their disgusting faces, I knew, without a shadow of a doubt, that this wouldn't be the last time.

I itched with violence. I could kill them for this. I wanted to.

Jamie glared at Aiden. "Don't make me *cut* you, Davis."

Aiden laughed. "With what, a cocktail sword?"

I rounded on him before I realized what I was doing. "Leave. Right now, before I hurt you."

Aiden closed the distance between us in seconds. Up close, he was even bigger. The muscles in his biceps twitched. "Why wait?"

Noah's hand was at Aiden's throat in an instant, and he pushed him up against the lockers. "You stupid motherfucker," Noah said to Aiden. "Jamie, get Mara out of here."

"Noah," I protested.

"Go!" he snapped.

Jamie grabbed my hand and pulled me away, past Anna. I heard the sound of bodies slamming into metal behind me and tried to turn, but Jamie was surprisingly strong.

"Noah can take care of himself, Mara."

I tried to pull away. "Aiden's huge."

Jamie flashed a small, bitter smile as he gripped my hand tighter and pulled me along. "But Noah fights dirty. He'll be fine. Promise."

He didn't let go until we stood next to the cul-de-sac, in front of his parents' car.

"Grounded likely means no phone or computer," Jamie said. "But if I encounter an owl, I'll try to smuggle a message to the outside, okay?"

I nodded, just as Jamie's dad rolled down his window.

"Bye, sugar," Jamie said, and kissed me on the cheek. "Don't let The Man keep you down."

And just like that, he was gone.

39

I stood there, completely dazed and staring at the empty campus. The one friend I'd made in the short time that I'd been here, aside from Noah, was gone. I felt a hand whisper on my back. I turned around.

Noah's beautiful face was a disaster. A bright red bruise bloomed beneath his left cheekbone, under a thicket of gashes that extended from his eyebrow to his ear.

"Oh my God," I whispered.

Noah flashed a deviant grin. Then winced. "Come on. We need to go." He steered me to the parking lot, glancing over his shoulder just once before we climbed into his car. Little beads of blood formed over his knuckles, then dripped on the console as he shifted the car into gear.

“Should we go to the hospital?

Noah smiled again. It looked painful. “You should see the other guy.”

“What did you do?”

“Oh, once he’s healed, he should be able to live a normal life.”

I raised my eyebrows.

“Kidding.” Noah brushed the hair from my cheek and tucked it behind my ear, and winced again. “He’ll be fine in a few days, I’m sorry to say,” Noah said, his jaw tightening. “He’s lucky I left him alive. If he threatens you again, I won’t.” Noah turned his eyes back to the road. “But in the meantime, I have to take my suspension tomorrow for that thing with Kent last week, and if Aiden or Anna tattles—well. I’m going to lay low, as it were.”

When we pulled into my driveway, Noah parked, but didn’t get out of the car. “I’ll see you Friday,” he said, lifting his sunglasses. “I don’t think your parents ought to see me like this. It wouldn’t help our case.”

“Our case?”

Noah reached around to clasp the back of my neck, and ran his thumb over the hollow below my ear. His breath caught with the movement. “I’d like to be around you for a while.”

My heart thrashed against my ribs at the feel of Noah’s hand on my neck. I was incoherent. What Jamie said and what Noah looked like and how close he was . . . the thoughts tumbled in my brain before I could make sense of them.

"Why did you sleep with Jamie's sister?" I blurted. Completely graceless. I wanted to punch myself in the face.

Noah's hand remained on my neck, but a look of amused contempt washed over his face. "What did he tell you?"

Well, I'd made my bed, and now I had to lie in it. I swallowed. "That you didn't like that he was with Katie, so you did it for revenge."

Noah studied my eyes. "And you believe him?"

All of sudden, my throat was dry. "Should I?"

He held my gaze, his hand still on my neck. "Yes. I suppose you should," he said tonelessly. Noah's eyes were dark, his expression unreadable.

I knew I should care about his answer. I knew that what Jamie had said meant something—that I was, and had been, a foolish girl who coveted something many girls had coveted and paid for before, and that I would pay soon. I should haul back and smack him, strike a blow for feminism or something or at the very least, get out of the car.

But then his thumb traced my skin and without quite realizing it, I leaned toward him and rested my forehead against his. Noah's lids dropped at my touch.

"You really should go to the doctor," was all I could say. I hated myself for it.

His smile was nothing but a turned up corner of mouth. His bottom lip was split. Noah looked at me then, and leaned in closer. His eyes fell on my lips. "I'm busy," he said in a low voice, pausing, lingering there with mere inches between us until I tilted my face closer to his without meaning to.

"I don't want to hurt you," I whispered, even though I was the one who would probably get hurt.

Our noses touched, and there was just one perfect, aching moment separating our mouths from each other. "You can't."

Someone knocked on the driver's side window, scaring me senseless. I broke away. Noah closed his eyes for a beat, then rolled down the window.

Daniel and Joseph stood there, Daniel's face contorted in mock disapproval, while Joseph grinned.

"Sorry to break it up," Daniel said, looking at me. "Just thought you'd want to know that Mom's five minutes behind us."

"What happened to your face?" Joseph asked Noah, clearly impressed.

Noah half-shrugged. "Got in a bit of a row."

"Cool."

"You want to come in?" Daniel asked Noah. "Get some ice for that?"

Noah glanced at the clock. "Five minutes?"

"She had to stop at the dry cleaners. You can make it if you hurry."

We got out of the car and the four of us headed into the house. Joseph unlocked the door and ran to the kitchen, presumably to get ice for Noah's face. Daniel rifled through the mail on the console table.

"What lucky institution of higher education accepted me today?" he asked, eyes on the envelopes. "Ah, Harvard. That's nice. And Stanford!" Daniel grabbed my hand and twirled me in a circle.

Noah peered at the pile. "And Northwestern. And NYU. You ought to go to NYU. More diversity. It's not healthy to have too many geniuses packed into one campus."

Daniel grinned. "You have a point. But it *is* nice to have options," he said, then placed the envelopes back down. He eyed Noah's cuts appreciatively. "Aiden made them call an ambulance, and insisted on being carried out on a stretcher," he said to Noah.

"I'd have preferred it if it were a coffin," Noah said.

"I heard his mother's calling for your expulsion, too, FYI."

Noah's eyes met my brother's. "The rest of the board will never approve."

Daniel nodded. "This is true."

My eyes darted back and forth between them. "What do you two talk about when I'm not around?"

"Wouldn't you like to know," Daniel said as he stuffed his keys in his pocket and grabbed his handful of validation. Joseph reappeared holding a Ziploc bag full of ice and handed it to Noah.

"Thanks," Noah said with a grin. Joseph looked like he won

the lottery. "I should go. I'll see you in a few days?" Noah said to me.

I nodded. "Don't forget to go to the doctor."

Noah shot me a look. "Good-bye, Mara," he said, and strolled off to his car. I narrowed my eyes as I watched him walk away, and closed the door once he was gone.

Daniel's arms were crossed when I turned inside. I peered at him. "What?"

"*You* need to go to the doctor," he said, looking at my arm.

I pressed the heels of my palms into my eyes. "Come on, Daniel."

"Come on yourself. When was the last time you changed the dressings?"

"A few days ago," I lied.

"Well, Mom said you have an appointment for a checkup. So, either I take you, or she does."

"Fine," I groaned and headed out the door. Daniel followed behind me.

"I heard about Jamie, by the way."

"You know what really happened?" I asked my brother. He nodded. I stared at my feet. "I can't believe Anna and Aiden did that to him. And they're going to get away with it." I felt a stabbing pain in my hands all of a sudden, and looked down. I'd been clenching my fists so that my nails dug into my palms. I tried to relax. "School is going to be misery without him."

"At least you have Noah."

I stared straight ahead. "It's not like I've exceeded my friend quota," I said quietly.

Daniel started the car and pulled out of the driveway. "I'm sorry I said that to you, you know."

"It's fine," I said, looking out the window.

"How are you doing otherwise?"

"Okay."

"When's your next therapy appointment?"

I glared at him. "Next Thursday. Did you tell Noah about it?"

"Of course not," Daniel said. "But I don't think he'd care."

I leaned my head back against the seat and turned away. "I'd rather he not know the depths of my crazy."

"Oh, come on. The guy's been in two fights in as many weeks. He clearly has some issues of his own."

"And yet, here you are, pimping me out to him."

"Nobody's perfect. And I'm not pimping you out. I think he's good for you. He's been through a lot too, you know."

"I know."

"And I don't think he really has anyone who he can talk to about it."

"Sounds like he's talked to you about it."

"Not really. Guys don't really hash things out like girls do. I just know enough—whatever. All I'm saying is that I think he'd get it."

"Yeah. Nothing like hearing the girl you just started dating is on antipsychotics."

Daniel took the opportunity to change the subject. "How are those going, anyway? Any side effects?"

"Not that I've noticed."

"Do you think they're working?"

With the exception of the disturbing phone call. "I think so."

"Good. So you think you'll be up for Sophie's surprise party Friday night? I'm planning a big shebang. Well, not so big. But a shebang nevertheless."

"I don't know," I said, thinking now about the phone call. The threat. Jamie. I wasn't sure I'd be in a partying mood. "Maybe."

"What about your birthday? You and Noah have any plans?"

"I didn't tell him," I said in a low voice, as I looked out the window at the passing cars. We were almost at the doctor's office. My stomach clenched at the realization.

"Why not?"

I sighed. "I don't want to make a big deal of it, Daniel."

He shook his head as he pulled into the parking lot of the doctor's office. "You should let him in, Mara."

"I'll take it under advisement." I opened the door to the office and Daniel followed behind me. I signed in on the clipboard and waited until they called my name. It was better than the hospital, but the same smell—that medical smell—made my breath quicken and my throat close. When the nurse took my blood pressure, my pulse thudded against the cuff as it constricted my arm. I gasped for breath and the nurse looked at me like I was crazy. Little did she know.

She led me into a room and pointed to the vinyl bench covered in doctor's office paper. I sat down, but the rustle and crunch of it annoyed me. The doctor walked in to see me a few minutes later.

"Mara?" she asked, reading her clipboard. Then she met my eyes and extended her hand. "I'm Dr. Everett. How's that arm?"

"Feels fine," I said, holding it out for her.

"Have you been changing your dressings every two days?"

Nope. "Mmm-hmm."

"How's the pain?"

"I actually haven't noticed it much," I said. Her eyebrows lifted. "I've been really busy with exams and school stuff," I said, by way of explanation.

"Distraction can be good medicine. Okay, Mara, let's have a look." She unwrapped the gauze from my elbow first, and worked her way down my forearm. Her forehead creased and she pursed her lips as the bandage unraveled further and further, revealing my pale, intact skin. She glanced over at her clipboard. "When did this happen?"

"Two weeks ago."

"Hmm. The ER doctor must have made a mistake. Probably an intern," she said to herself.

"What?" I asked, growing nervous.

"Sometimes first-degree burns are mistaken for second-degree, especially on the arms and feet," she said, turning over my arm and inspecting it. "But even so, the redness usually lasts for quite some time. Any pain when I do this?" she asked as she extended my fingers.

I shook my head. "I don't understand. What's wrong?"

"Nothing's wrong, Mara," she said, staring at my arm. "It's completely healed."

40

NOT HAVING AN ITCHY, SWEAT-COLLECTING bandage under my sleeve was the only bright spot in the next two days. Without Noah, and especially without Jamie, I had even less patience for school, and it showed. I snapped at my History teacher, who I loved, and came very close to punching Anna in the face when she walked past me and banged her bag into my shoulder. She'd gotten my only friend expelled. It would be the least I could do.

I resisted. Barely. But my dire mood followed me home. I just wanted to be alone.

When I walked in the house, I whipped out my sketch-book and went to the family room to draw. Working on the floor was always better for sketching, and my carpeted bedroom was not conducive.

About an hour after I'd started, Daniel peeked his head around the archway. "Hey."

I looked up from the floor and smiled without feeling.

"Have you thought about going to Sophie's party tomorrow night?"

I went back to smudging. Self-portraits are tough without a mirror. "Isn't there some kind of theme?"

"No," Daniel said.

"Oh."

"Does that mean you'll come?"

"No," I said. "Just wondering."

"You know Mom and Dad are going out tonight, right?" Daniel asked.

"Yup."

"And Joseph is coming with me to help get things ready for tomorrow."

"Yup," I said, without looking up.

"So what are you going to do?" Daniel asked.

"I am going to sit here. And draw."

Daniel arched an eyebrow. "You're sure you're all right?"

I sighed. "I just prefer my wallowing with a heaping dollop of self-pity, Daniel. I'll be fine."

"If it's your grades, I can talk to Mom for you. Soften the blow."

"What?" I hadn't really been listening before, but Daniel sure as hell had my full attention now.

"You haven't checked your grades?"

My heart started pounding. "They're up?"

Daniel nodded. "I didn't know you didn't know."

I shot up from the floor, leaving my sketchpad behind, and darted to my bedroom. I dove into my desk chair and swiveled around to look at the monitor. Anxiety skittered through my veins. I'd been confident a few days ago, but now . . .

As my eyes scanned the screen, I started to relax.

AP English: A

Bio: B+

History: B

Art: A

Spanish: F

Algebra II: B

I did a double take. Then scanned the screen again. F. Falls between D and G on the keyboard. F for first. F for failure. First failure.

I couldn't catch my breath and dropped my head between my knees. I should have *known*. God, was I stupid. But in my defense, I had never, ever failed a class before, and those things just don't seem possible until they actually happen. How was I going to explain this to my parents?

Shamed though I was, I hoped Daniel was still around. I

sprinted to the kitchen, my face hot. He'd left me a note on the refrigerator.

Went to set things up.
Call me and I can come back and get you.

I swore under my breath and leaned against the stainless steel, getting fingerprints all over it. And then it hit me.

Jamie.

He recorded my exam. He had proof that I aced it. I withdrew my cell phone from my pocket and pressed the picture Jamie installed for himself on my phone. A ram's head. Weirdo. I tilted my head toward the ceiling and prayed that he would pick up.

It went straight to voice mail.

"Grounded likely means no phone or computer," Jamie had said. "*But if I encounter an owl, I'll try to smuggle a message to the outside, okay?*"

My eyes filled with tears and I threw my cell phone at the wall, scuffing the paint and smashing the phone. Couldn't have cared less. There was an F on my transcript. An *F*.

I put my head in my hands and tugged on my face. Dark thoughts swirled in my brain. I needed to tell someone, to figure out what to do. I needed a friend—I needed my best friend, but she was gone. And Jamie was gone too. But I did have Noah. I walked over to my decimated phone and collected the pieces. I tried to put it back together. No luck. I took the house phone off the cradle and pressed the talk button, but then realized that I didn't even know his number by heart. I'd only known him for a few weeks, after all.

The tears dried on my face, making my skin stiff. I didn't finish my sketch. I didn't do anything. I was too upset, furious with myself for being so stupid but even angrier at Morales. And the more I stewed, the angrier I became.

It was all her fault. I'd never done anything to her when I started at Croyden, and she went out of her way to screw with my life. Maybe I could find out Jamie's address and get the MP3 from him, but would it help? Did Dr. Kahn even know Spanish? The exam was, as Jamie said, subjective. And even though *I* knew I nailed that answer, I also knew that Morales would lie.

I stared out the kitchen window at the black sky outside. I would deal with it tomorrow.

41

THE NEXT DAY BEGAN ABNORMALLY. I AWOKE starving at about four in the morning and went to the kitchen to make toast. I withdrew a half-gallon of milk from the refrigerator and poured myself a glass as the machine heated the bread. When the slices popped up, I ate them slowly, turning last night over in my mind. I didn't notice Joseph until he waved his hand in front of my face.

"Earth to Mara!"

A white drop fell from the triangle lip of the milk container. Joseph's words were muffled, invading my brain. I wanted to turn off the sound.

"Wake up."

I jumped, then slapped his hand away. "Leave me alone."

I heard a second person rummaging around in the kitchen and swiveled my neck around. Daniel withdrew a granola bar from the pantry and took a bite.

"Who peed in your Cheerios?" he asked me, mouth full.

I leaned over the table and put my throbbing head in my hands. It was the worst headache I'd had in weeks.

"Is Noah picking you up? His suspension should be over today, right?"

"I don't know. I guess."

Daniel looked at his watch. "Well, he's late. Which means I'm taking you. Which means you have to get dressed. Now."

I opened my mouth to inform Daniel that we had hours until school started, and to ask him what he was doing up so early, but caught sight of the microwave clock. Seven thirty. I'd been sitting at the kitchen table for hours. Chewing . . . for hours. I swallowed the cold bread and my panic over losing so much time.

Daniel looked at me out of the corner of his eye. "Come on," he said softly. "I can't be late."

I didn't see Noah's car in the parking lot when we arrived at school. Maybe he decided to take an extra day off. I drifted towards the campus, half-conscious. I didn't see Noah in English, or wandering the halls between classes, either. He was supposed to be there. I wanted to find out where Jamie lived and even though they hated each other, I didn't know anyone else well enough to ask.

Between classes, I made my way to the administration office to make an appointment with Dr. Kahn, and when the fated hour arrived, I entered his office armed with sound reasoning. I would argue for the grade I deserved. I would tell him about the MP3. I would stay calm. I would not cry.

The principal's office looked more like a distinguished gentleman's nineteenth-century study, from the dark wood paneled walls to the stacks of leather-bound books, and the bust of Pallas perched above the chamber door. Just kidding. About the books.

Dr. Kahn sat behind his mahogany desk, the green tint of the banker's lamp illuminating his preternaturally smooth face. He looked as undoctorly as it was possible to look, wearing khaki pants and a white polo shirt emblazoned with the Croyden crest. "Miss Dyer," he said, gesturing to one of the chairs opposite his desk. "What can I do for you today?"

I looked him in the eye. "I think my Spanish grade should be adjusted," I said. I sounded smooth. Confident.

"I see."

"I can prove I deserved an A on the exam," I said, and it was true. There *was* a recording of it. I just didn't have it.

"That won't be necessary," Dr. Kahn said, leaning back in his tufted leather chair.

I blinked. "Oh," I said, somewhat taken aback. "Great. So when will the grade be changed?"

"I'm afraid there's nothing I can do, Mara."

I blinked again, but when I opened my eyes, there was only darkness.

"Mara?" Dr. Kahn's voice sounded distant. I blinked again. Dr. Kahn had actually put his wing-tipped feet up on his desk. He looked so *casual*. I wanted to smack them off and pull his chair out from underneath him.

"Why not?" I asked through gritted teeth. I needed to stay calm. If I screamed, the F would stay.

But it was so tempting.

Dr. Kahn lifted a piece of paper from his desk and reviewed it carefully. "Teachers have to submit a written explanation to the administration whenever they assign a failing grade," he said. "Ms. Morales wrote that you cheated on your exam."

My nostrils flared, and red spots appeared in my vision. "She lied," I said quietly. "How could I cheat on an oral exam? It's ridiculous."

"According to her gradebook, your first scores were quite poor."

I couldn't believe what I was hearing. "So I'm being punished for doing better?"

"Not just better, Mara. Your improvement was pretty miraculous, don't you think?"

Dr. Kahn's words stoked my rage. "I got a tutor," I said through clenched teeth, as I tried to blink the spots away.

"She said she saw you sneaking glances under your sleeve

during your test. She said she saw writing on your arm."

"She's lying!" I shouted, then realized my mistake. "She's lying," I said in a lower, shaky voice. "I had a bandage on my arm when I took the test. From an accident."

"She also said she'd seen your eyes wandering during in-class assignments."

"So, basically, she can say I cheated without having to submit any proof?"

"I don't like your tone, Miss Dyer."

"Guess we're even, then," I said before I could stop myself.

Dr. Kahn raised his eyebrows slowly. His voice was infuriatingly even when he spoke. "Christina Morales has been a teacher here for over twenty years. She's tough, but fair—I can count on one hand the number of complaints from students."

I interrupted him. "They're too scared to say anyth—"

"You, on the other hand," Dr. Kahn continued, "have been here for mere weeks, and you have been late to class on multiple occasions, spoke back to your history teacher this morning—yes, I heard about that—and managed to get yourself thrown out of Ms. Morales's class after causing a huge disruption. Who would you believe?"

I literally saw red. I tried so hard not to scream that my voice, when I spoke, came out as a whisper. "Just—just listen. There's a recording of my exam. I'll get someone to translate it. We'll play it. Ms. Morales can—"

Dr. Kahn didn't even uncross his legs before interrupting

me. "Tell you what. I'll call Ms. Morales in later and I'll go over everything with her again. I'll let you know my final decision."

Dark thoughts swirled in my mind and time slowed to a crawl. I stood up from the chair, knocking it over, but my hands trembled too much to pick it up. This was—this whole thing was beyond unfair. And I was becoming unhinged. I threw open the door to his office and heard it slam into the doorstop before bouncing back. I didn't care. My feet felt like they were made of steel as I made my way to Spanish. I wanted to crush the grass into powder. Morales was going to get away with this. I hoped she choked on her lying tongue.

And I could see it with stunning clarity. Her eyes bulged and she staggered around her empty classroom, putting her bony fingers into her mouth, trying to figure out what was wrong. She turned blue, and made a funny hacking sound. It's hard to lie when you can't speak.

I wanted to face her. I wanted to spit in her eye. But as I flew up the stairs to her classroom, I knew I'd never go through with it. I'd curse at her, though. I rounded the corner and crossed the last few feet to the door, thinking of several epithets I wanted to fling in her direction. Today's Spanish class brought to you by the letter *C*.

There was no one in the classroom except for Jude when I skidded to a stop in front of the doorway. He was lying on the ground, pale with dust. A huge beam of wood lay on top of him, and I saw where the splinters met skin. His torso was all bloody, and some of it trickled down the side of his mouth. Making him look kind of like the Joker from *Batman.*

I blinked.

It was Jude's body no longer. It was the asshole that abused Mabel, lying on the floor, the side of his skull reduced to pink mush, his leg bent at a funny angle. Like a hick ballerina. The linoleum had turned to dirt and the flies choked his wounds.

I blinked again.

He was gone. In his place was Morales. She was lying on the floor, and her face was more purple than blue. This made sense, given my second-grade art lesson in primary colors. Red plus blue equals purple, and Morales was always red-faced. So help me, she now resembled the blueberry person from *Willy Wonka.* I tilted my head sideways and blinked at the bug-eyed body on the linoleum floor, certain she'd be gone like the others if I looked away. So I did.

But when I looked back, she was still there.

42

THE NEXT FIVE SECONDS FELT LIKE FIVE hours. The second bell rang, and I was pushed aside by a blond girl named Vera toting a guidance counselor behind her. Vera was crying. Hmm.

"She was choking when I got here but I didn't know what to do!" Vera blew a snot bubble as she cried, and the mucous dribbled down past her lips. Nasty.

"Everyone stand back!" Mrs. Barkan, the guidance counselor shouted. The doorway was overrun by students freaking out.

I heard a siren in the background and soon EMTs and police were pushing students out of the way, creating a little bubble of space around the classroom door. People were crying and shoving and generally annoying the hell out of me, so

I backed out of the throng. I trotted down the stairs two at a time until I hit the ground. I hadn't eaten lunch. I was starving and dizzy and I didn't sleep last night and so help me, this could *not* be happening. Did I even take my pill this morning? I couldn't remember.

I stumbled out from under the archway on to the sprawling green. The sun blinded me and I wanted to punch it in the face. And thinking that made me giggle. Then my giggle turned into a cackle. Soon, I was laughing so hard tears streamed down my face. My neck felt wet and I was out of breath and I dropped to the ground beneath a tree at the far corner of the campus, laughing madly and twisting on the grass, gripping my sides because they hurt, damn it, but it was just so funny.

Out of nowhere, a hand gripped my shoulder and folded me up into a sitting position. I looked up.

"Mara Dyer, isn't it?" Detective Gadsen said. His tone was curious and even, but his eyes were not friendly.

A blur of movement behind him attracted my attention. Noah appeared in my field of vision; when he saw who I was talking to, he stopped. I looked at my feet.

"How's the dog?" the detective asked.

It was all I could do not to look up in shock. I shifted my head to the side and my hair fell around my face in a curtain. The better to hide me with, my dear.

"What dog?"

"Funny thing," he said. "That dog you called Animal Services about a few weeks ago? After I talked to you, it just up and disappeared."

"That is funny," I said, even though it wasn't. Not at all.

"Was Ms. Morales your teacher?" he asked, without missing a beat.

Was? So she was dead, then. That, at least, was real. Impossible, but real. I nodded.

"This must be very difficult for you."

I almost laughed. He had no idea. Or maybe—maybe he did?

You have to admit, the paranoia was humorous. What could the detective possibly know? That I *thought* Morales should die and she died? Crazy. That I wanted the dog's owner punished for what he did to her and he was? Laughable. Thinking something does not make it true. Wanting something does not make it real.

"Yes, it is very difficult," I said, nodding again, making the hair fall farther over my face to mask my insane grin.

"I'm sorry for your loss," he said. My shoulders trembled with the attempt to stifle my laughter. "Did you know whether Ms. Morales was allergic to anything?"

I shook my head.

"Did you ever see her with an EpiPen?"

I shook my head, then stood up on shaky feet. I was a lawyer's daughter, after all, and even with my tenuous grip on reality, knew the conversation was over.

"I have to go," I said.

"Of course. Feel better, and I'm very sorry about your teacher."

I walked away. Away from the detective and away from Noah.

But Noah caught up. "What happened?" He looked unusually concerned.

"You didn't show this morning," I said without looking at him.

"Mara—"

"Don't. Just—don't." I stared straight ahead and focused on the route to class. "It's fine, Noah. I'm not mad. I just—I have to go. I'm going to be late for Bio."

"School's over," he said slowly.

I stopped. "What?"

"It's almost four." Noah's voice was quiet. "And last period was canceled. I've been looking all over for you."

Two hours. I'd lost more than two hours. I felt like I was falling, like someone pulled the ground out from underneath me.

"Whoa," Noah said as he placed his hand on the small of my back to steady me. I shook it off.

"I need to go," I said, feeling sick. But then another hand clapped my shoulder, and my knees almost buckled.

"Hey, guys," Daniel said, his voice serious. "Crazy day." I swallowed the bile rising in my throat. "You don't look so good, Mara," Daniel said. His tone was lighter, now, but there was a note of anxiety in it.

I wiped away a strand of hair that stuck to my forehead. "I'm fine. Just feeling a little sick."

"Right in time for your birthday," Daniel said, and gave a tight smile. "I'm sure that disappoints you."

"Your birthday?" Noah looked from me to Daniel.

I shot my brother a look of pure poison. He ignored me. "Mara turns seventeen tomorrow. March fifteenth, the little imp. But she's weird about it," Daniel explained, taking off his glasses and wiping something from the lens. "She gets all mopey every year, so it's my brotherly duty to distract her from her birthday ennui."

"I'll take care of it," Noah said immediately. "You're off the hook."

Daniel gave Noah a broad smile. "Thanks, bro, you're a sport." They exchanged a fist bump.

I couldn't believe my brother did that to me. Now Noah would feel obligated to do something. I wanted to punch them both in the face, and puke.

"All right," Daniel said, putting an arm around me. "I think I'd better take Mara home. Unless you feel like throwing up in Noah's car instead?" Daniel asked me. I shook my head.

"I'll pick you up tomorrow at eleven," Noah said to me, holding my gaze as Daniel led me away. "There are some things I need to say."

43

When Daniel and I arrived back at the house, my father's open accordion files were uncharacteristically strewn all over the dining room table. We heard the sounds of our parents arguing before we even shut the door. I motioned to Daniel to close it quietly.

"I think you need to ask for a hearing."

"Opening arguments are Monday, Indi. Monday. And there's an emergency evidentiary hearing right before that. The judge is not going to let me withdraw. There's just no way."

What happened?

"Call Leon Lassiter, then. Ask him to fire you. Tell him

you'll get him a referral. The judge might allow a continuance if he does. He'd want that, right?"

"I doubt it. He's keen to get this over with." I heard my father sigh. "You really think Mara's that bad?"

Daniel and I locked eyes.

My mother didn't hesitate. "Yes."

"Nothing's happened since the burn," Dad said.

"That we know about."

"You think there's something going on?"

"Have you seen her lately, Marcus? She's not sleeping. I think things are worse for her than she lets on. You being in the middle of a murder trial is not helping."

"Is it worth me being disbarred?"

My mother paused. "We can move back to Rhode Island if that happens," she said quietly.

I expected my father to laugh. Or to give an exasperated sigh. Or to say anything except what he actually said.

"All right," my father said, without pause. "I'll call Leon and let him know I'm out."

My stomach twisted with guilt. I made a move toward the kitchen, but Daniel grabbed my arm and shook his head silently. I narrowed my eyes to slits.

Trust me, he mouthed. We both stood stone-still as my father spoke.

"Hello, Leon? It's Marcus, yes, how are you? I'm not so great, actually." He then proceeded to give him the rundown.

I caught the words "unstable," "traumatic," and "psychiatric care." My eyes bored into Daniel's head.

After a few minutes, my father hung up the phone.

"Well?" My mother's voice.

"He's thinking about it. He's a good guy," my father said in a low voice, as my mother banged some cabinets open.

Daniel beckoned me close. "Listen to me," he whispered. "We're going to go in there, and you are going to act like this has been the best day of your life. Say nothing about Morales, okay? I'll handle it."

I didn't even have a chance to respond before Daniel closed the door behind us in one exaggerated movement. People probably heard the slam in Broward.

My mother's head popped out of the kitchen. "Hey, guys!" she said all too cheerfully.

"Hi, Mom," I said, plastering a false smile on my face myself. I was queasy and upset and guilt-ridden and having a hard time coming to terms with the fact that this was my life. We walked into the kitchen to find my father sitting at the table. His eyes were ringed with dark circles, and he looked thinner than usual. "Well, if it isn't my long-lost children," he said, smiling.

I wiped my clammy forehead and moved to give him a kiss on the cheek.

"How was your day, kid?"

Daniel gave me a loaded look from over his shoulder.

"Great!" I said, with too much enthusiasm.

"Mara's been helping me plan Sophie's surprise party," Daniel said, opening the refrigerator.

Oh?

"Oh?" my mother said. "When is that?"

He withdrew an apple. "Tonight," he said, taking a bite. "We're heading out in a couple of hours. You guys have any plans?"

My mother shook her head.

"Where's Joseph?" I asked.

"At a friend's house," Mom said.

I opened my mouth to suggest they go out, but Daniel beat me to it.

My mother eyed my father. "Your Dad's pretty busy, I think."

He looked back at her. There were a thousand unsaid words in their glance. "I think I could take the night off."

"Awesome," Daniel said. "You deserve it. Mara and I are going to go plan a bit, and then I'm going to take a quick nap before the party."

God, I could kiss Daniel right now. "Me too," I said, following his lead. I pecked my mother on the cheek, and whirled around quickly, before she could notice the thin sheen of sweat on my skin. I made my way to my bedroom.

"So you guys are set for the night?" my mother called after us.

"Yup!" Daniel yelled back. I nodded and waved behind me before turning the corner into the hallway. We met up there.

"Daniel—"

He raised his hands. "You're welcome. Just . . . relax, okay? You look like you're going to throw up."

"Do you think they bought it?"

"Yeah. You did good."

"But what about Dad's case? He can't drop it, not because of me—" I swallowed hard, and tried to steady my balance.

"I'll make a huge deal about how great you're doing tomorrow before Noah gets here. How much help you were with the party."

"You're amazing. Seriously."

"Love you too, sister. Go lie down."

Daniel and I departed for our respective rooms. It had grown dark out, and the hair prickled on the back of my neck as I passed the family pictures. I turned the other way, toward the French doors that looked out on our backyard. With the hall light on, the darkness outside seemed opaque and oddly, each time I approached the glass, I was seized with the sense that there was someone, something right outside—something slinking, something creeping, something—no. Nothing. Nothing there. I made it to my bedroom and darted over to my desk, to the bottle of Zyprexa sitting on it. After a week, my mother trusted me enough to keep the whole bottle in my room. I didn't remember if I'd taken one this morning. I probably hadn't. That's why the whole Morales thing—it was a coincidence that she died. Choked. A coincidence. I shook out a pill into my trembling hand, then tossed it to the back of my throat and swallowed without water. It went down slowly, painfully, leaving a bitter aftertaste on my tongue.

I kicked off my shoes and climbed into bed, burying my face in my cool cotton sheets. It was well after midnight when I awoke, for the second time in my life, to someone pounding on my bedroom window.

Déjà vu settled over me like a wet wool blanket, prickly and uncomfortable. How many times was I going to have to relive this? I was blind and nervous as I stepped out of bed and crept to my window. My heart lodged in my throat as I reached to open the blinds, readying myself to see Jude's face.

But Noah's fist was raised mid-knock.

44

HE WORE A RATTY BASEBALL CAP WITH THE brim pulled low over his eyes, and I couldn't see much of his face except to tell that he looked exhausted. And angry. I opened my blinds and the window and warm air gushed in.

"Where's Joseph?" he asked immediately, a note of panic in his voice.

I rubbed my aching forehead. "At a friend's house, he—"

"He's not there," Noah said. "Get dressed. We have to go. Now."

I tried to arrange my thoughts into a coherent order. The panic hadn't set in yet. "We should tell my parents if he isn't—"

"Mara. Listen to me, because I'm only going to say this

once." My mouth went dry, and I licked my lips as I waited for him to finish.

"We're going to find Joseph. We don't have much time. I need you to trust me."

My head felt thick, my brain cloudy with sleep and confusion. I couldn't form the question I wanted to ask him. Maybe because this wasn't real. Maybe because I was dreaming.

"Hurry," Noah said, and I did.

I threw on jeans and a T-shirt, then I glanced at Noah. He was looking away from me, toward the streetlight. His jaw tensed as he chewed on the insides of his cheek. There was something dangerous beneath his expression. Explosive.

When I was ready, I placed my hands on the windowsill and launched myself onto the damp grass outside my bedroom window. I swayed on my feet, off-balance. Noah reached out to steady me for half a second, then hurried ahead. I jogged to catch up with him. It took effort—like the swollen, humid air was pushing back.

Noah had parked in the driveway. He was the only one. Daniel's car was gone, my father's car was gone, and my mother's was missing too. They must have gone out separately.

Noah flung his door open and started it. I'd barely sat down before Noah floored the gas pedal. The acceleration pushed me back against the seat.

"Seat belt," he said.

I glared at him. When we pulled on to I-75, Noah still

hadn't lit a cigarette, and he was still silent. My stomach curdled. I still felt so *sick*. But I managed to speak.

"What's going on?"

He inhaled, then ran a hand over his rough jaw. I noticed then that his lip seemed to have healed in the past few days. I couldn't see his eyes from this angle at all.

When Noah spoke, his voice was careful. Controlled. "Joseph texted me. His friend canceled and he needed a ride home from school. When I showed up, he wasn't there."

"So where is he?"

"I think he's been taken."

No.

When I saw Joseph last it was at breakfast this morning. He'd waved his hand in front of my face and I said, I said . . .

Leave me alone. Oh, God.

Panic coursed through my veins. "Why?" I whispered. This wasn't happening. This wasn't happening.

"I don't know."

My throat was full of needles. "Who took him?"

"I don't know."

I pressed the heels of my palms into my eye sockets. I wanted to claw out my brain. There were two options, here: first, that this wasn't real. That this was a nightmare. That seemed likely. Second, that this wasn't a nightmare. That Joseph was really missing. That the last thing I said to him was "leave me alone," and now, he had.

"How do you know where he is?" I asked Noah, because I had only questions and out of all of them, that was the only one I could voice.

"I don't know. I'm going where I think he is. He might be there, he might not. That has to be enough for now, all right?"

"We should call the police," I said numbly, as I reached in my back pocket for my phone.

It wasn't there.

It wasn't there because I smashed it against the wall yesterday. Just yesterday. I closed my eyes, reeling as I lost my mind.

Noah's voice pierced through my free fall. "What would you think if someone told you they thought they might know where a missing child was?"

I would think that person was hiding something.

"They'd ask me questions I couldn't answer." I noticed for the first time that there was an edge to his voice. An edge that scared me. "It can't be the police. It can't be your parents. It has to be us."

I leaned forward and put my head between my knees. This felt nothing like a dream. Nothing like a nightmare. It felt real.

Noah's hand ghosted the column of my neck. "If we don't find him, we'll call the police," he said softly.

My mind was a wasteland. I couldn't speak. I couldn't think. I simply nodded, then looked up at the clock on his dashboard. One in the morning. We passed some cars as we sped on the highway, but when Noah turned off at an exit after over an hour of driving, the sounds of Miami died away. The few streetlamps we passed bathed the car in a yellowish light. We drove in silence and the lights became less and less frequent. Then they stopped altogether, and there was nothing but highway stretching in front of us, poorly illuminated by our headlights. The yawning darkness curved over us like a tunnel. I glanced over at Noah, my teeth clenched so I wouldn't cry. Or scream. His expression was grim.

When he finally parked, all I could see was tall grass in front of us, swaying in the hot breeze. No buildings. Nothing.

"Where are we?" I asked softly, my voice almost drowned out by the crickets and cicadas.

"Everglades City," Noah answered.

"Doesn't look like much of a city."

"It borders the park." Noah turned to me. "You wouldn't stay here, even if I asked you to."

It was a statement, not a question but I answered anyway. "No."

"Even though this is supremely fucking risky."

"Even then."

"Even though both of us might not—"

Noah's mouth didn't finish forming the sentence, but his eyes did. Both of us might not make it, they told me. Some nightmare. Bile rose in my throat.

"And if I—don't," Noah said, "do whatever you have to do to wake Joseph. Here," he said, thrusting his hand into his pocket. "Take my key. Type your address into the GPS. Just keep driving, all right? Then call the police."

I took Noah's key ring and shoved it into my back pocket. I tried to keep my voice from trembling. "You're freaking me out."

"I know." Noah moved to get out of the car and I did the same. He stopped me.

The smell of rotting vegetation assaulted my nostrils. Noah faced the sea of grass in front of us and pulled out his flashlight. I noticed then that his cuts were still there; they'd healed somewhat, but the bruise on his cheek made one side of his face look sunken. I shivered.

I was terrified. Of the swamp. Of the possibility that Joseph was actually in it. Of the chance that we might not find him. That he was missing, gone, had left me alone like I'd wanted, and that I would never get him back.

Noah seemed to sense my despair, and he took my face in his hands. "I don't think anything is going to happen. And we don't have that far to go, maybe a half kilometer. But remember—key, GPS. Get to the highway and keep going until you see your exit."

Noah dropped his hands and stepped into the grass. I followed him.

Maybe he knew more than he was sharing with me and maybe he didn't. Maybe this was a nightmare and maybe it wasn't. But either way, I was here in some dimension. And if Joseph was here too, I would get him back.

The water soaked through my sneakers immediately. Noah didn't speak as we trudged through the mud. Something he'd said teased my mind, but it melted into nothingness before I could catch it. And I needed to watch my footing.

Hordes of croaking frogs created a bass rumble all around us. When the gnats weren't biting me alive, the sawgrass attacked my skin. I itched everywhere, my nerve endings alive with it, my ears filled with buzzing. I was so distracted, so consumed by it that I almost walked straight past Noah.

Into the creek.

45

TANGLED ROOTS OF MANGROVE TREES SANK unseen into the black liquid, and on the opposite side, grass stretched in front of us for infinity. A sliver of moon hung in the sky, but I had never seen so many stars in my life. I could just make out the faint outline of a building close by in the darkness. Noah faced the body of still water.

"We need to cross it," he said.

It did not take a genius to figure out what that meant. Alligators. And snakes. But really, they could have been lurking in the distance between Noah's car and where we stood all along. So why not cross the creek? No problem.

Noah skimmed his flashlight over the surface of the water.

It reflected the beam; we could see nothing beneath it. The creek was maybe thirty feet wide across, and I couldn't tell how far it extended in each direction. The grass turned to reeds and the reeds turned to roots, obscuring my view.

Noah faced me. "You can swim?"

I nodded.

"All right. Follow me, but not until I'm across. And don't splash."

He walked down the steep bank and I heard him break the surface of the water. Noah carried the flashlight in his right hand and walked a good length before he had to swim. But then, he was easily six feet tall. I wouldn't make it that far. My stomach clenched in fear for both of us, and my throat was tight with anxiety.

When I heard Noah pull himself up out of the water, my knees almost buckled with relief. He shined his flashlight up, illuminating his face in a freaky glow. He nodded, and I descended.

I slipped and slid on the bank of the creek. My feet sank into the weedy water until they hit mud. It was oddly cool, despite the steamy temperature of the air. The water reached my knees. I took a step. Then my thighs. Another step. My ribs. The surface tickled the underwire of my bra. I waded cautiously, my feet tangling in the weeds at the bottom. Noah pointed his flashlight at the water ahead of me, careful to avoid my eyes. It was brown and murky under the beam, but

I swallowed my disgust and kept moving, waiting for the bottom to drop out from underneath me.

"Don't move," Noah said.

I froze.

His flashlight skimmed the surface of the water around me. The alligators appeared out of nowhere.

My heartbeat pounded in my ears as I noticed several disembodied points of light floating in the darkness on either side of me. One pair of eyes. Three. Seven. I lost count.

I was paralyzed; I couldn't go forward but I couldn't go back. I looked up at Noah. He was about fifteen feet away, but the water between us might as well have been an ocean.

"I'm going to get back in," he said. "To distract them."

"No!" I whispered. I didn't know why I felt like I had to be quiet.

"I have to. There are too many, and we have no time."

I knew I shouldn't have, but I tore my eyes from Noah's shadow and looked around me. They were everywhere.

"You have to get Joseph," I said desperately.

Noah took a step toward the bank of the creek.

"Don't."

He slid down over the edge. The beam of light bounced on the water and I heard him splash. When he held the flashlight steady, several pairs of eyes disappeared. Then they reappeared. Much, much closer.

"Noah, get out!"

"Mara, go!" Noah splashed in the water, staying close to the bank but moving away from me.

I watched the alligators swim toward him, but some of the eyes stayed with me. He was making it worse, the idiot. Soon both of us would be trapped, and my brother would be alone.

I felt one of them approach before I saw it. A wide, prehistoric snout appeared three feet in front of me. I could make out the outline of its leathery head. I was trapped and panicked but there was something else, too.

My brother was missing, alone, and more frightened than I was. He had no one else to help him, no one but us. And it looked like we might not get the chance. Noah was the only one who knew where to look, and he was going to get himself killed.

Something savage stirred inside me as the black eyes stared me down. Big, black doll's eyes. I hated them. I would kill them.

I didn't have time to wonder where the hell that thought came from because something changed. A low, barely perceptible rumble shook the water and I heard a splash off to my left. I whirled around, dizzy with the rush of violence, but there was nothing there. My eyes darted back to where the closest animal had been. It was gone. I followed the circle of light as Noah scanned the beam over the water. There were fewer pairs of eyes; I could count them now. Five pairs. Four. One. They all slipped away, into the darkness.

"Go!" I shouted to Noah, and I pulled up my feet to swim the rest of the way. I heard Noah propel himself out of the water. I thrashed in the murk, getting caught at one point in weeds, but I didn't stop. At the bank, my hands slid over tangled roots and I couldn't get purchase. Noah reached down and I grabbed his hand. He pulled me up, my legs scrambling against the earth. When I was out, I let go of his hand and fell to my knees, coughing.

"You," I sputtered, "are an idiot."

I couldn't see Noah's expression in the darkness, but I heard him inhale. "Impossible," he whispered.

I drew myself up. "What?" I asked when I'd caught my breath.

He ignored me. "We have to go." His clothes clung to his body and his hair stood on end as he roughed his hands through it. His baseball cap was gone. Noah started walking ahead and I followed, splashing through the wet reeds. When we reached a long stretch of grass, he took off at a run. I did the same. The mud sucked at my shoes and I panted from the exertion. Pain stabbed me under my ribs and I gasped for breath. I almost collapsed when Noah stopped in front of a small concrete shed. Noah's eyes scanned the darkness. I saw the outline of a large building far off in the distance and a cabin about forty feet away.

Noah looked at me, his face uncertain. "Which should we check first?"

My heart surged at the thought that Joseph could be so close, that we'd almost reached him. "Here," I said, indicating the shed. I pushed past Noah and tried to turn the knob of the door, but it was locked.

I felt Noah's hand on my shoulder and followed his eyes up to a tiny window beneath the overhang of the roof. It was basement sized; there was no way he would fit. *I* might not fit. The walls were smooth; there was nothing to step on to propel me up.

"Lift me," I said to him without hesitation. Noah laced his fingers together. He glanced back once, right before I stepped into his hands. I balanced myself on his shoulders before standing fully. As soon as I could, I grabbed the sill to steady myself. It was grimy, but there was a small point of light inside. There were tools propped up against the wall, a small generator, a few blankets on the ground and then—Joseph. He was on the floor in a corner. Slumped.

I had to choke back the swell of emotions; relief mixed with terror. "He's in there," I whispered to Noah as I pushed on the glass. But was he okay? The window stuck, and I mumbled a prayer to any gods that might be listening to let the thing open, just let it open.

It did. I reached my arms through and wiggled the rest of my body in. I crashed to the floor headfirst and landed on my shoulder. A bubble of hot pain exploded in my side and I clenched my teeth to keep from screaming.

I opened my eyes. Joseph hadn't moved.

I was wild with terror. I winced as I stood but gave no thought to my shoulder as I rushed over to my little brother. He looked like he was sleeping there, nestled in a pile of blankets. I inched closer, terrified that when I touched him he would be cold.

He wasn't.

He was breathing, and normally. Flooded with relief, I shook him. His head lolled to one side.

"Joseph," I said. "Joseph, wake up!"

I threw a light blanket off of him and saw that his feet were bound and his arms were tied in front of him. My head swam but I slapped my eyes into focus. I scanned the room, looking for something to cut the plastic twist ties on Joseph's wrists and ankles. I didn't see anything.

"Noah," I called out. "Tell me you brought a pocket knife?"

He didn't answer, but I heard the clatter of metal as it hit the tilted glass window. And bounced back outside. I heard Noah utter a string of expletives before the knife clattered against the window again. This time, it fell to the ground inside the building. I picked it up, unfolded it, and started sawing.

My fingers were raw by the time I cut through the ties on Joseph's hands, and they were numb when I finished working on his feet. I finally had the chance to look him over. He was still in his school clothes; khaki pants and a striped polo shirt. They were clean. He didn't look hurt.

"Mara!" I heard Noah's voice calling me on the other side of the wall. "Mara, hurry."

I tried to lift Joseph up but pain knifed through my shoulder. A strangled sob escaped my throat.

"What happened?" Noah asked. His voice was frantic.

"I hurt my shoulder when I fell. Joseph won't wake up and I can't lift him through the window."

"What about the door? Can you unlock it from the inside?"

And I'm an idiot. I hurried to the front of the concrete room. I turned the lock, opened the door. Noah stood on the other side of it, scaring the hell out of me.

"Guess that's a yes," Noah said.

My heart pounded as Noah walked over to Joseph and held him up under his shoulder. My brother was completely limp.

"What's wrong with him?"

"He's unconscious, but there's no sign of bruises or anything. He seems fine."

"How are we going to—"

Noah withdrew his flashlight from his back pocket and tossed it at me. Then, he hoisted Joseph over his shoulders, grasping behind his knee with one hand and his wrist with the other. He walked to the door like it was nothing and opened it. "Good thing he's a skinny bastard."

I let out a nervous laugh as we walked through, just before the beam of car headlights washed over the three of us.

Noah's eyes met mine. "Run."

46

We exploded into flight, our feet beating down the muck beneath us. The grass whipped my arms, and the air stung my nostrils. We reached the creek and I turned on the flashlight, skimming the surface of the water. It was clear, but I knew that didn't mean much.

"I'll go first," I said to the water. Almost daring the alligators to come back.

I sank down into the creek. Noah slid Joseph off of his shoulders and followed, careful to keep my brother's head above the surface. He tugged Joseph's body under his arm as he swam.

Somewhere in the middle, I felt something brush my leg.

Something large. I bit back a scream and kept moving. Nothing followed us.

Noah lifted my brother up for me to grab and I managed to hold him, barely, as my shoulder howled in agony. Noah pulled himself up the bank, took Joseph from me, lifted him again, and we ran.

When we reached Noah's car, he unloaded Joseph into the backseat first, then climbed in. I almost collapsed inside, suddenly shivering from the wet clothes pasted to my skin. Noah turned on the heat full blast, stomped on the gas pedal and drove like a lunatic until we were safely on I-75.

The sky was still dark. The steady thrum of the pavement underneath the tires threatened to lull me to sleep, despite the excruciating pain in my shoulder. It hung wrong no matter how I settled into the seat. When Noah placed his arm around me, curling his fingers around my neck, I cried out. Noah's eyes went wide with concern.

"My shoulder," I said, wincing. I looked behind me in the backseat. Joseph still hadn't stirred.

Noah drove with his knees as his hands skimmed my collarbone, then my shoulder. He explored it with his dirt-caked fingers, and I bit my tongue to keep from screaming.

"It's dislocated," he said quietly.

"How do you know?"

"It's hanging wrong. Can't you feel it?"

I would have shrugged, but, yeah.

"You're going to have to go to the hospital," Noah said.

I closed my eyes. Faceless people appeared in the darkness, crowding my bed, pushing me down. Needles and tubes tugged at my skin. I shook my head fiercely. "No. No hospitals."

"It has to be placed back into the socket." Noah worked his fingers into my muscles and I choked back a sob. He drew back his hand. "I didn't mean to hurt you."

"I know," I said through the tears. "It's not that. I hate hospitals." I started to tremble, remembering the smell. The needles. And then I let out a nervous laugh because I'd almost been eaten by giant reptiles but somehow, needles were scarier.

Noah ran a hand over his jaw. "I can put it back in," he said in a hollow voice.

I turned in my seat and then choked back the ensuing pain. "Really? Noah, seriously?"

His face darkened, but he nodded.

"That would be—please do it?"

"It's going to hurt. Like, you have no idea how badly it's going to hurt."

"I don't care," I said, breathless. "It would hurt just as much in a hospital."

"Not necessarily. They could give you something," Noah said. "For the pain."

"I can't go to the hospital. I can't. Please do it, Noah? Please?"

Noah's eyes flicked to the clock on the dashboard, and then

he checked the rearview mirror. He sighed and turned off the highway. When we pulled into a dark, empty parking lot, I checked the backseat. Joseph was still out.

"Come on," Noah said, as he got out of the car. I followed, and he locked it behind us. We walked a short distance before Noah stopped under a tangle of trees behind a strip mall.

He closed his eyes, and I noticed that his hands were balled into fists. The muscles in his forearms flexed. He shot me a dark look.

"Come here," he said.

I walked over to him.

"Closer."

I took another step, but I'd be lying if I said I wasn't afraid. My heart pounded in my chest.

Noah sighed and crossed the remaining distance between us, then stood, his chest against my back. I felt the length of his body pressed tightly behind mine and I shivered. From standing outside in my wet clothes or the feel of him behind me, I didn't know.

He circled one arm around my chest, aligned with my collarbone, and snaked the other beneath my arm so that his hands were almost touching.

"Hold very still," he whispered. I nodded, silent.

"Right then. One." He spoke softly into my ear, tickling me. I could feel my heart beating against his forearm.

"Two."

"Wait!" I said, panicking. "What if I scream?"

"Don't."

And then my left side ignited in pain. White-hot sparks exploded behind my eyes and I felt my knees buckle, but never felt the ground beneath me. I saw nothing but blackness, deep and impenetrable, as I floated away.

I woke up when I felt the car turn wide on the pavement. I looked up just as we passed under the sign for our exit.

"What happened?" I mumbled. My wet hair had stiffened in the artificial air, caked with filth. It crunched behind my head.

"I put your shoulder back in," Noah said, staring at the brightening road ahead of us. "And you fainted."

I rubbed my eyes. The pain in my shoulder had simmered to a dull, throbbing ache. I glanced at the clock. Almost six in the morning. If this was real, my parents would be awake soon.

Joseph already was.

"Joseph!" I said.

He smiled at me. "Hey, Mara."

"Are you okay?"

"Yeah. Just tired a little."

"What happened?"

"I guess I just fell into the ditch by the soccer field where you guys found me," he said.

I cast a furtive glance at Noah. He met my eyes, and gave a

slight shake of his head. How could he possibly think Joseph would buy that?

"It's weird, I don't even remember *going* there. How did you guys find me, anyway?"

Noah rubbed his forehead with his filthy palm. "Lucky guess," he said, avoiding my stare.

Joseph looked directly at me, even as he spoke to Noah. "I don't even remember texting you to pick me up. I must have hit my head pretty hard."

That must have been the companion lie to the one Noah told about the soccer field. And I could tell by Joseph's stare that he didn't believe either one. And yet he seemed to be playing along.

So I did too. "Does it hurt?" I asked my brother.

"A little. And my stomach feels kind of sick. What should I tell Mom?"

Noah stared straight ahead, waiting for me to make the call. And it was obvious what Joseph was asking—whether he should out me and Noah. Whether he should trust us. Because I knew that if Joseph did tell our parents the lie Noah told him, my mother would lose it. Absolutely.

And she would ask questions. Questions Noah said he couldn't answer.

I looked behind the seat at my little brother. He was dirty, but fine. Skeptical, but not worried. Not scared. But if I told him the truth about what had happened—that someone, a stranger, had taken him and tied him up and locked him in a shed in the middle of the swamp—what would that do to him? What would he look like then? A memory returned of his ashen, downcast face in the hospital waiting room after I burned my arm, of his body slumped and stiff and small in the waiting room chair. This would be worse. I could think of few things more traumatic than being kidnapped, and I knew from experience just how hard it would be to come back from something like that. If he even could.

But if I didn't tell Joseph, I could not tell my mother. Not after my arm. Not after the pills. She would never believe me.

So I decided. I looked at Joseph in the rearview mirror. "I don't think we should mention it. Mom will freak out, I mean—freak *out*. She might be too scared to let you play soccer any more, you know?" Guilt flared inside of me at the lies, but the truth could break Joseph, and I wouldn't be the one to do it to him. "And Dad will probably sue the school or something. Maybe just use the pool shower outside, get into bed, and I'll tell her you didn't feel well last night and asked me to come pick you up?"

Joseph nodded in the backseat. "Okay," he said evenly. He didn't even question me; he trusted me that much. My throat tightened.

Noah pulled onto our street. "This is your stop," he said to Joseph. My brother got out of the car after Noah shifted it into park. I followed suit before Noah could open the door.

Joseph walked to the driver's side window and reached in. He shook Noah's hand. "Thanks," my brother said, flashing a dimpled grin at Noah before heading to our house.

I leaned down to the open passenger window, and said, "We'll talk later?"

Noah paused, staring straight ahead. "Yes."

But we didn't get the chance.

I met up with Joseph back at the house. All three cars were in the driveway now. Joseph showered outside, then we crept in through my bedroom window so as not to wake anyone. My brother was smiley, and tiptoed down the hallway with exaggerated steps like it was a game. He closed his bedroom door and, presumably, went to bed.

I had no idea what he thought, what he was thinking about all this, or why he let me off so easily. But I ached with exhaustion and couldn't begin to work through it. I peeled off my clothes and turned on my shower, but found that I couldn't even stand. I sank down under the stream of water, shivering despite the heat. My eyes were blank, vacant as I stared at the tile. I didn't feel sick. I wasn't tired.

I was lost.

When the water ran cold, I got up, threw on a green T-shirt and striped pajama bottoms, and went to the family room, hoping the television could dull the droning non-thoughts in my brain. I sank into the leather couch and turned on the TV.

I scrolled through the guide but saw little besides infomercials, while the news hummed in the background.

"Locals reported a massive fish kill this morning in Everglades City."

My ears pricked at the mention of Everglades City. I closed the guide, my eyes and ears riveted to the plastic-looking anchorwoman as she spoke.

"Biologists called out to the scene are saying it's most likely due to oxygen depletion in the water. A startling number of alligator corpses are thought to be the culprit." The video switched to a freckled, blond woman in khaki shorts with a microphone pointed at her bandana-covered mouth. She stood in front of an eerily familiar looking body of murky water; the camera panned in on the white-bellied, dead alligators floating in it, surrounded by hundreds of fish. "An abundance of decomposing matter in the water soaks up a large amount of oxygen, killing off fish in the area in a matter of hours. Of course, in this case, whatever killed the alligators could have killed the fish. A chicken and the egg puzzle, if you will."

The anchor-mannequin spoke again: "The possibility of illegal dumping of hazardous waste is being investigated as well. Herpetologists at the Metro Zoo are expected to do necropsies on the animals over the next couple of days, and we'll be sure to report the results right here. In the meantime, tourists might want to steer clear of the area," she said, holding her nose.

"You aren't kidding, Marge. That has got to stink! And now over to Bob for the weather."

My arm shook as I held out the remote and turned the television off. I stood, swaying on alien feet, as I made my way to the kitchen sink for some water. I pulled a cup from the cabinet and stood at the counter, my mind reeling.

The place they showed on camera didn't look exactly the same.

But I was there in the middle of the night; surely it would look different in the daytime.

But maybe it was somewhere else entirely. Even if it wasn't, maybe something *had* poisoned the water.

Or maybe I hadn't been there at all.

I filled the plastic cup and brought the water to my lips. I accidentally caught my reflection in the dark kitchen window.

I looked like the ghost of a stranger.

Something *was* happening to me.

I heaved the plastic cup at the dark glass and watched my reflection blur away.

47

BEFORE

I WOKE UP THE NEXT DAY IN A SKELETAL, INSTITUtional bed inside the Tamerlane State Lunatic Asylum. The mattress beneath me was torn to pieces and filthy. The bed frame groaned as I shifted and I looked down at myself. I was dressed in black. Someone kissed my neck behind me. I whipped around.

It was Jude. He smiled, and snaked his arm around my waist, pulling me closer.

"Come on, Jude. Not here." I ducked under his arm and stood up, tripping over the debris and insulation on the floor.

He followed me, and backed me up against the wall.

"Shhh, just relax," he said, as he lifted his hand to my cheek and went for my mouth. I turned my head away. His breath was hot on my neck.

"I don't want to do this right now," I said, my voice hoarse. Where was Rachel? Claire?

"You never want to do this," he mumbled against my skin.

"Maybe because you do it so badly." My stomach clenched as soon as the words were out of my mouth.

Jude was still. I chanced a brief look at his face; his eyes were vacant. Lifeless. And then he smiled, but there was no warmth in it.

"Maybe it's because you're a tease," he said, and his smile faded. I needed to leave. Now.

I tried to extract myself from between his body and the wall by pushing against his chest with my palms.

He pushed back. It hurt.

How was this happening? I'd learned over the past two months that Jude had his dick moments—entitled, spoiled, obnoxious—typical Alpha male garbage. But this? This was a whole new level of fucked up. This was—

Jude pressed me against the dusty, crumbling wall with the full weight of his body, cutting off my train of thought. I felt the individual hairs rise on the back of my neck and assessed my dwindling options.

I could scream. Rachel and Claire might be close enough to hear me, but they might not. If they weren't—well. Things would get uglier.

I could smack him. That would probably be stupid, as I'd seen Jude bench-press twice my body weight.

I could do nothing. Rachel would come looking for me eventually.

Door number three seemed the most promising. I went limp.

Jude did not care. He crushed into me with more force, and I fought the swirling hysteria rising in my throat. This was wrong, wrong wrong wrong wrong. Jude crushed his mouth against mine, panting, and the force of him pushed me deeper into the wall, setting loose small clouds of dust that billowed around my body. I felt nauseous

"No," I whispered. I sounded so far away.

Jude didn't answer. His pawing hands were rough and clumsy under my coat, under my sweatshirt, under my shirt. The cold of his skin against my stomach made me gasp. Jude laughed at me.

It sparked a cold, rocking fury inside of me. I wanted to kill him. I wished that I could. I pulled one of his hands off my body with a force I didn't know I had. He replaced it, and without thinking I hauled off and smacked him.

I did not even have the opportunity to register the sting on my hand before I felt it on my face. On *my* face. Jude's blow came so fast and so fierce that it seemed to take me minutes, or hours, to realize he'd even hit me back. My eyeball felt like it was dangling from my socket. The pain bit at me from the inside. My whole being was hot with it.

Shaky-limbed and crying—was I crying?—I began to sink. Jude pulled me up, up, and pinned me, trapped me against the wall. I trembled so furiously against it that bits give way against my hands, my arms, my legs. Jude trailed his tongue over my cheek, and I shuddered.

Then Claire's voice rang out, cutting the charged, silent air. "Mara?"

Jude backed away just a little, only a little, but my feet would not move. My cheeks were cold and itchy with tears and his saliva that I couldn't wipe away. My breath was ragged, my sobbing silent. I raged at myself for not knowing the hollow stranger standing near me. And I raged at him for hiding himself so well, for tricking me, trapping me, crushing me. I felt something tug at the edges of my mind, threatening to pull me down.

A pair of footsteps a few feet away brought me back. Claire called my name again on the other side of the doorway; I couldn't see her, but I clung to that voice, tried to shake off the infuriating helplessness and powerlessness that clogged my throat and weighed down my feet.

Her flashlight danced around the room and finally landed on Jude as he stepped out from behind the wall, raising tiny cumulus clouds of dust.

"Hi," she said.

"Hey," Jude replied with a calm, even smile. It was impossibly more frightening than his rage. "Where's Rachel?"

"She's looking for the blackboard room to add our names

to the list," Claire said quietly. "She wanted me to come back and make sure you guys weren't lost."

"We're good," Jude said and beamed, flashing those all-American dimples. He winked at her.

The shrieking violence inside of me escaped in only a faint, wretched whisper. "Don't leave."

Jude stared hard into my face, his eyes reflecting pure anger. He didn't give me a chance to speak before turning back to Claire. He grinned and rolled his eyes. "You know Mara," he said. "She's a little freaked out. I'm taking her mind off of it."

"Ah," Claire said, and chuckled softly. "You two kids have fun." I heard her footsteps retreat.

"Please," I said, a little louder this time.

The footsteps paused for a moment—one bright, hopeful moment—before picking up again. Then they faded into nothingness.

Jude was back. His meaty hand pushed against my chest, crushing me back into the wall. "Shut up," he said, and unzipped my coat in one harsh motion. He unzipped my sweatshirt in another. Both garments hung limp from my shoulders.

"Don't move," he warned me.

I was frozen—completely, stupidly incapacitated. My teeth chattered and my body shook with anger against the wall as Jude fumbled with the button on my jeans, popping it out of the buttonhole. I had only one thought, just one, that had crawled like an insect into my brain and beat its wings until I could hear nothing else, think nothing else, and until nothing else mattered.

He deserved to die.

As Jude unzipped my fly, three things happened at once.

Rachel's voice called out my name.

Dozens of iron doors slammed shut in a deafening clang.

Everything went black.

48

THE SOUND OF MY MOTHER'S VOICE SHOCKED me awake.

"Happy birthday!" She stood next to my bed and smiled down at me. "She's awake, guys! Come on in."

I watched numbly as the rest of my family paraded into my room, carrying a stack of pancakes with a candle in the middle. "Happy birthday," they sang.

"And many moooooreeee," Joseph added, with jazz hands.

I put my face in my hands and tugged on my skin. I didn't even remember going to sleep last night, but here I was in bed this morning. Waking up from my dream-memory-nightmare about the asylum.

And about the Everglades?

What happened last night? What happened *that* night? What happened to me? What happened?

What happened?

My father pushed the plate at me. A tiny droplet of wax rolled down the side of the candle and lingered, trembling like a lone tear, before it hit the first pancake. I didn't want it to fall. I took the plate and blew the candle out.

"It's nine thirty," my mother said. "Enough time for you to eat something and shower before Noah picks you up." She brushed a strand of hair out of my face. My eyes wandered to Daniel. He winked at me. Then my gaze shifted to my father, who didn't look as thrilled with this plan. Joseph beamed and waggled his eyebrows. He didn't look tired. He didn't look afraid.

And my shoulder didn't hurt.

Did I dream it?

I wanted to ask Joseph, but I didn't see how to get him alone. If it had happened, if he had been taken, I couldn't let my mother know—not until I spoke to Noah. And if it hadn't happened, I couldn't let my mother know. Because she would have me committed for sure.

And at this point, I would be completely unable to argue with her.

I hovered on the edge of the dream and the memory, unable to tell which was which, as I accepted my family's kisses and my present, a digital camera. I thanked them. They left. I pushed one leg out of bed, then the other, and planted my feet on the floor. Then one foot, then the next foot, until I reached my bathroom. Rain lashed the small window and I stared straight at the shower door, hovering between the vanity and the toilet. I couldn't look in the mirror.

I remembered that night. Only when I was unconscious, apparently, and only in pieces, but they were taking on the shape of something enormous and terrifying. Something ugly. I rooted around for the rest of the memory—there was Jude, that asshole, that coward, and what he tried to do and then, and then—nothing. Blackness. The memory slipped away, retreating into the inscrutable vastness of my frontal lobe. It taunted me, niggled at me, and I was angry with it and the world by the time Noah knocked on the front door to pick me up.

"Ready?" he asked. He held an umbrella, but the wind unsteadied his arm. I examined his face. The bruise was gone, and there were only the smallest traces of the lacerations above his eye.

They couldn't have healed that much in one night.

Which meant that last night had to have been a nightmare. All of it. The asylum. The Everglades. Had to have been.

I realized then that Noah was still standing there, waiting for me to answer. I nodded, and we made a break for it.

"So," Noah said once we were both in the car. He pushed

back his damp hair. "Where to?" His voice was casual.

That confirmed it. I stared past him, at a plastic bag caught in the neighbor's hedge across the street, being battered by the rain.

"What's wrong?" he asked, studying me.

I was acting crazy. I did not want to act crazy. I swallowed the question I wanted to ask about the Everglades last night because it wasn't real.

"Bad dream," I said, and the corner of my mouth curved into a slight smile.

Noah looked at me through rain-jeweled lashes. His blue eyes held mine. "About what?"

About what, indeed. About Joseph? About Jude? I didn't know what was real, what was a nightmare, what was a memory.

So I told Noah the truth. "I don't remember."

He stared at the road ahead of us. "Would you want to?"

His question caught me off guard. Would I want to remember?

Did I have a choice?

The sound of the doors rang in my ears. I heard the tug of my zipper as Jude pulled it down. Then Rachel's voice echoing in the hall, in my skull. Then she was gone. I never heard her again.

But maybe . . . maybe I did. Maybe she came for me, and I just didn't remember it yet. She called for me, and maybe she came before the building crushed her—

Before it crushed her. Before it crushed Jude who crushed me. My mouth went dry. Some phantom memory teased my brain, announcing its presence. This was important, but I didn't know why.

"Mara?" Noah's voice reunited me with the present. We were stopped at a red light, and rain pounded on the windshield in waves. The palm trees on the median swayed and bent, threatening to snap. But they wouldn't. They were strong enough to take it.

And so was I.

I turned back to Noah and focused my eyes on his. "I think not knowing is worse," I said. "I'd rather remember."

When I spoke those words, it hit me with exquisite clarity. Everything that had happened—the hallucinations, the paranoia, the nightmares—it *was* just me needing to know, needing to understand what happened that night. What happened to Rachel. What happened to me. I remembered telling as much to Dr. Maillard just a week and a half ago and she smiled at me, telling me I couldn't force it.

But maybe, just maybe, I could.

Maybe I could choose.

So I chose. "I need to remember," I said to Noah with an intensity that surprised us both. And then, "Can you help me?"

He turned away. "How?"

Now that I knew what was wrong, I knew how to fix it. "A hypnotist."

"A hypnotist," Noah repeated slowly.

"Yes." My mother didn't believe in it. She believed in therapy and in drugs that could take weeks, months, years. I didn't have that kind of time. My life was unraveling, my *universe* was unraveling, and I needed to know what happened to me *now*. Not tomorrow. And not Thursday, at my next appointment. Now. Today.

Noah said nothing, but dug into his pocket for his cell phone as he drove with one hand. He dialed and I heard it ring.

"Hello, Albert. Can you get me an appointment with a hypnotist this afternoon?"

I didn't comment on Albert the butler. I was too excited. Too anxious.

"I know it's Saturday," he said. "Just let me know what you find out? Thanks."

He hung up the phone. "He's going to text me back. In the meantime, did you have anything you wanted to do today?"

I shook my head.

"Well," he said, "I'm hungry. So how about lunch?"

"Whatever you want," I said, and Noah smiled at me, but it was sad.

When we turned on to Calle Ocho, I knew where we were going. He pulled into the parking lot of the Cuban place and we darted into the restaurant, which was still insanely busy despite the epic flood.

I felt well enough to smile at the memory of the last time we ate here as we waited near the dessert counter to be seated. I heard the hiss and spit of onions meeting hot oil, and my mouth watered as I scanned the bulletin board next to the counter. Ads for real estate, ads for seminars—

I moved closer to the board.

Please join Botanica Seis for the seminar "Unlocking the Secrets of Your Mind and of Your Past," with Abel Lukumi, ordained high priest. March 15th, $30.00 per person, walk-ins welcome.

Just then, our waiter appeared. "Follow me, please."

"One second," I said, still staring at the flier. Noah caught my eye and read the text.

"You want to go?" he asked.

Unlocking secrets. I turned the phrase over, chewing on my lower lip as I stared at the flier. Why not? "You know what? I do."

"Even though you know it's going to be New Age, spiritual nonsense."

I nodded.

"Even though you don't believe in that stuff."

I nodded.

Noah checked his cell phone. "No word from Albert. And the seminar starts in," he checked the flier and then his phone, "ten minutes."

"So we can go?" I asked, a real smile forming on my lips this time.

"We can go," Noah said. He let our waiter know that we wouldn't be sitting, and turned to the counter to order something to go.

"Do you want anything?" he asked. I felt his eyes on me as I looked in the glass case.

"Can I share with you?"

A quiet smile transformed Noah's face. "Absolutely."

49

THERE WAS NO STREET PARKING NEXT TO THE Botanica, so we parked three blocks away. The torrential downpour had reduced to a heavy mist, and Noah held the umbrella over me. I moved it so that it was between us, and we pressed together underneath it. The familiar thrill of his proximity made my pulse gallop. We were closer than we had been in days. I didn't include the shoulder incident from last night because it didn't happen. My shoulder didn't hurt.

I was warm next to Noah, but shivered anyway. The charcoal clouds did something to the atmosphere of Little Havana. The Domino Park was abandoned, but a few men still huddled in the rain next to the mural at the entrance, under the eaves of one of the small tents. Their eyes followed us as we passed. Smoke curled from the entrance of a cigar shop nearby, mingling with the rain and the incense from the computer repair store in front of us. The neon sign buzzed and hummed in my ear.

"This is it," Noah said. "1821 Calle Ocho."

I looked at the sign. "But it says it's a computer repair store."

"It does indeed."

We peered into the shop, pressing our faces to the cloudy glass. Electronics and dissembled computer parts mingled with large terra cotta urns and an army of porcelain statues. I looked at Noah. He shrugged. I went in.

A bell jangled behind us as we entered the narrow storefront. Two young boys peeked out from above a glass counter with no adults in sight.

My eyes wandered inside the store, over the rows of shelves lined with plastic bins. Inside the bins, in no discernible order, there were halved coconut husks, bear-shaped containers of honey, several types of shells, rusty horseshoes, ostrich eggs, absorbent cotton, tiny jingle bells, packages of white plastic flip-flops, beads, and candles. Stacks of candles of every size, shape, and color; candles with Jesus emblazoned on the front, and candles with naked women emblazoned on the front. There were even dozens of varieties of ice cream sundae candles. And . . . handcuffs. What was this place?

"Can I help you?"

Noah and I turned around. A dark-haired young woman on crutches appeared in a door frame between the main storefront and a back room.

Noah raised his eyebrows. "We're here for the seminar," he said. "Is this the right place?"

"*Si*, yes, come," she said, beckoning us over. We followed her into another narrow room with plastic patio chairs arranged on the white tile floor. She handed us two pamphlets and Noah handed her money. Then she disappeared.

"Thanks," I said to him as we sat in the back of the room. "I'm sure this wasn't how you planned on spending your Saturday."

"I'll be honest, I was hoping you'd suggest the beach," he said and shook out his damp hair, "but I consider live entertainment a close second."

I grinned. I was starting to feel better, more normal. More sane. My eyes wandered around the white room. Hospital white, and the fluorescent lights made it brighter. It contrasted oddly with the furniture—grandma furniture, really. A brown and yellow armchair, a pea green cabinet, more shelves with candles. Strange.

Someone coughed to my left; I turned my head and a pale, thin man dressed in a white robe, wearing white flip-flops and with a white triangular hat on his head, sat in the row in front of us. Noah and I exchanged a look. The other attendees were more normally attired; a heavyset woman with short, curly blond hair in jean shorts fanned herself with a pamphlet. Two identical middle-aged men with mustaches sat in the far corner of the room, whispering to each other. They wore jeans.

Just then, the speaker walked up to the podium and introduced himself. I was surprised to see him wearing a crisp suit, given that he was supposed to be a priest. A priest of what, I did not know.

Mr. Lukumi arranged his papers before smiling broadly and scanning the few filled seats. Then our eyes met. His went wide with surprise.

I turned around, wondering if someone behind me had caught his attention, but no one was there. Mr. Lukumi cleared his throat, but when he spoke, his voice shook.

I was being paranoid. Paranoid paranoid paranoid. And stupid. I focused on the lecture and on Noah, as he took an exaggerated interest in what was being said. I'm not sure what I expected, but hearing Mr. Lukumi discuss the mystical properties of candles and bead necklaces wasn't it.

Noah cracked me up as he pretended to actively listen; nodding and murmuring at the most inappropriate moments. We passed the Cuban sandwich he'd bought back and forth during the seminar and at one point, I struggled so hard not to laugh that I almost choked on it. If nothing else, I was having some badly needed, well deserved fun after the hellish week.

When the talk ended, Noah went to the front of the room

to chat up Mr. Lukumi as the handful of other attendees filtered out. I went to explore.

There was only one small window in the room, and it was partially hidden by a shelf. An overflow of rain gurgled out of a storm drain, sounding like a muffled plug-in fountain through the glass barrier. My eyes scanned the labels of dozens of tiny bottles and jars of herbs and liquids in front of me; "mystic bath," "recuperation of love life," "luck," "confusion."

Confusion. I reached out to inspect the bottle just as something squawked behind me. I whipped around and, in the process, dislodged a poured candle from the shelf. It fell in slow motion then smashed against the tile, the glass casing splitting into a thousand little diamond shards. Noah and Mr. Lukumi both turned in my direction, just as a small silver cup with jingle bells on it tipped over.

Mr. Lukumi's eyes flicked to the cup, then to me. "Get out," he said, as he approached.

His tone stunned me. "I'm sorry, I didn't mean—"

Mr. Lukumi crouched and examined the broken glass, then raised his eyes to mine. "Just go," he said, but his voice wasn't angry. It was urgent.

"Wait a minute," Noah said, growing annoyed. "There's no call to be rude. I'll pay for it."

Mr. Lukumi rose from his crouch and reached for my arm. But at the last second, he didn't take it. His tall figure loomed over mine. Intimidating.

"There is nothing for you here," he said slowly. "Please leave."

Noah appeared at my side. "Back up," he said to Mr. Lukumi, his voice low. Dangerous. The priest did so without pause, but his eyes never left mine.

I was beyond confused, and speechless. The three of us stood still a few feet from the doorway. One of the children giggled in the other room. I tried to orient myself, to figure out what I'd done that was so insulting and examined Mr. Lukumi's face in the process. His eyes met mine, and something flashed behind them. Something I didn't expect.

Recognition.

"You know something," I said to him quietly, not sure how I knew. I registered Noah's surprise in my peripheral vision as I stared Mr. Lukumi down. "You know what's happening to me." The words felt true.

But I was crazy. Medicated. In therapy. And believing that was what had led me here to a hole in the wall with a medicine man made more sense than the impossible idea that there was something very, very wrong with me. Something worse than crazy. Mr. Lukumi dropped his gaze and my conviction began to slip away. He was acting like he knew. But what did he know? *How* did he know? And then I realized that it didn't matter. Whatever insight he had, I was desperate for it.

"Please," I said. "I'm—" I remembered the tiny bottle clenched in my sweaty fist. "I'm confused. I need help."

Mr. Lukumi looked at my fist. "That won't help you," he said, but his tone was softer.

Noah's expression was still wary, but his voice was calm. "We'll pay," he said, digging into his pocket. He had no idea what was going on, but he was going along with it. With me. Reckless Noah, game for anything. I loved him.

I *loved* him.

Before I could even dwell on the thought, Mr. Lukumi shook his head and motioned us toward the door again, but Noah withdrew a fat wad of bills from his pocket. As he counted them out, my eyes went wide.

"Five thousand to help us," he said, and pressed them into Mr. Lukumi's hand.

I wasn't the only one shocked by the money. The priest hesitated for a moment before his fingers curled over the cash. His eyes appraised Noah.

"You do need help," he said to him, shaking his head before closing the door behind us. Then his eyes found mine. "Wait here." Mr. Lukumi headed to a back door I hadn't even noticed. How deep did this place go?

He finally disappeared, and the sound of squawking and clucking met my ears.

"Chickens?" I asked. "What are those—"

A nonhuman scream cut off my question.

"Did he just—" My hands curled into fists. No. No way.

Noah tilted his head. "What are you getting so upset about?"

"Are you joking?"

"The *medianoche* we just ate had pork in it."

But that's different. "I didn't have to hear it," I said out loud.

"No one likes a hypocrite, Mara," he said, a sad shadow of a smile turning up one corner of his mouth. "And anyway, you're running this show. I'm just the financier."

I tried not to think about what might or might not be happening in the back room as the sandwich turned sour in my stomach. "Speaking of finances," I said, swallowing carefully before I continued, "what the hell were you doing with five thousand dollars on you?"

"Eight, actually. I had grand plans for today. Hookers and blow aren't cheap, but I suppose animal sacrifice will have to do. Happy birthday."

"Thanks," I deadpanned. I was starting to feel more normal. Relaxed, even. "But seriously, why the money?"

Noah's eyes were focused on the back door. "I thought we'd stop in the art district to meet a painter I know. I was going to buy something from him."

"With that much money? In cash?"

"He has cash vices, shall we say."

"And you'd enable them?"

Noah shrugged a shoulder. "He's supremely talented,"

I looked at him with disapproval.

"What?" Noah asked. "Nobody's perfect."

Since Noah's money was now being used to support animal

sacrifice as opposed to someone's cocaine habit, I dropped the subject. My eyes roamed the room.

"What's the deal with all the random stuff here?" I asked. "The rusty horseshoes? The honey?"

"It's for Santeria offerings," Noah said. "It's a popular religion here. Mr. Lukumi is one of the high priests."

Just then, the back door opened and the high priest himself appeared, carrying a small glass in his hands. With a picture of a rooster on it. Terrible.

He pointed at the ugly brown and yellow flowered armchair in the corner of the room. "Sit," he said as he ushered me toward it. His voice was dispassionate. I obeyed.

He handed me the glass. It was warm. "Drink this," he said.

My bizarre day—my bizarre life—was getting weirder and weirder. "What's in it?" I asked, eyeing the mixture. It looked like tomato juice. I'd pretend it was tomato juice.

"You are confused, yes? You need to remember, yes? Drink it. It will help you," Mr. Lukumi said.

I flicked my eyes to Noah and he held his hands up defensively. "Don't look at me," he said, then turned to Mr. Lukumi, "But if anything happens to her afterward," he said carefully, "I will end you."

Mr. Lukumi was unruffled by the threat. "She will sleep. She will remember. That is all. Now drink."

I took the glass from him but my nostrils flared as I brought it to my mouth. The salt-rust smell turned my stomach, and I hesitated.

This whole thing was probably fake. The blood, the botanica. Mr. Lukumi was humoring us for the money. The hypnotist would probably do the same. It wouldn't help.

But neither did the pills. And the alternative was waiting. Waiting and talking to Dr. Maillard, while my nightmares got worse and my hallucinations became harder to hide, until I'd eventually be pulled out of school—dashing any hope of graduating on time, of going to a good college, of having a normal life.

What the hell. I tilted the glass and winced when my lips reached the warm liquid. My taste buds rebelled at the bitterness, the metallic iron flavor. It was all I could do not to spit. After a few painful gulps, I wrenched the cup from my lips but Mr. Lukumi shook his head.

"All of it," he said.

I looked at Noah. He shrugged.

I turned back to the glass. This was my choice. I wanted this. I needed to finish it.

I closed my eyes, tossed my head back and brought the glass to my mouth. It clicked against my teeth and I swallowed the thin liquid. I chugged it when my throat protested, screamed at me to stop. The warmth dribbled over both sides of my chin and soon, the glass was empty. I sat upright again and held the cup in my lap. I did it. I smiled, triumphant.

"You look like the Joker," Noah said.

That was the last thing I heard before I blacked out.

50

When I awoke, I faced a wall of books. My eyes felt puffy and swollen with sleep and I rubbed them with my fists like a little girl. Lamplight from an alcove stretched across the room, reaching for my exposed legs at the foot of the bed.

Noah's bed.

In Noah's room.

Without any clothes on.

Holy shit.

I wrapped the flat sheet tighter around my chest. Lightning flashed, illuminating the roiling surface of the bay outside the window.

"Noah?" I asked, my voice shaky and hoarse with sleep. My last memory was the taste of that rank concoction Mr. Lukumi gave me to drink. The warm feel of it dribbling down my chin. The smell. And then I remembered cold, being cold. But nothing else. *Nothing* else. My sleep was dreamless.

"You're up," Noah said as he padded into view. He was limned in the light from his desk, his drawstring pants hanging low on his hips and his T-shirt hugging his lean frame. The light cast his elegant profile into relief; sharp and gorgeous, as if he'd been cut from glass. He moved to sit on the edge of his bed, about a foot away from my feet.

"What time is it?" I asked him. My voice was thick with sleep.

"About ten."

I blinked. "It was almost two when the seminar ended, wasn't it?" Noah nodded. "What happened?"

He shot me a loaded glance. "You don't remember?"

I shook my head. Noah said nothing and looked away. His expression was even, but I saw the muscles working in his jaw. I grew increasingly uncomfortable. What was so bad he couldn't—oh. Oh, no. My eyes flicked down to the sheet I'd wrapped around myself. "Did we—"

In an instant, Noah's face was full of mischief. "No. You tore your clothes off and then ran through the house screaming 'It burns! Take it off us!'"

My face flushed hot.

"Kidding," Noah said, grinning wickedly.

He was too far away to smack.

"But you did jump in the pool with your clothes on."

Fabulous.

"I was just glad you didn't choose the bay. Not in this storm."

"What happened to them?" I asked. Noah looked bemused. "My clothes, I mean?"

"They're in the wash."

"How did I—" I blushed deeper. Did I take them off in front of him?

Did *he* take them off?

"Nothing I haven't seen before."

I buried my face in my hands. God help me.

A soft chuckle escaped from Noah's lips. "Fret not, you were actually very modest in your intoxicated state. You undressed in the bathroom, wrapped yourself in a towel, crawled between my sheets, and slept." Noah shifted on the bed, and the oddest crunching came from underneath him. I looked, really looked, at the bed for the first time.

"What," I asked slowly, as I eyed the animal crackers strewn all over it, "the hell?"

"You were convinced they were your pets," Noah said, not even trying to suppress his laughter. "You wouldn't let me touch them."

Jesus.

Noah raised the light quilt, careful not to disturb my sheet, and folded it so none of my pets would spill onto the floor. He walked over to his closet and retrieved one of his plaid shirts and a pair of boxer briefs and held them out to me casually. I gripped the bed sheet covering my skin with one hand and took his clothes with the other as Noah walked back to the alcove. I slipped the shirt over my head and the boxers over my legs but I was acutely, keenly aware of his presence.

In point of fact, I was acutely, keenly aware of everything. The places where Noah's flannel shirt billowed and curved against my body. The cool cotton sheets beneath my legs, which really felt like silk. The smell of old paper and leather mingled with the rumor of Noah's scent. I saw, felt, smelled everything in his room. I felt alive. Vital. Incredible. For the first time in forever.

"Wait," I said as Noah slipped a book from a shelf and headed toward the door. "Where are you going?"

"To read?"

But I don't want you to.

"But I need to go home," I said, my eyes meeting his. "My parents are going to kill me."

"Taken care of. You're at Sophie's house."

I loved Sophie.

"So I'm . . . staying here?"

"Daniel's covering for you."

I loved Daniel.

"Where's Katie?" I asked, trying to sound casual.

"Eliza's house."

I loved Eliza.

"And your parents?" I asked.

"Some charity thing."

I loved charity.

"So why are you going to read when I'm right here?" My voice was a challenge and a tease and I was shocked at the sound of it. I didn't think, I wasn't thinking—about what had happened last night or today or what would happen tomorrow. It didn't even register. All I knew was that I was there, in Noah's bed, wearing his clothes, and he was too far away.

Noah tensed. I could feel his eyes travel over every inch of my bare skin as he stared at me.

"It's my birthday," I said.

"I know." His voice was low and rough and I wanted to swallow it.

"Come here."

Noah took a measured step toward the bed.

"Closer."

Another step. He was there. I was waist high, wearing his clothes and tangled in his sheets. I looked up at him.

"Closer."

He ran his hand through my still-wet hair, and his thumb drew a semicircle from my brow to my temple to my cheekbone, moving over my neck. He fixed his gaze on me. It was hard.

"Mara, I need to—"

"Shut up," I whispered as I grabbed his hand and tugged, and he half-kneeled, half-fell into bed. I didn't care what he was going to say. I just wanted him close. I twisted my arm to curl him behind me and he unfolded there, the two of us snuggled like quotation marks in his room full of words. He laced his fingers in mine and I felt his breath on my skin. We lay there in silence for some time before he spoke.

"You smell good," he whispered into my neck. He was warm against me. Instinctively, I arched back into him and smiled.

"Really?"

"Mmm-hmm. Delicious. Like bacon."

I laughed as I twisted to face him and raised my arm to hit in one move. He caught my wrist and my laugh caught in my throat. A mischievous grin curved my mouth as I raised my other hand to hit him. He reached over me and caught that wrist too, gently pinning my arms above my head as he straddled my hips. The space between us boiled my blood.

He leaned forward slightly, still touching me nowhere and smelling like need and I thought I would die. His voice was low when he spoke.

"What would you do if I kissed you right now?"

I stared at his beautiful face and his beautiful mouth and I wanted nothing more than to taste it.

"I would kiss you back."

Noah parted my legs with his knees and my lips with his tongue, and I was in his mouth and *oh*. Abandon all hope, ye who enter here. I felt myself unfold, turned inside out by his insistent mouth. When Noah pulled back I gasped at the loss, but he slid his hand beneath my back and lifted me, and we were sitting and his head was dipping and our mouths were colliding and I pushed him down and lingered above, hovered before I crashed into him.

I felt delicious for an eternity. I smiled against Noah's lips and ran my fingers through his hair and withdrew at some point to see his thoughts in his eyes, but they were closed, his lashes resting on his stone cheek. I lifted higher to see him better, and his lips were blue.

"Noah." My voice was rude in the stillness.

But he wasn't Noah. He was Jude. And Claire. And Rachel and dead and I saw them all, a parade of corpses underneath me, pallor and blood in lunatic dust. The memory sliced through my mind like a scythe, leaving behind lucid, unforgiving clarity.

Twelve iron doors slammed shut.

I slammed them shut.

And before the blackness, terror. But not mine.

Jude's.

One second, he had pressed me so deeply into the wall that I thought I would dissolve into it. The next, he was the trapped one, inside the patient room, inside with me. But I was no longer the victim.

He was.

I laughed at him in my crazed fury, which shook the asylum's foundation and crushed it. With Jude and Claire and Rachel inside.

I killed them, and others, too. Mabel's torturer. Morales.

The realization slammed me back into Noah's bedroom, with his motionless body still beneath me. I screamed his name and there was no answer and I freaked the fuck out in earnest. I shook him, I pinched him, I tried to wrestle into his arms but they held no asylum for me. I dove for his headboard and with one hand fumbled for his cell, furious and terrified. I reached it and began dialing 911 while I raised my other arm and backhanded him across the cheek, connecting with skin and bone in a furious sting.

He woke up with a sharp intake of breath. My hand hurt like a bitch.

"Incredible," Noah breathed, as he reached his hand up to his face. The beautiful taste of him was already fading from my tongue.

I opened my mouth to speak, but there was no air.

Noah looked far away and hazy. "That was the best dream I have ever had. Ever."

"You weren't breathing," I said. I could barely get the words out.

"My face hurts." Noah stared past me, at nothing in particular. His eyes were unfocused, his pupils dilated. From the dark or something else, I didn't know.

I placed my trembling hands on his face, careful to balance my weight above him. "You were dying." My voice cracked with the words.

"That's ridiculous," Noah said, an amused smile forming on his mouth.

"Your lips turned blue." Like Rachel's would have, after she suffocated. After I killed her.

Noah raised his eyebrows. "How do you know?"

"I saw it." I didn't look at Noah. I couldn't. I unstraddled him and he sat up, glancing his hand across the dimmer, brightening the room. Noah's eyes were dark, but clear now. He stared at me plainly.

"I fell asleep, Mara. You were sleeping next to me. You pulled me into bed and I was behind you and . . . God, that was a good dream." Noah leaned back against the headboard and closed his eyes.

My head spun. "We kissed. You don't remember?"

Noah smirked. "Sounds like you had a good dream as well."

What he was saying—it made no sense. "You told me I smelled—like bacon."

"Well," he said evenly. "That's awkward."

I looked at my hands lying limp in my lap. "You asked if

you could kiss me, and then you did. And then I—" There were no words to translate it, the dead faces I saw on the insides of my eyelids. I wanted to rub them out, but they wouldn't leave. They were real. It was all real. Whatever the Santeria priest did had worked. And now that I knew, now that I remembered, all I wanted was to forget.

"I hurt you," I finished. And it was only the beginning.

Noah rubbed his cheek. "It's all right," he said, and pulled me back down, curling me into his side, my head on his shoulder and my cheek on his chest. His heart beat under my skin.

"Did you remember anything?" Noah whispered into my hair. "Did the thing work?"

I didn't answer.

"It's all right," Noah said very softly, his fingers brushing my ribs. "You were just dreaming."

But the kiss wasn't a dream. Noah *was* dying. The asylum wasn't an accident. I *killed* them.

It was all real. It was all me.

I didn't understand why Noah didn't remember what happened seconds ago but I finally understood what had happened to me months ago. Jude trapped me, crushed me against the wall. I wanted him punished, to feel *my* terror of being trapped, of being crushed. So I made him feel it.

And abandoned Claire and Rachel.

Rachel, who sat with me for hours under the giant tire in our old school's playground, our thighs gritty with dirt, as I confessed an unrequited fifth-grade crush. Rachel, who sat still for my portraits, who I laughed with and cried with and did everything with, whose body was now turned into so much meat. Because of me.

And not because I went along with the Tamerlane plan, even knowing it could be dangerous. Not because I failed to scratch at some vague tickle of premonition. It was my fault because it was actually, literally my fault—because I crumpled the asylum with Rachel and Claire inside like it was nothing more than a wad of tissues in my pocket.

I reeled at the delusions I'd invented after murdering Mabel's owner and Ms. Morales. I was not crazy.

I was lethal.

Noah's hand worked in my hair and it felt so wonderful, so painfully wonderful that it was all I could do not to cry.

"I should go," I managed to whisper, even though I didn't want to go anywhere. I didn't want to *be* anywhere.

"Mara?" Noah leaned up on his elbow. His fingers traced the outline of my cheekbone, stroking my skin awake. My heart did not beat faster. It did not beat at all. I had no heart left.

Noah studied my face for a moment. "I can take you home, but your parents will wonder why," he said slowly.

I said nothing. I couldn't. My throat was filled with broken glass.

"Why don't you stay?" he asked. "I can go into another room. Say the words."

The words wouldn't come.

Noah sat next to me, the bed shifting under his weight. I felt his warmth as he leaned in, brushed my hair aside, and pressed his lips to my temple. I closed my eyes and memorized it. He left.

The rain lashed his windows as I buried myself in his sheets and pulled the covers up to my chin. But there would be no shelter in Noah's bed or in his arms from the howling of my sins.

51

SITTING NEXT TO NOAH WHILE HE DROVE ME home the next morning was the worst kind of torture. It hurt to look at him, at his sun-drenched hair and his worried eyes. I couldn't talk to him. I didn't know what to say.

When he pulled into my driveway, I told him I didn't feel well (truth) and that I would call him later (lie). Then I went to my room and closed the door.

My mother found me that afternoon in my bed with the blinds shut. The sun slotted through them anyway, casting bars against the walls, the ceiling, my face.

"Are you sick, Mara?"

"Yes."

"What's wrong?"

"Everything."

She closed the door and I turned over in the membrane of my sheets. I'd been right; something *was* happening to me, but I didn't know what to do. What *could* I do? My whole family moved here for me, moved here to help me get away from my dead life, but the corpses would follow wherever I went. And what if the next time it happened, it was Daniel and Joseph instead of Rachel and Claire?

A cold tear slid down my burning cheek. It tickled the skin next to my nose but I didn't wipe it away. Or the next one. And soon, I was flooded with the tears I never cried at Rachel's funeral.

I didn't get up for school the next day. Or the next. And there were no more nightmares, now. Which was unfortunate, because I deserved them.

The oblivion when I slept was blissful. My mother brought me food but otherwise left me alone. I overheard her and my father speaking in the hallway but didn't care enough to be surprised by what they said.

"Daniel said she was doing better," my father said. "I should have withdrawn from the case. She's not even eating."

"I think—I think she'll be all right. I spoke to Dr. Maillard. She just needs a bit of time," my mother said.

"I don't understand it. She was doing so well."

"Her birthday had to have been hard for her," my mother said. "She's a year older, Rachel isn't. It makes perfect sense for her to be going through something. If nothing changes by her appointment Thursday, we'll worry."

"She looks so different," my father said. "Where'd our girl go?"

When I went to the bathroom that night, I turned on the light and looked in the mirror to see if I could find her. The husk of a girl not-named Mara stared back at me. I wondered how I would kill her.

And then I dove back into bed, my legs shaking, teeth chattering, because it was just so scary, too scary, and I didn't have the guts.

When Noah appeared in my room later that evening, my body knew it before my eyes could confirm it. He had a book with him: *The Velveteen Rabbit*, one of my favorites. But I didn't want him there. Or rather, *I* didn't want to be there. But I wasn't about to move, so I lay in bed, facing the wall, as he began.

"Long June evenings, in the bracken that shone like frosted silver, feet padded softly. White moths fluttered out. She held him close in her arms, pearl dewdrops and flowers around her neck and in her hair," he said.

"'What is Real?' asked the boy. 'It is a thing that happens to you when a girl loves you for a long, long time. Not just to play with,'" Noah said. "'But really loves you.' 'Does it hurt?' asked the boy. 'Sometimes. When you are Real you don't mind being hurt.'

"She slept with him, the nightlight burning on the mantelpiece. Love stirred."

Hmm.

"Swayed gently," he said. "A great rustling. Tunnels in bedclothes, an unwrapping of parcels. Her face grew flushed—"

So did mine.

"Half asleep, she crept up close to the pillow and whispered in his ear, damp from—"

"That is not *The Velveteen Rabbit*," I said, my voice hoarse from disuse.

"Welcome back," Noah said.

There was nothing to say but the truth. "That was awful."

Noah responded by defiling Dr. Seuss. *One Fish, Two Fish, Red Fish, Blue Fish,* became an instructional rhyme on fellatio.

Fortunately, Joseph walked into my room just as Noah recited his next title. *The* New *Adventures of Curious George.*

"Can I listen?" my brother asked.

"Sure," Noah said.

Filthy visions of the Man in the Yellow Hat and his monkey desecrated my mind.

"No," I said, my face muffled by my pillow.

"Don't pay attention to her, Joseph."

"No," I said louder, still facing my wall.

"Come sit next to me," Noah said to my brother.

I sat up in bed and shot Noah a scathing look. "You can't read that to him."

A smile transformed Noah's face. "Why not?" he asked.

"Because. It's disgusting."

He turned to Joseph and winked. "Another day, then."

Joseph left the room, but he was smiling as he went.

"So," Noah said carefully. I was sitting up, cross-legged and tangled in my sheets.

"So," I said back.

"Would *you* like to hear about Curious George's new adventures?"

I shook my head.

"Are you sure?" Noah asked. "He's been *such* a naughty monkey."

"Pass."

Then Noah gave me a look that broke my heart. "What happened, Mara?" he asked in a low, quiet voice.

It was nighttime, and maybe it was because I was tired, or because I'd started talking. Or because it was the first time he ever asked me, or because Noah looked so heartbreakingly, impossibly beautiful sitting on the floor beside my bed, haloed by the light of my lamp, that I told him.

I told him everything, from the beginning. I left nothing out. Noah sat stone still, his eyes never leaving my face.

"Jesus Christ," he said when I was finished.

He didn't believe me. I looked away.

"I thought I was mad," Noah said to himself.

I snapped my eyes to his. "What? What did you say?"

Noah stared at my wall. "I saw you—well, your hands, anyway—and heard your voice. I thought I was going mad. And then you showed up. Unbelievable."

"Noah," I said. His expression was remote. I reached out and turned his head to me. "What are you talking about?"

"Just your hands," he said, taking my hands in his and turning them over, flexing my fingers as he inspected them. "You were pressing them against something but it was dark. Your head ached. I could see your fingernails; they were black. Your ears were ringing but I heard your voice."

His sentences knotted together in a way that didn't fit. "I don't understand."

"Before you moved here, Mara. I heard your voice before you moved here."

The memory of Noah's face that first day of school arranged itself into an unthinkable shape. He looked at me like he knew me because—because somehow, he did. Any words I could have spoken next vanished from my tongue, from my brain. I could not make sense of what I was hearing.

"You weren't the first one I saw. Heard. There were two others before, but I never met them."

"Others," I whispered.

"Other people I saw. In my mind."

His words sunk like a stone in the air around us.

"I was driving the first time, at night," he said in a rush. "I saw myself hit someone; but it was on a completely different road, and it wasn't my car. But I headed straight for her. She was our age, I think. Pinned behind the steering column. She didn't die for hours," Noah said, his voice hollow. "I saw everything she went through, heard everything she heard, and felt everything she felt, but was somehow still on my road. I thought it was a hallucination, you know? Like at night when you're driving sometimes, and you imagine going over the shoulder, or hitting another car. But it was real," Noah said, and his voice was haunted.

"The second one was very ill. He was our age as well. I dreamed one night that I was preparing food for him, then fed him, but the hands weren't mine. He had some sort of infection and his neck hurt so badly. He was so sore. He cried."

Noah's face was drawn and pale. He leaned his head into his hand and rubbed it, then ran his fingers back through his hair, making it stand on end. Then he looked up at me. "And then in December, I heard you."

The blood drained from my face.

"I recognized your voice on your first day at school. I was giddy at the impossibility of it. I thought I was going insane, imagining sick and dying people and *feeling* it, feeling an echo of what they must have felt. And then you showed up, with the voice from my nightmare, and you called me an ass," Noah said, smiling faintly.

"I asked Daniel about you, and he told me, vaguely, what had happened before you moved here. I assumed that's what I saw. Or dreamed. But I thought if—I don't know. I thought if I knew you, I might be able to understand what was happening to me. That was before Joseph, obviously."

My mouth felt like it was filled with sand. "Joseph?" That wasn't real.

"A couple of weeks ago, in the restaurant, I had a—a vision, I suppose," he said, sounding embarrassed. "Of a document, a deed from the Collier County archives." Noah shook his head slowly. "Someone—a man wearing a Rolex—was pulling files, photocopying, and he lingered on that document. I saw it like I was the one looking straight at it," he said, inhaling deeply. "It had a property address, a location. And when I saw it, I got a screaming headache, which is typical. I just couldn't stand all the *sounds*. So I left you until it passed." Noah raked his fingers through his hair. "A couple of days later, when I got home from school, I passed out. For hours—I was just gone. When I woke up, I felt high. And I saw Joseph asleep on the cement, before someone closed a door. And whoever it was wore the same watch."

I sat still, my feet tucked underneath me, growing numb as Noah went on.

"I didn't know if it was real or if I'd dreamed it, but after what happened to you, I thought it might actually be happening. In real time. Looking back, with the others, I'd always seen some indication of where they were—which hospital, which road. But I never realized it was *real*." Noah's eyes fell to the floor. Then he closed them. He sounded so tired. "And so with Joseph, I took you with me—just in case I passed out again, or something else." His jaw tightened. "When it turned out that he *was* there, how could I explain that to you? I thought *I* was mad." He paused. "I thought I took him."

I heard an echo of Noah's voice from that night. *"Do whatever you have to do to wake Joseph."*

He said that before we even saw him.

"Holy shit," I whispered.

"I wanted to tell you the truth—about me, about this—before he was even taken. But then when he was, I didn't know what to say. I honestly I thought I was responsible somehow. That maybe I was the one hurting everyone I'd seen, and repressed the memories . . . or something. But then whose headlights were those in the Everglades? And why would they pull into the drive by the shed?"

I shook my head. I didn't know. It made no sense. I'd thought I was crazy, but realized I wasn't. I thought Joseph's kidnapping wasn't real, but it was.

"I didn't take him," Noah said. His voice was clear. Strong. But his intense stare was still fixed on the wall. Not on me.

I believed him, but asked, "So who did?"

For the first time since Noah started speaking, he turned to me.

"We'll find out," he said.

I tried to assemble all of this information into something that made sense. "So Joseph never texted you," I said. My heart beat faster.

Noah shook his head, but flashed the barest suggestion of a smile at me.

"What?" I asked.

"I can hear that," Noah said.

I stared at him, bewildered.

"You," he said quietly. "Your heartbeat. Your pulse. Your breath. All of you."

My pulse rioted, and Noah's smile broadened.

"You have your own sound. Everything does; animals, people. I can hear all of it. When something, or someone's hurt, or exhausted, or whatever—I can tell. And I think—fuck." Noah lowered his head and tugged on his hair. "So, this is going to sound mad. But I think maybe I can fix them," he said, without looking up. But then he did, and his eyes fell on my arm. On my shoulder.

Impossible.

"When you asked why I smoke, I told you I've never been ill. It's true—and when I've gotten into rows, I hurt for a while and then—nothing. No pain. It's over."

I looked at him, disbelieving. "Are you saying that you can—"

"How's your shoulder, Mara?"

I had no words.

"You'd be in quite a lot of pain right now, even once it was back in its socket. And your arm?" Noah said, taking my hand and extending it. He traced his finger down from the indent of my elbow to my wrist. "You'd still be blistering, and probably starting to scar," he said, his eyes roaming over my unbroken skin. Then they met mine.

"Who told you about my arm?" I asked. My voice sounded far away.

"No one told me. No one needed to. Mabel was dying when you brought her to me. She was so far gone, my mother didn't think she'd survive the night. I stayed at the hospital with her and I don't know, I held her. And heard her heal."

"It makes no sense," I said, staring at him.

"I know."

"You are telling me that somehow, you've seen a handful of people who were about to die. You could feel an echo of what they felt. And that whenever my heart—or anyone else's—races, you can hear that."

"I know."

"And somehow, you can hear what's broken in people, or what's wrong, and fix it."

"I know."

"While the only thing I'm capable of is—" *Murder.* I could barely think it.

"You had visions as well, no? Saw things?" Noah's eyes studied mine.

I shook my head. "Hallucinations. Nothing was real except the nightmares, the memories."

Noah paused for a beat. "How do you know?"

I thought back to every hallucination I had. The classroom walls. Jude and Claire in the mirror. The earrings in the bathtub. None of them had actually happened. And the events I thought *didn't* happen—the way I'd excused Morales's death and the death of Mabel's owner—did.

I did have PTSD. That was real. But what had happened, what I did, what I could do, was also real.

"I just know," I said, and left it at that.

We stared at each other, not laughing, not smiling. Just looking; Noah serious, myself incredulous, until I was seized by a thought so potent and so urgent that I wanted to scream it.

"Fix me," I commanded him. "This thing, what I've done—there's something wrong with me, Noah. Fix it."

Noah's expression broke my heart as he brushed my hair from my face, and skimmed the line of my neck. "I can't."

"Why not?" I asked, my voice threatening to crack.

Noah lifted both of his hands to my face, and held it. "Because," he said, "you aren't broken."

I sat perfectly still, breathing slowly through my nose. Any sound would shatter me. I closed my eyes to stop myself from crying, but the tears welled anyway.

"So," I said as my throat constricted.

"So."

"Both of us?"

"Seems that way," Noah said. A tear trickled onto his thumb, but he didn't move his hands.

"What are the odds of—"

"Highly unfavorable," Noah cut me off.

I smiled under his fingers. They were painfully real. I was so aware of him, of us, lost and confused and with no new understanding of what was happening or why.

But we weren't alone.

Noah moved closer and kissed my forehead. His expression was calm. No, more than that. It was peaceful.

"You must be starving. Let me get you something from the kitchen."

I nodded, and Noah stood to leave. When he opened my bedroom door, I spoke.

"Noah?"

He turned.

"When you heard me before—before I moved here. What did I say?"

Noah's face grew somber. "'Get them out.'"

52

"I MUST SAY, I THINK I RATHER LIKE THIS SLEEPING arrangement."

I didn't think I would ever tire of hearing Noah's voice in the nether darkness of my bedroom. The weight of him in my bed was unfamiliar and thrilling. He leaned against two of my pillows and had me curled into his side, sharing my blanket. My head rested on his shoulder, my cheek on his chest. His heartbeat was steady. Mine was insane. I think I knew that it wasn't safe for him here. With me. But I couldn't bring myself to pull away.

"How did you work this out, anyway?" I still hadn't left my room or seen my mother since she'd been in to check on me earlier that afternoon, before Noah's confession. Before my confession. I wondered how we were getting away with this.

"Well, technically, I'm sleeping in Daniel's room right now."

"Right now?"

"As we speak," Noah said, curving his arm around my back. It rested just below the hem of my shirt. "Your mother didn't want me driving home so late."

"And tomorrow?"

"That's a good question."

I leaned up to see his face. It was thoughtful, serious, as he stared at my ceiling. "Whether you'll be here tomorrow?" I kept my voice even. I knew by now that Noah didn't play games. That if he was going to leave, he would leave, and be honest about it. But I hoped that wasn't what he was going to say.

He smiled softly. "What happens to us tomorrow. Now that we know we're not insane."

It was the ultimate question, one that haunted me since last week, since I remembered. What was next? Was I supposed to do something with it? Try to ignore it? Try to stop it? Did I even have a choice? It was too much to deal with. My heart beat wildly in my chest.

"What are you thinking?" Noah shifted on to his side and tightened his grip on my back, pressing me into him, aligning us perfectly.

"What?" I whispered as my thoughts dissolved.

Noah shifted closer and tilted his head as if he was going to whisper something to me. His nose skimmed my jaw instead, until his lips found the hollow beneath my ear.

"Your heart started racing," he said, tracing the line of my neck to my collarbone with his lips.

"I don't remember," I said, consumed now with the feel of Noah's hand through the thin fabric of my pants. He slid his hand up behind my knee. My thigh. He tilted his face up to look at me, a wicked smile on his lips.

"Mara, if you're tired, I can hear it. If you're hurt, I can feel it. And if you lie, I will know it."

I closed my eyes, just now beginning to fully realize what Noah's ability meant. Every reaction I had—every reaction I had to *him*—he would know. And not just mine—everyone's.

"I love not having to hide it from you," Noah said, hooking his finger under the collar of my shirt. He pulled the fabric to the side and kissed the bare skin of my shoulder.

I pushed him back slightly so I could see his face. "How do you deal with it?"

He looked confused.

"Hearing and feeling everyone's physical reactions around you constantly. Don't you go crazy?"

If he didn't, I certainly would, knowing that as long as I was near him, I had no secrets.

Noah's eyebrows drew together. "It just becomes background noise, mostly. Until I focus on one person in particular." His finger grazed my knee, and he drew it up the side of my leg, over my hip, and my pulse raced in response.

I smiled. "Stop it," I said, and pushed his hand away. He grinned broadly. "You were saying?"

"I can *hear* everything—everyone—but I can't feel them. Only the four I told you about, and only when they—you—were injured. You were the first one I met, actually, then Joseph. I saw you, where you were, and felt a reflection, I think, of what you both were feeling."

"But there are a lot of injured people out there." I stared at him. "Why us?

"I don't know."

"What are we going to do?"

A smile turned up the corner of Noah's mouth as he traced mine with his thumb. "I can think of a few things."

I grinned. "That won't help me," I said. And as I said it, a wave of déjà vu rolled through me. I saw myself clenching a glass bottle in a dusty shop in Little Havana.

"I'm confused," I said to Mr. Lukumi. "I need help."

"That won't help you," he said, looking at my fist.

But he *had* helped me remember then.

Maybe he could help me now.

I was on my feet in an instant. "We have to go back to the botanica," I said, darting to my dresser.

Noah gave me a sideways glance. "It's well after midnight. There won't be anyone there now." His eyes studied mine. "And anyway, are you even sure you want to go back? That priest wasn't particularly pleasant the first time around."

I remembered Mr. Lukumi's face, the way he seemed to know me, and grew frantic.

"Noah," I said, rounding on him. "He knows. That man—the priest—he knows about me. He *knows*. That's why what he did worked."

Noah raised an eyebrow. "But you said it didn't work."

"I was wrong." My voice sounded strange, and the quiet room swallowed my words. "We have to go back there." Gooseflesh pebbled my arms.

Noah came over to where I stood, pulled me close, and stroked my hair until my breathing slowed, watching my eyes as I calmed down. My arms hung limp at my sides.

"Isn't it possible that you would have remembered that night anyway?" he asked quietly.

I narrowed my eyes at him. "If you have a better idea, let's hear it."

Noah took my hand and laced his fingers in mine. "All right," he said, as he led me back to bed. "You win."

But it felt, somehow, like I had already lost.

53

THE NEXT MORNING, I WOKE UP NEXT TO Noah.

With my arm draped over his waist, I felt his ribs move under the thin fabric of his T-shirt as he breathed. It was the first time I'd ever seen him like this—the first time I could study him unhindered. The swell of his biceps under his sleeve. The few curls of hair that peeked out from the ripped collar of his abused shirt. The necklace he always wore had slipped out during the night. I looked closely at it for the first time; the pendant was just a slim line of silver—half of it hammered into the shape of a feather, the other half a dagger. It was interesting and beautiful, just like him.

My eyes continued to wander over the inhumanly perfect

boy in my bed. One of his hands was clenched in a fist next to his face. A sliver of soft light illuminated the strands of his dark, tousled hair, making them glow gold. I breathed him in, the scent of his skin mingling with my shampoo.

I wanted to kiss him.

I wanted to kiss the small constellation of freckles on his neck, hiding next to his hairline. To feel the sting of his rough jaw under my lips, the petal-soft skin of his eyelids under my fingertips. Then Noah let out a soft sigh.

I was drunk with happiness, intoxicated by him. I felt a stab of pity for Anna and for all the girls who may or may not have come before, and what they lost. And that birthed the follow-up thought of just how much it would hurt me to lose him, too. His presence blunted the edges of my madness, and it was almost enough to make me forget what I'd done.

Almost.

I slid my hand down to Noah's and squeezed it. "Good morning," I whispered.

He stirred. "Mmmm," he murmured, then half-smiled with his eyes closed. "It is."

"We have to go," I said, wishing we didn't, "before my mother finds you in here."

Noah rolled over and leaned on his forearms above me, not touching for one second, two, three. My heart raced, Noah smiled, then slipped out of my bed and out of my room. We met up in the kitchen, once I was dressed and brushed and generally presentable. Sandwiched between Daniel and Joseph, Noah grinned at me over a cup of coffee.

"Mara!" My mother's eyes went wide when she saw me standing, and dressed, in the kitchen. She quickly composed herself. "Can I get you anything?"

Noah gave me a surreptitious nod of his head.

"Um, sure," I said. "How about" —my eyes scanned the kitchen counter— "a bagel?"

My mother grinned and took one from the plate, popping it into the toaster. I sat down at the table across from the three boys. Everyone seemed to be pretending I hadn't sequestered myself in my bedroom for the past few days, and that was fine with me.

"So, school today?" my mother asked.

Noah nodded. "I thought I'd drive Mara," he said to Daniel. "If that's all right."

My eyebrows knit together, but Noah shot me a look. Under the table, his hand found mine. I stayed quiet.

Daniel stood and smiled, walking over to the sink with his bowl. "Fine with me. This way, I won't be late."

I rolled my eyes. My mother slid a plate over to me, and I ate quietly next to her and Joseph and Noah, who were talking about going to the zoo this weekend. Their bright moods were palpable in the kitchen that morning, and I felt love and guilt swell in my chest. The love was obvious. The guilt was for what I'd put them through. What I might still put them through, if I didn't figure out my problem. But I pushed that thought away, kissed my mother on the cheek, and made my way to the front door.

"Ready?" Noah asked.

I nodded, even though I wasn't.

"Where are we really going?" I asked as Noah drove, knowing full well that it couldn't be school. It wasn't safe there for me. Because I wasn't safe around anyone else.

"1821 Calle Ocho," Noah said. "You wanted to go back to the botanica, didn't you?"

"Daniel's going to notice we're not in school."

Noah shrugged. "I'll tell him you needed a day off. He won't say anything."

I hoped Noah was right.

Little Havana had somehow become our familiar haunt, but nothing about it was familiar today. Crowds of people surged through the streets, waving flags in time to the drumbeat of the music blaring from an unidentified source. Calle Ocho was closed to traffic, so we had to walk.

"What is this?"

Noah's sunglasses were on, and he scanned the colorfully dressed multitudes. "A festival," he said.

I glared at him.

"Come on, we'll try to push through."

We did try, but it was slow going. The sun beat down on us

as we cut a precarious path through the people. Mothers holding the hands of children with painted faces, men shouting over the music to one another. The sidewalks were crowded with tables, so customers could watch the festivities as they ate. A group of guys leaned against the wall of the cigar shop, smoking and laughing, and the domino park was filled with onlookers. I scanned the storefronts for the odd assortment of electronics and Santeria statutes in the window but didn't see it.

"Stop," Noah called out over the music. He was four or five feet behind me.

"What?" I walked back to where he stood, and on the way, bumped into someone, hard. Someone in a navy baseball cap. I froze.

He turned around and looked up from under the brim. *"Perdon,"* he said, before walking away.

I took a deep breath. Just a man in a hat. I was too jumpy. I made my way over to where Noah stood.

Noah took off his sunglasses as he faced the storefront. His face was expressionless, completely impassive. "Look at the address."

My eyes roamed over the stenciled numbers above the glass door of the toy store. "1823," I said, then took a few steps in the other direction, to the next one. My voice caught in my throat as I read the address. "1819." Where was 1821?

Noah's face was stone, but his eyes betrayed him. He was shaken.

"Maybe it's on the other side of the street,"I said, not believing it myself. Noah said nothing. My eyes roamed the length of the building, inspecting it. I made my way back to the toy store and pressed my nose up to the cloudy glass, peering in. Large stuffed animals sat in a duck-duck-goose arrangement on the floor, and marionette puppets were frozen mid-dance in the window, congregating around a ventriloquist dummy. I stepped back. The shop had the same narrow shape as the botanica, but then, so did the stores on either side of it.

"Maybe we should ask someone," I said, growing desperate. My heart raced as my eyes scanned the shops, looking for anyone to ask.

Noah stood facing the storefront. "I don't think it would matter," he said, his voice hollow. "I think we're on our own."

54

MY SENSE OF DREAD INCREASED EXPONENTIALLY as we drove down the dark, palm-tree lined driveway to the zoo.

"This is a bad idea," I said to Noah. We had talked about it on the ride back from Little Havana, after I called my mother and told her we were going to hang out at Noah's after school—which we didn't go to—for a change of scenery. Since there was no way to track down Mr. Lukumi, if that was even his real name, and no one else we could go to for help unless we both wanted to be committed, we had to figure out what to do next. I was, of course, the top priority; I had to figure out what prompted my reactions if I was going to have any hope at all of learning to control them. We agreed that this was the best way, the easiest way to experiment. But I was still afraid.

"Just trust me. I'm right about this."

"Pride goes before the fall," I said, a small smile on my lips. Then, "Why can't we test you first, again?"

"I want to see if I can counteract you. I think that's important. Maybe it's why we found each other. You know?"

"Not really," I said to the window. My hair clung in sweaty tendrils to the back of my neck. I twisted it into a knot to get it off my skin.

"Now you're just being contrary."

"Says the person with the useful . . . thing." It felt weird to name it, name what we could do. Inappropriate. It didn't do the reality justice.

"I think there's more you can do, Mara."

"Maybe," I said, but doubting it. "I wish I had your thing, though."

"I wish you did, too." Then after a pause, "Healing's for girls."

"You're awful," I said, and shook my head. An obnoxious grin curved Noah's mouth. "It's not funny," I said, but smiled anyway. I was still anxious, but it was incredible how much better I felt with Noah there, with him knowing. Like I could deal with this. Like we could deal with it together.

Noah parked at the curb of the zoo. I didn't know how he managed to get us after-hours access, and didn't ask. An outcropping of sculpted rocks greeted us as we walked in, towering over a manufactured pond. Sleeping pelicans dotted the water, their heads tucked under wings. On the opposite side, flamingoes, pale pink in the halogen auxiliary lights, stood in clumps on the opposite side of the walk. The birds were silent sentries, failing to notice or comment on our presence.

We wound deeper into the park, hand in hand as a hot breeze ruffled the foliage and our hair. Past the gazelles and antelopes, which stirred as we approached. Hooves stamped the ground, and a low nickering swept through the herd. We increased our pace.

Something rustled in the branches above us but I couldn't see anything in the dark. I read the exhibit sign: white gibbons to the right, chimpanzees to the left. As soon as I finished reading, a shrill scream pierced the air and something crashed through the brush toward us. My feet and my heart froze.

The chimpanzee stopped short right at the moat. And not one of the cute, tan-faced charmers usually conscripted into the entertainment industry; this one was enormous. It sat, tense and coiled at the precipice. It stared at me with human eyes that followed us as we started walking again. The hair stood up on the back of my neck.

Noah turned into a small niche and withdrew a set of keys from his pocket as we approached a small structure disguised by large plants and trees. The door read EMPLOYEES ONLY.

"What are we doing?"

"It's a work room. They're preparing for an exhibit on insects of the world or something," Noah said as he opened the door.

I hated the idea of killing anything, but at least bugs reproduced like—well, like roaches—and no one would miss a few.

"How'd you work this out?" I asked, looking behind us. My skin prickled. I couldn't shake the feeling that we were being watched.

"My mother's done some volunteer work here. And gives them an obscene amount of money."

Noah flipped on the lights, illuminating the long metal table in the center, and closed the door behind us. Metal shelves lined the walls, holding bins and plastic tubs. Noah walked around, his eyes scanning their small labels. I was rooted to the doorway, and couldn't read them from where I stood.

Finally, Noah held up a translucent plastic box. My eyes narrowed at him.

"What are those?"

"Leeches," he said casually. He avoided my stare.

A wave of disgust rolled through me. "No. No way."

"You have to."

I shuddered. "Pick something else," I said, and rushed to the far side of the room. "Here." I pointed at an opaque tub with a label I couldn't pronounce. "Somethingsomething scorpions."

"Those are poisonous," Noah said, studying my face.

"Even better."

"They're also endangered."

"Fine," I said, my voice and legs beginning to tremble as I walked over to a transparent box and pointed. "The big-ass spider."

Noah walked over and read the label, still holding the box of leeches close. Way too close. I backed away. "Also poisonous," Noah said evenly.

"Then that will be plenty of incentive."

"It could bite before you kill it."

My heart wanted to escape from my throat. "A perfect opportunity to practice your healing," I choked out.

Noah shook his head. "I'm not going to experiment with your life. No."

"Then pick something else," I said, growing breathless with terror. "Not the leeches."

Noah rubbed his forehead. "They're harmless, Mara."

"I don't care!" I heard the insects in the room beat their chitinous wings against their plastic prisons. I began to lose it and felt myself sway on my feet.

"If it doesn't work, I'll take it off immediately," Noah said. "It won't hurt you."

"No. I'm serious, Noah," I said. "I can't do it. They burrow under skin and suck blood. Oh my God. Oh my God." I wrapped my arms around my body to stop it from shaking.

"It will be over quickly, I promise," he said. "You won't

feel anything." He reached his hand into the tank.

"No." I could only croak this in a hoarse whisper. I couldn't breathe. Multicolored spots appeared behind my eyelids that I couldn't blink away.

Noah scooped up a leech in his hand and I felt myself sink. Then . . .

Nothing.

"Mara."

My eyes fluttered open.

"It's dead. Unbelievable," he said. "You did it."

Noah walked over with his palm open to show me, but I recoiled, scrambled up against the door. He looked at me with an unreadable expression, then went to discard the dead leech. When he lifted the bin to replace it back on the shelf, he stopped.

"My God," he said.

"What?" My voice was still nothing but a shaky whisper.

"They're all dead."

"The leeches?"

Noah put the bin back on the shelf with an unsteady hand. He walked among the rows of insects, eyes scanning the transparent tubs and opening the others to inspect them.

When he reached the spot he started in, he stared at the wall.

"Everything," he said. "Everything's dead."

55

THE STENCH OF ROT FILLED MY NOSTRILS, AND a voice buzzed in my ear.

"Biologists are reporting that the fish kill in Everglades City was most likely due to oxygen depletion in the water."

Images of bloated, belly-up alligators appeared in my dark consciousness.

"A startling number of alligator corpses are thought to be the culprit."

I had done that. Just like I'd done this.

Noah surveyed the destruction with empty eyes. He couldn't look at me. I couldn't blame him. I wrestled with the doorknob and bolted into the darkness. An assault of screeches and howls and barks met my ears. At least the slaughter was limited.

I was disgusted by myself. And when Noah followed me outside, I saw that he was too.

He avoided my eyes and said nothing. The sight of his hands curled into fists, of his revulsion, stung my heart and made me cry. Pathetic. But once I started, I couldn't stop and didn't really want to. The sobs scorched my throat, but it was a good kind of pain. Deserved.

Noah was still silent. Only when I dropped to the ground, unable to stand for a second longer, did he move. He grabbed my hand and pulled me up, but my legs trembled. I couldn't move. I couldn't breathe. Noah wrapped his arms around me but as soon as he did, I just wanted them off. I wanted to run.

I struggled against his grip, my thin shoulder blades digging into his chest.

"Let me go."

"No."

"Please," I choked.

He loosened his grip by a fraction. "Only if you promise not to run."

I was out of control, and Noah knew it. Afraid I'd do even more damage, he had to make sure I didn't ruin anything else.

"I promise," I whispered.

He turned me to face him, then set me free. I couldn't bring myself to look at him, so I focused on the pattern of his plaid shirt, then at the ground.

"Let's go."

We walked wordlessly amid the snarls and shrieks. The animals were all awake, now; the antelope had herded together at the edge of their exhibit, stamping and shifting in fear. The birds flapped, frantic, and one pelican dove straight into an outcropping of rock as we approached it. It fell to the water and emerged, dragging its broken, limp wing beside it. I wanted to die.

The second we reached Noah's car, I lunged for the handle. It was locked.

"Open it," I said, still not meeting his gaze.

"Mara—"

"Open it."

"Look at me first."

"I can't handle that right now," I said through clenched teeth. "Just open the door."

He did. I folded myself into the passenger seat.

"Take me home, please."

"Mara—"

"Please!"

He started the car and we drove in silence. I stared at my lap the whole way but as we slowed down, I finally looked out the window. The scenery was familiar, but wrong. When we passed the gated entrance to his house, I shot him a steely glare.

"What are we doing here?"

He didn't answer, and I understood. Since my confession, Noah had only been humoring me. He said he believed me, and maybe he did really believe that there was something off, something wrong with me. But he didn't get it. He thought I'd been dreaming when I kissed him and he almost died. That Rachel, Claire, and Jude were killed when an old, decrepit building collapsed on them. That Mabel's owner could have fallen and cracked his skull open, Ms. Morales could have died of shock, and the whole thing might just add up to a series of terrible coincidences.

But he couldn't think that now. Not after tonight, after what I'd just done. That could not be explained away. That was real. And now, Noah was ending it, and I was glad.

I would figure out the next step by myself.

He parked the car in the garage and opened the passenger door. I didn't move.

"Mara, get out of the car."

"Can you do it here? I want to go home."

I needed to think, now that I was completely and utterly alone in this. I couldn't live this way, and I needed to make a plan.

"Just—please."

I got out of his car but hesitated by the door. The dogs sensed something wrong with me the last time I was here, and they were right. I didn't want to be anywhere near them.

"What about Mabel and Ruby?"

"They're crated. On the other side of the house."

I exhaled and followed behind Noah as he entered a corridor and climbed a narrow staircase. He reached to take my hand but I flinched at his touch. Feeling him would only make this harder for me. Noah kicked the door open and I found myself in his room. He turned to face me. His expression was quietly furious. "I'm sorry," he said.

This was it. I had lost him, but was surprised to find that instead of anguish, or misery, I just felt numb.

"It's okay."

"I don't know what to say."

My voice was cold, removed when I spoke. "There's nothing *to* say."

"Just look at me, Mara."

I raised my eyes to his. They were savage. I would have been afraid if I didn't know better. The scariest thing in the room was me.

"I'm so, infinitely, forever sorry," he said. His voice was empty, and my chest constricted. He shouldn't feel guilty about this. I didn't blame him. I shook my head.

"No, don't shake your head," he said. "I fucked up. Egregiously."

The word escaped from my throat before I could stop it. "What?"

"I never should have let it get that far."

My expression morphed into shock. "Noah, you didn't do anything."

"Are you joking? I tortured you. I *tortured* you." There was a quiet rage in his voice. His muscles were tense and coiled; he looked like he wanted to smash something. I knew the feeling.

"You did what had to be done."

His voice was laced with contempt. "I didn't believe you."

I had known that.

"Just tell me this," I said. "Were you lying about what you could do?"

"No."

"So you *elected* not to do anything?"

Noah's expression was hard. "It was too fast. The—sound—or whatever, was different from the last time with Morales."

"Morales?" I said dully. "You heard that?"

"I heard—something. You. You sounded *wrong*. But I didn't know why or what it was or what it meant. And with Anna and Aiden, when Jamie got expelled, you were off, too, but I didn't know what was happening. I didn't understand it; only that he threatened you, and I wanted to break him for it. This time, tonight, wasn't the same, and I don't think the alligators were either."

My mouth went dry as Noah confirmed what I'd done. He ran both of his hands over his face and back through his hair.

"There was too much going on—too much noise of everything else in the marsh. I didn't know if they'd just disappeared, but I—I had a feeling something had happened." He paused, and his face went still. "I'm sorry," he said flatly.

I felt sick listening to him—my throat closed and I couldn't breathe. I needed to get out of there. I made for Noah's door.

"Don't," Noah said, crossing the room. He reached for me but I shied away. He took my hand anyway and walked me over to his bed. I acquiesced, knowing that this would be our last conversation. And as much as that hurt me, even though I knew it was necessary, I found myself unable to break away just yet. So we sat side-by-side, but I pulled my hand from his. Noah turned away.

"I thought—I thought maybe you were just seeing what was about to happen; that you were seeing things sort of like me. I thought you just felt guilty about Rachel."

Just what my mother would say.

"I didn't get it, and I pushed you, and then I pushed you further."

He looked at me from underneath those lashes and his stare pierced the cavity where my heart used to be. He was furious with *himself*, not me. It was so wrong, so backward.

"It wasn't your fault, Noah." He started to speak, but I placed my fingers over his beautiful, perfect mouth, aching at the contact. "This was your first time seeing it. But it wasn't *my* first time doing it. If I don't—" I caught myself before I told him what I thought I had to do. What I *did* have to do. "I can't handle seeing the look on your face the next time it happens, okay?"

Noah glared at me. "It was because of *me*, Mara, because of what I made you do.

"You didn't make me kill every living thing in that room. I did that all by myself."

"Not everything in that room."

"What?"

"You didn't kill everything in that room."

"With the exception of us, I did."

Noah laughed without amusement. "That's it. You could have killed me. I tormented you, and you could have ended it by ending *me*. But you didn't," he said, and brushed my hair away from my face.

"You're stronger than you know."

His hand lingered on my cheek and I closed my eyes in anguish.

"I know we don't know how or why this is happening to you—to us," he said. "But we *will* figure it out."

I opened my eyes and stared at him. "It's not your responsibility."

"I fucking *know* it's not my responsibility. I want to help you."

I inhaled sharply. "What about tomorrow? Someone's going to wonder what killed hundreds of endangered species."

"Don't worry, I'll—"

"Fix it? You'll fix it, Noah?"

As I spoke the words, I knew that that was exactly what he thought. That despite all rationality, he did think he could fix me, like he could fix everything else.

"Is that how you see this working? I'll screw up and you'll take care of it, right?" I was just another problem that could be solved if only we threw enough time or practice or money at it.

At me. And when the experiment failed—when *I* failed—and people died, Noah would blame *himself*, hate *himself* for not being able to stop it. For not being able to stop me. I wouldn't do that to him. So I said the only thing I could.

"I don't want your help. I don't want you." The words felt mutinous on my tongue. And they hit him like a slap in the face.

"You're lying," Noah said, his voice low and quiet.

Mine was cold and distant. "I think it would be better if I didn't see you again." I didn't know where the strength to say such a thing came from, but I was grateful for it.

"Why are you doing this?" Noah said, piercing me with an icy stare.

I began to lose my composure. "You're really asking me that question? I murdered five people."

"By accident."

"I wanted it."

"God, Mara. You think you're the only person to want bad things to happen to bad people?"

"No, but I am the only person who gets what she wants," I said. "And Rachel, by the way, wasn't a bad person. I loved her, and she did nothing to me, and she's dead anyway and it's my fault."

"Maybe."

I whipped around. "What? What did you just say?"

"You still don't know if the asylum was an accident."

"Are we back there again? Really?"

"Listen to me. Even if it wasn't—"

"It wasn't," I said through clenched teeth.

"Even if it wasn't an accident," Noah continued, "I can warn you the next time you get close."

My voice went low. "Just like you warned me before I killed Morales."

"That's not fair, and you know it. I didn't know what was happening then. I do now. I'll warn you the next time it happens, and you'll stop."

"You mean, you'll make me stop."

"No. It's *your* choice. It's always your choice. But maybe if you lose your focus, I can help bring you back."

"And what if something happens and you're not there?" I asked.

"I'll be there."

"But what if you're not?"

"Then it would be my fault."

"Exactly."

His expression went carefully blank.

"I want a boyfriend, not a babysitter, Noah. But let's say I agree to this plan, and you're there but can't stop me. You'll blame yourself. You want that on my conscience too? Stop being so selfish."

Noah's jaw tensed. "No."

"All right. Don't. But I'm leaving."

I stood to leave but felt Noah's fingers on my thighs. The pressure of his grasp was feather-light on my jeans, but I was frozen.

"I'll follow you," he said.

I looked down at him, at his hand-stirred hair above his grave face; his lids were half-closed and heavy. Sitting on his bed, he was level with my waist. A thrill traveled along the length of my spine.

"Get off," I said, without conviction.

The ghost of a smile touched his mouth. "You first."

I blinked and stared at him carefully. "Well. Isn't this a dangerous game."

"I'm not playing."

My nostrils flared. Noah was provoking me. On purpose, to see what I'd do. I wanted at once to smack him, and to rake my fingers through his hair and pull.

"I won't let you do this," I said.

"You won't stop me." His voice was low, now. Indescribably sexy.

My eyes fluttered closed. "Like hell I won't," I whispered. "I could kill you."

"Then I'd die happy."

"Not funny."

"Not joking."

I opened my eyes and focused on his. "I'd be happier without you," I lied as convincingly as I could.

"Too bad." Noah's mouth curved into the half-smile I loved and hated so much, just inches from my navel.

My head was foggy. "You're supposed to say, 'All I want is

your happiness. I'll do whatever it takes, even if it means being without you.'"

"Sorry," Noah said. "I'm just not that big of a person." His hands traveled up the side of my jeans, up to my waist. The pads of his fingertips grazed the skin just underneath the fabric of my shirt. I tried to steady my pulse and failed.

"You want me," Noah said simply, definitively. "Don't lie to me. I can hear it."

"Irrelevant," I breathed.

"No, it isn't irrelevant. You want me as much as I want you. And *all* I want is you."

My tongue warred with my mind. "Today," I whispered.

Noah stood slowly, his body skimming mine as he rose. "Today. Tonight. Tomorrow. Forever." Noah's eyes held mine. His stare was infinite. "I was made for you, Mara."

And at that moment, even though I didn't know how it was possible or what it meant, I believed him.

"And you know it. So tell the truth. Do you want me?" His voice was strong, confident as he voiced the question that sounded more like a statement.

But his face. In the slightest crease and furrow of his brow, barely perceptible, it was there. Doubt.

Did he really not know? As I tried to comprehend the impossibility of that idea, Noah's confidence began to fray at the edge of his expression.

Right would have been allowing his question to go unanswered. Letting Noah believe, impossible though it was, that I didn't want him. That I didn't love him. Then this would all be over. Noah would be the best thing that almost happened to me, but he would be safe.

I chose wrong.

56

I WRAPPED MY ARMS AROUND NOAH'S NECK AND buried myself in him.

"Yes," I whispered into his hair as he held me.

"What's that?" I could hear the smile in his voice.

"I want you," I said, smiling back.

"Then who cares about anything else?"

Noah's hands on my waist, on my face, felt so familiar, like they belonged there. Like they were home. I pulled back to look at him and see if he felt it, but when I did, I shattered into a million pieces.

Noah believed in me. I didn't understand until then, right then, how much I needed to see it.

I shivered at the lovely scrape of his jaw on my skin. His

lips skimmed my collarbone and when he shifted his hips into mine, I became senseless. I knotted my fingers in his warm hair and crashed my mouth into his. When I tasted his tongue, the world fell away.

But then the bitter air of the asylum stung my nostrils. Jude's face flickered behind my eyelids and I pulled away, gasping.

"Mara, what's wrong?"

I didn't answer him. I didn't know how. We'd come so close to kissing a thousand times before, but something almost always stopped us—myself, Noah, the universe. Before now, the only time we'd succeeded, I was sure, positive that he almost died. My heart rebelled at the idea, even though I knew I was right. What was happening to me? To him, when we kissed?

"What is it?" he asked.

I needed to say something, but that's not the kind of thing you can just bust out with.

"I'm—I don't want you to die," I stammered.

Noah looked appropriately confused. "All right," he said, and pushed back my hair. "I won't die."

I looked at the floor, but Noah ducked his head and caught my eyes. "Listen, Mara. There's no pressure." His hands brushed down my face. "This," he said, as they trailed down my neck. "You." My arms. "Are enough." He laced his fingers into mine and held my stare. I knew he meant it.

"Just knowing you're mine." He released my hand and lifted his to my face, glancing his fingers over my lips. "Knowing that no one else gets to touch you like this," he said. "Seeing the way you look at me when I do. And hearing the way you sound when I do.

A slight, uneven smile played on his lips. Just looking at them was not enough.

Seized by boldness and frustration, I grasped Noah's hand and pulled him to his bed. I pushed him until he was sitting and climbed into his lap, ignoring his raised eyebrows as I straddled him. My hands furiously worked the buttons on his plaid shirt but fumbled. My dexterity had vanished along with my decorum.

Noah placed one of his fingers under my chin and tilted my head. "What are you doing?"

"We can do other things," I breathed, as I slipped his shirt off his shoulders. I wasn't completely sure if that was true but I was completely sure that at that moment, I didn't care. I was desperate to feel his skin against mine. I was desperate to try. I gripped the hem of my T-shirt and started to pull it up.

Noah reached down and clasped my wrists gently. "You want to sleep with me, but you won't kiss me?"

Well, yeah. I opened my mouth to speak, then closed it, because I thought that might not fly.

Noah lifted me off of his lap. "No," he said, and shrugged his shirt back on.

"No?" I asked.

"No."

I narrowed my eyes at him. "Why not? You've done it before."

Noah looked away. "For fun."

"I can be fun," I said quietly.

"I know." Noah's expression leveled me.

"You don't trust me," I said quietly.

Noah measured his words before he spoke. "You don't trust yourself, Mara. I am not going to die if you kiss me; I told you that already. But you still think I'm going to. So, no."

"You're kidding me," I said, incredulous. Noah, Noah *Shaw*, was slamming on the brakes.

"Does this look like my kidding face?" Noah composed his expression into one of mock seriousness.

I ignored it and stood up. "You don't want me."

Noah threw his head back and laughed, rich and loose. A blush crept up into my cheeks. I wanted to punch him in the throat.

"You have no *idea* what you do to me," he said as he stood. "I could barely keep my hands off you last night, even after seeing what you'd been through this week. Even after knowing how wrecked you were when you told me. And I'm going to spend an eternity in hell for that dream I had about you on your birthday. But if I could call it up again, I'd spend it twice."

He took my hand and turned it over in his, studying it. "Mara, I have never felt about anyone the way I feel about you.

And when you're ready for me to show you," he said, brushing my hair to the side, "I'm going to kiss you." His thumb grazed my ear and his hand curved around my neck. He leaned me backward and my eyes fluttered closed. I breathed in the scent of him as he leaned in and kissed the hollow under my ear. My pulse raced under his lips.

"And I won't settle for anything less."

Noah pulled away and drew me up with him. I was disoriented, but not enough to ignore the cocky grin he was wearing.

"I hate you," I muttered.

Noah smiled wider. "I know."

57

I COULDN'T GO TO SCHOOL THE NEXT DAY, EITHER—that much was obvious. Who knew what triggered the deaths—was a stray thought enough? Or did I have to envision it? And what about the animals that died, even though I never explicitly wanted them to? What about Rachel?

I needed to rebuild my world and figure out my place in it before I would be safe around the general population. I told my mother that I wanted to stay home, that going back to school yesterday was a little too much for me and I wanted to wait until after my appointment with Dr. Maillard today to try it again. Given my recent behavior, she was happy to oblige.

I made it to lunch without incident. But as I stood in the

kitchen midway through making myself a sandwich, someone started pounding on the front door.

I froze. They didn't go away.

I crept soundlessly to the foyer and looked through the peephole. I let out a sigh of relief. Noah stood on my front step, disheveled and furious.

"Get in the car," he said. "There's something you need to see."

"What? What are you—"

"It's about your father's case. We need to make it to the courthouse before the trial's over. I'll explain, but come."

My mind raced to catch up but I followed Noah without hesitating, locking the door behind me. He didn't stand on ceremony and I flung open the passenger door and dove in. Noah backed out of the driveway in seconds, then reached into the backseat and withdrew a newspaper. He dropped *The Miami Herald* in my lap as he wove between lanes, ignoring the irritated honking that followed.

I read the headline: CRIME SCENE PHOTOS LEAKED ON FINAL DAY OF PALMER TRIAL. I scanned the photos; a few of the crime scene and one of Leon Lassiter, my father's client. Then I skimmed the article. It gave a detailed overview of the case, but I was missing something.

"I don't understand," I said, focusing on Noah's clenched jaw and angry stare.

"Did you look at the photos? Carefully?"

My eyes roamed the pictures, disturbing though they were.

Two of them showed Jordana Palmer's dismembered body lying piecemeal in the tall grass, with chunks of flesh ripped from her calves, her arms, her torso. The third was a landscape, taken from the distance, with markers showing the position and location where the body was found. The little concrete shed where Noah and I had found Joseph was cast in a penumbral shadow by the flash.

My hand fluttered to my mouth. "Oh my God."

"I saw it when I went to go buy cigarettes during lunch. I tried to call but there was no answer at the house, and of course you still don't have a mobile. So I drove straight here from school," he said in a rush. "It's the same shed, Mara. Exactly the same."

I remembered Joseph, lying on the concrete floor in a nest of blankets, his hands and feet bound by twist ties. And how Noah and I were almost too late to save him.

To save him from ending up exactly like Jordana. My stomach rolled with nausea.

"What does this mean?" I asked, even though I already knew.

Noah ran his hands through his hair as he sped, pushing ninety-five. "I don't know. The photograph they have of Lassiter shows him wearing a Rolex on his right hand. When I saw the documents in the Collier County archives in my mind, whoever was pulling files had the same watch," he finished, before swallowing. "But I'm not sure."

"He took Joseph," I said, my voice and mind hazy.

Noah's expression was hard. "It doesn't make sense, though. Why would he go after his own lawyer's child?"

My mind flooded with images. Joseph, the way he must have looked when he was waiting for a ride home from school the day he was taken. My parents, as they spoke in tense voices about my father dropping the case. My father speaking to Lassiter—

That same night.

"My father was going to drop his case," I said, strangely removed. "Because of me. Because I was falling apart. He spoke to him that afternoon."

"Still doesn't make sense. Your father would have dropped it for sure if one of his children disappeared. The judge absolutely would have ordered a continuance."

"Then he took him because he's sick," I said, my voice a twisted hiss. My mind raced, tumbling ahead before my mouth could catch up. I flashed back to before I knew about the case, before this had all happened. To my brother watching the news one afternoon, as Daniel lifted an unmarked envelope.

"Where did this come from?" Daniel asked.

"Dad's new client dropped it off, like, two seconds before you got here."

Lassiter knew Joseph. Knew where we lived.

"I'll kill him." I spoke the shocking words so softly I wasn't even sure I'd said them aloud. I wasn't even sure I'd thought them, until Noah's eyes turned on me.

"No," he said carefully. "We're going to go to the courthouse and find your father and have the trial continued. We'll tell him what happened. He'll withdraw from the case."

"It's too late," I said. The words congealed on my tongue, and the weight of them pulled me down. "The trial's over today. Once the jury's out—it's over."

Noah shook his head. "I called. They're not out yet. We can make it," he said, his gaze flicking to the clock on the dashboard.

I turned the paper over in my hand, examining it as my dark thoughts grew and spread and swallowed up any possible alternative.

"Whoever leaked these photos did it to influence the jury. They did it because my father—because Lassiter—is winning. He's going to be acquitted. He's going to be free."

I couldn't let it happen.

But would I really be able to stop it?

I had wanted Jude dead, and he was. And I'd killed Morales and Mabel's owner just by wanting it, thinking about it, about her choking, his head smashed in. I grew nauseous at the imagery, but swallowed hard and forced myself to remember, to try to understand so that if I needed to, I could do it again. The collapsed building, the anaphylactic shock, the head injury; those were the causes of the deaths.

I was the agent.

Noah's voice snapped me back into the moment. "There is

something profoundly wrong here. I know it, which is why I came to get you. But we don't have a fucking *clue* what's going on. We have to get to the courthouse and speak to your father."

"Then what?" I asked, my voice hollow.

"Then we'll give statements about Joseph's kidnapping, and Lassiter will be indicted for it."

"And he'll be out on bail again, just like this time. And what evidence can we give?" I said, my voice rising. I hadn't meant to say—to think—my earlier words, but a crazed enthusiasm was taking over. Adrenaline flowed through my veins. "Joseph doesn't remember a thing except for the lies we told him. And I'm on antipsychotics," I said, my voice growing steadier and steadier. "No one's going to believe us."

Noah switched tactics, no doubt because I was right. In a low voice, he said, "I brought you because I trusted you. You don't want to do this."

As Noah asserted his knowledge of what I wanted, my mind rebelled. "Why not? I've killed people for less than murdering and butchering a teenage girl and kidnapping my baby brother." I grew incomprehensibly giddy.

"And last week—that was you at peace with it, then?"

Noah's words stopped me in my tracks. But then. "Maybe I'm a sociopath, but I don't feel sorry about Mabel's owner. At all."

"I wouldn't either," Noah admitted. The muscles worked in his jaw. "Jude deserved it, too, you know."

I tilted my head at him. "Did he? You say that because he almost hurt me—"

"He did hurt you," Noah said, suddenly fierce. "Just because it could have been worse doesn't mean he didn't hurt you."

"He didn't rape me, Noah. He hit me. He kissed me. I killed him for that."

Noah's eyes darkened. "Good riddance."

I shook my head. "You think that's fair?" Noah said nothing, his eyes a thousand miles away. "Well, the way you feel about him is the way I feel about Lassiter."

"No," he said, as he turned off the highway on to a bustling street. I could see the courthouse in the distance. "There's a difference. With Jude, you were alone and terrified and your mind reacted without you even knowing it. With him it was self-defense. With Lassiter—it would be an execution."

The air swallowed his words as he let that sink in. Then he said, "There are other ways to solve that problem, Mara."

Noah swung into the shaded parking lot next to the courthouse and cut the engine. We flew out of the car, my mind turning over his words as we ran up the courthouse steps.

There were other ways to solve the problem, Noah had said. But I knew they wouldn't work.

58

I WAS BREATHLESS BY THE TIME WE REACHED THE wide glass front doors. After Noah went through the metal detector, I emptied my pockets into the little plastic bin and held out my arms so the security guard could wand me. I bounced a little on the balls of my feet, beyond anxious.

Our footsteps echoed down the enormous hall, mine following Noah's, and I swung my head in both directions, checking the room numbers as I went. Noah stopped at room 213.

I wiped the sweat from my face with my sleeve. "Now what?"

Noah walked over to a hallway and made the first left. I

hovered in the background as he spoke to a young guy sitting at the front desk. I couldn't hear what he was saying, but I examined his face. It told me nothing.

When he was done, he returned to my side and began walking in the direction we came in. He didn't say a word until we were outside, back on the courthouse steps.

"What happened?" I asked him.

"The jury's been out for two hours."

My feet turned to stone. I couldn't move.

"It's not too late," Noah said, his voice quiet. "They may come back with a conviction. Hell, Florida's a death penalty state. You might get lucky."

I bristled at Noah's tone. "He went after my brother, Noah. My family."

Noah placed his hands on my shoulders and forced me to look at him. "I will protect him," Noah said. I tried to turn away. "Look at me, Mara. I will find a way."

I wanted to believe him. His confidence was unshakable, and it was tempting. But Noah was always sure. And he was sometimes wrong. In this case, I couldn't afford it.

"You can't protect him, Noah. This is not something you can fix."

Noah opened his mouth to speak but I cut him off. "I've been so *lost* since Rachel died. I've tried to do the right things. With Mabel, Morales—I did everything the right way; calling Animal Control, telling the principal. But nothing worked until I did it *my* way," I said, and my own words sparked something inside of me. "Because everything that's happened—it's been about me from the beginning. Understanding who I am and what I'm supposed to do. *This* is what I'm supposed to do. It's what I have to do."

Noah looked down, directly into my eyes. "No, Mara. I want to know why this is happening to us, too. But this isn't going to help."

I looked at Noah, incredulous. "It doesn't matter for you, can't you see that? So you get headaches and you see hurt people. What happens if you never figure it out? Nothing," I said, and my voice cracked.

Noah's eyes went flat. "Do you know what it means that we were able to help Joseph?"

I didn't speak.

"It means the two others I saw were real. It means I didn't help them and they died."

I swallowed and tried to compose myself. "It's not the same thing."

"No? Why not?"

"Because now you know. Now you have a choice. I don't. Unless I can channel it—use it, maybe, for a purpose—things will keep getting worse. I make everything worse." A tear rolled down my burning cheek. I closed my eyes, and felt Noah's fingers on my skin.

"You make *me* better."

My chest cracked open at his words. I stared into Noah's perfect face and tried to see what he saw. I tried to see us—not individually, not the arrogant, beautiful, reckless lost boy and the angry, broken girl—but what we were, who we were, together. I tried to remember holding his hand at my kitchen table and feeling for the first time since I'd left Rhode Island that I wasn't alone in this. That I belonged.

Noah spoke again, cutting my thoughts short. "After you remembered, I saw what it did to you. It won't compare to knowing you did it on purpose." Noah closed his eyes and when he opened them, his expression was haunted. "You're the only one who knows, Mara. The only person who knows me. I don't want to lose you."

"Maybe you won't," I said, but I was already gone. And when I looked at him, I saw that he knew it.

He reached for me anyway, one hand curving behind my neck, the other skimming my face.

He would kiss me, right now, after everything I'd done. I was poison, and Noah was the drug that would make me forget it.

So of course I couldn't let him.

He saw it in my eyes, or maybe heard it in my heart, and dropped his hands from my body as he shifted back. "I thought you only wanted to be normal."

I looked at the marble steps beneath my feet. "I was wrong," I said, trying not to let my voice crack. "I have to be more than that. For Joseph." And for Rachel. And for Noah, too, though I didn't say it. Couldn't say it.

"If you do this," he said slowly, "you'll become someone else."

I looked up at Noah. "I already am someone else."

And when he met my eyes, I knew that he saw it.

In seconds, he broke our stare and shook his head. "No," he said to himself, then, "No, you're not. You're the girl who called me an asshole the first time we spoke. The girl who tried to pay for lunch even after you learned I had more money than God. You're the girl who risked her ass to save a dying dog, who makes my chest ache whether you're wearing green silk or ripped jeans. You're the girl that I—" Noah stopped, then took a step closer to me. "You are *my* girl," he said simply, because it was true. "But if you do this, you'll be someone else."

I struggled for air as my heart broke, knowing that it wouldn't change what I had to do.

"I know you, Mara. I know everything. And I don't care."

I wanted to cry when he said it out loud. I wished that I could. But there were no tears. My voice was unexpectedly hard when I spoke.

"Maybe not today. But you will."

Noah held my hand. The simplicity of the gesture moved me so much that I started to doubt.

"No," Noah said. "You made me real, and I will hurt for you and because of you and be grateful for the pain. But this? This is forever. Don't do this."

I sat down on the steps, my legs too shaky to keep me upright. "If he's found guilty, I won't."

"But if he's acquitted—"

"I have to," I said, my voice breaking. If he went free, he might go after my brother again. And I was the agent. I could stop it. I was the only one who could.

"I don't have a choice."

Noah sat down next to me, his expression grim. "You always have a choice."

We said nothing for what seemed like hours. I sat on the unforgiving stone and the unnatural coolness of it penetrated my jeans. I turned the night of the collapse over and over again in my mind, until the thoughts and images whirled like a cyclone.

Like a cyclone. Rachel and Claire were caught up in my fury, which was too explosive, too wild to have any focus.

But that was not the case today.

When the doors clicked open behind us, we were up in an instant as a throng of people flooded the courthouse steps. Reporters with microphones, cameras, flashbulbs, and cameramen shining their painful lights in my father's direction. He was in front.

Lassiter was behind him, beaming. Triumphant. Cool anger coursed through my veins as I watched him approach, followed by police. With guns in their holsters. And in an instant, I knew. I knew how to keep everyone else here safe while I punished Lassiter for what he tried to do. Before he could hurt anyone else.

My father made his way to a podium so close to where we stood, but I shifted out of his way, out of his field of vision. Noah held my hand, squeezed it, and I didn't pull away. It didn't matter.

Microphones jabbed at my father's face, vying for dominance, but he took it all in stride. "I have a lot to say today, as I'm sure you can all guess," my father said, and there was a murmur of laughter. "But the real winners here are my client, Leon Lassiter, and the people of Florida. Since I can't hand over a microphone to the people of Florida, I'm going to let Leon say a few words."

I saw the gun. The matte black metal was so plain and unremarkable. The metal was dull on my fingertips. The grooves on the grip dimpled my palm. It almost looked like a toy.

My father stepped out of the way, moving his head to the right, and Leon Lassiter's took its place. I was right behind him.

It was strange the way it felt; the weight unfamiliar and somehow dangerous. I looked down the muzzle. Just a hole.

"Thank you, Marcus." Lassiter smiled and clapped my father on the shoulder. "I am a man of few words, but I wanted to say two things. First, that I am grateful, so grateful, for my lawyer Marcus Dyer."

I pointed the gun.

"He took time away from his life, his wife, his children to

get justice for me, and I am not sure I'd be standing here right now if it wasn't for him."

Blackness seeped into my field of vision. I felt arms holding me, felt the brush of lips by my earlobe, but I heard nothing.

"Second, I want to tell the parents of Jordana—"

And then the oddest thing; before another thought appeared against the backdrop of my mind, someone began popping popcorn right there at the courthouse. *Pop pop pop pop*. The sound was so loud that my eardrums tickled. Then rang. Only then did I hear the screaming.

Moments later I could see again, and there were bowed heads, ducked and tucked under hands and knees. The hand holding mine was gone.

"Put the gun down!" someone shouted. "Put it down now!"

I was still standing. I looked straight ahead, straight in front of me, and saw a pale arm extended in my direction. Holding a gun.

It clattered to the steps. A wave of screams erupted with the bounce.

I didn't recognize the woman standing in front of me. She was older, her face splotchy and red, with streaks of mascara trailing down her skin. Her finger pointed at me like an accusation.

I heard the voice of Rachel in my mind, the voice of my best friend.

"How am I going to die?"

"He killed her," the woman said calmly. "He killed my baby."

Officers surrounded the woman and gently, reverently placed her hands behind her back. "Cheryl Palmer, you have the right to remain silent."

The piece semi-circled the board, sailing past A *through* K, *and crept past* L. *It settled on* M.

"Anything you say can and will be used against you in a court of law."

Landed on A.

The sound died away, and the pressure lifted from my hand. I looked beside me, but Noah wasn't there.

Zigzagged across the board, cutting Rachel's laughter short. R.

Panic overcame me, threatened to pull me under as I searched for him with feral eyes. There was a flurry of activity to my right; a swarm of EMTs buzzing around the leaking body on the courthouse steps.

Then back to the beginning. To A.

Noah knelt beside it. My knees almost buckled to see him alive, not shot. Relief flooded me, and I took another step just to be closer to him. But then I glimpsed the body lying on the ground. It was not Leon Lassiter.

It was my father.

59

A MACHINE BEEPED TO THE LEFT OF MY father's hospital bed as another on his right hissed. He'd been joking an hour ago, but the pain medication had put him back to sleep. My mother, Daniel, Joseph, and Noah were all huddled around the bed.

I hung back. There was no room for me.

I had never been there to witness it before, that exquisite moment when my thoughts became action. Just yesterday, I surveyed the chaos—the chaos I wanted—and stood there helpless as my father's blood flooded over the white marble stairs. A grieving mother was arrested, taken from her broken family to be locked away. But she was a danger to no one.

I was a danger to everyone.

A doctor poked his head into the room. "Mrs. Dyer? Can I speak with you for a moment?"

My mother stood up and tucked her hair behind her ear. She had spent the night at the hospital but looked like she'd been here for a thousand years. She made her way over to the door where I stood, and slipped around behind me, her hand brushing mine. I winced.

The doctor's words trailed through the open door. I listened.

"I have to tell you, Mrs. Dyer, your husband is one lucky man."

"So he's going to be okay?" My mother's voice was stretched to the breaking point. Tears welled in my eyes.

"He's going to be fine. It's a miracle he didn't bleed to death on the way here," the doctor said.

I heard a sob escape my mother's throat.

"I've never seen anything like it in all my years of practice."

My gaze flicked to Noah. He sat next to Joseph and stared at my father, his eyes shadowed and dark. They didn't meet mine.

"When can he come home?" my mother asked.

"A few days. He's recovering from the bullet wound beautifully, and we're really just keeping him here for observation. To make sure he doesn't get an infection and that the healing continues. Like I said, he's one lucky man."

"And Mr. Lassiter?"

The doctor's voice lowered. "He's still unconscious, but there will probably be significant brain damage. He might not wake up."

"Thank you so much, Dr. Tasker." My mother ducked back into the room and headed over to my father's bedside. I watched her as she fit seamlessly into the little tableau, where she belonged.

I took one more look at my family. I knew every laugh line on my mother's face, every smile that Joseph had, and every shift of expression in Daniel's eyes. And I looked at my father, too—at the face that taught me how to ride a bicycle, that caught me when I was too scared to jump into the deep end of the pool. The face that I loved. The face I'd let down.

And then there was Noah. The boy who fixed my father but couldn't fix me. He had tried, though. I knew that now. Noah was the one I never knew I'd been waiting for, but I chose to let him go. And I chose wrong.

All of my choices had been wrong. Everything I touched I would destroy. If I stayed, it could be Joseph or Daniel or my mother or Noah, next. But I couldn't just disappear; with my parents' resources, I'd be found in hours.

My mother sniffed then, stealing my attention. And I realized—I could tell her. I could tell her the truth about what I'd done, with Mabel's owner and Morales and in the Everglades. She would surely have me committed.

But was a mental hospital where I belonged? I knew my parents—they'd make sure I went somewhere where there would be art therapy and yoga and endless discussions about my feelings. And the truth was that I wasn't crazy. I was a criminal.

All of a sudden, I knew where I needed to go.

I looked at each of them once more. I said a silent good-bye.

I slipped out of my father's hospital room just as Noah's head turned in my direction. I wove through the hallways, cutting a path through the nurses and orderlies as I went. Past the waiting room, still peppered with a few reporters from the day before. I walked past everyone, straight to Daniel's car, parked under a murder of crows that had alighted on a cluster of trees by the parking lot. I got into the car and turned the key in the ignition. I drove until I reached the Thirteenth Precinct of the Metro Dade Police. I got out of my car, closed the door behind me, and walked up the stairs so that I could confess.

Detective Gadsen had been suspicious the last time we spoke, and I would simply confirm what he might already guess to be true. I would tell him that I had crushed Mabel's owner's skull. That I stole Morales's EpiPen, and released fire ants inside her desk. I was too young to be sent to prison, but there was a solid chance I'd end up in the juvenile detention center. The plan wasn't perfect, but it was the most self-destructive thing I could think of, and I so badly needed to self-destruct.

I could hear nothing but the throb of my heartbeat as my feet hit the concrete. The sound of my breathing as I took what I hoped would be my last free steps. I walked into the building and up to the front desk and told the officer I needed Detective Gadsen.

I didn't notice the person behind me, not until I heard his voice.

"Can you tell me where I can report a missing person? I think I'm lost."

My legs filled with lead. I turned.

He looked at me from under the brim of that Patriots cap he always wore and smiled. A silver Rolex glinted on his wrist.

It was Jude.

Jude.

In the police station. In Miami.

Five feet away.

I closed my eyes. He couldn't be real. He wasn't real. I was hallucinating, just—

"Through those doors and down that hallway," the cop said.

My eyes flew open, and I watched the officer point behind me.

"First door on the left," he said to Jude.

I looked slowly from the officer to Jude as my veins flooded with fear and my mind flooded with memories. The first day at school, hearing Jude's laugh and then seeing him forty feet away. The restaurant in Little Havana, watching him appear after Noah left and before that boy Alain sat in his seat.

The night of the costume party? The open door to our house?

Another memory flickered in my mind. *"Investigators are*

having trouble recovering the remains of eighteen-year-old Jude Lowe due to the wings of the landmark that are still standing, but could collapse at any moment."

It was impossible. Impossible.

Jude raised his hand to wave at the officer; he caught my eye and his watch caught the light.

My mouth formed Jude's name, but no sound came out.

Detective Gasden appeared then and said something, but his voice was muffled and I didn't hear it. I barely felt the pressure of his hand on my arm as he tried to lead me away.

"Jude," I whispered, because he was all I saw.

He walked toward me and his arm brushed mine lightly, so lightly, as he passed.

I felt myself fracture.

He pushed open the doors. He didn't turn around.

I tried to reach him as the doors swung shut, but I found that I couldn't even stand. "Jude!" I screamed. Strong hands held me up, held me back, but it didn't matter. Because no matter how I looked then, broken and wild on the floor, for the first time since that night at the asylum, my biggest problem wasn't that I was losing my mind. Or even that I was a murderer.

It was that Jude was still alive.

end of volume one

acknowledgments

I owe many people many thanks for their unwavering support of *Mara Dyer* and me:

To my editor, Courtney Bongiolatti, for doing everything right. You have been Mara's champion from the beginning and I could not be more grateful.

To my publisher, Justin Chanda, for taking a big chance on my strange little book, and for loving the creepy stuff as much as I do.

To my agent, Barry Goldblatt, for being my white knight and not believing in the word "impossible."

To my incredible publicist, Paul Crichton, to Chrissy Noh, Siena Koncsol, Matt Pantoliano, Lucille Rettino, Laura Antonacci and the entire talented team at Simon & Schuster for their boundless enthusiasm and dedication, and to Lucy Ruth Cummins, for designing the cover that blows *everyone* away.

To Beth Revis, Rachel Hawkins, Kirsten Miller, and Cassandra Clare for their generosity, to Kami Garcia, for literally more than I can say, to Jodi Meadows and Saundra Mitchell for their pitch perfect advice, to Kody Keplinger for making me feel like I belong, and to Veronica Roth, the Dauntless, for being one of the bravest people I know.

To all of my kind and witty and intelligent blog and Twitter friends: You have made every second of this wild ride more fun. Thank you for sharing my journey and for honoring me by allowing me to share yours.

To my rescuers, in every sense of the word—you know who you are. The world is a better place because you're in it.

To my readers: Amanda, Noelle, Sarah, Ali, and Mary for your insight. And to the tireless soldiers in my Beta Army: Emily L. for loving Noah first, Emily T. for loving Noah without being asked, Christi, for telling me "no" when I needed to hear it, Becca, for being my plot goddess, Kate, for numerous eleventh hour miracles, and to Natan, for always counting my bullets. I would count the ways in which I am grateful, but I don't have enough fingers and toes. And we know that's all I'm good for. To Stella, for couch space in over a decade's worth of apartments, and to Stephanie, for doing it all first. I don't say it enough, but I love you.

To the people who make me feel like I've won the family lottery every day: My one and only Tante, Helene, and Uncle Jeff, for Pesach. For Dulong. For Jacob, Zev, Esther, Yehuda, Simcha, and Rochul. To Jeffrey, for *so* much, to Bret and Melissa for *The Blair Witch*, among other awesome things, to Barbara and Peter for being Barbara and Peter, to Aunt Viri and Uncle Paul for inspiring my favorite line in the sequel, and also that whole lifetime-of-support thing, and to Yardana Hodkin—I adore you.

To Andrew, for giving me the best gifts. For being so much nicer than I could ever hope to be. You deserve a medal or ten. Thousand.

To Nanny and Zadie, Z"L. You would love how this is all turning out.

To Janie and Grandpa Bob, for being my biggest cheerleaders from the moment I was born and every day since.

To Martin and Jeremy, for being the second and third show

ponies in a line. For always being in my heart, even though we're far apart. For making me thrilled to not have sisters.

And to my mother, for reaching things on high shelves. For *The Joss Bird*. For Brandy. For helping me be a singer and not an acrobat. For being the ultimate woman of valor. Words will never be enough.

Last but certainly not least, thank *you* for reading this book. I can't wait to share what happens next.

Turn the page
for a sneak peek
at the thrilling sequel

I woke up on the morning of some day in some hospital to find a stranger sitting in my room.

I sat up gingerly—my shoulder was sore—and studied the stranger. She had dark brown hair that bled into gray at the roots, and hazel eyes with webs of crow's feet at the corners. She smiled at me, and her whole face moved.

"Good morning, Mara," she said.

"Good morning," I said back. My voice was low and hoarse. It didn't sound like my own.

"Do you know where you are?"

She obviously didn't realize that the floor directory was positioned directly outside the window behind her, and that from the bed, I had a clear view. "I'm at the Lillian and Alfred Rice Psychiatric Unit." Apparently.

"Do you know who I am?"

I had no idea, but I tried not to show it; she wouldn't have asked me if we'd never met, and if we *had* met, I should remember her. "Yes," I lied.

"What's my name?"

Damn. My chest rose and fell quickly with my breath.

"I'm Dr. West," she said evenly. Her voice was warm and friendly but not at all familiar. "We met yesterday, when you were brought in by your parents and a detective by the name of Vincent Gadsen."

Yesterday.

"Do you remember?"

I remembered seeing my father lying pale and wounded in a hospital bed after he was shot by the mother of a murdered girl.

I remembered that I was the one who made her do it.

I remembered going to the police station to confess to stealing my teacher's EpiPen and releasing fire ants in her desk, which is why she died of anaphylactic shock.

I remembered that it wasn't true—it was fiction. A lie I would feed the police so they would keep me from hurting anyone I loved again. Because they wouldn't believe I wished my teacher dead and that not long after, she died. Choked to death on a swollen tongue, exactly the way I imagined she would.

I remembered that before I could tell anyone any of this, I saw Jude at the Thirteenth Precinct of the Metro Dade Police Department. Looking very much alive.

But I did not remember coming here to the hospital. I didn't remember being brought. After Jude appeared, I remembered nothing else.

"You were admitted yesterday afternoon," the stranger—Dr. West—said. "The detective called your parents when they couldn't get you to stop screaming."

I closed my eyes and saw Jude's face as he walked by me. Brushed past me. Smiled. The memory stained the backs of my eyelids, and I opened them quickly, just to see something else.

"You told them that your boyfriend, Jude Lowe, who you thought died in a building collapse in December, is alive."

"Ex," I said quietly, fighting to stay calm.

"Excuse me?"

"Ex-boyfriend."

Dr. West tilted her head slightly and employed her carefully neutral psychologist expression, one I recognized well since I'd seen it often on my psychologist mother. Particularly in the past few months.

"You said that *you* caused the abandoned asylum in Rhode Island to collapse, crushing your best friend, Rachel, and Jude's sister, Claire, inside. You said Jude sexually assaulted you, which is why you tried to kill him. And you said he survived. You said he's here."

She was perfectly calm as she spoke, which magnified my panic. Those words in *her* mouth sounded crazy, even though they were true. And if Dr. West knew, then so did—

"Your mother brought you here for an evaluation."

My mother. My family. They would have heard the truth too, even though I hadn't planned to tell it. Even though I didn't *remember* telling it.

And this was where it got me..

"We didn't begin yesterday because you were sedated."

My fingers wandered up to my shoulder, exposed in my short-sleeve white T-shirt. That explained why it was sore. There was a Band-Aid on my skin, covering what must have been the injection site.

"Where is she?" I asked, picking at the Band-Aid.

"Where is who?"

"My mother." My eyes scanned the hallway through the glass, but I didn't see her. The hall looked empty. If I could just find her, maybe I could explain.

"She's not here."

That didn't sound like my mother. She didn't leave my side once when I was admitted to the hospital after the asylum collapsed. I told Dr. West as much.

"Would you like to see her?"

"Yes."

"Okay, we can see if we can work that out later."

Her tone made it sound like it would be a treat for good behavior, and I didn't like it. I swung my legs over the bed and stood up. I was wearing drawstring pants, not the jeans I last remembered myself in. My mother must have brought them from home. Someone must have changed me. I swallowed hard. "I think I want to see her now."

Dr. West stood up as well. "Mara, she isn't here."

"Then I'll go find her," I said, and started looking for my Chucks. I crouched to look under the bed, but they weren't there.

"Where are my shoes?" I asked, still crouched.

"We had to take them."

I rose then, and faced her. "Why?"

"They had laces."

My eyes narrowed. "So?"

"You were brought here because your mother thought you may be a danger to yourself and others."

I bit down hard on my bottom lip. "I really need to talk to her," I said then, struggling to keep my voice even.

"You'll be able to."

"When?"

"Well, I'd like you to speak with someone first, and have a doctor come in, just to make sure you're—"

"And if I don't want to?"

Dr. West just looked at me. Her expression was sad.

My throat wanted to close. "You can't keep me here unless I consent," I managed to say. I knew that much, at least. I was a lawyer's daughter and I was seventeen years old. They couldn't keep me here unless I wanted to be kept. Unless—

"You were screaming and hysterical and you slipped. When one of our nurses tried to help you up, you punched her."

No.

"It became an emergency situation, so under the Baker Act, your parents were able to consent for you."

I whispered so I wouldn't scream. "What are you saying?"

"I'm sorry, but you've been involuntarily committed."

From #1 New York Times bestselling author
KRESLEY COLE
KRESLEY COLE
POISON PRINCESS
THE ARCANA CHRONICLES
KRESLEY COLE
ENDLESS KNIGHT
THE ARCANA CHRONICLES
LET THE CARDS FALL WHERE THEY MAY. . . .
KRESLEY COLE
DEAD OF WINTER
THE ARCANA CHRONICLES
thearcanachronicles.com
PRINT AND EBOOK EDITIONS AVAILABLE
SIMON & SCHUSTER BFYR
TEEN.SimonandSchuster.com